W9-BZA-317

DEATH IN ROUGH WATER

OTHER MYSTERIES BY FRANCINE MATHEWS
FEATURING MERRY FOLGER

Death in the Off-Season

DEATH

in

ROUGH
WATER

A Merry Folger Mystery

FRANCINE MATHEWS

WILLIAM MORROW AND COMPANY, INC.
New York

Library of Congress Cataloging-in-Publication Data

Mathews, Francine.
    Death in rough water : a Merry Folger mystery /Francine Mathews.
        p.   cm.
    ISBN 0-688-13473-4
    I. Title.
PS3563.A8357D42   1994
813'.54—dc20   95-13826
                                                            CIP

Printed in the United States of America

First Edition

1   2   3   4   5   6   7   8   9   10

BOOK DESIGN BY JUDITH STAGNITTO-ABBATE

Love bears all things, believes all things,

hopes all things, endures all things.

— FIRST LETTER OF PAUL

TO THE CORINTHIANS, 13 : 7 – 8

❧

This book is dedicated to Mark,

who bears, believes, hopes, endures.

ACKNOWLEDGMENTS

E ARLY ONE MORNING IN
July 1994, I walked through Nantucket and up Washington Street to the
Town Pier, which runs from South Beach out into the harbor and its
seasonal congregation of fifteen hundred moored vessels. I was searching
for Nantucket's marine superintendent, Dave Fronzuto, to ask why the
island had no commercial trawling fleet. We talked for some time—of
the added expense of trawling from an island, of tourist boaters, Nantucket politics, hot-water showers, and ice machines; and then I strolled
the length of the pier to look at the *Ruthie B.*—a Western-rigged commercial dragger, the last of its kind to call Nantucket home. Though I
make free use of the Town Pier and its harbormaster, the events and
intrigue recorded here never, of course, occurred; and Dave Fronzuto is
in no way to be confused with my character Mitch Davis, though both
are Coast Guard veterans.

The marine superintendent was the first of many helpful Nantucketers who took valuable time in the height of the tourist season to chat
with me about island life, official and unofficial. Detective David Smith
of the Nantucket police discussed everything from Nantucket's crime
statistics to its new enhanced 911 system, while Fire Chief Bruce Watts,
an islander by birth, answered questions I hadn't thought to ask about
emergency response. His insight and information were invaluable. Gordie
McClay, Bosun's Mate First Class of the Coast Guard Service, Brant Point
Station, was kind enough to talk to me about commercial fishing regulations, the service's information database, and jurisdiction around New
England waters. Ted Jennison of Glidden's Island Seafood gave me the
scoop on the August tuna auctions and the price of swordfish—impossible though it is to obtain these days in Nantucket waters. Waleska Ortiz

of Boston's Registry of Vital Records and Statistics explained the arcana of restricted birth certificates and court orders.

Fiction is, by its very nature, a transformation of fact; and thus, any use to which I put the information gleaned from these kind people is entirely my own responsibility.

Mimi Beman of Mitchell's Book Corner has been profoundly supportive and cheering of a novice author; her knowledge of the island and her Nantucket room, in the back of the store, provided useful guides to the island's fishing culture and history.

My agent and friend Rafe Sagalyn is the most dedicated of professionals; he knows how much I rely upon him. My editor, Carrie Feron, has my deepest gratitude for performing the task few in her profession have mastered—*actual editing*. And finally, thanks to my mother, Betty Barron, who trekked the Northland Cranberry bog in the rain, Madaket in the fog, and the Jetties in the sun, all in the name of research; and to my husband, Mark Mathews, who continues to give meaning to so much of what I do.

I don't think we need feel guilty about the killing we do; we do it for life's sake: our own. But I guess for that very reason the killing may put a scared and thoughtful fisherman in mind of his own span.

❧

—JOHN HERSEY, *BLUES*

PROLOGUE

⚜

THE NIGHT WIND WAS
blowing unusually cold for late May, and the stars were blotted out by
a bank of cloud. Captain Joe Duarte took the measure of the waters, felt
the plunge of his deck, and knew he should head for port. The mounting
weather made black sea and sky one, a pitching cocoon through which
his trawler labored and rolled. The *Lisboa Girl* had just crossed over what
Duarte knew as the Leg—part of the intricate underwater landscape of
the Georges Bank he'd been fishing since the age of fifteen. He had
turned sixty-eight three months past, and though much had changed in
the fifty-three years he'd been on the water, he still called the Bank's
bottoms, its gullies and peaks, by the old names made familiar from
decades of studying charts in storm and sun: Cultivator Shoals, Billy
Doyle's Hole, Little Georges, Outer Hole.

The younger men, using location indicators fed down from the stars,
thought in numbers instead of words. They moved over the crags of the
seabed as a blind man feels Braille, sensing the humps and dips that
clutched at their nets. Had they been told to head to the Leg instead of
out on the loran's 2500 line, they'd have been lost.

The captain knew the Georges Bank like the profile of a beloved
woman, something no numbers on a screen could ever replace. The
charted names of the bottoms would remain with him, like the half-
remembered Portuguese words of his babyhood, an artifact of a vanished
age. Like his boat. And himself, for that matter. He was among the last
of Nantucket's commercial fishermen, and the last of the Duartes to go
down to the sea, something they had been doing in Portugal and the
New World for over five hundred years.

The *Lisboa Girl*, three decades old and Joe's second trawler, was one
of only two remaining draggers to call Nantucket home. She was an

Eastern-rigged wooden vessel, meaning that her pilothouse was aft and she launched her nets over the side rather than to the stern. A more dangerous and old-fashioned boat to fish from than the steel-hulled Western-riggers—in heavy seas like this, she'd have to come to a stop and turn broadside to the wind to prevent the net from drifting under the hull and fouling the propeller.

The captain pulled open the pilothouse porthole and stuck his head into the rising wind. It was time to quit fishing and head for port. His rheumatic bones ached, and his eyelids stung with weariness. Maybe it was time to quit for good, like all the rest.

He was the last of a generation. The younger men skippered boats that cost upwards of three hundred thousand dollars, paid for with mortgages higher than they'd take on a house, and faced insurance charges of forty thousand dollars a year. Fishing from an island port like Nantucket tacked a surcharge on everything they needed to survive. They weren't fools. They left for the mainland ports of Hyannis and Provincetown, Gloucester and New Bedford, and the Nantucket fleet slowly died.

Joe Duarte had watched the others go with a grim pride. His boat was paid off. He'd inherited his house on Milk Street. He could afford to stay in the town where he was born—where, at fifteen, he learned his trade from his father and grandfather, and had the youth whipped out of him by the bitter cold of winter fishing. He found the mainland ports too crowded and the towns too suburban. In his more poetic moments, he said they lacked an essential romance. Returning to the harbor of a January night, past Great Point Light arcing its reassurance into the early dusk, he saw the glow from hundreds of Nantucket windows rising out of the midwinter Atlantic with a surging of the heart and a gladness born of deep love. He knew the value of what he had earned with his blood and his years.

Only I've no one to give it to, he thought. *So much for pride. All it buys is loneliness. I've got to call Del. Blood is blood, after all.*

"Holy Christ, would you look at that!"

Jackie Alcantrara, his first mate, was bent over the gray face of the fish-finder, studying the shifting shapes of the schools twenty-five fathoms below. The image rippled like a field of summer wheat. "It's gotta be cod, Joe. A friggin' fish convention. Let's go." He moved to the door of the pilothouse impatiently, shouting orders to the two crewmen on the night watch.

Joe Duarte stuck his head around the door and squinted in the glare of the working lights. It was impossible to see much of the Atlantic beyond, but he could feel the pitch of the waves, grown sharper in the last few minutes, and the wind that was tugging at his sparse white hair. They were heading into fifteen-foot seas, over sharp peaks on the sandy bottom, and the net would be torn to shreds. There were no other boats in sight. They were one hundred and fifty miles from land.

Loneliness is a type of death. I must call Del.

"Jackie!" he yelled over the din of the gantry winch, which was paying out the net and the pair of half-ton steel doors that dragged it to the bottom. "Jackie!"

The mate turned to him impatiently, bullet head thrust forward in resentment. He had been a captain himself until last year, and taking orders from Joe was something he fought every day.

"Get the net outta the water, *now!*"

"What the hell are you talking about, old man?"

"I'll not have a couple thousand dollars' worth of new net torn apart in a gale, you understand? Get it up!"

Jackie stood stock-still, his jaw working fiercely, his overdeveloped upper body emphasizing all that was squat and Cro-Magnon about him; then he turned and drove a hand flat against the pilothouse wall with a shuddering violence.

"Christ *Almighty*," he said. "When are you gonna go home and die, old man? Tell me that! There's ten tons of cod down there, more than we've seen in months, more than anybody's seen at one time in more trips out than we can count. We're making money here, and you talk about a net!"

The bastard. I'd never have spoken to my captain like that. No respect, these days. No gratitude. I'd better call Felix Harper, too.

On the one hand, everything Jackie said was true. For years, cod on the Bank had steadily dwindled. During the day, they hung around in the mid-depths where only the huge factory ships could reach them; but at night, they dropped back to the bottom, and the *Lisboa Girl* dropped her nets after them through all the hours of darkness. Joe was turning his back on money. But he could sense the weather's gathering menace, and no amount of fish was worth the safety of his boat and men. Jackie was young. He would learn from the weather, from the ones who didn't come home, from the sudden silences on the radio frequencies in the midst of an unexpected gale.

"First Mate Alcantrara," the captain shouted into the wind, "for the last time, *bring in the net*, or I will do it for you." He ducked back into the pilothouse and counted to five. Then he looked through the porthole for Jackie. The mate had gone over to the crewmen and was shouting and gesturing; but still the net was being payed out. *Bullheaded young cuss.* A huge wave broke over the bow as the *Lisboa Girl* dove into a trough, spraying the men standing midships by the gantry.

Joe abandoned the pilothouse and reeled his way across the heaving deck, his hair instantly wet from the blown seas, his face turning red with suppressed rage.

"Tell me what I have to do to get an order obeyed here," he said to Jackie. The mate shrugged and looked away, muttering into the storm. Joe turned to the young Norwegian working the winch. "Get that net back on deck, Lars, double-time, you understand?"

"Sure, Cap'n," the blond crewman said, casting a glance at the first mate. "If you say so. But there's an awful lot of fish down there."

"There's a lot of bones, too," Joe said through his teeth, "and not all of them ancient. Bring it up."

Lars, a Norwegian incorrectly known around Nantucket as the Swede, turned back to the controls and eased the lever through neutral into reverse. The winch gave a groan audible even over the force of the wind, and the net started to wind wetly out of the water.

"That's it," Jackie burst out beside him. "I'm through. There's nothing worse than a man who's too afraid to make money. Why don't you stay home and leave the cod to people who know what they're doing?"

Joe Duarte's rage hiccuped inside of him as he shot a look at Jackie's ugly face, but it was quickly replaced by a terrible weariness. He *was* old, too old to be walking a sea-slick deck in the pitching dead of night, too old to slam an obnoxious twenty-eight-year-old on the jaw, too old to weigh whether the catch or his life was more important.

"You think you know what you're doing, huh?" he said. "You think you know how to run a boat?"

"Damn sight better'n you do, old man," Jackie retorted.

"At least I've got a boat to skipper," Joe said, with satisfaction, "instead of a wreck at the bottom of Cape Cod Bay. You didn't learn from that bit of trouble, did you, Jackie boy? You never learn anything. Your skull's too hard and your brain's too small. You can get off my boat, and good riddance."

He had expected the first mate's scowl of rage and the words bubbling at his lips; had expected him to take a swing at him, even, sealing the fate of their sundering after a year of strained partnership. But he hadn't expected the look of horror that washed over the man as he stared at something behind Joe himself, over his head, or the cry of warning that was torn from him too late.

Oh no. God, no. Del.

The full force of the steel otter door, rising much too fast from the roiling sea, caught the captain in the back of the skull. It was a massive blow that knocked sense from him with the swiftness of a snuffed candle flame. He crumpled at his crewmen's feet, at the base of the gantry, the otter door swinging wildly overhead as the Swede struggled to secure it. Jackie reached for Joe Duarte just as the boat heeled over, wallowing in a trough and pitched sideways by the weight of the swinging door; but the stunned man slid out of the mate's reach like a leaf blown by the wind, over the side and into the black water, his white head another bit of froth on the surging waves.

"Joe!" Jackie cried, the howling of the wind drowning his voice. "Joe!"

But Joe Duarte was past all hearing.

CHAPTER ONE

"I

T COMES AS NO SUR-
prise to any of us, dear friends," Father Acevedo was saying, "that Joe
Duarte stayed in the water rather than attend his own funeral. He used
to say that if the Lord wanted him at Mass instead of on the Georges
Bank on Sunday, He'd have sent the fish to church." He paused for the
anticipated laughter. "I think we know where the fish are today, dear
friends, and we know that Joe Duarte is right where he'd want to be."

The sentiment, however apt, failed to strike a note of cheer in the
crowd. It *missed*, somehow, like the funeral conducted without a body;
like the blowing gusts of frenzied rain that hammered the first summer
flowers into their muddy beds. Father Acevedo meant well. He was Portuguese himself, born and raised on the Cape, and his father had fished
with the Provincetown fleet. He'd known Joe Duarte for six years. But
when a man was lost at sea, fear cut deep in the hearts of his confederates, a fear hard to laugh off. No one who fished for a living wanted
to die for it.

Detective Meredith Folger scanned the faces lining the pews and
aisles of St. Mary's. A few shocked smiles met the priest's sally, but most
of the mourners simply looked uncomfortable. She caught the eye of
Jackie Alcantrara—Joe Duarte's first mate, the one who'd jumped into
the Atlantic after him and come back empty-handed. He'd taken a knock
on the head, and the hospital had shaved his skull; the man looked more
like a bull than ever, she thought. His heavy-featured face had gone
white under his tanned skin, and he wasn't laughing. Merry dropped her
eyes to her lap and wished the funeral Mass were done.

Joe's relatives had come from all over Massachusetts—the Ed Duartes
from Gloucester, the Luis Duartes from Mattapoisett, and up front, behind the first pew, the Manny Duartes out of New Bedford, the ones his

daughter, Del, had been living with. They were all fishermen. A good number of townsfolk had also braved the rain to say goodbye to Cap'n Joe, though few among them still made their living from the sea. There were Portuguese names all over the island, but they tended to be printed on the sides of pickup trucks rather than boats. Not a family among them failed to fish every summer, however—for pleasure or sport, or the occasional killing in the Japanese tuna auctions.

Father Acevedo beamed all around and raised his hands, signaling the end of his homily, and the congregation rose for the Prayer of the Faithful. Merry craned for a look at Adelia Duarte as she stood in the first pew, her two-year-old, Sara, singing a quiet nonsense song to her doll, and marveled again at her calm dignity. She had been absent from the island almost three years, since the pregnancy that had alienated her father; to return under circumstances like these must be an unbearable strain. Yet she showed no signs of the gnawing guilt and regret that her neighbors probably hoped to see—none of the remorse of the prodigal daughter, eyes downcast and shoulders trembling, returned to her home when all hope of reconciliation was forever lost. She had yet to endure the post-funeral reception, when the wives of her father's friends would invade the house with their casseroles and sympathy, sincere or false, a suffocating flock of femininity blessed with men safe and alive.

Merry smiled, and just as swiftly smoothed her features back into anonymous solemnity. Everyone in the church was trying not to stare at Adelia and her baby, and failing miserably. She was too much her father's child to care what Nantucketers said or thought about her life; she was probably looking forward to the struggle.

She had, after all, chosen to wear red today.

"A pretty enough little thing," Jenny Baldwin was saying, her eye on Sara Duarte, who was wandering wide-eyed through the forest of adult legs filling Joe Duarte's living room, "though rather small. But then she *is* illegitimate, and I always find that babies born out of wedlock are *not* robust, don't you? And where did she get that red hair?" she continued, not waiting for Merry's response. "Not from the Duartes, certainly."

"Agnes's hair was auburn," Merry said, recalling Adelia's mother.

"Was it?" Jenny said vaguely. "She died before my time, I'm afraid. Too bad. If she'd lived, perhaps Adelia wouldn't have been quite so—

unrestrained. But a girl raised as she was . . ." She clicked her tongue in mock sympathy and raised one eyebrow in the general direction of the red dress. She was the sort of woman who'd learned to click her tongue before she'd learned to form sentences. "Of course, Tom and I were always ready to do anything we could for her—"

"If you'll excuse me, Mrs. Baldwin," Merry said, her own black brows lowering, "I'd like to talk to Adelia, and I haven't much time before I'm due back at the station. You understand."

"You were great friends once, weren't you?" Jenny Baldwin said, her bleached blue eyes awash with interest.

She's wondering if I know who the baby's father is, Merry thought with distaste. "Yes," she said, "but we've grown far closer since she left the island. Absence has a way of revealing your true friends."

She set down her club soda and crossed the room in search of the red dress, which seemed to have vanished into the kitchen. She had been less than frank with Jenny Baldwin, but anger brought out her contrary streak. Del Duarte was a childhood friend. They had grown apart during the past decade, some of which Merry had spent at Cape Cod Community College, the Massachusetts Police Academy, and her first tour in New Bedford. By the time she'd come back to Nantucket six years ago, Del had her own life. Her pregnancy took her off-island three years later. Merry had no idea who'd fathered baby Sara.

A wall of bodies obscured her view of Adelia. She eased her shoulder past stocky, weathered Tom Baldwin, Jenny's husband, raising her hand to the small of his back and hoping he'd ignore her. Instead, he turned his head and smiled.

"Merry!" he said. "Good to see you."

"And you, Tom. Where've you been hiding?"

"Oh, inside a foundation or two," he said, his tanned skin crinkling at the corners of his eyes. He'd made more money than most during the eighties' development boom, and from the look of the signs around town announcing his current projects, he'd plowed the profits back into his business. Merry doubted he'd worked the inside of a cement cellar for years.

"I hope no one commits a crime today," he said, glancing over at her father, the police chief, who stood surrounded by a knot of Joe Duarte's older friends. From the way he held his hands in the air, spaced about eighteen inches apart, Merry knew John Folger was regaling them with the tale of his latest near-conquest of an elusive bluefish.

"We left Ralph Waldo by the phone in case a cat got stuck in a tree."

"How's your granddad doing?"

"Very well, thanks. He never seems to get any older." At eighty-two, Ralph Waldo Folger was competent and eager enough to resume his duties as police chief—relinquished to his son some twenty years before—so that Merry and John could attend Joe Duarte's funeral. She knew he'd be safely tucked up in his favorite armchair, one eye on the storm and one ear on the police radio.

"Sad about Joe," Tom said, twirling the ice cubes in his drink, "but at least he lived a long life."

"Right," Merry said shortly. Adelia's father had been sixty-eight. An age Tom Baldwin would consider young once he reached it.

"I don't suppose Adelia will be staying on the island long," he continued. "The house should sell quickly, this time of year—"

"—and on this block of Milk Street," Merry finished. "I know. Everyone says the same thing. *Perfect* summer cottage for a young investment banker from New York. But I haven't had a chance to talk to her long enough to find out whether she's planning to sell or not." She caught sight of Del through the space left by a turning head, and with a smile for Tom Baldwin, wove her way toward the kitchen.

It was like Joe Duarte's daughter to be calmly scrambling an egg in the middle of chaos. She stood by the stove, her long dark hair a shining band against the brightness of her dress, the only cheerful thing in an otherwise drab bachelor kitchen. It was a galley space, narrow and dark, with an ell for a small Formica-and-steel table with three outmoded chairs. The stubby refrigerator was rounded and domed in the mode of the 1940s, the counters were badly fauxed marble, and the linoleum on the floor was bleached of its original color—yellow, probably. A frieze of brown age spots overlaid the wallpaper like the back of an octogenarian's hand; Joe had apparently intended to strip it from the walls, since one section was torn off and hung to the floor with the pathetic droop of a three-day-old lily. The young investment banker from New

York would have to sink some money into the place. Merry touched Del lightly on the shoulder, and Del turned to her with an expression partly of relief and partly of weariness.

"*Eh, filha,*" she said, "Good of you to come after all these years."

Hey, girl. The affectionate Portuguese phrase stripped away the years as suddenly as a breath of wind, and Merry reached out to hug Adelia. "You look great," she said. "I can't tell you how sorry I am about Joe."

Del nodded and looked beyond her to the crowded living room. "Can you believe this circus?"

"It's like a bad joke—'How many people can you fit into a Nantucket cottage?' "

"Depends how many have eaten today, right?" Del said, laughing. "Joe'd have thrown them all out an hour ago."

"Or left them the house and camped on the boat."

"But that's what it means to be dead," she said, glancing up at the ceiling. "He's a captive audience somewhere, for the first time in sixty-eight years." Her eyes shifted quickly to the egg drying in the pan. "Whoops. She likes them soft, salmonella or no. Sara!"

She reached for a plate and scraped the egg onto it, looking around for her daughter. Merry saw her face change as Tom Baldwin shouldered his broad chest through the kitchen door, Sara Duarte giggling on one arm. "Here she is!" he said, swooping her into a chair fitted haphazardly with a booster-seat cushion. He turned to Adelia, one hand reaching for the plate. The Baldwins had no children, Merry remembered, but it must not be from choice; Tom clearly enjoyed them. He smoothed Sara's deep red curls, the color of mahogany, and settled himself into a chair, fork at the ready. Merry leaned against the wall and smiled at Del. She didn't smile back.

"I'll feed her, if you don't mind, Tom." Adelia took the fork out of his hand and stood over his chair, her lips compressed.

"Sure," he said, rising quickly. "Just thought you could use a hand."

"I'm never too busy to feed Sara," she said, and sat down. Tom looked at Merry, shrugged, and backed out of the kitchen.

"Feeling a little tense?" Merry said, drawing up the remaining chair as Adelia lifted a forkful of egg toward Sara's obliging mouth. "Or did Tom hit a nerve?"

"Tom's just being Tom," she said wearily. "Hale and hearty and bending over backward to show everybody that Sara would love to have a daddy. That poor Del has her hands too full, trying to raise her kid alone. Why didn't she put her up for adoption, like everyone told her to? So couples like the Baldwins, poor guys, could have a baby of their own? But no. Adelia was always so stubborn, so bullheaded. Never knew what was good for her, and never would listen when people tried to tell her. *Que pena.*"

"You don't really believe they think that, Del," Merry said.

"Oh, I *know* they do." Adelia put down the fork in frustration. Her large dark eyes looked at Merry speculatively, and then she dropped her head to rub at her temples. "And I've got a headache that will not quit."

Sara kicked her feet against the tabletop, wanting another forkful of egg, then gave up and reached for it with her fingers.

"Okay, so maybe I'm a little raw," Del said, sitting back in the chair. "But you don't know, Mere, how hard it is to come back—and how tough it is just to stay cool." The brown eyes blurred with tears. "To look like I don't give a damn. I can't even cry for Pop in peace—I'm too busy keeping up my end. I can't lose it in public. Everybody'd nod and say I feel as guilty as sin. So I try to be a rock instead. You know, half these people are here out of nosiness. Paying their respects to Pop is just an excuse. They want to know how I handle Sara. And how bad I feel about Pop."

"So how *do* you feel?"

"Pretty lousy," she said, laughing shortly. "You know me. I'm always feeling guilty over things I've only *thought* of doing, never mind things I've actually done. I can't get it out of my head that I didn't call him on his birthday. I *should* have called him, Merry. It was three months ago. I thought about it that day, *and I decided not to.* Can you believe that? As if he'd be around next year to call instead. I'm such an idiot."

"Del—you can't think like that."

"Then I guess I can't think at all."

Merry was silent for a moment. She'd known Del for twenty-odd years. Despite the distance that had grown between them, she was probably her closest friend on Nantucket. And she knew that if their roles were reversed, she'd have felt the same way. Never mind that Joe Duarte hadn't called his daughter in years; he'd had the last laugh. He'd *died,* the ultimate upping of the ante in a war of silence.

"It'll be over soon," she said, reaching for Del's hand. "You'll be home in New Bed before you know it."

Del squeezed her fingers in response, released them, and drew a deep breath. "Well, yeah, that's what I'd like to talk to you about," she said. "I'm thinking about staying."

"You are?" It was the last thing she'd expected. "So you're not selling the house. From the way the real estate talk is going, you've got at least ten buyers in the living room alone. Do you want your old job back?"

"With Tom?" Del shook her head. Three years ago, she had been Tom Baldwin's personal assistant, and was, by all accounts, invaluable. She was smart, efficient, and organized—the latter something Tom had struggled and failed to be.

Del reached for a napkin to wipe Sara's face. It was smeared with egg, like the sunrise smile of a clown. Sara pursed her lips and leaned away, her hands balled into fists.

"He hired a sub for me when I left, and he's not gonna fire her just because I'm back in town."

"Even if you could stand it," Merry said.

Del grinned. "Yeah, there's that," she said. "I'd probably go nuts. Too much a part of the past, you know?" She looked at Merry, weighing her words. "I've got a better idea. I'm going to take Pop's boat out and fish."

"You? *Fish?*"

"Swordfish, actually. You know what they're getting for harpooned ones? It's like a yuppie craze. Somebody figured out that a harpooned fish dies quicker and tastes better than one caught by the long-liners' nets, and the restaurants are paying through the nose for it. At least they are in New Bed."

"Then you know they are here." Nantucket's restaurants were expensive, trendy, and geared to a seasonal crowd intent on spending money for pleasure. "But Del—a harpoon?"

"I've thrown one before," she said, smiling. "You know how Pop was. He wanted a son and he got me. So he tried his best to turn me into a boy. I've been throwing a harpoon with him on the weekends since I was ten. He'd leave the *Lisboa Girl* at dock and take out the *Praia*—his thirty-footer—with me in the bow to spot. We caught a bunch over the years. You learn the knack. And you never forget the thrill."

"Aren't swordfish pretty scarce?"

"Yeah, well, that's a problem," Adelia said, looking momentarily troubled. "We'll just have to see. My cousins in New Bed started harpooning on the side, and they're not doing too badly. I went out with them a couple of times to get my arm back in gear, and it reminded me how much I missed being on the water. Pop used to say the harpooner's arm was passed down through the blood, you know, ever since the whaling days. Knowing the sea and loving it is something Duartes are born with." She paused and looked at Merry soberly. "Pop's dead. I can't bring him back. But now he's gone, I miss a lot of things I thought I'd forgotten. Like hard work and cold spray and the fight to the death. I want Sara to grow up a Duarte."

"You think you can make a living?"

"I hope. The darn swords aren't spawning, Mere. But people keep buying 'em, don't they? The scarcer they get, the more they cost, and that's gotta be good for me."

"But not for the fish," Merry said.

Adelia shrugged. "Pop always said what went around came around. Look at the striped bass. Or the blues. They disappear for years, and then one day they're back like a case of the clap. I can't waste time worrying about saving the swords. If I'm harpooning, I'll get maybe three fish a month. That's not gonna kill 'em off."

"Three a *month*? You'll be lucky to get three a season," Merry said.

"It's that bad, huh?"

"It's worse. Nobody I know is fishing for swords these days. They're all after the sushi market." The Japanese paid exorbitant prices—up to twenty thousand dollars a fish—for prime tuna at auction. But the best tuna was caught in August, when the Atlantic had warmed enough to allow the massive fish to keep their layer of fat, so prized in Asia. "If the swords play out, you could switch to tuna fishing later in the season. They're not as endangered."

Del thought for a minute, and then shook her head. "One fish a month. *Que coisa.* Stack that up against an average long-line seiner's haul, and tell me who's more of a threat to the fish."

She had her heart set on this business. Merry ran her fingers through her blond hair—still damp from the rain and the persistent humidity that came with it—and decided to concentrate on essentials. "Who's going to crew for you?"

"I haven't figured that out," she admitted. "I'll think about crew tomorrow. There has to be some guy on the island who's strong enough to work for a woman."

"I'm not so sure," Merry said carefully. "Precious few are willing to take orders from one."

"Nothing's changed down at the station, *eh filha?*"

Merry was the only female detective on the Nantucket force, and one of the few women at the station, barring some traffic cops and summer interns.

Adelia's sudden smile was like a snapshot of childhood. "Maybe you'll come fish," she said. "We could be the only girl crew on Nantucket. Think about it. We'd be a tourist attraction."

Merry shook her head. "We Folgers like to say that police work is handed down through the blood. Something we're born with."

"I was afraid of that. Got any ideas about crew?"

"I might. Give me a few hours." She paused, and eyed the baby. "You'll need child care."

"I know." Adelia lifted Sara out of her chair and straightened the hem of her dress.

"She's beautiful, Del," Merry said, squatting down to Sara's eye level. She had the meltingly soft skin and the faint flush of rose in her cheeks that come with the two-year-old's territory. Her eyes were Merry's exact shade of green. She smiled slowly at Merry and reached a hand out to squeeze her nose.

"Yeah. Hard to believe she comes from me," Adelia said soberly. Glancing up, Merry saw pain flicker in her eyes. "She's a sweetheart. Gives nobody trouble. Which you could never say about me."

"What are you doing tonight?" Merry said, rising and dusting off her knees. "After this crowd clears out, I mean."

"Having dinner at your house, if I'm lucky."

"Good. I know just the person to take care of Sara." She gave her friend a swift kiss, touched a hand to the child's head, and was gone.

It was only when the last of the guests had left, and she had begun to collect the scattered glasses lying about the living roon, that Adelia realized Jackie Alcantrara was still in the house. Was it a slight cough, an overly loud exhalation of air, that had drawn her to her father's "snug," as he called it? Or the creeping sense of being not quite alone?

The little den at the back of the house had never seemed big enough for more than one person; she'd rarely ventured farther than the threshold, even when she'd been desperate for her father's notice. The space was still dwarfed by the cracked Naugahyde recliner at full stretch and the huge old desk in one corner, piled to its gills with papers, bills, and photographs of prize catches; and there was a strong odor of pipe tobacco embedded in the fibers of the room that brought her father back in a sharp rush. Thumbtacked to the fake dark paneling was a picture of herself, taken at Great Point Rip when she was fifteen, holding high her first surf-caught blue.

She leaned in the doorway, kept by habit from entering the room, a dishtowel flung over one shoulder and a brace of wineglasses in her hands. Jackie was bent over the desk, rifling through the papers, too intent on his search to notice her approach. At the sight of him—close-cropped bullet head, large animal hands cracked and roughened by weather, awkward, bulky body—she felt sharply afraid. She had made no mention to Merry Folger of the doubts that had troubled her since Joe's death; in daylight, among friends, they seemed slightly hysterical, and that was not her style. But doubt haunted her brain nonetheless. Standing before her now, Jackie was the embodiment of her worst suspicion.

"Tell me what you're looking for, and maybe I can help," she said.

He straightened as if he'd been shot, his face suddenly crimson, and shoved his hands in his pockets without a word.

"What's up, Jackie?"

He shrugged. "You might as well hear it from me as anyone else," he said, avoiding her eyes. "Your dad promised me his boat, when he was gone, since he had no sons and he figured you wouldn't be back after . . . And you're a woman, anyway. It's not like you'd need it."

"His *boat*?" Adelia said, aghast. "The *Lisboa Girl*?"

Jackie nodded.

"But it's paid for. Free and clear. There's no mortgage," she added, as if this would make it plainer. Boats free of debt were an increasing rarity among New England fishermen, and though Joe Duarte's was old, it was worth at least a hundred thousand dollars. "He musta been nuts. Maybe he'd give you a break on the price, but—"

"The word was *give*," Jackie said firmly, his color rising again. "And not just the *Lisboa Girl*, but the *Praia* as well."

"You're dreaming! There's no way he'd give you both." It was the *Praia* she'd been intending to use for swordfish harpooning.

"Dreaming? *I'm* dreaming?" Jackie said. "And what have you been doing for the past three years, Del, besides spreading your legs for any man in a pair of pants? While you were hanging around New Bedford with your bastard, I was working myself to the bone to keep your dad on the water." He came toward her, his blunt skull and bear paws made suddenly menacing by the smallness of the room and the viciousness of his words. Despite herself she leaned backward into the hall, a sick mingling of rage and fear building in her throat.

"I earned that boat, every foot of her, and the *Praia* too. If it weren't for me, Joe Duarte would've been finished months ago, and much you cared about it. So don't tell me what I know and don't know, or what you're due from a man you couldn't trouble yourself to look after." He was swaying slightly on his feet, as though he still felt a deck heaving beneath him, and Adelia knew he'd drunk quite a bit that afternoon.

"You've got your nerve, coming back here with that brat after what you've done, acting like you've never left and nobody the wiser." His voice had grown harsh, the words slurring with anger. "You'll get what's coming to you, Del—that's the truth, and everybody knows it. There's not a man on the water won't think it's justice when Joe Duarte's will is read."

"His will," Adelia said dully, understanding now the rifled papers. "*Que coisa.*"

"I witnessed it for him. So I know what it says. I just figured I'd find it before you did, in case you decided to put a match to it and sit pretty."

"Like I'd do that, Jackie. If Pop wanted you to have the boats, he wanted you to have the boats. But you won't find anything in the desk— Pop gave up trying to, years ago. Now get out of my house."

Adelia felt suddenly weary, as though she were ancient beyond belief, and had survived the last century without a single night's sleep. *Pop gave away his boats. My boats.* It was God's little joke, spiking her plans and cursing her with characters like Jackie. Of course, her father had thought she'd never need her birthright. She'd left him, as Jackie said. The anger in the man before her must have been nothing compared to Joe Duarte's.

"I'll call Felix Harper in the morning." She turned away from the room. "He's Pop's lawyer. He'll be able to answer all your questions." *And mine,* she thought.

"I'll call him myself," Jackie said, and brushed past her heavily on his way to the door. She smelled the sour odor of stale whiskey. One reason for the unprovoked abuse; he'd probably regret it in the morning. Not that he'd ever tell her.

"You do that," she said, watching him swing down the shining-wet brick path and through the picket-fence gate onto Milk Street, his figure hunched against the violent gusts that still battered the island. Her mother's peonies were sodden starbursts against the grass, the hydrangea heads were bowed to their knees in a welter of rain. She looked up at the heavy sky, the lowering dusk, and let the storm's wet fingers brush back her hair. The weather had settled in. Even Joe's seabed must be uneasy tonight, with such turbulence sweeping the air above. The thought of him lost and alone in the Atlantic sent a sharp stab of pain through her stomach.

She closed her eyes and considered dinner at the Folgers' with relief and something else—a renewed conviction. Hysterical or no, her fears would have to be shared before they could be banished. She could not endure another night of the thoughts that had plagued her ever since Joe Duarte's death.

CHAPTER TWO

A DELIA DUARTE CLOSED
her door on the stormy dusk just as Merry Folger was drawing up to the
geranium-colored portal of Peter Mason's two-hundred-year-old saltbox.
The house, with its hundred acres of cranberry bog and sheep pasture,
was tucked into the island's moors and surrounded by Nantucket Conservation Foundation lands; but despite its isolation in the late-afternoon
gloom, it looked snug and welcoming. Yellow light shone from the
windows, the scent of woodsmoke spiraled from the chimney—and Merry's spirits, dampened by funereal thoughts and contagious melancholy,
immediately rose. She turned off her car's ignition and thrust open the
door.

She was still wearing the quiet navy suit she'd thought proper for
the Mass, and her pumps sank into the crushed quahog shells that covered the drive. She jumped quickly to the brick steps and rang the bell,
feeling the sudden rush of anticipation that always preceded the sight of
Peter. Ney was barking from somewhere within the house. That meant
Peter was probably home.

"Detective!"

Not Peter, but Rebecca the housekeeper, her close-cropped iron-gray
hair as grim as ever, her blue eyes snapping with interest, and her smile
wide with pleasure. Rebecca, who would love to see Peter settled with a
nice young woman and had been trying to get Merry to the house on
various pretexts all year. First, the laundry-room window she thought was
forced, and demanded that Merry inspect herself—a window that clearly
had not been raised or otherwise violated in years. Next, the matter of
the missing suitcase, filled, Rebecca swore, with her most personal documents, that had disappeared from the barn storage room. The suitcase
was discovered not much later, safely shelved in the stone depths

of the storm cellar. After that, Rebecca started talking about her failing memory, and Merry made a point of stopping at the farm without being summoned—knowing how long the gray island winters could be for a woman of Rebecca's years, living with only Peter and his foreman, Rafe da Silva, for company.

"Now isn't that the prettiest thing!" Rebecca said, admiring her suit as she stood aside to allow Merry across the threshold. "You didn't find *that* on-island."

"Ann Taylor," Merry said automatically, and ran her fingers through her damp blond curls. "I've just been to Joe Duarte's funeral."

"That was today?" the housekeeper said. "And I never remembered. I'll have to send that poor girl a card all the same. You'll be wanting to see Peter, of course," she said briskly. "He's on through to the study."

But the sound of voices had drawn Peter Mason from his fire, and when Merry turned toward the hallway leading to the warmth of his favorite room, she found him leaning against the doorjamb, index finger in his book, studying her quietly.

"Merry," he said. "What a pleasure." The way he said the final word made her catch her breath and flush to her black eyebrows, but he'd already turned back into the room and couldn't possibly have noticed. She followed him and took the seat he offered, feeling the comfort of the place steal over her in warm waves. The fire was of driftwood, its multicolored flames cheerily psychedelic, and the flowered chintz of the sofa was bright against the storm beyond the windows. Rebecca had disappeared, and Merry felt herself relax into the place and the moment with something like relief. She hadn't realized how tense the funeral and the crowd at Adelia's had made her.

"I've been having scotch," he said. "Something about the rain and the damp—when it's raw, I need to drink something warm-colored. Like sherry. Or scotch. What'll it be?"

"Sherry, I think," she said, and he smiled. A few months ago she'd have refused even a beer, conscious of how it might look for a cop to drink on the job; but she wasn't on the job today, and Peter Mason was no longer a suspect in his brother's murder. "I just got out of Joe Duarte's funeral."

"Of all days," Peter said, glancing out the window. "My own father was buried on a raw day in January. You never forget it."

"Particularly when you've no one to bury," Merry said. "Just word of a death you tell yourself to believe. That's how it was with Billy." Her brother had been eighteen when he'd shipped to Vietnam, jumped on a grenade, and never come back. She shook herself slightly and accepted the delicate crystal glass Peter handed her, filled with sherry the color of amber, and let the first sip pool on the tip of her tongue. Like the last warm days of September captured in a bottle. She sighed and closed her eyes, leaned back into the sofa's softness, and kicked off her shoes.

"How's your friend taking it?"

"Del? Like a rock. Mostly because everyone who knew her father is hoping she'll fall apart. The prodigal daughter, the outcast returned too late—you know."

He nodded, and slid into his club chair. "Something appropriately operatic."

"She knew what it would be like, and I think she's strong enough to handle it. How she feels when everyone goes home and she turns out the lights is another story."

"Were they close?"

"Del and her dad? They were once. After her mother died, they were all each other had. One reason Joe took it so hard when she got pregnant and left. Although he'd stopped speaking to her by that time."

Peter's brow was furrowed. "Because of the baby?"

"Because she wouldn't tell him whose it was. She probably knew he'd go after the guy with a shotgun and try to make him marry her, and I doubt Del wanted to marry Sara's father. If she had, she'd be married by now. But instead she wanted to have the baby in peace and ignore all the questions. That wasn't Joe's style."

"And he probably died regretting it," Peter said.

Merry nodded. "Just like Jose da Silva will." The father of Peter's foreman had banished Rafe from his fishing boat and his family after Rafe was falsely accused of murder, and despite the passage of six years and Rafe's imminent marriage, the two had still not spoken. "That's partly why I'm here."

One of Peter's hawkish eyebrows rose. "I'd so hoped it was to drink sherry with me. I thought it might just be possible, since I hadn't heard Rebecca needed a silver tea service found, or a valuable set of pearl earrings recovered from my sock drawer. But never mind. Tell me what you intend for the da Silva family while I refill your glass."

Merry studied his back as he stood at the bookshelf-cum-bar, decanting the wine with practiced ease, and wondered what he did poorly. She had never witnessed an awkward moment in Peter Mason's life—except, perhaps, those first few after the discovery of his brother's body in his flooded bog. He had been enraged and embittered then, at Rusty Mason more than anyone else, and anger made him careless with words. She hoped she wasn't going to make him angry now.

"How much do you depend upon Rafe?"

He stoppered the sherry decanter before replying. "As a friend or as a foreman?" he said, after a moment.

"As a foreman, I suppose."

"I've come to rely on him increasingly over the years, to the point where I doubt I could replace him entirely if and when he leaves me."

"You seem certain he will," she said, feeling relieved.

"Change is a norm, Merry; permanence an illusion." His gray eyes went flat and cold for an instant, and he sat down again opposite her. "I never expect to hold the people I care about for very long."

She turned away, reading an old pain in his eyes, and sipped again at her sherry. Peter's fear of hurt never failed to disturb her. It was too much like her own.

"But I still have a thorough knowledge of every stage of production at Mason Farms," he continued. "It's vital, and it's frankly impossible to run a profitable concern without the owner having his finger on the pulse of the place. I value the bog and the sheep enough to make sure that I do—if only so I don't look stupid every time Rafe takes a vacation."

"How busy are you right now?"

"Not terribly. The vines have flowered, and the fruit should set fairly soon. After that it's just a matter of irrigation and time. The harvest isn't until October. As for the sheep, they're past lambing, and the shearing, again, can wait until fall. So I'd say we're through the spring rush and into the deceptive lull of early summer." He set his glass down and looked at her steadily. "Now. Why don't you tell me what you plan to do with Rafe."

"Adelia needs somebody to crew for her."

"To crew *for* her?"

Merry nodded. "I know. It's unusual. The most women are ever allowed to do on a fishing boat is cook, right? I'm sure Rafe thinks so. But he's the best person I could think of. He's dying to get back on the water—at least, I imagine he is. I've never known a fisherman to leave fishing without dreaming of it the rest of his waking days. And this is perfect. Adelia's going to harpoon swordfish—"

"She's going to *what* swordfish?"

"Harpoon them." Her voice sounded small even to herself. "You don't know her, Peter, so this must seem crazy. But trust me. It's not."

"And a woman wielding a barbed hook on a stick needs somebody to steer the boat, I presume?"

"That's about it."

"I can't believe Rafe will be happy as a glorified taxi driver."

"Maybe not. Maybe he will. I just wanted your permission, as his employer, to present the idea. He needn't go full-time, even. Just those days you think you can spare him. Adelia knows Rafe from way back. She's bound to respect him; the da Silvas have always been considered the best of the old breed. She'd be thrilled to have his help whenever he could get away."

"By all means, ask him," Peter said. "With my blessing. Just don't be hurt if he laughs you out of the room."

The last time Merry had entered the loft over the barn, she had argued bitterly with Rafe and left in tears. She had still been in love with him then and hurt by his efforts to distance her. The memory of last fall still had the power to embarrass her. But it no longer tugged at her heart.

This afternoon she found Rafe drawn up to his desk, dark head bent under the circle of lamplight falling on a pile of paperwork, a mug of coffee steaming gently. He was playing the radio, one reason he hadn't heard her shoes on the barn's wooden stairs, and he started involuntarily at her presence.

"Merry! How's the Girl Scout doin'?"

Her childhood nickname. She smiled. "Not bad. And yourself?"

He threw down his pen and spun around in the chair, thrusting its caster feet across the bare wooden floor. "Saw you at the funeral."

"But didn't bother to say hello."

"I got outta there kind of quickly. Didn't want to run into my dad. He and Joe were buddies from way back. Went to school together."

"Joe's entire first-grade class must have been in the living room. I said hello to Jose. He looked good."

"Yeah, pride agrees with the Old Bastard," Rafe said, slapping a sheaf of papers into a neat, squared pile. "Amazing we can live on an island of six thousand people and avoid each other. But da Silvas were always masters when it came to blood feuds. My great-great-grandfather kept one running in Portugal for three generations."

Merry pulled up a chair. "Do you miss it, Rafe?"

"Fighting with my father? Not at all. I'm smarter than that, Merry."

"I meant working for him. Fishing for a living. Going out with the boats in the darkness of early morning, all that."

Rafe stopped his rapid motions at the desk and stared at her, thinking, his easy humor sobered in an instant. "All the time," he said. "Even though I know my father sold his boat two years ago to a guy trawling out of Hyannis. I keep thinking it should've been mine."

"It should have," Merry said, shocked.

Rafe looked moodily at his hands, the fingers spread wide on his denimed knees, and expelled a breath. When he met her eyes again, he was smiling. "What's in the blood doesn't die easily, Merry. Particularly pride."

"Or the love of fishing." Merry swallowed and looked at her shoes. A scalloped stain of darker blue between sole and upper showed where the rain had done its work. "Adelia is thinking of staying on," she said.

"Yeah? She gonna work for Tom Baldwin again?"

"I don't think so. She's talking about swordfishing."

A short bark of laughter, whether of contempt or disbelief Merry couldn't say. "Harpooning, actually," she continued, "off the *Praia*. Joe's thirty-footer."

"Trust a woman to come up with a harebrained scheme like that."

"You don't think she can do it?"

"I'm not saying she couldn't do it. Provided there were any swordfish to catch. Nobody's sending boats out after 'em in these waters, Merry. All the sword on the local market's picked up off Long Island. She can't make a decent living. Then she'll be scrambling around trying to get a part-time job in high season, when they've been promised to kids from Ireland and Australia for months, and she'll be desperate."

She knew what he meant. Local summer jobs increasingly went to members of the British Commonwealth, anxious for some time in the United States and applying through overseas agencies. Some had work permits, some did not. It was beyond the strength of the Nantucket police to do the work of the Immigration and Naturalization Service and round up illegal aliens. So her father told his patrolmen to look the other way, and the restaurant owners paid ten bucks an hour for their dishwashers. Like everything imported on Nantucket, the summer help was pricey.

"That's pretty harsh," she said.

"Yep. It is. But I'm betting that's how it'll go."

"Maybe nobody's catching swordfish because nobody's looking for it."

"Well, the reverse could also be true. And who's she gonna get to crew for her, anyway? It'd be different if she had a brother. But no guy is gonna work for a Jonah."

A Jonah. Seaman's term for landlubber, drawn from Jonah and the whale. All women were by definition Jonahs to the men who fished Nantucket's waters.

"I thought maybe you might," Merry said quickly, getting the words out in a rush before she had time to regret them.

"*Me?* You crazy? I wouldn't set foot on that boat if it were dry-docked and for sale. No way, Meredith. I may miss fishing, but not that bad."

"Come on, Rafe. At least give it a thought."

"No."

"Flat-out?"

"You heard me. I'd be the laughingstock of every self-respecting boat in the harbor, not to mention getting chaffed by Tess for spending my days with another woman. Took me long enough to get her to the altar as it is. I don't want to screw things up a month before the wedding."

Tess Starbuck had agreed to marry Rafe the previous Christmas, one more reason Merry had put all feeling for the foreman behind her.

"Peter thinks it's a great idea," she said.

"You ran this by Pete?" At that, Rafe laughed outright. "I just bet he thinks it's a great idea. I just bet. Get *him* on the boat then, he's so sensitive with women."

"Rafe," Merry said, heard the pleading note in her voice, and stopped. She took a breath and started again. "Adelia seems committed to this.

Maybe with a little time she'll find somebody permanent to crew for her, somebody she can hire on a steady basis. Everybody knows you have a real job here at the farm; nobody would think you were doing anything more than a nice favor for an old friend. And if *you* help her—it'll give her credibility. A little bit of acceptance, maybe. Until she gets her head above water and decides whether she's good at this—or should sell the house and go back to New Bed. You see what I'm saying?"

Rafe folded his tanned arms across his chest and stared at her quizzically. "Yep. I see what you're saying. You're trying to make me feel bad so I'll do something I don't want to. You'll be pulling out all the stops and talking about Billy next."

The grenade her brother had jumped on in Vietnam had landed at Rafe's feet. It was Rafe, not Merry, who never failed to mention that he owed his life to Billy.

"Del's got that little girl. Cutest thing you ever set eyes on. But nobody wants to give her a break. I think she hasn't done much to deserve that. I think it's time somebody like you—independent, respected, mature enough to work with a woman—gave her that break."

He sighed heavily. "Merry, Merry. You're too darn emotional to be in the police business, you know that?"

"Yep."

He scratched his beard, rolled the abandoned pen under his fingers, took a swig of coffee, and thought it over.

"Just for a few days?"

"You know you'd love to be out on a boat again. Don't tell me you wouldn't."

"Might be fun to see the look on the Old Bastard's face, come to that." He turned back to his papers. "I'm not saying yes. So don't tell Del anything I wouldn't want you to. I'm just saying—I'm not saying no."

CHAPTER THREE

❦

R ALPH WALDO FOLGER
lifted the lid from his beloved spaghetti sauce, breathed deeply of garlic, beef, and tomatoes, and sighed. The recipe was his wife's, mastered during the final years when arthritis had swollen Sylvie's hands and crippled her legs, barring her from the things she had loved—needlework, garden, and kitchen, in that order. The slow illness, Ralph had told Merry, was God's way of teaching him how to live without her grandmother; had she been taken from him abruptly, he'd have been lost. Instead, they continued to collaborate, in a sense, every time he unfolded one of the yellowed slips of paper on which she had recorded her secrets in her spidery Swedish hand. And so it was that on a night of terrible spring storm the Thursday before Memorial Day weekend, he could grace the house on Tattle Court with the mouth-watering smell of Bolognese.

In contrast to the unrelenting rain and the early fall of dark, the kitchen was warm and filled with a soft golden light. It was a square space nearly one hundred and fifty years old, with somewhat newer wooden cabinets and white-enameled fixtures overlaid with a faint yellowing from age. The walls were painted a strong sea blue that looked shady in summer and cozy in winter, while the floor was of oak that creaked and sloped with the settling of the house. In the center of the room was a large oval table, scarred and darkened from decades of use, where the Folgers read their morning papers, piled their discarded mail, left purses and hats and crumpled brown bags of forgotten lunch. As a child, Merry had done her homework here, and Sylvie had put up jar after jar of brightly colored preserves. The room was the soul of the house.

A sudden shriek nearly jolted Ralph Waldo out of his shoes—Sara Duarte, exercising her lungs. Her small hands waved a fork and spoon in midair, and her legs, clad in bright green courduroy, were energetically kicking the rungs of the aged Folger high chair. "Skettie!" she crowed. "Sara want *skettie!*"

Ralph Waldo smiled, his strong teeth a bright slash through his already tanned skin. Sara stopped kicking and waving, mesmerized by the sight of him. He knew how utterly strange he must seem to her—six feet tall, white-haired, his brows bristling over a trimmed beard—a Santa in sports clothes, like a card sent from a retirement community in Florida. But Sara Duarte was too little to know of Santa yet; her wonder must be wordless, complete in itself without the necessity of metaphor. This was what it was to be absolutely young.

"Meredith Abiah!" he bellowed in the general direction of the stairs. "There's a child needs feeding!"

A pause in distant conversation and a hasty clatter of footsteps. The girls were coming down.

He had never gotten past thinking of them as the girls. As children they had tucked themselves into Merry's dormer room to gossip and share secrets and confide their most embarrassing hopes. That they were both over thirty now and long past the age of slumber parties meant little to Ralph Waldo; time had ceased to serve as a responsible marker of age. He felt as fit as he had at sixty—well, perhaps as fit as he had at seventy—and so the girls' passage through their twenties had happened almost imperceptibly. Even this little one seated at his table, impatient for spaghetti, did not age Adelia in Ralph Waldo's eyes. Sara was simply another girl, with years and years before her, and Ralph could think of nothing more delightful to have in the house.

Merry had tackled him in the living room before Del and her baby arrived that evening.

"I've got a favor to ask of you, Ralph," she'd said.

Merry's favors had a way of becoming commitments.

"Does this have to do with Adelia, perchance?"

"How do you envision your summer?"

"My summer?" His favorite season. The time of tomato plants and bluefish on the grill and early-morning walks to Bartlett's produce truck at Federal and Main, followed by a satisfying lunch and nap in his Adirondack chair. "Same as always, I expect. Puttering at this, meddling with that."

"How'd you like some company?"

"What are you proposing, Meredith?"

"It's just that Adelia is thinking of staying."

"And what would she want with an old man's company?"

"Child care. She's got to work, and if she works, she's got to have someone reliable to take care of Sara. You're the most reliable person I can think of."

"A two-year-old?" He quailed momentarily, remembering Merry at that age. Legs that ran as fast as a sandpiper's, and always in the most dangerous direction. A constant stream of semi-intelligible language, punctuated by questions that rarely had adequate answers. The occasional storm of temper that ended in tears and a sudden fall into sleep. The smallness of a soft hand encased in his (to a child) enormous one, and all the sweetness of discovering the world anew, shining and wondrous as it hadn't been in years. Would he be reduced to ferrying her around on his bicycle, as he had seen so many tourist grandpas do, small fists beating on the broad back, the demands relentless for "a *story*, Grandpa, a *story*"?

"It would only be temporary," Merry said, "until Del got her feet under her and could find a good alternative."

Ralph looked with despairing love at his granddaughter. Her green eyes under the black brows and blond hair were terribly intent.

"Temporary," he repeated, knowing how false that word usually turned out to be.

"I swear."

Of course he said yes.

"I'm starving," Merry said now, automatically stepping around Tabitha the cat and a cluster of recyclable containers piled willy-nilly on the floor. Tidiness was not the Folgers' strong point. "I feel like I haven't eaten in ten years."

"Me, too," Adelia said. "Ralph, if I could have had anything tonight, it would have been Sylvie's spaghetti."

Ralph beamed. "I thought you might. A favorite thing from childhood is the best way to banish sadness. Your dad loved Sylvie's sauce himself, as I recall, so we'll pretend for a few moments we're all together under one roof, as we were in the old days."

Merry felt her throat constrict as she reached for the grated cheese. Her mother had died when she was ten, Adelia's when she was six. With

John Folger running the police force and Joe Duarte out on the water
for days at a time, home life was a sporadic thing. Ralph Waldo, however,
had tried to fill the gap. He was never too occupied to build a fort or
look for plovers' eggs on the beach; it was *Ralph* who was the best thing
from both their childhoods. But for the life of her, Merry had no idea
how to tell him so.

Adelia reached for his hand and squeezed it. "Can I have the cheese,
Ralph?"

This would have to do for the moment.

"You two get caught up?" her grandfather asked.

They looked at one another and said nothing. Ralph raised one eyebrow and then concentrated on twirling the pasta around his fork. Sara
clattered her spoon against the table with determined purpose, and Adelia
reached over to cut the spaghetti into baby-sized bits.

"Del thinks there's something wrong with her father's death," Merry
said quietly. She put her fork down, folded her hands under her chin,
and looked sidelong at her friend.

"Beyond the obvious fact that sixty-eight is too young, you mean?"

She nodded.

"Adelia, my dear," Ralph Waldo began, and then stopped. No point
in telling a Portuguese Nantucketer that the sea was a fickle mistress; and
none in reminding her that men as good as Joe Duarte were lost up and
down the coast every year. If her mourning took a turn toward denial,
so be it. "What exactly do you mean by *wrong?*"

"I can't get it out of my head," she said. "Ever since the word came
that he was gone, I knew something wasn't right. They said Pop was hit
by one of the otter doors and knocked overboard. That with the size of
the swell and the weight of his clothes, he sank like a stone. That Jackie,
who jumped in after him when he saw him fall, was almost drowned
himself trying to find him. But none of it makes sense. Joe Duarte was
too good a fisherman to—"

"Have an accident?"

"—to mess with his crew's job. And he was a damn sight too smart
to have a net down in rising weather. He'd have smelled it coming, seen
it in the set of the waves, and been on his way home before it hit."

"People make mistakes, Del."

"Not this stupid, Ralph. Believe you me," she said, drumming a red-lacquered fingernail on the tabletop, "my Pop was killed."

Ralph Waldo grunted and glanced at Merry.

Del looked from one to the other, her anger mounting. "*Que pena,*" she said. "Maybe Joe Duarte was hit over the head and thrown in the water, but not by the net doors and not by the swell. He was murdered."

Ralph cleared his throat abruptly and knit his brows, turning the edge of his pasta bowl with one broad thumb as he spoke.

"How many folks crewed for your dad, Adelia?"

"Four. The *Lisboa Girl* is a sixty-five-footer."

"Had they been with him long?"

"Nope. Since most guys nowadays want to fish from the mainland, Pop was having trouble keeping a crew together for longer than a season. I don't know any of them, except Jackie, and he's only been first mate for a year."

"That's right," Merry said. "He'd moved off-island."

"Until he sank the boat he was skippering over on the Cape's backside," Del said. "At least, that's what I heard from my cousins. I was in New Bed at the time."

"He sank a boat, and your dad took him on as first mate?"

"Like I said, with only two boats trawling out of Nantucket, it's tough to find *anybody* to crew. Particularly anyone with experience. Besides, Pop and Jackie's dad, Sylvester, were cronies from way back. Ever since Sylvester died of a heart attack, Pop's tried to look out for Jackie."

"My dear," Ralph said gently, "for what you're saying to be true, the entire crew would have to be lying. And to keep their stories straight, under such pressure, is quite beyond the power of most of the chuckleheads running trawlers for a living. And as I recollect from the newspaper account, the crew was interviewed by the Coast Guard, and the stories agreed."

Adelia nodded and looked away. "It sounds crazy, right?"

"I'm not saying that makes it any less likely, understand." He waved his spaghetti fork for emphasis. "Quite the contrary. But even if we accept, for the moment, that your father was helped into the water, where's the *why* of it? Why would an entire crew want to murder their captain?"

"Maybe they figured they'd get a new one they liked better," Adelia said, "and got paid to do it."

"Meaning?"

"Pop left Jackie the *Lisboa Girl* and the *Praia* free and clear in his will. *Both boats.* Or so Jackie says. I'm calling the lawyer to make sure."

There was a silence. Ralph cleared his throat and shoveled a forkful of pasta into his mouth as a cover for thought.

"He didn't have to leave 'em to me," Del said. "I could've seen him leaving them to Manny or Luis. They're blood, and they coulda used the break. They're running other people's boats because they can't afford the mortgages and the insurance."

"Jackie's come into a fortune," Merry said quietly. "And a way to restore his reputation as a skipper."

"You know what I'm saying, *filha*," Del interjected. "If Jackie wanted a boat, Pop signed his death warrant."

"*If* Jackie killed him," Ralph Waldo said. "Did he know that he stood to inherit?"

"He told me he'd witnessed the will."

Ralph Waldo heard the pain in her voice. Jackie had been Joe's confidant at a crucial moment—when he hadn't given his daughter a thought.

"Think of it," Del pressed. "Guys are lost overboard every year. Especially in storms. All he had to do was pick his moment."

Neither Ralph nor Merry answered, and silence fell around the table, punctuated only by the lilting waver of Sara Duarte singing as she fingered her pasta. Her spoon was abandoned to one side of her plastic mat, and her hands were covered with dark red sauce. Impatiently, Adelia seized a paper napkin and wiped her child's hands clean, moving on to the smeared cheeks, despite Sara's protests.

"I had a gut feeling things were screwy back in New Bed," she said. "But when I heard what Jackie had to say—and the way he said it, tough as nails and like he'd just been caught peeing in the bushes—I just knew Pop was murdered." She threw down the napkin and looked at them both, her eyes sharp and stubborn. "So you guys think I'm crazy. I'm not gonna let it slide. Pop deserves better. And I'm the only one who cares about him, now."

Later, when the dishes were washed and Ralph Waldo was putting the last scouring on the stainless-steel sink, Merry saw Adelia out the door and joined him in the kitchen with a towel.

"Leave them to drain," he said. "There's nothing here needs any particular consideration."

"So what do you think?" she said.

"I think, Meredith Abiah, that your friend is succumbing to the culture of her forebears."

"Which one is that?"

"In my day, the Portuguese fishing community was always rife with rumor and innuendo. If they weren't talking about good and bad luck— who was carrying it and who was spreading it—they were drumming up the latest conspiracy theory about price-fixing in the Boston fish markets. The Portuguese take nothing at face value that they can embroider and embellish. Joe Duarte was getting on in years, he made a mistake, or a series of mistakes, and he paid a heavy price. But it surprises me not at all, Meredith, that his daughter doesn't believe it." He held out his hands for Merry's towel and she handed it to him, hoisting herself up on the Formica counter, legs dangling.

"That business about Jackie and the boats is pretty weird," she said. "It might be worth looking into."

"You mean the boat he sank, as well as the boats he stands to inherit?"

Her eyes gleamed. "Exactly. Here's a guy who's involved in two boat accidents in one year. Even Del can be forgiven for thinking he's carrying bad luck. Or that there's more here than meets the eye. I'm getting pretty interested in his seamanship myself."

"You don't think Joe was murdered, Meredith Abiah?"

"No," she admitted. "Much as I'd like to back Del, I can't say that I do. But she may not drop her vendetta against Jackie until I can prove he had nothing to do it."

"Even proof may mean nothing," Ralph Waldo said. "The Duartes are pretty good haters." He spread the towel on the counter to dry and flipped off the light. The sound of rain pattering on the kitchen's roof filled the darkened room. "It can't hurt to help an old friend, I suppose."

But Merry was looking over Ralph's shoulder at the open door. Her father's voice swept into the room along with the roar of the storm.

"In my experience, helping an old friend is always a prelude to disaster," John Folger said. He was standing half in and half out of the kitchen, wrenching off his sodden shoes. "Which old friend are we helping now?"

"Joe Duarte," Merry said. "Adelia wants us to find his murderer."

CHAPTER FOUR

MERRY TURNED INTO THE
Coast Guard compound at Brant Point, its square buildings looming as
purely white as a Greek fishing village in the glare off the harbor. She
had walked down Easton Street from the station at South Water, osten-
sibly to avoid the traffic from the eleven-thirty car ferry, but in truth
she'd have clutched at any excuse to be outside. The previous day's storm
had given way to a brilliant May morning of sun and high cumulus, with
a fresh breeze that sent the sailboats' riggings clanging metallically
against their masts. It was the sort of spring day that came all too rarely
on an island affectionately called the Gray Lady for its persistent fogs.

Everywhere about the compound lay desks and cot frames torn out
of their rooms, grayed mattresses piled high, chairs overturned on their
sides; spring cleaning for the Coast Guard, Merry guessed. She turned
away from the postcard perfection of the boat basin and ran up the steps
of the main building, lifting her sunglasses to the top of her head as she
pulled open the heavy door.

The interior of the station was dim and cool, blinding her for a
moment as she stood in the doorway, blinking and searching for a point
of focus.

"Detective Folger."

Terry Samson's high-pitched, cracking voice, a voice no man de-
served, and certainly not the compact fighting weight that was Terry.
He was standing by the refrigerator in the midst of the station's eating
area, holding a pitcher of lemonade, looking for all the world like Tom
Cruise in *Top Gun*. The sunglasses worn inside were a bit much.

"What can I do for you?" The words fell somewhere between a
screech and a whine.

Merry winced involuntarily and turned it quickly into a smile. "Terry. I figured you'd be out on patrol."

"Not this shift. I'm on tomorrow—always seem to draw more Saturday nights than anyone else, and I'm beginning to think the system's rigged. Do me a favor and investigate."

"I'm actually here on a case, if you've got the time to help me," Merry said.

"Anything I can do, Merry, you know that. This concern the boatborne drug ring Woods Hole keeps yammering about?"

Drug ring. First word *she'd* heard. That might be something to offer her father, since he'd told her in no uncertain terms to leave the Duarte mess alone. In John Folger's opinion, the state police should handle Joe's death if it was suspect—and the DA in Barnstable wouldn't like the Nantucket force jumping turf. Merry had enough on her plate anyway, he said. Even now, she was supposed to be calling on an elderly woman in Dionis who claimed to have had her geraniums stolen from their pots. Some plate.

"You keep a record of boating accidents, right?" she asked Terry.

"Sure. We have written reports—recent and archived—and a computerized database that went on-line last year."

"Does it show accidents all over New England, or just around Nantucket?"

He took a swig of lemonade straight from the jug, let out a deep sigh, and closed the refrigerator door. "We're part of the Woods Hole Group here, Merry. That covers everything from the Cape Cod Canal to Point Judith, Rhode Island. Anything that happened in these waters would be in the archived reports. The LEISII—that's the computer database—could turn up a broader range, depending on what you're looking for." He shoved the sunglasses to the top of his head, ruffling his hair in an unwittingly endearing fashion, and waited for information.

"I'd like you to check your accident reports from last year," she said. "A boat that went down off the Cape, I think."

"Commercial or pleasure?"

"Commercial, actually."

"That helps. We keep track of commercial captains anyway—if they're licensed." He looked at her quizzically. "This some sort of insurance fraud deal?"

Merry restrained herself from wincing again as his voice cracked, and shook her head. "It's nothing like that, Terry, just a check on a couple of stories I've run into in another matter."

"Okay. *Don't* tell me until it's all over. How far back you want to go?"

She thought quickly. Adelia said Jackie had come on as first mate the previous spring; for the sake of thoroughness, she'd better survey from the first of the previous year. "Last January, I guess," she said.

Not surprisingly, the bulk of the commercial fishing accidents occurred during the rough weather of late winter and early spring, when the Atlantic was fiercely cold, the swell was dramatic, and the water was the color of a submarine's steel hull. These were the months when the New England fishing community eked out a living, waiting for the return of the summer schools, competing with the Spaniards and the Norwegians and the Russians for whatever bottom fish remained in international waters. Tough as the work was, nobody could afford to stay home.

Since Jackie's boat had sunk off the Cape, the written report had been sent to Woods Hole, and it would take a few days to retrieve. Terry turned instead to the computer database, punched in Jackie's name, and turned up two accident reports within seconds. One was as recent as last week, and concerned Joe Duarte; as first mate, Jackie's name was on record as the point of contact. The second dated from last April. Terry pushed back his chair, waved Merry toward the screen, and said, "It's all yours."

Jackie had sunk the *Seaman's Folly* just off Wellfleet Harbor during a sudden storm on April 16. The Coast Guard had made short work of the details. The report said only that while attempting to race for port, the captain had struck an unmarked wreck in seven fathoms of water, and the boat had foundered rapidly. The five-man crew was saved, owing to a timely SOS. The boat's owner—a corporation called SeaCon—lost its investment and Jackie lost his job.

Merry looked up from the monitor, deflated. What had she expected? A red flag hidden in the efficient prose? The hint that a criminal act had gone undetected?

A *pattern.* That's what she'd hoped to see: something that linked the accidents. But whatever might be hidden in Jackie Alcantrara's past, the Coast Guard report wasn't telling.

She looked back at the screen. Mortgaged boats carried insurance by law, and as with any accident, the proof of the policy and its under-writer were recorded in the report. The SeaCon Corporation had placed its trust in a company called Water Rights. Maybe it was worth inves-tigating the claim's outcome.

"Thanks, Terry," she said, rising and glancing at her watch. "You've been very helpful. I'll take you to lunch when all this is over and fill in the gaps."

"And I promise to praise your detecting skill without claiming any part in the victory," he said.

If I can stand to listen to your voice, poor man, she thought, and sped toward Emily Teasdale and her missing geraniums.

"Needs more balsamic vinegar." Tess Starbuck passed Peter Mason the spoon with an air of conviction.

He sipped the liquid tentatively and screwed up his face. "Needs *sugar,* surely?"

Tess sighed and handed him a piece of lettuce. "You're not in the habit of drinking salad dressing straight from the bottle, are you? Try it with something grassy-flavored, and imagine warm duck breast slivered on top. An autumnal taste is what we're going for here."

Rafe leaned in the doorway, arms crossed, and decided not to involve himself in the debate. Too many cooks, and so forth; and besides, his allegiance was murky: his bride-to-be or his boss of six years. The two of them had been experimenting with the cranberry-based dressing for much of the afternoon. It was one of a series of concoctions intended for bottling under a new Mason Farms Comestibles label. Tess had per-suaded Peter to play the role of partner, promising to showcase his pro-duce, cranberries, and spring lamb in ways certain to wow the New York food critics. They were to test the line at the Greengage this summer, and eventually launch it upon an unsuspecting world.

Thank God for Memorial Day weekend and the start of the tourist trade, Rafe thought, and felt a sudden sense of blasphemy. He'd always decried the yearly invasion of off-islanders, claiming they took and spoiled and gave nothing back; but Tess's business had changed his mind. Her livelihood was directly dependent upon the summer people, and the good opinion of a few powerful critics in the mainland enclaves of Boston, Manhattan, and Washington, D.C.

He hated the worry lines around Tess's eyes and the heightened streaks of gray in her rich hair. She was forty-three years old, and had suffered the vagaries of sudden death and accident. First there was her husband, Dan, lost overboard from his scalloper two years back in a nor'easter; and then there was her son, Will, haunted by his father's death and struck down in a vicious attack the previous September. He had survived, but his motor skills were impaired and his after-school hours were spent in physical therapy rather than the hoped-for Nantucket Whalers football practice. By late April, he had finally seemed his old self, despite the migraine headaches that still swept over him without warning, leaving him lost and silent in his darkened attic room for days at a time.

Throughout the off-season, Tess had struggled to make ends meet and nurse her son back to health; the Mason Farms line had been born of frustrated creativity and financial need. Whether Peter had decided to back her out of kindness or a hereditary business sense Rafe couldn't say, but he was grateful regardless.

"This'd be great with the lamb-and-apple sausage, too," Peter said, chewing the lettuce ruminatively. "But that'd be more of a spring salad."

"Right. Slice it thin, layer it with the chèvre, and put it on baby field greens." Tess turned from him briskly and sought out the vinegar. "I can see using the dressing with melon and papaya and some green chilies in a fruit salsa, too. But I'll work on that tomorrow, okay?"

"The restaurant opens tomorrow," Peter said.

"Salsa takes maybe twenty minutes. If it works, I'll serve it for lunch. I'll get it to you and add it to the file." Tess was keeping an informal compilation of recipes, thinking long-term of *The Greengage Way*, her pet cookbook project.

"We should enter these in the cranberry festival cook-off," Peter said.

"By October, I'll have the kinks worked out. *Something* should win a first-prize ribbon."

Rafe handed Tess a towel. "I'll run you home."

"I thought Will got his license," Peter said.

"He did." She dried her hands briskly. "Why do you think I've got no car?"

*   *   *

On the way back to town in Peter's Range Rover, Tess was quiet and abstracted. *Thinking about the food*, Rafe decided. She had come to her business late in life, but it was her passion, born of innate talent and the thrill of making money from what she loved.

"You look tired, hon," he said. "Whaddya say we hit the Brotherhood for a burger and a beer?" The Brotherhood of Thieves was a favorite of tourists and natives alike; they took no credit cards, no checks, and no reservations, and every day the line of hopeful diners snaked out the door and up Broad Street. The place never failed to cheer Tess.

She slid over and leaned her head against his shoulder. "Can I have a Sam Adams?"

"You can have two."

"Nobody's in town yet, really. It'll be our last chance to have the Brotherhood to ourselves."

Once on Broad Street, he managed to find a parking space—something else that would vanish with Memorial Day weekend—and got a table for two in a dim corner of the Brotherhood's subterranean space. It was only five, but neither he nor Tess had eaten lunch, and the prospect of food was stimulating. There was a fire burning on the hearth, perfect for the end-of-May chilliness that came off the water of an evening, and Rafe leaned back in his chair with a sigh.

"Get a beer in my hand now, and I'll feel like I've died and gone to heaven."

"You work hard today?"

"Nope." He grinned. "But I was probably thinking too much."

"About what Merry said?" Tess's eyes dropped to her hands. She was worrying at her engagement ring, sliding it nervously back and forth. Sometimes Rafe wished he'd given her a car or something practical instead, but he shuddered to think what she'd have done with a steering wheel in times of mental foment.

"You think it's a bad idea," he said flatly.

"Not because I'm jealous, Rafe. You don't think that, do you?"

"Of course not," he lied.

"I'm too much of an adult not to trust the man I love, even if he's spending eight hours in the sun on a small boat in the middle of the

Atlantic with a woman ten years my junior who's known for her loose morals."

"Adelia Duarte's never been known for loose morals," he said, "and you know it, Tess. She made a mistake, is all—" He bit his tongue. The last thing Tess needed to hear was his defense of a woman she'd decided to mistrust.

"Hi, folks!" A cheery college kid of a waiter, on the island early and clearly ready to enjoy the summer. "Have you seen our specials on the blackboard?"

"Yep," Rafe said, to stem the endless recitation of ingredients he knew would follow. "And I think we've decided."

"Great! What can I get for you this evening?"

He looked at Tess; her arms were crossed and her eyes stared into the fire stonily. "The lady'll have a New Yorker and a Sam Adams," he said, "and I'll have a Bostonian with the same." He slapped the menus shut and handed them to the waiter with a smile. The kid nodded at both of them and headed for the kitchen.

Tess stood up immediately and stalked after the waiter, all her fury in her thin form. She grabbed him by the elbow. *Changing her dinner*, Rafe thought. She'd probably really wanted the bacon cheeseburger he'd ordered for her—it was her standing meal at the Brotherhood—but God forbid that the defender of Adelia Duarte should be right about anything.

Tess slumped back down in her seat, eyes still glued to the flickering hearth.

"So if you're not jealous, why are you in such a hissy fit?"

"Because I can't believe you'd be so stupid as to alienate Peter Mason," she said. "Running around after swordfish—which believe me, I know as a restaurateur are scarce as hens' teeth—when you can make a steady income and have the stability you do after six years at Mason Farms—" She put her face in her hands in frustration, and Rafe saw with alarm that she had begun to cry.

"Tess," he said, reaching a hand to her shoulder gently, "Peter doesn't mind. This is a slow point in the farming season. I've got some days free. There's no harm in it, girl. And I'd be helping out an old friend."

"I'm just so afraid," Tess said. Her voice was muffled by her fingers.

"Of what?"

"Of you. Of the whole fishing thing. I know you, Rafe—you've never gotten over your love of that life. It's in your blood. The slow season will turn into the high season, and you'll be out there just one more day, and pretty soon you won't be there when Peter needs you for the cranberry harvest, and you'll just gradually slip away. Back to boats and the craziness of the fishing grounds and the relentless work and the lousy money."

"Tess—"

"Well, I've lived that life, Rafe." Her head came up out of her hands, and he saw the reddened wetness where she'd rubbed at her eyes. "I lost Dan to it. We never had a dime we hadn't spent three times over, and we were never out of debt a single day of our married lives. He handed me that debt at the side of his grave, and I'm still not close to paying it off. I've only added to it. Can't you see that financial security is the one thing I need in my life?"

"I thought what you needed was me," he said, feeling suddenly cold.

"Not if you're on a fishing boat." She averted her eyes. "I vowed never to get involved with that life again. I can't face the instability and the possibility of—loss. You could die out there like Dan did. Like Joe Duarte did, for God's sake. Don't you people ever learn?"

"Dan and Joe were exceptions," Rafe said falteringly.

"And you never believe that anything will happen to you, do you?" She laughed, a short, humorless sound. "I'm just starting to make a foothold in a world I love, and I *will not* allow myself or my son to be dragged back down. I want Will to grow up knowing there's something more to life besides gutting fish and mending nets."

"Is that an ultimatum?"

She looked back at him wordlessly.

"Is it, Tess?"

"I don't know."

"Well, you think about it. Because July twenty-third isn't far away. And when I marry, Ms. Starbuck, I intend it to be for richer, for poorer, in good times and in bad, in farming or on the water. And I intend it to be for keeps." He pushed back his chair, pulled out his wallet, and threw twenty dollars on the table. "Wouldn't want you to worry about the bill," he said, and turned away.

There was a sharp ping on his back followed by a metallic clink at his feet. She'd thrown her engagement ring as he walked out the door.

CHAPTER FIVE

P ETER MASON WATCHED
Rafe and Tess down the drive from his open front door, then shut it
carefully. He intended to pursue the salad dressing—this time as accom-
paniment to the marinating chicken breasts Rebecca had left on the
counter for his supper. He would grill and slice them into the lettuce
he'd pulled from the garden that morning, open a bottle of Kendall-
Jackson chardonnay, and tuck into a healthy meal that felt like Memorial
Day weekend. All it lacked was company.

He stopped in the act of opening the kitchen door and thought
about it, gray eyes focused on the kitchen clock. For some reason the
numbered dial had been overlaid with Merry Folger's face. What was he
waiting for? He'd been haunted by the blond detective throughout the
winter, the strongest proof he could find that he'd recovered from a dec-
ade-long obsession with his college sweetheart. Seeing Alison after his
brother's murder had finally put to rest the long ache; he no longer
mourned his broken engagement. Instead, he'd exchanged Christmas
cards with her. And lately, when the form of a woman invaded his
dreams at night, exquisite and pulsating and unreachable as the sky, she
had borne the sharp cheekbones, the eyes cool as water under leaves, of
Meredith Folger.

But what of Merry herself? What, in fact, of her feelings for Rafe?
On every occasion that Peter had seen her during the past eight months,
she had seemed much as usual—friendly, warm, and carefully professional. He shut the refrigerator door without retrieving the lettuce and
threw himself into a kitchen chair.

It was important, after all, to approach emotion with logic. Never
mind that the two had nothing to do with each other. It was part of his

classical education to consider a problem objectively and to fear any action not preceded by thought.

Consider, for example, whether it would be better to risk himself with Merry and be rejected, or to remain silent and hope that she would eventually fall in love with him of her own accord. He searched his mind for historical precedent. What would Napoleon have done in such a situation? Taken the former course, obviously, and hoped the stars and his brilliant maneuvers were enough to win the day. Risking oneself had all the appeal of romanticism and the daring wager. He'd spent too many years being protective and sensible. It was time for rasher acts.

He reached for the phone hanging on the kitchen wall and dialed information. He didn't even know her number at home, though she'd called him from there once or twice the previous fall; and he realized suddenly just how official how much of their contact had been. For an instant his resolve fled, and then the voice of the operator came on the line, forcing him forward.

She arrived looking as cool and elegant as if she'd just stepped from a luxury hotel instead of the kitchen on Tattle Court, where in fact she'd been feeding Sara Duarte her supper. She had changed from her jeans into a jade-green washed silk sheath—nothing expensive, but clean-lined and simple enough on her tall, thin frame that it looked like a million bucks. The color exactly matched her eyes. Peter drew a sharp breath when he saw her step out of her new unmarked police Explorer, struck by the fact that she had gone to some effort over his invitation, and too amazed even to think what that might mean.

She looked for him in the window, and smiled when she saw him; and all he could think was, *Where does she get off being so calm?*

The dinner had turned into something more elaborate than grilled chicken salad during the hour preceding her arrival, and he hoped he hadn't gone overboard, didn't look too eager, with his smoked bluefish pâté and his corn muffins and the new red potatoes sliced into his baby Bibb lettuce—but Merry was a good little eater and dove into the food with a sigh of delight, allowing him to refill her glass with the chilled chardonnay, moisture pearling the side of the crystal until she pressed it against her forehead and closed her eyes, in a gesture at once so sensual and childlike that it tightened his throat.

He had promised himself he would not push her this evening; he feared losing her entirely by being too hasty. So he looked away from the moist glass filled with wine and studied the early roses beyond his window as she told him about Adelia Duarte and her father and the possibility of a murder case, however unlikely, and however much the province of the state police. What he wanted was to reach across the table and take hold of her long, thin fingers, the hands that were tanned and weathered from a lifetime in sun; wanted to kiss her palm and then the forehead she had tried to cool with her glass. He shut his eyes.

"So we're going tomorrow. Do you want to come?"

He blinked and looked back at her, and for an instant, perhaps, she saw the intensity of the entire world staring out from under his hawklike brows. He recognized it in her face, the way her features went blank in surprise and then recovered. She took a sip of wine.

"Go where? I'm sorry, I'm afraid I was thinking of something else."

"Swordfishing. With Rafe and Adelia and me. It'll be a wonderful day on the water—like nothing you've ever done. Say you'll come, Peter."

He held her eyes a minute, assessing. She didn't blink. "Maybe I will," he said.

They left the Town Pier off South Beach at six in the morning, when the sun laid a white light on the water and the coffee in Rafe's thermos tasted very good. Peter and Merry were braced by the long steel pulpit jutting from the bow, Rafe was at the helm, and Adelia studied the charts. The *Cormorant* was a forty-four-foot sportfishing boat she'd chartered cheap from one of Joe Duarte's cronies, past all fishing now and only too glad to earn something from the custom Brownell he kept loitering at its mooring. They made their way through the harbor to the narrow channel between the jetties and Nantucket Sound beyond. Out past Point Rip, a huge submerged sandbar that signaled its presence with white-rilled waves and a darker shadow on the nautical charts. Then into the broad depth of the Great Round Shoal Channel, and finally, when the coffee was long gone and they'd progressed to Rebecca's muffins, toward the deceptive and shifting bars of the Great Round Shoal itself, northeast of the island, where entire schools lurked in the shimmering depths and many a boat had run aground in decades past.

An hour went by. The great swords were elsewhere.

"Let's head for the wreck of the *Andrea Doria*," Rafe said.

"That's forty miles south." Del looked annoyed.

"If they're in Nantucket waters, they're basking over that ship." Rafe chewed his beard, holding in his temper.

Del scanned the horizon an instant, then shrugged. *"Ta bom,"* she said. "Let's go."

Rafe throttled the engines higher and turned the boat toward the waters beyond Siasconset.

Two hours or so passed in surging motion. Adelia took the wheel, one eye on the charts, and Rafe came forward to where Peter sat, quiet in the rush of the wind and sun, his face speckled with the white spots of dried salt from the spray shushing over the Brownell's bow. He was wearing faded Nantucket Reds and Docksides, his traditional sailing togs, with a heavy sweatshirt to ward off the chill. Despite the sun the wind had raised gooseflesh along his tanned thigh, something he seemed not to notice.

"Happy?" he asked Rafe.

Rafe shrugged. "I'd be happier if Tess weren't in such a snit."

"Take her some swordfish steaks this evening and tell her I caught the thing," Peter said. "Maybe she'll get over it."

"Fat chance. If we even *see* a sword today."

"That rare?"

"That rare. Some people say they've been overfished, by the Spanish long-liners in particular. Those boats'll put out a thousand hooks at a time and take everything they can get. Others say the swords are just too cagey to be caught anymore. One thing's for certain—the fish that're coming in to market are half the size of the ones caught a couple decades ago. Either they're not living as long before they're caught, or the bigger ones have learned to stay away from the fishing lanes. Whatever it is, they're the king of the sportfishing business, I'll tell you that. A good swordfish can weigh half a ton and be fifteen feet long—not that we see many of 'em anymore. But you go up against one of these babies traveling fifty miles an hour, with your feet in that pulpit and a harpoon in your hand, you'd better not blink. Sometimes they even attack the boat. It's the only thing comes close to Moby Dick."

Peter looked toward Adelia, who was studying gauges on the bridge. She had the short, sturdy body of a Portuguese fisherman, the muscled arms and the strong legs. She looked bred into this life, as indeed she was. Her long dark hair was pulled through a baseball cap—a *swordfishing* cap, as Rafe had reminded him—and her face was intent and efficient.

"She doesn't look like she blinks much," Peter said.

"Sure don't. But we'll have to see."

"We're at thirty fathoms, Rafe," Adelia called out.

"What's the water temperature?"

"Hovering right around seventy."

"That's it. Start lookin'." He turned to Peter. "Back in the eighties, when I was still working my cousin's boat out of New Bed, the swords used to bask along this thirty-fathom line. Two miles north, two miles south, you won't find 'em; but if they're here, they're *here*, you see what I mean."

He sent Merry into the tower at the ship's midsection to scan the blue-green sea, and took over the wheel. Adelia made her way to the bow and climbed into the pulpit, rolling her shoulders in anticipation. She lashed the harpoon horizontally across the bowsprit and fed the line aft, where it lay coiled in a barrel, one end tied to a bright yellow float. Peter glanced up at Merry and saw her puzzled look. He decided to join her.

"What exactly are you supposed to be looking for?"

She turned to him with something like despair. "I haven't the foggiest."

"Rafe!" he shouted below. "What're we looking for up here?"

"Dorsal fin breaking the surface, you idiot. Or a bunch of gulls hovering over something in the water. That might mean the sword is fishing himself. Lot of menhaden and blues in these waters, and swords love 'em. Or with all this sunlight, you should be able to see the body cruising below the surface. Shaped like a torpedo, or a shark—you remember *Jaws*. The sun'll pick out the colors. Smaller ones're blue, big ones look dark gray."

"I see one!" Merry cried excitedly, pointing and jumping in the tower. "Over there, Peter! See it?"

He craned to look and registered something long and blue, almost ten feet it seemed, a few boat lengths away. The dorsal fin was breaking the surface.

Adelia was poised and craning from the pulpit as Rafe brought the boat in alongside the enormous fish, floating just under the surface of the waves like a submerged log. Merry had gone completely still, and Peter realized with a start that she had taken his hand and was holding it tightly.

"Forget it, Rafe!" Adelia yelled. "Shark."

Merry dropped Peter's hand, deflated and relieved at once, he thought, and let out a deep breath.

"Let's keep looking," he said. "You scan that side, I'll scan this."

An hour went by, with Rafe cruising first southeast, then northwest, along the thirty-fathom line. It was noon, the sun high and warm, the breeze cooling now instead of chill. Peter and Merry switched sides, then gave up and descended from the tower to eat some lunch and rest their eyes. They had seen nothing but unbroken ocean—not a tuna, not another shark, and certainly not a swordfish.

It was only once they had torn into Rebecca's cheese-and-tomato sandwiches that Adelia, glancing idly to starboard, caught the first roiling of the fin through the water. "Three o'clock!" she yelled, leaping to the pulpit and drawing the harpoon across her body, dart facing to starboard. "Three boat lengths."

The fish began to run, and Rafe brought the boat around quickly and steadily, down-sun from the fish, a giant, gray-slick mass slicing rapidly toward the bow. Merry and Peter were poised on either side of the fifteen-foot pulpit, tensed and wordless.

"Sword it is," Adelia said, leaning far over the protective bar, harpoon poised. Her scarlet nails flashed in the sunlight. "A nice little one. A marker."

"What's a marker?"

"Hunnerd 'n' fifty pounds or so."

Peter's gaze shifted from the woman to the fish, watching as she led the broadbill with her dart, left hand gripping the shaft, right palm on the harpoon's heel. The fish came closer. Del's shoulders moved. *Strike.*

She seemed poised like a gymnast on the shaft running straight down into the water, the fish frozen by the pin thrust near its dorsal fin. Her shoulders heaved up and thrust downward a second time, almost falling over the pulpit's side, driving the dart deeper into the fish's flesh. Then she yanked the shaft of the harpoon upward, pulling it free from the dart and the line attached to it, just as the big fish surged off into the water.

"There he goes," she said, almost hoarsely, and slid down against the pulpit's rails. Peter, mesmerized by the entire sight, only now came alive and climbed up into the pulpit to offer her a hand. Almost stumbling from relieved tension, Adelia ducked back into the boat and gave a war whoop of victory.

The sixty-fathom line was running out rapidly from its barrel, and in a few more seconds, the yellow floater zipped over the side of the boat and skittered across the waves. The fish was diving, diving, desperate for sanctuary; but the constant tugging against line and dart would eventually wear down its strength.

For fifteen minutes the diving and the plunging continued. Then the yellow ball no longer jiggled on the surface. Somewhere in the depths the great fish had fallen still. Rafe slowly brought the boat alongside the yellow floater, and the rest of them moved to the stern, securing the ball on deck and beginning the arduous task of hauling the line back on board. They had nearly two hundred pounds of fish to pull to the surface, hand over hand, and there was life in the great beast yet. Three times the line they collected was run out by the fish's dying throes, and four times they hauled it in.

"It's a tug-of-war," Merry said.

"Exactly." Rafe was the anchorman behind the rest of them, muscles bulging against the force of the fish, the taut line chafing his leathery palm. "This is where it comes down to us or him. He knows it, we know it. Come on, boy," he said. "I ain't gonna stand here forever."

The dorsal fin and tail broke the surface; the fish circled a few times off to starboard, and then finally rolled on its side. The purplish, fluorescent scales glowed vividly in the sun. Merry gasped as she saw the great dark eye, alive and seemingly fixed directly on her, and found to her dismay that she was crying. Despite her island childhood, she had known such creatures only by rumor, and to witness one fight for its existence was profoundly moving. She glanced at Adelia. All she saw on the other woman's face was weariness, excitement, exultation. She was truly her father's daughter, then. Merry could not have done this daily for anything in the world; it would drain and break her within a week.

"Let's bring him alongside," Rafe said, leaving the tail of the rope in Peter's hands. He towed the fish against the side of the boat and lassoed the tail. Then it was a matter of block and tackle, winching the massive weight into the air until it hung alongside, head alone remaining in the water. The purple scales had begun to fade to a silvery gray.

"Seven, eight feet. Two hundred pounds, easy," Adelia said. She reached into her pocket for a knife, leaned over the side, and slit the fish's throat. The water darkened suddenly with blood. Merry turned her face into Peter's shoulder, felt his arm come up around her, and closed her eyes.

They headed for home, the fish soaked with buckets of seawater and shrouded in wet canvas to keep it fresh.

"I probably made a thousand bucks today," Adelia said. "With the price of harpooned swordfish right now, at least a thousand bucks."

Peter whistled.

"Of course, I spent a couple hundred on fuel. And I'm splitting what's left over with Rafe. But still. I could get by with one fish a week. If I'm lucky, maybe I'll find two."

Rafe snorted from his post at the wheel. "This could be the first and last fish you see all season, Del. Don't get cocky."

Merry said nothing, staring out at the late-afternoon light as they rounded Great Point. There was ugliness in police work, but rarely of her own making; what got her up in the morning was the hope of stemming some of the violence. Or redressing it, if violence had already been done. She was not equipped to enjoy it, and she could never have embraced it, as Adelia clearly did. Despite the warmth of the day, she pulled the sweatshirt draped across her back closer around her neck, and retreated into herself.

Adelia was sipping a Coke on the bridge, watching Rafe navigate the channel into Nantucket Harbor.

"So that's the famous Peter Mason," she said.

"I don't know about famous. Rich, yeah. But that just happened to him, same as it *didn't* happen to you and me. An accident of birth."

"And he likes it that way."

Rafe shot her a glance. "What do you want to know, Del?"

She smiled and shook her head. "Merry wrote to me a couple of times during that murder case last year," she said. "He gave her some trouble, didn't he?"

"He was just trying to keep a lid on things," Rafe said, "what with getting shot himself and not knowing whether his brother was killed by mistake. And Merry may not have told you, but there was a time when she thought Peter ran Rusty over and left him to drown in the bog. That doesn't make for warm feelings."

"*Que pena.*"

"Whaddya mean, too bad?"

"He's fallen for her like a ton of bricks."

Rafe hawked and spit into the sea by way of answer.

"How long you lived with this guy?" Del said, laughing. "You tellin' me you can't see it?"

"If I'm blind, that makes two of us," Rafe said, looking over his shoulder. "Merry doesn't have a clue."

CHAPTER SIX

"**N**AME?"

"Joshua Field."

"Spell it."

The kid in the Birkenstocks, Greenpeace T-shirt, and two-hundred-dollar faux-nineteenth-century horn-rimmed spectacles complied, albeit with disdain. Perhaps she still smelled of fish, Merry thought; she couldn't tell. Her olfactory threshhold had long since been passed. For reasons she was about to learn, Joshua Field had thrown fish guts and blood over her head as she debarked from Del's boat. A quick dousing under the Town Pier's hot-water shower hadn't done much to cleanse her. Her gorge rose at the memory of the slimy mess, and she stared at Field malevolently. He failed to look dismayed.

Never mind. He'd still be sitting in a holding cell when she was warm in her bath.

"Age?"

"Twenty."

"Occupation?"

"Student. At BU."

"Address?"

"Three-twenty Commonwealth Avenue, Apartment Three-A, Boston."

She leaned back in her desk chair and glanced out her office door at the station's upstairs conference area. Only one other guy was in on this late Saturday afternoon of Memorial Day weekend; the rest were either off-duty or out pounding the streets as the first wave of summer residents landed on Nantucket. She'd hoped to have dinner with Peter after Rafe had docked the Brownell, but in the midst of unloading the great fish and figuring out how to get it to the scales and the wholesalers, Joshua Field attacked. After a moment's stunned silence, Peter punched him flat on his back, an act that galvanized Merry into action; she arrested Field for assaulting a police officer and told Peter to go home.

"So tell me, Field, why's a kid like you pouring fish guts over a police officer's head?"

"I didn't know you were a cop."

"I figured that. Let me rephrase the question. Why fish guts at all? Couldn't you just have run over somebody's mailbox at night, or scribbled graffiti on the side of the Finast?"

"You think this was a petty act of vandalism?" he said, in tones of shock. "It was a *symbolic* act." He leaned forward, his face a mixture of self-satisfaction and fanaticism, and drew a piece of paper from his pocket.

He's going to pound the table, Merry thought, and closed her eyes.

"The slaughter of the swordfish population is a travesty, a disgrace, and a black mark on this nation's soul," Field proclaimed, pounding the table. "Spawning stocks of Atlantic swordfish have declined dramatically in recent decades, by almost three-quarters their 1970s level. Long-line seining by international shipping conglomerates contributes to the overfishing of the already dwindling population. Congress, in the pockets of the commercial fishing industry, has failed repeatedly to adopt amendments to the Marine Mammals Act that might rein in the catch of swordfish and save the species. Unless the heedless greed of the commercial fishermen is thwarted, unless the fishing industry itself is made to pay for the destruction it has wantonly visited upon one of the noblest creatures in the sea, the swordfish will be extinct by the year 2000."

"Whoa, whoa, whoa, Josh."

"Joshua."

"I like the part about heedless greed, but I still don't see where the fish guts come in."

He sighed and thrust his glasses higher on the bridge of his nose. "National action, pressure on political organs, and the galvanization of the press are important, of course," he said, "but the fish are being slaughtered in ports throughout New England. We need to hurt the fishermen where they live. We need to make them feel the consequences of their acts. If the carnage touches them personally, perhaps they'll begin to listen."

"Forgive me, Joshua," Merry began, and then stopped, studying his face. "This is a cause that clearly means a great deal to you. Are you a marine biology major or something?"

"Political science."

"Oh. Well, as I said—forgive me, but fish guts are something fishermen see every day. Sort of like a butcher sees bones. They're not going to be moved by it. I admit it had an effect on *me*—but as I've explained, I'm not normally fishing for a living. Try it again on one of the commercial guys and all you're likely to get for your trouble is a pretty severe beating. Okay?"

"If that's what the cause requires of me, I see no reason to shirk it," he said. "I'm not going to run in the face of big business and its thugs."

"Oh, for crying out loud—there *is* no big business in fishing on Nantucket. Do you know whose boat you attacked today? A single mother's. She has a two-year-old to feed. She's not hauling in several tons of swordfish a day in long-line nets. In fact, she's harpooning them one by one, which is highly labor-intensive, and actually in demand among restaurants right now. Did you know that?"

"I'm a vegetarian."

"Look, Joshua—the point is this. It takes far more effort and ingenuity and skill to harpoon a single swordfish a week than it does to net thirty. If restaurants are paying high prices for *harpooned* fish, then more and more fishermen are going to abandon long-line seining and try to catch them with harpoons. But there's no way they'll be able to catch them in the same volume. Now, doesn't it sound like my friend Del is the best news your swordfish have had in years? If the trend toward harpooning continues, the population is bound to recover over time. Do you see what I'm saying?"

He stared at her stonily. She struggled on. "And another thing. You're wrong about the lack of controls. The National Marine Fisheries Service closely monitors the swordfish population, among others, and sets limits on the season. They close off spawning grounds to fishing during certain times of the year. It's not as bad as it seems."

"Are you done with me?" he said.

"Just about. There's the matter of the night in a cell you get to spend with us."

* * *

Merry fingerprinted Joshua Field on the station's invisible-ink palm-print roller, then took full-face and profile mug shots. It was just a few steps to the holding pen, where she could legally keep him for twenty-four hours; longer than that, and he'd have to be flown off-island by the sheriff, since the station had no prisoner shower. Not that Joshua Field merited a prolonged arrest; she hoped only to teach him a minor lesson. Whether he would learn it was another question. He seemed almost impressed with the eight-by-ten area allotted him for the night. Merry left Field to contemplate his nobility in the company of a mattressless steel cot bolted to the floor and a stainless-steel latrine, and thankfully went home.

The phone rang as she was wrapping herself in her terry robe, hair fragrant and skin softened, feeling remote from the varied events of a day that had begun in the duskiness of 5:00 A.M. Ralph had some leftover spaghetti waiting for her in the kitchen, and nothing in the world—not even dinner with Peter—sounded half as good.

"Meredith!"

"Yes, Ralph?"

"Telephone."

It was Peter, his voice dark and hesitant on the line.

"Wow. Twice in two days. I'm honored, Mr. Mason."

"Are you all right?"

"Having had my bath, I feel almost wonderful."

"What was with that little creep?"

"Protesting the near-extinction of the swordfishing industry. I mean the swordfish. They are *not* the same thing in the young man's mind."

"Oh, my God."

"Peter, are you telling me that you never protested anything while you were at Princeton?"

"Well—" He had the grace to sound embarrassed. "I *did* throw chicken blood on Nassau Hall once to protest the university's investment portfolio."

"Its *investment* portfolio? How like a Mason."

"Because of their South African investments," he said patiently. "A few years after I left, they divested, but I doubt I had much to do with it. And that still doesn't explain why the kid got you, of all people."

"I suppose he meant to hit Del, only he didn't know any better. He wasn't all bad."

"You kept him overnight?"

"I did. But I think he'll actually enjoy it. Any sort of martyrdom for the cause will make him feel rather special."

"At least he wasn't able to follow you home."

"Peter! You can't be serious. He was completely harmless."

"I'm not so sure, Merry." He hesitated, as if weighing his next words. "I wouldn't want anything to happen to you. Promise me you'll be careful, okay?"

Seemingly innocent words, the words any friend might offer another. But they kept her abstracted and silent over her spaghetti that night, and twice she had to ask Ralph to repeat what he had said.

She was on duty the next day, Sunday. She released Joshua Field, took an address and phone number where he could be reached, and watched him hoist his backpack onto one shoulder and head off toward town. Then she set about tidying the file of a case she'd closed a few weeks back—a fairly simple burglary investigation. She'd been assigned nothing major since, and it was time her brain was put to use. The station was pretty quiet, and Merry felt restless. She glanced at her father's darkened office, considered the hour—one o'clock—and picked up the phone.

Jackie Alcantrara had gone down to the Town Pier to work on the *Lisboa Girl*, his wife told Merry. The lawyer wouldn't let him operate it until it was officially his—meaning after the will had been probated and he'd paid some form of inheritance tax to the state, and God alone knew where *that* money would come from, with Jackie unable to fish—but he wasn't a man to sit at home when there was work that could be done, and one of the things that needed doing was mending net. Merry thanked her, picked up her enormous shoulder bag, and headed for the Town Pier.

The sixty-five-foot *Lisboa Girl* was about thirty years old, Merry guessed—pushing the limit of her intended life span, but kept, through careful dry-docking every few springs, in the sort of shape that allowed her to survive the following January's weather. She was moored not at a slip but at the far end of the dock, one of the few spots that accommodated her size; near her sat the dark blue *Ruthie B.*, Nantucket's only other dragger. The *Lisboa Girl's* hull was of cypress, painted white with racing stripes in the colors of the Portuguese flag; but the steel frame of the gantry bolted amidships was frightful with rust, as were the otter doors that lay at its feet, detached from the net. It was clear to all eyes that this was a boat with a commercial purpose, a workhorse sharply distinct from the thousand-odd other boats moored off South Beach. Industrial or no, Merry found her a cheerier sort of craft than the newer million-dollar steel-hulled draggers that commonly fished out of New Bedford and other mainland ports. And most important, she was an *unmortgaged* boat, free of the necessity of insurance that could cost an owner tens of thousands of dollars a year.

The perfect boat for Jackie, in other words.

To her right, the beach curved sharply out into the water and ended in Monomoy, where splendid old houses and private docks ran down to the harbor; to her left, the two-hundred-foot yacht *Athena*, a dark green corporate cruiser, rocked gently at her mooring on the backside of Old South Wharf. Merry could see the crowds of day-trippers from the Hy-Line ferry tours milling like brightly colored ants among the fishing-shack boutiques that lined the wharf; but a breathless quiet still held where she stood on the Town Pier. It was almost empty this Sunday afternoon, with only the occasional *thunk, thunk* of a flip-flop on the wooden planking or the guttural interruption of a boat engine to break the peace.

She scanned the *Lisboa Girl's* deck for Jackie, and saw only a heap of net unrolled from its drum. He had been mending, but wasn't now. Lunch, perhaps? She called his name.

A close-cropped head popped into view through the pilothouse door. A long look, not unfriendly, but not welcoming either. For an instant she thought he'd pretend she was a stranger, and duck back inside. But Jackie wasn't entirely stupid. He'd grown up with Merry, though they'd rarely had the inclination to chat.

"You here to see me?" he finally said.

"Yeah. How are you, Jackie?"

"What's it about?"

"I'd like to come aboard."

He shrugged. "Do as you like. It's kind of a mess."

The dragger was crafted low to the water, wide-girthed and rounded as a dory. Merry stretched a foot to the side, grabbed a rail, and hoisted herself on deck. Jackie was slow in moving to help her.

"I understand congratulations are in order," she said. "Hear you're captain now."

A wariness in his eyes. "Who told you that?"

"Felix Harper. Joe's lawyer. And your wife mentioned it when I talked to her just now. Cap'n Joe certainly was a generous man."

"There's a lot'll say I earned it," Jackie said. "The old man was slipping those last months. Probably why he ended up the way he did. His crew was all that stood between him and retirement, and he knew it. I figure I got what I was due."

Merry walked in front of the pilothouse and across the deck, to the side where the steel gantry rose in all its ugly purpose. She imagined the net hauled out of the air, taut and straining overhead; thought of the added weight of swinging steel doors tipping the ship seaward in heavy weather; and felt how suddenly Joe Duarte must have slid off the canted deck. The knowledge of it came over her like vertigo, a mingling of dizziness and fear. She reached down to steady herself against the boat's side and closed her eyes.

"This isn't a social call, is it?" Jackie said. She felt his muscular bulk looming over her, and looked up at him, summoning a smile.

"Yes and no," she said. "I realized at Joe's funeral how little I know about fishing, even though I grew up here. I decided I'd like to know more." She touched the rough surface of the detached otter doors. "What do these things do, anyway?"

"The doors?" He crouched down next to her. "You have to understand trawling to understand the doors. The net's shaped like a funneled bag, with the narrow end closed by a string." He reached for a length of net and pulled it toward them by way of illustration. "The open end is raised upward by floaters, while the closed end trails along the seabed. That's why we spend so much time mending net," he said, smiling for the first time, "because there's so much junk along the bottom. Rocks pulled up by scallopers, pieces of trash left by other boats, even the sand hills will put a hole in a net. The bigger boats have rollers on theirs that sort of keep the net off the bottom, but the *Lisboa Girl* isn't big enough to handle those."

"And the doors?" Merry said.

"The doors—they weigh the net down. One on either side of the net, eight-hundred pounds apiece. That's hardwood sheathed in steel, that is, and you don't get much heavier that that. They slice into the water like a pair of hatchets when the net's payed out. The floaters, now," he said, pointing to the net's upper rim, "keep the top of the net mouth rising while the doors hold the bottom down, and what you end up with is an opening that doesn't close."

"Don't the fish swim out once they realize they're in a net?"

"Doesn't work that way. Fish strike upward when they're panicked, and what they hit is mesh. And the net's being dragged along by the boat at about two knots, so they're scooped into the closed end."

Merry nodded. "So how long do you leave the net in the water before you haul it in?"

"Maybe an hour," he said, "depending. Sometimes half an hour, sometimes two. You scope out the fish on the fish-finder, and you figure how long it takes to get a good haul." He hoisted himself to his feet and headed for the pilothouse. Merry followed.

It was a snug space for wheel and charts, with a bank of electronic equipment ranged along an instrument console. Merry's black brows came together as she looked at them.

"It's like an attack submarine."

"The *Lisboa Girl's* not young, but Joe kept her up-to-date," Jackie said. "That's the loran, for satellite navigation—can't fish without it these days. And this is the automatic pilot, that's the sonar, for depth-finding, and that there's the fish-finder." He flipped a switch and she saw a screen full of murkiness. "Nothing much to see here at dock, o' course, but you get the idea."

"I didn't know it was so high-tech."

"When you're out alone on the Georges Bank in ten-foot seas, taking ice on the bow and the rigging, and you've got a hundred miles to port, you want everything you can get between you and disaster. You trust your men, you trust your boat, and you trust your equipment; but you never, never trust the sea." He leaned back against the chart table and gave her a level stare. "Now why don't you tell me why you're here."

Merry said nothing for an instant, assessing his calm for signs of the volatile temper Adelia had warned her about. "I'm here because Del

Duarte can't get over Joe's death, and I have to help her put it behind her."

"By learning about fishing?"

"By asking you again what happened that day."

"I told the Coast Guard everything."

"But Del doesn't believe it, Jackie. She can't accept the idea that Joe Duarte was fallible, that he could have made a mistake that cost him his life. She's asked us—the Nantucket police—to open a murder investigation."

His fingers clenched spasmodically on the wooden table and then released. He thrust himself away from the charts and pulled open the pilothouse door.

Merry followed him outside and found him standing by the gantry with its now-impotent steel slabs. *The scene of the crime,* she thought.

Jackie swung around abruptly and faced her, the muscle in his jaws working, his gray eyes flat and cold. "You telling me that bitch is accusing me of murder?"

"No," Merry said. "I'm telling you that no one at the station thinks there's any truth in it, but to satisfy Del and calm her down—to help her come to terms with her father's death—we've got to go through the motions."

"To hell with the motions," he shot back. "I've got a living to make, and if she sets out to tie up my boat, she'll regret it. You tell her that from me." He emphasized his point with a blunt forefinger, thrust accusingly in Merry's face. "Del's a spoiled little girl. She needs to grow up and face reality. Just because she left her old man in the lurch is no reason to start blaming me when he goes and dies. Shit." He turned away and spit over the bow, all his venom in the arc of phlegm.

Merry took a deep breath, seeing the rigidity in his shoulders, the stiffness of his neck. "Well, Jackie," she said, "in somewhat gentler terms, that's what I'm trying to do. And it'll help all of us get past this faster if you answer my questions."

There was a short silence, during which he continued to stare out toward the mouth of the harbor, and she held on to her calm by folding her arms across her chest, her hands clutching her elbows.

"Seems a guy can't even make a living anymore," he said. "Between the lawyers and the police and the friggin' stupid women. *I just want to fish*. You know? I want to go out and do what I know how to do. This sitting around is killing me."

Merry refrained from telling him that the sooner he talked to her, the sooner he might be able to claim his boat; it wasn't exactly true. Her father wasn't opening a murder investigation. Nothing would stop the probate of Joe Duarte's will. But as long as Jackie thought Del might—

"Okay," he said, thrusting himself away from the gantry. "Shoot."

She got out a notebook, pen, and her half-glasses. "The weather was pretty bad that day, wasn't it?"

"The storm that hit the island the day of Joe's funeral was nothing compared to what swept through the Bank three days before."

"But Joe decided to stay and fish."

Jackie's eyes shifted away. "We'd been out for two days and were almost ready to turn for home. The weather came up sudden, and I don't think anybody expected it. Besides, he'd seen a lot of rough sea over the years. You worry about January. You don't worry so much about May."

"You had a net down."

"Most of the other boats had pulled out and were heading for port. We were in about twenty-four fathoms of water, around the Leg—"

"What's a fathom?"

"Six feet."

"And the Leg?"

"—is just a spot on the Bank, round about the twenty-five-hundred line on the loran. That don't mean nothing to you, I know, but it's the only grave marker Joe'll ever have."

"Go on."

"We'd run into some nice-sized cod. They're gettin' rarer and rarer anywhere, even on the Bank, which was famous for 'em, so we wanted to fish while we were still making money, and damn the swell. But Joe got nervous about the weather—he'd lost all his balls this winter, God knows how we got any fish at all—and ordered the net pulled in. The Swede—he's a kid 'bout twenty-three, and Joe had him working the winch—he's so excited about all the fish down there, and pissed about Joe, that he doesn't ease up on the throttle, and the doors come rocketing out of the water twice as fast as they should. Here, look at these."

He reached down and picked up the net, pointing to the yellow chafing strips tied to it at varying intervals. "These are made of fiberglass to toughen the net while it's dragging along the bottom." His blunt, calloused finger moved higher, to some strips of rag. "But these *here* are like flags—haul three in together, and you know the doors are coming up out of the water. The Swede was only hauling in about fifty feet of net. He shoulda seen these rags, and eased off the throttle. But he's feeling angry about the fish that got away, and he gets careless." He threw the net aside in disgust.

"So the doors slammed into this thing here," Merry said, tapping the gantry, "much faster than they should. Where was Joe?"

Jackie dropped his eyes and rubbed at his nose with chapped, red fingers. *Gaining time,* Merry thought.

"He was at the helm, at first," Jackie said, "like he shoulda been. But when he sees what's happened, he runs out fast and starts giving orders. Doors that weigh this much, unsecured and swinging wild, can capsize a boat, and the cap'n wasn't about to let that happen. He got in the way, what with the crew trying to secure the doors—you've got maybe thirty seconds to do it, and Joe figured we weren't doin' it right—and all of sudden he's reaching an arm in to do it himself. The boat heels over, the left door comes walloping in, and Joe's out cold from an eight-hundred-pound slap to the head."

He fell silent, and looked away over the mass of fishing boats to either side of the *Lisboa Girl,* to the mouth of the harbor and the sea beyond. "It looks real nice out there today," he said. "A real Chamber of Commerce view. But unless you've seen it, Merry, you'll never understand what high seas in a storm and chaos on deck can be like. How sixty feet of old wooden boat can feel like a milk carton, shuddering with every wave that comes against the bow, lurching into the troughs, while the sea rises like a wall in front of you, swamping your men and tearing at the net you're trying just to get on board. And trying to get on board quickly, so's the catch don't send the entire boat capsizing with the next wallow." He turned back to her and dropped his eyes again. "Joe didn't panic, exactly. He just picked the wrong moment to try'n run things."

Jackie was definitely uncomfortable about something, but whether it was his memories—or his version of them—Merry couldn't say. "You went into the sea after him?"

He nodded. "Not that it did any good. He wasn't wearing a life jacket—nobody does, the padding's too dangerous around the winches.

You get caught in a line and you'll lose an arm. What with the knock on the head and the size of the seas, he never had a chance. He had his boots and his slicker on; and they'd have weighted his body and sent him to the bottom. Almost sent me down, in fact, 'cause I forgot to haul off my boots when I went in after Joe. But at least I wasn't unconscious."

"How'd you get that?" she asked, pointing to his head wound.

He felt it gingerly. "They had to use a grappling hook to haul me back on board, and they hit me in the head with it before they managed to catch my clothing. No big deal. The hair'll grow back." He gave her the vestige of a smile. "I was lucky it wasn't January. The water in May is around fifty degrees, but at least it isn't freezing. Man only lasts a few minutes in January water."

Merry felt her stomach clench and looked up at Jackie Alcantrara. "Did you get a good price for the trip?"

He shrugged. "Nothing like what Joe's life was worth."

For the first time, amid all the bluster about the boat being his due, about Joe Duarte being past his prime, about Jackie himself being all that had stood between the Captain and disaster, Merry saw something like pain for the dead man in the living one's eyes. She read it as a form of truth, and decided that despite Jackie's deliberate omissions and half-truths, he probably had not killed Adelia's father.

"You know how many good men get caught by those doors over the years?" he said. "I could read you a list. Men retired now with one arm, men knocked unconscious and overboard like Cap'n Joe. He wasn't God, Detective. What happened to him has happened a thousand times. You tell Del that, from me. And you tell her I won't be taking no murder rap for what the sea's done on its own."

CHAPTER SEVEN

"**H**OW'S BUSINESS?"

Tess turned from tossing the last of the chicken lobsters, claws waving frantically, into a boiling vat of water and squinted at the kitchen's back screen door. The light was behind the face thrust around the jamb, blotting out the features, but she recognized Rafe's voice and the outline of his shaggy head. He'd affected a breezy nonchalance, as though Friday's blowup and Saturday's fishing hadn't occurred, but there was an edge of tension to the words nonetheless.

"Not bad," she said, turning back to the lobsters. "In fact, I don't have time to talk right now."

"Did you get the steaks?"

"Yep."

"How were they?"

"Don't know. Gave them to the cat."

"Tess! Those things're are worth a fortune!"

He had a right to be aghast. Almost thirty pounds of swordfish arrived on her doorstep the previous evening, enough to serve the entire restaurant at a tidy profit; and though she had no cat, as Rafe well knew, she hadn't kept the steaks either. She sent them out to the VFW's Memorial Day dinner in 'Sconset, with her compliments and no explanation.

"Do you really think I'd accept anything from that woman?" she said now. "After she's done her best to destroy my happiness?"

"Oh come on, Tess, be reasonable," Rafe said in exasperation. "The steaks were from me. My share of the catch. I had as much to do with landing it as Del did."

"You're quite the partners, I hear."

"Now what's that supposed to mean?"

"You took her to dinner yesterday."

"We got a burger with Peter, and we went dutch, if you want to know. Now stop acting like a three-year-old and ask me into the kitchen."

She turned toward him abruptly, kitchen knife in hand, and despite himself, he leaned back from the doorway apprehensively.

"Do me a favor, Rafael da Silva," she said, advancing on the screen door. "Get out of my backyard and don't come around here again. We have nothing to talk about. Not until you know what you want, who you want, and why. Is that clear?"

"Tess!"

She shut the back door firmly in his face, despite the heat of the un-air-conditioned kitchen, and sat down suddenly in an available chair. *Damn Adelia Duarte,* she thought. *Damn her thirty-year-old body and her Portuguese blood and her adorable two-year-old and her love of the sea. Damn her for being everything I'm not, and for spending entire days with him. I hate her.*

The inner door swung open, and her chief waiter, Sammy, looked at her with pleading eyes. "Tess, table five is frantic for their orders. I placed them half an hour ago. Whaddya say we give them their food before they revolt, huh?"

I hate her. I wish she had never come back.

The door swung closed. From the stove the timer suddenly blared, announcing the end of the lobsters' martyrdom.

I wish she were dead.

She put aside the kitchen knife with shaking hands and closed her eyes.

Merry glanced at her watch and turned the gray Explorer toward home. A thorough canvass of the docks had told her that most of Joe Duarte's crew had left the island for work on boats elsewhere—one in Mattapoisett, another in New Bedford. She'd managed to find the last and best man to talk to—the Swede, the twenty-three-year-old winch operator who'd made such a mess of things—scraping the barnacles from a pleasure yacht still dry-docked in the Washington Street boatyard. He pushed sunglasses to the top of his white-blond head, crossed his arms over his deeply tanned and completely bare chest, and told her his name was Lars Olafson. He was really from Norway, and he'd been knocking around the New England seaports looking for work since the age of seventeen.

If she believed Lars, he hadn't missed the marker rags on the net; the winch itself was to blame. The throttle hadn't been working properly, and even when Cap'n Joe rushed up and all hell broke loose with the doors, no one could get the thing to slow down. They'd finally thrown the proverbial wrench in the works—jammed the winch itself—but by that time the skipper was over the side and Jackie had gone in after him.

"So how'd it happen?" Merry had asked.

The Swede shrugged. "The engineer didn't ship that trip—had a bad cold, and his vife vooden let him outta ta house. Maybe tings didn' get checked out right."

Or perhaps they did, Merry thought, if the object was murder. Had Jackie fixed the winch so that it would malfunction, anticipating Cap'n Joe's reaction and the probable consequences? Here was a way to kill someone without the entire crew being aware of it—no need for consistent stories, no silence bought with money, no risk of acting with confederates one could not entirely trust. But how risky the method itself would have been! The chances of the wrong crew member being struck by the doors—of other lives being lost beside Joe's, or *instead* of Joe's—were very great. Would Jackie gamble that heavily with so little certainty of gain?

Merry couldn't be sure. But she declined the Swede's offer of a drink, tore her eyes from his flashing white grin, and turned toward home with less conviction of Jackie Alcantrara's innocence than she'd had a few hours before.

"We're going out again tomorrow," Adelia said, spooning some of Ralph Waldo's kale-and-bean soup into Sara's mouth. "Rafe says he's got the time, and that we might as well see if we can do this more than once. He wants to get the word out to the local wholesalers that they don't have to count on importing all their swordfish."

Merry shook herself out of half-listening to the wail of sirens coming from town and focused her attention on Del. "Could you sell to restaurants directly? What about the Greengage?"

Ralph Waldo flashed her a look of warning and shook his head. Adelia's spoon dipped as she went for Sara's mouth, and soup dribbled onto the mat.

"Shoot!" she said. "Can I have a sponge, Ralph?"

He tossed her one as Merry looked from one to the other. "What's wrong with the Greengage?" she said.

"Tess Starbuck thinks I'm the Devil in a Blue Dress," Adelia said carefully. "She doesn't want Rafe fishing anymore, and I'm the reason he is. She gave him back his ring and warned him off the property."

"You're kidding." Merry sat down quickly, a knot in her stomach. There was a time when she'd been jealous of Tess, and wished that Rafe had never met her; but those days were long past. Now she felt responsible. If she hadn't talked Rafe into helping Del, Tess might still be planning a July wedding.

"This is terrible," she said. "I've got to talk to her."

"I'd stay out of it, Meredith Abiah," Ralph Waldo said. "No good ever comes in meddling with affairs of the heart. Tess is a big girl. Acting childish right now, maybe, but she doesn't need anybody to tell her what's what."

"So is she jealous of you, or just mad that Rafe's fishing?"

"I'm not sure," Adelia said. "Maybe both. But I think if anybody talks to her, it should be me. I put a note in her box today, asked her to lunch. All I need is another person out to get me."

Merry looked at Ralph Waldo. He lifted an eyebrow. "Are you talking about Jackie?"

Del shrugged. "I dunno. That's what makes it so weird." She stood up and reached for her purse, fishing around in its depths. "You can take the girl outta the office," she said, pulling out a Filofax, "but she'll take a piece of it with her." Her red-tipped fingers flipped through the calendar quickly and extracted a folded sheet. "Came under the door this morning."

Someone had glued letters cut from magazines onto a piece of lined notebook paper.

"The oldest trick in the book," Merry said, showing it to Ralph Waldo. The two of them bent their heads over the note. In the sudden silence, the persistent whine of the sirens seem to amplify, drifting up through the streets from the waterfront. *That's fire, not police,* Merry thought, and then studied the paper before her.

ADELIA DUARTE NEW BEDFORD WAS TOO HOT TO HOLD YOU, BUT NANTUCKET ISN'T YOUR HOME ANYMORE. GET OUT OF TOWN AND TAKE YOUR BRAT WITH YOU.

It was signed *The Avenging Angel*—again in clipped magazine letters, but culled this time from flowing italic script. An author with an egotistical streak, a desire for self-dramatization.

"So should I be worried?"

"Yes," Merry said. "Not unduly worried, of course, but more so than a person whose mail is a bit more orthodox." She looked up at her friend, her eyes sober. "You think this is from Tess?"

"Could be," Adelia said slowly. "It's the same old stuff about Sara and my morals. The sort of crap a woman would care about."

"It just doesn't sound like Tess Starbuck," Ralph Waldo said. "Too self-righteous."

"Jealousy can turn the nicest person into a raving lunatic," Merry said. "Particularly if she thinks she's got a lot more to lose than just Rafe. Tess's whole life, really, is at stake here—a father for Will, financial security, her happiness. It's not beyond the realm of possibility. That's what makes it so disturbing." She perused the letter again. "I'm not sure I *want* you to go talk to her, Del. She might not be very reasonable."

"*If* she sent the note," Ralph Waldo reminded her.

"Got any other likely candidates?"

"Adelia, my dear, perhaps you should sleep here tonight," Ralph Waldo said.

"Thanks, Ralph." She retrieved the note and tucked it back in the Filofax. "I'm okay. It takes a lot to scare a Duarte. I'm staying on Nantucket, and so is Sara, and no vicious creep with a poisoned pen is going to drive us away."

"Did Joe ever install a good system of bolts?" Ralph Waldo asked.

"Good enough," Del said shortly.

"I wonder," Merry said to her grandfather, "if the creative genius wore gloves."

"Probably not. Most folks don't think paper holds fingerprints."

At that, the phone rang shrilly from the kitchen wall. Ralph leaned over and caught it. "Folgers', " he said shortly. And then his face changed.

"Meredith," he said, covering the mouthpiece with a broad palm, "your father wants you down at the Town Pier. It's on fire, and everything within shouting distance—boats, sheds, you name it—is going up like a torch."

CHAPTER EIGHT

❧

M ERRY FOLGER STOOD aghast on the shore of South Beach, overwhelmed by the orange flames engulfing the Town Pier. The roar and heat of the fire rolled toward her like the onset of a hurricane, battering her face, assaulting her eardrums, drowning the curses and shouts of the men grappling with hoses on the blackened sand. The crackling light cast a distorted reflection of boats rippling across the harbor, colored it red, and then tore it to pieces with ravenous jaws. Merry's gaze was riveted suddenly by a blinding flash out past the pier—a ball of flame spiraling upward from a boat's gas tank— and then a concussive *boom!* that startled her out of her skin. Her heart racing, she took a deep breath. And bent double with coughing.

Ash and the acrid odor of burning plastic sifted through the air. Merry narrowed her eyes to slits, pulled the tail of her T-shirt out of her jeans, and held it to her mouth. Ninety-five percent of the craft moored off South Beach—some nine hundred boats even this early in the season—had fiberglass hulls. Fiberglass was toxic when burned. She could pass out just from breathing, die a few moments later.

The pier, soaked in tar and oil from generations of vessels, was burning as though designed for the purpose. One glance told Merry it could not be saved. She turned to survey the half-moon of beach. Shadowy figures up and down the shore were avoiding the protective barricades, wading out into the water, and swimming to their boats in the hope of saving them. Her throat constricted at the sight. Patches of oil flamed on the water, unmoored boats drifted in all directions, and any swimmer in the night harbor ran the risk of injury. Her efforts would be better spent on crowd control. But where was her chief?

She strained to distinguish her father's figure from the crowd battling the fire, with no success. South Beach was only about twenty feet deep at its widest point, and the scorched sand was a bewildering morass of bodies, hoses, trucks, and debris. Access to the pier was blocked by the airport crash truck, one of the few island vehicles designed to approach intense heat without its windshield cracking. Inside the cab, the operator was outlined against the flames and the sweeping arc of foam the truck was spraying desperately at the burning boats.

The fire chief, Walt Munn, had reacted quickly, Merry thought. Only four men at a time out of the department's staff of eighteen worked each ten-hour shift at the firehouse, but tonight there were at least thirty battling the flames in front of her. Fire department vessels equipped with water cannons divided their spray between the docks and the buildings immediately bordering the beach—the houses on Washington Street, the marina sheds, the harbormaster's office and public showers. Between the guys on the shore and the ones on the boats, Munn must have called in volunteers as well as full-time crews, and still it was not enough. In the hellish glow off the water, Merry saw despair and exhaustion on the men's sooty faces.

But the chaos of South Beach was nothing compared to what was happening beyond the waterline. The Coast Guard was trying, and failing, to maintain order. As far as the eye could see in the fire-lit night, boats were heading for the jetties and the open sound, almost ramming one another in the mad scramble to put danger behind them.

It was, from any point of view, a disaster.

"Meredith!"

It took an instant to recognize her father, so soot-begrimed and sweaty was his skin; his regulation blue Nantucket police uniform was equally fouled. The lower half of his face was obscured by a gas mask.

"Dad!" She dropped her shirt and sucked a lungful of air; big mistake. Coughing, she closed her streaming eyes and breathed into the handkerchief John Folger shoved in her hand. He was one of the few men she knew who still carried one. She made a mental note to start carrying one herself, and tied it thankfully over her nose and mouth. "What can I do?" she shouted over the din of the flames.

Her father lifted the mask from his face and rubbed a hand across it, leaving wet black marks on his nose and cheeks. "It's like a steam bath inside this thing," he said. Merry held her breath and passed him the handkerchief. He mopped his forehead and mouth and handed it back to her, damp and smoke-laden. She tied it over her face anyway.

"Keep these idiots back from the wharf area," John Folger said, gesturing toward the crowds of sightseers who had walked down from town for a better view of disaster. "All we need is some kid from a New York suburb exploding with a boat while he's trying to get a picture." He handed her a bullhorn and made as if to move on.

"How'd it start?"

He stopped and fixed her in his vivid blue gaze. "That's what I want you to find out tomorrow," he said, "after it's turned to ash. I want you with Hank Burrows, and I want you in charge of our end of the case. There's a fortune in boats lost tonight, Meredith, and I don't need some off-islander suing the town for negligence. We have to fix blame and fix it well."

Hank Burrows was the deputy fire chief. He was also the island's trained arson expert. A disaster at one of the piers was the town's worst nightmare; the fire department had planned for it, and drilled with the police and Coast Guard in fear of it, and adopted the grim hope that preparation would render the eventuality unlikely.

"So you don't think it was an accident," Merry said.

He laughed shortly, a contemptuous sound meant for the arsonist, not her. "A cigarette may have taken out Yellowstone, but for this, you'd need a drum of lighter fluid and a plenty long fuse. The fire was reported half an hour ago, just after it got dark. I got here in five minutes, maybe less. And it was already beyond saving."

Merry swallowed. That someone could have set this was difficult to believe. Nantucketers had a terrified respect for fire—the legacy of the Great Fire of 1846, which had raged for an entire night and consumed the heart of town, fifteen square blocks. No islander could forget that, despite a century and a half's passage.

She stared at her father's retreating back an instant, pushed aside the handkerchief, and lifted the bullhorn to her lips. "Clear the area," she bellowed, her voice transformed and falling away from her, one more inhuman sound in the general cacophony. "Stand away from the police line. You are in extreme danger. . . . "

A boat exploded five hundred yards away from her, sending plastic and metal and sheets of fire sky high with a deafening boom, and the crowd gasped. A few people cheered. In the slight illusion of silence that ensued, the pause following the concussion, Merry and the thrill seekers watched the scattered pieces of what had been a Boston whaler rain down like a fountain in the roiling, angry harbor. She had instinctively ducked and clapped her hands over her ears when the boom fell upon her; and now, recovered, felt slightly foolish. She glanced around to see whether anyone was laughing at her, shrugged, and put the bullhorn back to her lips.

It was three in the morning before the fire was under control, but the sightseers had straggled home long before that. In the dead watches of the night only the islanders remained—the exhausted firemen, the owners of houses threatened on Washington Street, the police struggling for order. Daylight would show that over a thousand feet of pier and three hundred boats had been destroyed—a cold and objective statistic. But the ruins were still warm and smoking at dawn, and there was nothing objective about the anger Merry saw on the faces around her, the frustrated rage of those forced to clean up after another's devastating mess.

It was after Merry left, on the 4:00 A.M. turn of the tide, that the body drifted to shore.

CHAPTER NINE

🐚

Merry woke at seven, only a few hours after she had stumbled into bed, and forced her smoked-pained eyelids to open. The shower had done little to erase the deep intensity of odor that permeated her hair and skin; now her bed would reek of it, though her closet had escaped. She had shed her clothing in the backyard.

The sound of Ralph whistling from the kitchen below drifted up the stairs, and she fell back into her smoky pillow with a sigh of weariness. If God were just, her grandfather would forsake the bacon and eggs today in favor of more subtly scented foods. She didn't think her nostrils could stand the combined assault of melted fiberglass and Ralph's usual morning fare.

When she appeared in the kitchen a half hour later, her blond waves falling damply helter-skelter to her chin, Ralph Waldo paused by her chair and thrust his nose in the general direction of her scalp.

"I'm going to have to shave it off," she said. Her voice was hoarsened by smoke inhalation, despite the gas mask she'd eventually managed to find; she coughed and tasted smoke.

"Not a bit of it, young woman. Takes me back a century or two to the first days of whaling. The smell from a tryworks melting down blubber must have approximated the odor of your hair. Wear it proudly."

"And wear it somewhere else, right?"

"It'll pass off. Another few days, you'll be right as rain."

"Or would be, if Dad hadn't made the fire my summer project."

"I think it's becoming the entire town's," Ralph said soberly. He studied her face and decided she was awake enough to handle more news. "Your dad's set up a crisis center at the station, right in the middle of the garage." The police station on South Water was actually the old firehouse, converted to police use in 1980, and at the center of it remained a large space intended for a hook-and-ladder. The police usually left it empty.

"For boat owners tracking their lost vessels?"

Ralph Waldo set warm cranberry muffins and a bowl of blueberries in cream before her, the two freshest scents in the world. "The station switchboard has been jammed all night. Your father never made it home."

Merry took a bite of muffin and closed her eyes appreciatively. "We'll be dredging for rudders and somebody's boat-rail barbecue all summer long."

"There's something else," Ralph Waldo said. "They've found a body."

Merry's spoonful of blueberries stopped in mid-ascent. She stared at him, her face expressionless. "Just one?"

He nodded. "It's enough."

"Drowned?"

"I don't know."

"It's incredible there aren't dozens, the way people panicked last night," Merry said bitterly. "We train and train for a disaster like this, and when it happens, we realize we should have trained more. There should have been some way to keep people out of the water." She raked her hands across her face, trying to force the bone-deep weariness to recede. "Was it a man or a woman, Ralph?"

"They think it was a man."

"That bad, huh?"

"Must've been caught in a burning boat."

"Jesus." She pushed away the bowl of blueberries, nauseated by her own smokiness and the images it conjured up. Blackened, unrecognizable skeletons, the skin shrink-wrapped by heat over the bones, the teeth gaping. Bodies caught in seaweed and stinking masses of fish gone belly up from so many hours of heat on the water.

"I can't face it, Ralph."

"Try to eat something, Meredith Abiah," he said gently. He only used her middle name—from Ben Franklin's mother, a Nantucket Folger—when he felt tender or indignant. She was thankful it was the former this morning. Though she never allowed her father to see her weaknesses if she could help it, Ralph saw everything, and usually refrained from judgment.

"I was just getting interested in Joe Duarte's death," Merry said, lifting her head and meeting his bright blue eyes. "That threatening letter Del got only makes her doubts more justified. But all that seems irrelevant now, doesn't it?"

"That reminds me," Ralph said. "In the bustle over the fire, she left her Filofax behind her. You'll be wanting to drop it off, I expect." He pulled up a chair and teased an edge from one of her muffins. "I thought we'd agreed her notions were a lot of malarky."

"We had. But then I talked to the Swede—one of Joe's crew—after I talked to Jackie Alcantrara. Their stories didn't match up."

"Funny. I don't remember that from the newspaper accounts."

"The Swede wasn't interviewed. He was off-island at the time—I checked. And since he was technically responsible for the mess, I suppose it's always been his word against the others'."

"He worked the winch?"

She nodded. "Jackie says he was careless and brought the metal doors in too wild and too fast. That's why Joe jumped in to lend a hand; then he got hit and went over."

"It's happened often enough before."

"That's what Jackie said. Only the Swede doesn't agree. He says the winch *couldn't* be stopped—that it had to be jammed. Something had gone wrong with it."

"Something that didn't show up in the rest of the trip?" Ralph said skeptically. "It wasn't the first haul they'd pulled. They'd been out two days, or so the newspaper said."

"That's true. But things can break down, can't they? Or be tampered with?"

"Maybe." Ralph reached one long arm to the stove and pulled his percolator toward her cup. "Maybe this Swede is feeling too responsible, and thinks he'll shift the blame. Remember, Meredith, nobody else on the crew mentioned jamming the winch. Everybody said it was human error."

"Ralph," she said quickly, eyes on his coffeepot, "I don't think I can take the smell today. But thanks anyway." She rose, napkin to her lips, and ran her fingers through her hair in what passed for a Merry combing. "And you may be right about the winch. But it doesn't really matter, does it? We've got a body on South Beach, and an unholy mess to clean up."

"Take a muffin with you," he called after her.

She spent the morning down on South Beach with the Nantucket Fire Department. John Folger remained at the site only long enough to tell her what to do, then departed for his crisis center and another twenty-four hours of work. Hank Burrows had requested the help of an arson expert from Boston, who was arriving that afternoon; until then the scarred wreckage of pilings and hulls was cordoned off from all but the tide. What threatened to drift out to sea was dragged ashore in pieces by volunteers working with the exhausted Coast Guard crews. Uncertain what might be relevant, they saved everything they could. All police personnel were on call, including the twenty summer interns. John Folger had pulled them off foot patrol and set them to the task of labeling debris as the fire department's divers retrieved it from the water.

The banality of the morning after, Merry thought, *when even disaster can be handled with logistics and a yellow legal pad.*

She was given the job of finding witnesses among the boat owners and residents of Washington Street. It wasn't hard to do; most of them were on the beach that morning, scavenging among the detritus for signs of a familiar vessel, gone past recalling. There were insurance forms to fill out, and dreams to be mourned; but most of all, there was anger to vent, and the wide-open beach was the place to do it.

On her third canvass she found Marty Bremen. He was a weather-beaten guy of fifty, a New Yorker by birth, who spent every summer in a house on Union Street he'd first visited as a boy. His family had been renting from the same owners for two generations. He installed his wife and kids every Memorial Day weekend, put the boat in the water, and flew back to the city for the work week.

"This year," he said, "I should have waited a day to take the *Gemini* off its trailer. But yesterday was perfect fishing weather—"

"You were out on the water?"

He nodded. "Shoulda stayed out all night, in retrospect."

He'd left the pier in the late afternoon with his eldest son, a kid of fifteen who was just getting the passion for blues, and they'd come back late with their lights on.

"What time was that?"

"Geez, I dunno. Eight-thirty, nine, maybe? Just light enough to still see, and dark enough not to see much."

"Did you notice anything wrong at the pier?"

"Not on our approach, no. But the explosion came when I was mooring up. Like an idiot, I tried to help, instead of heading right back out to sea."

"You're sure it was an explosion?"

"Couldn't have been anything else, Detective. A loud boom, like a gas tank exploding, and a helluva sheet of flame. Like those pictures of car bombs in Beirut from a couple of years back."

"Where'd it come from?"

He turned and gestured vaguely toward the ruin of the pier. "From the other side of the dock, couple of boats down from mine. I didn't get a clear view of what happened, but Charlie Rounseville"—at this, Marty looked past Merry's shoulder in search of Charlie—"was having a party on his yacht, *Calypso*, only a few slips away. The explosion must have shaken more than the martinis."

Charlie Rounseville was a tall, rangy-looking fellow in his mid-thirties who was making something of an event of the search for his boat; he had what amounted to a tailgate picnic set up on the back of his Range Rover and was offering wine to various passersby. Last night's party, it seemed, had simply shifted venue. Merry was wearing her police uniform, something that, as a detective, she rarely donned; but official authority went with it, she figured, and authority was needed in the aftermath of chaos. Charlie Rounseville was hardly awed, however, and greeted her with an outstretched glass.

"Officer! May I offer you a sip of something on this most desperate of days?"

Merry smiled and declined. "I understand you're Charlie Rounseville."

"The same. But you have the advantage of me, Miss—"

"Detective. Detective Meredith Folger. I'm in charge of the police side of this investigation."

"So there's an investigation?" He turned to his assembled partiers with a broad smile. "I win the bet, Jamie," he tossed off to a rotund gentleman with thinning blond hair. Jamie raised his glass in salute. "I told them it was arson."

"What made you so sure?"

"My own eyes, Detective. Sure you won't have a glass?" He uncorked a bottle of California chardonnay and sloshed it into what looked like a plastic champagne flute. "Salvaged the portable picnic basket from the boat when all hell broke loose," he confided. "These were in it. Seemed best to bring the perishable stuff back to the beach instead of Mother's good crystal."

"Mr. Rounseville," Merry broke in, "could we start from the beginning?"

"Certainly. Certainly. It's the end, after all, that's so damnably depressing. What would you like me to tell you?"

Charlie Rounseville owned a house on Orange Street. He had made what Merry gathered was a vast amount of money in the 1980s bond market and had devoted the first half of the nineties to spending it on himself and his fluctuating circle of acquaintances.

"I understand you had a party last night."

"A drinks-and-canapés do for a few friends."

Merry looked past him toward the tailgate. Three couples stood morosely on the sand, plastic wineglasses in hand. "These are your guests?"

"They're staying up at the house," Charlie said. "New Yorkers all. I'd intended a brilliant launch of the summer season, you understand, but losing my fifty-foot yacht was not part of the plan."

"You were still having drinks when the explosion occurred?"

"We'd intended to go on to dinner in town, but the night was *lovely*, Detective. And Jamie's stories are so ludicrous. Time got away from us. I suggested midnight steak and eggs back at the house, and we bagged the reservation at Twenty-one Federal."

"And what time would you say the fire occurred?"

"Nine o'clock or so."

"You're sure it was nine o'clock?"

"Thereabouts. Jamie!" Charlie called. "When did your blasted watch go off? He always has it set," he confided to Merry in a wine-scented mutter, "so he can call into his office for messages. The damn thing beeps every five minutes."

"Every quarter hour," Jamie said indignantly.

"See? Absolute idiot. What quarter hour was it when the bomb or whatever it was blew?"

"Eight-forty-five."

"Some use, anyway," Charlie said, turning back to Merry.

"So you think it was a bomb."

"Sure of it."

"Could you describe it for me, please?"

"Well—" He hesitated. "My slip is—was—number nine. The boat in seven—that's just next to mine on the left as you're facing the dock"— he waved toward the blackened skeleton of the pier—"was a pretty little antique sloop named the *Sea Devil*, belonged to a woman, Nancy Harding. It's hard to picture now, of course. The explosion came from number five, just to the left of her. A huge boom! And then the sounds of falling debris and crackling flame right after. We were sitting on deck, some of us, while the rest were in the cabin. The boat rocked and pitched like we'd been hit by a typhoon. I remember looking over my shoulder and seeing a wall of flame jumping from number five into Nancy's sloop. The furled sails went up first, and then it was the mast, and for some reason the planking between the two slips was blazing. I jumped onto the dock and threw my wine at it, as I recall. Silly thing. Alcohol can't have helped."

"Probably not," Merry said gently, "but it's the sort of impulse we all have. The first thing that comes to hand, and so forth."

"Exactly. Well, then some people got out of their boats and started throwing buckets of water on the flames, but they seemed to simply get higher. Marty Bremen had the presence of mind to call the fire people, though it took him a bit of time to run down the dock and do it. A few of the more intelligent, or more selfish, got back in their boats and headed out to sea. They're the ones who were saved. The rest of us just tried to form a bucket brigade to douse the fire, but—" Charlie stopped and took a sip of wine, his expression gone from fatuous to grimly weary.

"I don't know this for certain, you understand," he said, "but I've been thinking about it ever since. *We couldn't put the fire out.* I think there was oil all over the place. Water was useless against it. And that's what made me think of a bomb, of course. At first I thought it might have been anything—ash from one of our cigarettes floating on the wind, and hitting a gas spill in that dinghy. But now I'm convinced. Something like ash on gasoline wouldn't have had the explosive power. Reminded me of my days in the army. There was TNT in that dinghy, Detective; I'm sure of it. Just as I'm sure there was oil on the dock. Anyone who'd go to the trouble to set up the one would be sure to leave the other."

"You boat owners seem to know one another's boats," Merry said. "Who owned the dinghy that exploded?"

"That's just it," Charlie said. "Most of these slips are rented for the season, but a few are left vacant by the mooring company for occasional rentals. I'd never seen this dinghy before, and it wasn't the kind that's usually here."

"Do you remember when it tied up yesterday, and who was in it?"

He shook his head. "Seems to me it hadn't moved for most of the weekend. At least, not during the times that I was down here. We were out on the water most of Saturday, but stayed around the house until the cocktail hour yesterday. I can't really help you there."

"Could you describe it for me?"

He snorted in derision. "Not a prize possession of anybody's, I'd have to say. More like a vessel to sink than to sail. A little wooden dinghy, maybe twelve feet, couple of decades old, with oars and a lot of old crap stowed in the bottom. Needed scraping and painting desperately. The sort of dinghy you see all the time, and never look at twice."

And I'll bet the skipper's description matches, Merry thought. *A nondescript Any Man in faded polo and cutoffs, probably a former Navy Seal with a talent for explosives. Or maybe just a guy who's worked construction and knows how to blast some rock. The sort of guy no one would notice, the sort of guy no one did.*

CHAPTER TEN

❦

WILL STARBUCK WAS OUT
of breath from pedaling the four and a half miles between his door and
Mason Farms. He would not have noticed the distance last year, but that
he was able to ride the bike at all this Memorial Day weekend was cause
for thankfulness. The previous fall, a murderous trap had knocked Will
from his ten-speed, leaving him with a fractured skull and damaged co-
ordination. This was his first trip to Peter's under his own power in over
six months.

He laid the bike in the tall grass by the drive and pounded up the
back steps to the kitchen. Rebecca was ironing, and that particular smell
of damp linen and moist metallic heat had crowded spring out of the
room.

"Where are you going in such a hurry?" she exclaimed, setting the
iron down and pursing her lips.

"Peter here?"

"He's in the study."

Will shot down the hallway before she could ask another question
and paused long enough before Peter's closed door to permit an impatient
knock. Before the invitation to enter was half spoken he'd turned the
knob.

"Will!" Peter was in his favorite armchair, a last mug of coffee to one
side and his tanned face just lifting from a nursery catalogue. "Where's
the fire?"

"So you know about it then," he said, disappointed. "I thought I'd be
the first to tell you."

"There's such a thing as the news," Peter reminded him, "although
rarely does it offer such spectacular footage of Nantucket." He flipped
the catalogue closed, stood up, and stretched his hands over his head.

"Matter of fact, I ran by South Beach this morning. Got up early, saw the pictures on TV, and thought of the boat Adelia Duarte rented. We used it only two days ago. I can't believe it's gone."

Will felt himself flush. Peter had an uncanny way of voicing the things he most wanted to discuss but lacked the courage to say. He met the older man's eyes and looked down, feeling exposed and young.

"What is it?"

"I just wondered," he said, "if maybe Rafe wouldn't be fishing anymore. I sort of miss seeing him around here."

"It hasn't been that long," Peter said, momentarily amused. "Only a weekend." Then he read the unhappiness in Will's face and adopted a more sober expression. "I imagine you miss him around the Greengage," he said. "I remember from my own parents. Three days of silence and tension can be a lifetime."

"It's just that it's making my mom crazy," Will burst out. "She's moping around the house, ignoring everybody, and she's not cooking right. People's orders have been late all weekend. She's mixing them up. The restaurant is really important to her, you know? Only now—it's like it doesn't matter. It's a lousy way to start the season." He kicked at a coffee table leg and slumped down on Peter's sofa. "I keep thinking Rafe'll come by, and she'll snap out of it. Or that I should get him over to the house. But what if I screw things up?"

"You're afraid you'll make it worse."

Will nodded. "Then it'll be my fault. If I leave them alone, it's their problem. But how can I leave them alone? It's my wedding, too!"

"You're right, of course. I hadn't thought of it that way."

"Pete," he said imploringly, and then hesitated, his face flushing. "Do you think *you* could . . ."

"Talk to them? But what if *I* screw things up?" Peter smiled. "Playing matchmaker isn't my strong suit, Will. I'm better at nursing grudges. Besides, what could I do? Tess doesn't want Rafe fishing. She particularly doesn't want him fishing with Adelia Duarte. I'm afraid that kind of attempt to control Rafe only makes him resist her harder. If it comes up now—this clash of wills and methods—it's bound to come up later. Better they learn how to live with it before the wedding."

"If there *is* a wedding," Will said.

"Has your mother canceled any of the arrangements?"

He shook his head. "Nope. But maybe she just hasn't thought of it yet. She isn't very organized these days. She's talking to herself like a total space. I'll ask her a question, and she won't even answer. It's worse than when Dad died." He paused. "Rafe's made her really happy, I guess. I don't want that to change. Things were pretty bad a year ago."

"I know."

"Where is Rafe, anyway?"

"He's gone into town," Peter said. "To see a guy named Jackie Alcantrara."

"Who's he?"

"The man who owns a boat Rafe's thinking of renting."

"Give me one reason to help Del out," Jackie was saying. "What's she ever done but shaft me?"

"So the *Praia* wasn't lost in the fire?"

Jackie shrugged and said nothing. He'd told Rafe he'd been working on the *Lisboa Girl* when the fire started, and from his excellent position at the far end of the pier, had had no difficulty in fleeing the harbor early. But Rafe didn't know whether the *Praia* had been moored off South Beach or not.

"You don't have to help Del out," he said, starting over. "You can view it as money in your own pocket."

"Or the lawyer's."

"You own the boat," Rafe said patiently, "or will. Any rent the lawyer collects will be deposited in the estate. It'll go to you eventually. It's a way to make money when you're just sitting at dock."

"That Felix Harper guy won't even let me take the *Lisboa Girl* out. What makes you think he'll rent the *Praia* to Del?"

"I called him."

"You did? Without asking me?"

"You own the boat, Jackie, not the lawyer."

"Shit." Jackie pulled a toothpick out of his mouth and stared venomously at the point. "Everybody's trying to run my business. *Felix*. You know what that means? In Latin? *Happy*. I guess he's pretty happy right now, all the money he stands to make before I get what's my due."

"He told me he's planning to call you. Thinks there's no reason why you can't work the *Lisboa Girl* a similar way—pay rent to the estate and take her out to fish." Anticipating Jackie's pique, Rafe had suggested the idea to Felix Harper. "Until Joe's will is probated, that's the only solution. So he's not giving Del any special favors. He's treating her the same as you."

"Me, pay rent to work the *Girl*? Pay it to myself? What a bunch of crap. It's killing me, da Silva. You know the blues they're hauling in right now? The schools started early this year. I'm burning money every day I sit at home."

"Then view the rent as money in the bank, and get back on the water. Or go to the Cape and hire out on somebody's crew. The legal stuff'll only take a few months."

"Nobody'd need me," Jackie said, shoving the toothpick back in his mouth and rolling it from side to side with his tongue. "*You* know what that's like." This was the only reference, slight as it was, that he made to Rafe's past. "People think you carry bad luck, they don't want you on their boat."

"Do you?"

"Do I what?"

"Carry bad luck?"

He shrugged, but Rafe saw the truth in his studied indifference. No fisherman, any more than a baseball player, was likely to discount luck. There were the obvious codes everyone knew—a knife stuck in a mast was a bad omen; a hatch cover placed upside down was equally fool-hardy; but whistling on deck was sure to raise the wind. Jackie was probably making rituals even now from the way he wore his socks, the route he took while on the boat, whether he positioned his fisherman's cap with the bill forward or back. One day his luck would break.

"Where's the *Praia* now?" Rafe pressed.

Jackie said nothing for a minute, then shifted his flat gray stare to Rafe's. There was no emotion in his eyes, neither anger nor bitterness nor amused contempt. They reminded Rafe of a fish.

"Whaddya want with that slut, anyway?" Jackie said. "Heard you're getting married. You settin' Del up on the side in case you get bored?"

Rafe twitched with the impulse to slam him, and then subsided into self-control. What Jackie wanted, after all, was a fight. He was dying to punch somebody over something and feel like a winner for once.

"You like just lookin' at those boats? Or you gonna make some money off 'em?"

"Ah, hell," Jackie said, and spat. "The *Praia*'s on a trailer at the Washington Street boatyard—or was, before last night. Talk to the goddam lawyer. Maybe Del'll harpoon herself in the head one of these days and solve all our problems."

The Boston arson expert, Jim Hayes by name, was pacing the sand with his head bent and his hands on his hips, looking for signs. What exactly the signs might portend, Merry couldn't begin to say. He was a little man, five feet six at most, but they were all—the other police officers, firemen, herself—studying him as though he were an oracle of Delphic stature.

He arrived by helicopter just after one, and listened to the fire chief's report of last night's blaze and her account of the morning's interviews. That the fire was caused by some sort of blast seemed apparent, and Hayes said nothing that might counter the assumption.

Survey done, he looked up and searched the attentive faces, his own lighting up when he spied Merry's.

"Detective!"

She crossed the sand to where he stood. "Yes, Mr. Hayes?"

"I'd like to get some police divers down."

"I think we can help you."

"The tides have been through here once since the fire, of course," he said, "but I imagine heavy debris won't have moved far from the harbor floor."

"The water isn't so very deep there anyway," Merry said reasonably. "It ranges from two to eleven feet at mean low tide."

"Where are we now?"

"The tide was almost out when the fire started," she said, "so it was low again this morning around nine A.M. It's heading in right now, and should be high in another two hours."

"Good." He turned to walk toward the waterlogged remains of the marine superintendent's office.

"Mr. Hayes?"

"Yes?"

"What are our divers looking for that the fire department hasn't already found?"

"The dinghy that blew up, of course. And pieces of the bomb."

"You really think they'll find *that* after the fire that swept through here?"

"Detective," he said, walking back to her with his chin jutting out and his eyes angry, "do the words 'Pan Am 103' mean anything to you?"

Merry looked blank.

"The plane. Blew up in 1988 over Lockerbie, Scotland. Two hundred fifty-nine people killed on the plane, eleven on the ground. Debris scattered over thirty-six hundred square miles. The Scottish police managed to find the bomb *timer*, Detective. A piece of Swiss electronics no bigger than your little fingernail. They could reconstruct the entire device by the time they were done. Compared to that, this should be a piece of cake. The stuff's been sitting in a fish bowl out there, and the collapse of the pier has worked as a natural barrier to the drift of the tide. So yes, I *expect* your divers to find every last fuse and battery. And they'll answer to me if they don't."

He marched off, leaving Merry feeling silly and somewhat out of her depth.

After she'd heard all that Charlie Rounseville had to say, she'd headed directly for the harbormaster's office in search of the marine superintendent, Mitch Davis. She found only Scottie Flanagan, a scalloper by winter and Mitch's assistant during the summer months. He was spiking his coffee mug with scotch and staring gloomily out at his defunct responsibility. The two-year-old office, only recently completed, had been doused with water and saved from last night's flames, but the blond shingles were darkened with smoke and everything inside was completely begrimed with ash. The heat and the force of the water hoses had shattered the windowpanes; the floor was swimming with broken glass and sodden paper. Merry noticed Scottie's brown bag of coffee had spilled, sending dark grinds all over the filing cabinet. The suggestion they made of rifled garbage added to the general air of dereliction. She tried not to wonder if the coffee he was drinking had come from the floor.

"Would you look at this, Meredith?" he said, the usage of her first name a sign of his lifelong friendship with the Folgers. "And it's not like

Visitor Services won't help us rebuild. They will." Visitor Services had built the new office and the hot-water showers in the first place, with part of the funds Nantucket skimmed from the hotel taxes paid by tourists. A million dollars was taken in the previous season; three quarters of that was returned to the town by the state. Visitor Services had the happy task of plowing it back into facilities that handled summer people.

"It's just the mess of it all," Scottie continued, including Merry in the sweep of his disgust. "And the mess out there, which is worse." He gestured toward the hulk of the docks. "The town'll be sued by every son of a bitch who lost a boat, you know that? And where's Mitch? That's what I'd like to know."

"He hasn't shown up?"

"Not today. He was here most of the night, but weren't we all. Coulda seen *Elvis,* you looked hard enough."

"Scottie, it's probably arson."

"Oh, for God's sake."

"Be happy. That's a criminal offense. If we find the guy, the town'll be awarded damages, and the boat owners can sue for civil redress. So cheer up. But first, tell me who'd be likely to want to see this place burn."

"The wharf?" He looked blank.

"I admit, it seems far-fetched. But think for a minute. Who holds a grudge against you or Mitch?"

"That's crazy, Merry. Scottie Flanagan's everybody's friend."

When he's in the bar, and he's buying, she thought. "I know, Scottie. I know. But if, as we think, the fire was deliberately set, then someone went to a lot of trouble to make life lousy for you and Mitch. Have you thrown anybody out of the marina? Crossed anybody in business? Slept with somebody's wife?"

She'd added the last as a joke, to conjure a smile from the old man; he had been talking a good line about the boatmen's wives for decades of summers now, but she knew he was completely devoted to his Betty.

Scottie's weathered features were puckered with thought.

"There's something," Merry said. "Come on, tell me."

He looked up at her from under his eyebrows, like a hesitant dog. "Nothing but the same old bizness, Mere. Can't believe somebody'd set a fire over it."

"You never know. What is it?"

"Just the board of selectmen, is all."

"The *selectmen?*"

Nantucket's local form of government was a board of selectmen, who met every Wednesday to consider island business. They controlled the purse strings as well. Any proposal to initiate, fund, or terminate anything had to be approved by the board.

"They never were happy 'bout those hot-water showers," Scottie said. "You know Mitch went around the back way to get 'em."

"He went to Visitor Services."

"Exactly. After the selectmen refused him money in the town budget for two years running. They figured taxpayers shouldn't have to foot the bill for boaters' showers. As if boaters were Haitian refugees or somethin' 'stead of the richest class of tourists we see all summer. Used to be a saying around the pier, here, Meredith, that started with the New York Yacht Club. *'You can sail to Nantucket with a five-dollar bill and a clean shirt and never change either.'* The point being, nowhere to get change, and nowhere to take a bath. It was downright embarrassin', with the quality of people picking up moorings every year out there."

"I can imagine."

"Never had ice, even, for their food lockers. Mitch changed that. Buys his ice from a guy out near Surfside, when all the rest of the ice companies import it from the Cape. Sold eleven hundred bags of ice last Fourth of July from that unit right out there." The coffee cup waved toward the blackened remains of an ice cooler. "We're supportin' local business. Do the selectmen see that? Not on your life. But Visitor Services did. We *still* have Nantucketers sneering at our new office, and complaining about their tax dollars going to folderol, when it was tourist money paid for everything."

Merry tried to quell his outrage as best she could. It was unlikely that a deranged local politician had torched the pier in a misguided assault on the showers, but she filed Scottie's words away nonetheless. She made a mental note to call Mitch Davis, and turned to the subject of slip five.

Scottie was able to retrieve a Xerox copy of his dock plan from the waterproof filing cabinet. It was a simple diagram he used to record transient rentals, showing the numbered slips and the names of the owners whose boats had claimed them for the entire summer. There were sixty-five in all. She noted slip five was, as Rounseville had said, vacant for the season. Twelve other slips up and down the pier had been similarly at liberty.

"That was the slip next to Nancy Harding's sloop—poor Nancy, that's quite a loss, that is," Scottie said, glancing at the penmark Merry had left by slip five. "Insurance money won't come close to solving the problem of how she'll replace such a pretty little vessel. There aren't many of them in good condition to be found anymore, even if she wanted to buy another."

"Slip five was rented this weekend, I gather," Merry said.

"I guess so."

"You don't know?"

"Mooring company handles the rentals. Boaters call up the Lewises— they're the operators—on the boat radio and tell them they're comin' in, and the Lewises collect the fees by launch every evening. No one particular is here to greet every boat."

Merry's heart sank. "You're kidding."

"Is it important?"

"Very."

"You saying it was that boat caused all this trouble?"

"The party on the *Calypso* saw it explode."

"I'll be damned."

"Try to think, Scottie. Were you here when the boat came in? Did the owner ask for the mooring company's number?" She searched for a marker meaningful to the old man. "Did he buy ice, maybe?"

"Don't remember the boat coming in," he said doubtfully. "Just that there was one there after it'd been empty awhile."

"That'd be when? Friday?"

"Thursday night. If he'd come Friday, the slip'd have been rented."

"And you don't remember the operator?"

"You'll have to call Cindy Lewis for that. I remember the boat, though. Hardly worth docking, come to think of it; little dinghy with an outboard putt-putt and a pair of oars. He wasn't going much past Coatue with that. At forty bucks a day for a slip, he'd have done just as well to have dropped anchor out in the harbor."

"Did he come in and out much?"

"Not that I noticed."

"Try to think, Scottie. Maybe you saw him Sunday."

"I don't watch every boat that moves in the harbor, Meredith," he said testily. "I've my radio to listen to, and my paper to read." He closed his eyes and was silent a moment. "I'd have to say the boat was there all day Sunday. I was up and down the docks a bit, and I never saw it gone."

"And Saturday?"

"That's it," Scottie said, his eyes flying open. "*Saturday.*"

"What about it?"

"You saw him yourself, Meredith. Here at the dock, when you got back from fishing with Del. He's the one who poured fish guts over your head."

Standing now on the beach, watching Jim Hayes disappear toward the fire truck, Merry thought again of what Scottie Flanagan had told her. Not a minute had she found to follow up the lead on Joshua Field; the arson expert's arrival intervened. But she had radioed a request that the youth be brought in for questioning. It was time she checked on the station's progress. She had those divers to send for, anyway. She headed for her Explorer and raised the dispatcher.

"Sunny, I need the Potts brothers and their diving gear down at South Beach," she said. Tom and Phil Potts were islanders and members of the division of criminal investigation, detectives like herself. But unlike Merry, they were avid divers. The Nantucket force was too small a concern to keep professional divers on staff; they just made use of the material at hand. Jim Hayes didn't need to know that, however. "Any word on the Field kid?"

"I sent a uniformed officer over to the Baldwin place," the dispatcher said, her voice fogged and broken by static, "but nobody's home. Probably at the beach."

"The Baldwin place?"

"That's the address he left. Tom and Jenny Baldwin."

"I didn't know," Merry said. "It was just a street address in Monomoy."

"We'll have somebody try again later, okay?"

CHAPTER ELEVEN

❦

PETER MASON SHOWED UP on the beach right around the time the Potts brothers did. He took one look at the way Merry's cheekbones stood out sharply under her green eyes and recognized her exhaustion. Whenever Merry pushed herself too far, her bones seemed to rise to the surface and betray the inherent frailty of her long, thin frame. He resisted the impulse to put his arm around her shoulders and settled for inviting her to lunch.

The Potts brothers were safely in the hands of Jim Hayes, she had asked every last question she could ask, and the prospect of sitting down for an hour far from the smell of burned plastic and dead fish was too much to deny.

"Can I have a beer?" she said.

"You can have two."

"That'll put me to sleep."

"I've been hoping you'd pass out in my car."

Merry looked at him closely. Peter adopted many moods with her, but he had never flirted before. It was a day for strange revelations and unexpected turns of events.

"So you think this Field kid was crazy enough to set fire to the wharf?"

They were sitting in Arno's, a lively restaurant on Main, where they'd had to wait only fifteen minutes for one of the two tables by the window. This was the *good* table, the one for four people on the opposite side of the room from the reception desk and the line of hopeful tourists. Arno's was noisy with the clatter of cutlery against china and unceasing conversation, amplified by the wood floors and two-storey brick walls. There were monumental unstretched canvases tacked to the brick, done in charcoal and pastels, of 1920s bathing beauties and tennis stars and family groupings rendered nostalgic by outdated clothing. Merry relaxed into the din and the color, the normalcy of tourist life, though it was clear from snatches of conversation floating around them that nearly everyone was discussing the previous night's disaster.

"What I don't understand is why he'd do it the night after he was released," she said, lowering her voice and looking about her significantly. "Sort of stupid, don't you think?"

"He'd have been smarter to have a confederate in his organization set off the bomb while he was safely in a police cell."

"Organization?"

"Aren't these protesters great joiners? He can't have come up with the idea of swordfish all by himself."

"No. It's not likely, is it? But still. I'd only released him Sunday morning, and twelve hours later he's allegedly blowing up the wharf and causing the death of one unidentified possible male. Daddy is not going to be pleased with my judgment."

"Maybe he's a nut."

"My father's many things, but insane is not one of them." Without seeing Peter's meaning she went on, "Oh, God, I don't know. The whole thing is crazy. What bothers me, Peter, is that I just can't envision Joshua doing it. Fish guts is one thing. Even minor vandalism—say he knocked a hole in somebody's dory and sank it, for instance, or cut the lines and set a boat adrift. But a *bomb*? It's too sophisticated."

"Hardly," Peter said. "A bomb is just a battery attached to an open circuit and some explosive. Something—a timer, a trigger—closes the circuit, and it detonates. Any kid who got through high school physics could manage as much."

"Except that it's not his style," Merry said. "He's much more likely to stand on Main Street with a bullhorn and harass the tourists. He finds protest glamorous. He's burnishing his image as a political Quixote. He's not someone violent looking for an outlet. Do you understand?"

"I think so. But that doesn't controvert what Scottie Flanagan told you," he said gently.

"No," Merry said. "Dammit, it doesn't."

"Eat your sandwich."

It was a Canadian bacon Reuben, one of the house specialties. But she was beginning to think she should have ordered something less smelly. Her stomach was still a little sensitive to olfactory overload.

"You're completely shot, Merry." Peter's fingers felt for hers, a cool, dry caress that was gone almost before she registered it. "You haven't touched a thing but the beer. On an empty stomach, it'll go straight to your head. I admit to the worst intentions where you're concerned—I find the image of you helplessly tipsy a serious temptation—but you *are* still on duty, and charming as your uniform is, I prefer to ravage you in green silk. So eat, and keep us both honest for the time being."

Merry seemed turned to stone by this extraordinary speech, staring at Peter while he calmly ate his Caesar salad. That he should regard her as anything like a love object was impossible. For an instant she felt dizzy with nameless sensations and closed her eyes.

When she put a word to her feeling for Peter, she called him a friend, and hoped that he considered her the same. Anything else positively terrified her. Peter seemed beyond her in so many ways—his wealth, his education, his experience of the world. And that was only half of it; there was his extraordinary sexual attraction and his decision, for years, not to use it idly. She had learned enough to know that he had loved only a few women. She thought of them as the Chosen.

Peter came from a tribe that got what it wanted, regardless of cost. The ruthless calculation in his genes was like the strength of his frame: consciously controlled through years of effort. Merry sensed nonetheless that he looked out at the world from gray eyes as piercing and predatory as a hawk's. She thought she had surprised an unfamiliar intensity in those eyes more than once during Friday's dinner, and had dismissed it as unlikely. But now she wasn't so sure. And the uncertainty—the panicked *thrill* of wanting and not wanting—gnawed at her empty stomach.

She picked up the Reuben without another word and tore into it.

"Merry! How nice to see you," Jenny Baldwin said. "Won't you come in?" It was Tuesday morning, and Merry was standing on the Baldwin doorstep in Monomoy. At her side, or rather looming over her five feet ten, was Howie Seitz, the previous summer's police intern from Northeastern's Criminal Justice program. He had graduated the Friday before Memorial Day and come directly to the island, the only new hire her father had been able to make. That John Folger had chosen Howie of all people surprised Merry;

but she had to admit she'd grown to like the big clod. Seitz had been one of the volunteers on South Beach the night of the fire; to be in on the chase a few days later gave him a definite sense of importance.

"I'm afraid this isn't a social call, Mrs. Baldwin," she said. "Am I correct in believing you have a youth by the name of Joshua Field resident in your house?"

"My, aren't we formal, Meredith," Jenny said, amused. "What's Josh done now?"

"Is he inside?"

"Don't tell me you're still mad about those fish guts."

"I'm too busy to hold a grudge, Mrs. Baldwin. Where is Joshua?"

Jenny held wide the screen door and motioned them into the house. The harbor's blue water gleamed from a window at the end of the long center hall, airy and cool. Merry felt rather than saw the faded chintz sofas, hydrangea blooms in large green bowls, rag rugs scattered across worn board floors.

"Josh!" Jenny called up the staircase. "Detective Folger is here to see you!"

There was an instant's silence from above, as though a small animal were crouched in its burrow, awaiting a dog's renewed digging. Then, to Merry's surprise, there came the sound of Joshua Field's easy descent of the steps. She'd half expected him to try an upstairs window, one that gave out on an eave of the roof, perhaps, or the back porch's overhang. But no. Martyr ever, he was coming to meet his doom.

At his appearance she wasted no time. "Mr. Field, I'd like you to accompany us to the station for some questioning in connection with the fire that consumed the Town Pier Sunday night."

There was a silence, during which Joshua Field broke into a grin and Jenny Baldwin's hand came up to her throat.

"You're not arresting him!" she said, her voice shrill and strangled. "Tom won't stand for—"

"No, Mrs. Baldwin, I am not arresting him. I would merely like to record a statement as to his whereabouts and knowledge of Sunday night's events. Mr. Field?"

The strongest impression Merry retained of the afternoon was not of Joshua Field's supercilious smile, nor of his aloof passivity as Howie helped him into the backseat of the police cruiser, but of Jenny Baldwin standing motionless by the door as they pulled away, her expression blank, one hand poised uselessly on the knob.

Joshua Field, it turned out, was Tom Baldwin's nephew. He had decided to spend the summer between his junior and senior years working construction at one of Tom's sites on the island, using the happy circumstance of free room and board as a means to wage his anti-swordfishing campaign. He was about to leave for work when Merry nabbed him; and his chief concern, once he was conveyed to the Water Street station, was whether he could call his foreman and tell him he'd be late.

"Make that absent for the rest of the day," Merry said.

"You can't seriously be going to hold me for this," Joshua said calmly. "It's police harassment. You have a fire at the wharf, and you decide to pick on the kid who dumped fish guts on your head. It's not going to be tolerated, Detective. Certainly not once my uncle returns from Boston tonight and hears about it. He'll have your job."

"Mr. Field," Merry said patiently, running a hand through her long bangs, "the police chief is the only person who controls my job, and the chief happens to be my father. And believe me, he remembers your uncle best as a skinny little kid he used to haul out of cars for necking with girls at the end of various unpaved roads. Your uncle isn't likely to scare my father. Arson, on the other hand—particularly arson with the sort of price tag of destruction tied on the Town Pier, arson that has left at least one person dead—makes him very mad."

"I *hate* it when the chief's mad," Howie Seitz offered distantly.

They were, by this time, seated across a plain wooden table in the station's upstairs conference area, which doubled as the sole interview room. Merry punched a tape recorder's button and Howie opened his notebook. "Mr. Field, I'm going to record your statement for police records. I would like to note that those present for the Nantucket police are Detective Meredith Folger and Patrolman Howard Seitz. Mr. Field, could you please state your full name and date of birth . . ."

What the hour and a half of repeated questions, attacks from varying angles, and ingenuous suppositions on Merry's part boiled down to was a firm denial of any involvement in anything like a bombing on the part of Joshua Field. Yes, he'd moored the old dinghy at the pier on Thursday night; he and his uncle had hauled it out of the tall grass at the edge of the Monomoy property and taken it across the harbor to the slips, since the Baldwin dock had been destroyed during last winter's storms and Tom had not yet been able to repair it. Tom's other boat was already at the pier, and it seemed a simple thing to place the dinghy there. They'd meant to hire the slip for the entire season, but since Tom was leaving for Boston and in a hurry, he'd handed Josh some cash and told him to reserve the next few days until he got back. They'd lost both the dinghy and Tom's forty-foot fishing boat in the fire; he'd be the last person to have triggered a bomb when his uncle's pride and joy was moored nearby.

"Are you aware," Merry asked him, "that witnesses saw your dinghy explode at approximately eight-forty-five P.M. Sunday night, seriously damaging the neighboring vessel and triggering the fire that engulfed the wharf within seconds?"

For the first time, Field looked disconcerted, but he recovered quickly with a characteristic shrug. "I can't explain it," he said. "I wasn't near the boat all day. After you released me, Detective, I went home, had a shower, and fell asleep, since I didn't catch a wink in that cell all Saturday night. Aunt Jen can swear that I was in my room until dinnertime, when I got up and ate with her. Afterward we saw the movie"—Merry didn't have to ask where, "the movie" usually meaning the older of Nantucket's two theaters, the Dreamland—"which let out at ten-fifteen. I think you can check all of that."

He was right, of course. She had no direct proof linking Joshua Field to any bomb that might have been in his boat, merely the wharf manager's identification of him as owning the dinghy that exploded. It was for this reason she refrained from arresting him; she knew she could never keep him in the station beyond the length of his statement. It was just possible that someone else had chosen the dinghy as the least noticeable boat in which to plant a bomb; but how had the bomber known Joshua was unlikely to take the dinghy out on the day in question? Or was the bomb placed at random a few minutes before exploding? Far more plausible was the idea of Joshua setting up the apparatus, then avoiding the wharf for the remainder of the day in order to establish his alibi. But until she could prove it—

"Thank you, Mr. Field," she finally said. "That will be all for today. But I would ask that you remain on the island and be available for police questioning during the next few days."

"Don't worry, Detective," he said condescendingly. "I'm not likely to run from *you*. Or your father."

His words were punctuated by Howie's shooting to his feet, his cap in his hands. "Chief Folger," he said. "*Sir.*"

Merry looked around. Her father stood at the door of the conference area, his face impossibly weary. He'd slept for maybe four hours the previous night, arriving home after she'd gone to bed and leaving again before she was up.

"Yes, sir?" she said, reading his intention on his face.

"Could I see you in my office, Detective?"

"Of course. Howie," she said, "show Mr. Field downstairs. Then write up your notes and transcribe the tape."

"Sure, Mere," he said. "I mean, Detective."

She followed her father to his office and waited until he'd shut the door firmly behind him and dropped with an explosive sigh into his chair. It rocked back against the wall, adding further grime to the already dark gouge he'd carved in the plasterboard over the years.

"What is it?" she said.

"That little twerp tell you anything?"

"Not much. Says the boat's his, but the bomb isn't. We've nothing to link him to it."

"I know. God Almighty."

"Dad?"

He ceased rubbing his aching eyes and stared at her blearily. "The crime lab in Boston just called. They've identified the body."

Merry waited.

"It's Mitch Davis."

"Mitch?" She was bewildered. "Scottie Flanagan said he couldn't find him yesterday, but I didn't know he was actually *missing.*"

"His wife has been calling the emergency center every hour on the hour. Mitch never came home Monday morning." John Folger cleared his throat. "We faxed his dental records to Boston a few hours ago."

"So what was the marine superintendent doing on a burning boat?" Merry mused.

"Especially after he was dead," her father said.

Merry's head came up. "What?"

"Mitch was murdered. Boston found a thirty-eight slug in the back of his skull."

CHAPTER TWELVE

ＡDELIA DUARTE PULLED
the dark green sweatshirt over her head and reached back to flip her
long hair free. She could hear the faint tolling of the Unitarian Church's
curfew bell drifting over town from Orange Street, and out of long habit,
she counted the fifty-two strokes. Nine o'clock on a Wednesday night.
Early for bed, but she and Sara were both worn out, and Rafe would be
knocking on her door at seven. She was tired tonight with something
deeper than physical exhaustion. She had ignored her pain over Joe
Duarte's death for too long, and the strain was beginning to show.

A faint breeze stirred the threadbare priscilla curtains at her window
and sent the ancient shade slapping against the glass. She turned and
sniffed the air, wondering if a storm was kicking up; but the scent of the
wind was clean. Good weather brought breezes to Nantucket at this time
of year; it was when the rainclouds descended that the world seemed to
hold its breath.

Del was fresh from the bath after a day spent cleaning house. She
had begun with her father's "snug" and its bulging rolltop desk and
worked her way to the attic shelves. Joe Duarte's lifetime accumulation
of junk had been sorted, packed in boxes, and set out back near the trash
cans for disposal; less easily discarded were the collections of mounted
fish, the decades-old photographs of trolling buddies long gone, and the
carefully stored memories of her dead mother. These last had given her
pause.

She found the simple white cardboard box high on a shelf in the
guest-room closet, its ancient and exuberant script proclaiming it to be
from Filene's. *For Del* was written on the lid. Her mother's wedding dress.
Had he forgotten it was there? Or kept it in the hope she'd retrieve her
respectability someday and walk down the aisle on his arm? Del

closed her eyes to steady herself a moment, overcome by a wave of sadness and anger, and opened the box.

Resting on top of the yellowed silk was a photograph of Joe and Agnes, freshly married and posed on the steps of St. Mary's, grinning broadly in postwar fashion. She raised it to the window, wanting to see more clearly in the fading afternoon light. All that her parents could not have known was written on their hopeful faces. No sense of the back-breaking work, the stormy nights her mother had spent in fear, the inevitable disappointments, her early death.

Del closed the box and set it back on the shelf, smoothing the aged cardboard gently with her fingertips. She was not ready to explore further. Or to examine the welter of emotions that had plagued her for three years. Even now the memory of that morning—she queasy with an eight-week-old fetus, unable to stand the smell of tobacco that clung to her father's shirt and hair, and Joe blank with disbelief, a line of pain between his brows—even now the thought of it made her feel like vomiting. The sick fear and pride had kept her wrapped in silence, unable to look back, unable to pick up the phone, waiting for some sort of bridge she could not build herself.

Now that Joe Duarte had gone farther than she ever dreamed, into the darkness of the abyssal sea, she kept at bay the memory of his stubborn pride, his ignorance of Sara, his rejection of her, and finally—most bitter in its disregard—his legacy to Jackie Alcantrara. She rejected anger for the simpler anguish of loss. And always, more guilt.

Without me, your dad would've been finished months ago. Jackie's words rang over and over in Del's mind. Had her absence hastened Pop's drift toward old age? Had pain worn away at his mental strength, his drive for living—dulled the edges of his fisherman's sixth sense? *Was this why he had died?*

She did not know what his final days were like. And the not knowing was a large stone she stumbled over whenever he came to mind. She had cleaned the house partly in the hope that she would find something—a letter, perhaps, addressed to her in his crabbed hand. But there was nothing. Pop was gone. He was past explanation or redress, past anger or forgiveness, past being hugged or told that he was loved.

The search for his murderer was a way of setting to rights all that Del had made wrong between them. That her father was equally responsible for the silence she disregarded. He was past blame, after all. She was not. She would avenge him like a Portuguese heroine of old, draw blood for blood, and pour it on the waters that had closed over his stunned white head. Perhaps then she would feel less as though she had killed him.

Del drew on her sweatpants, sighing deeply, the weight at the center of her chest easing somewhat with renewed resolve. She looked around the room, at the walls grayed with neglect, at the windows crying out for cleansing, at the familiar candlewick bedspread her mother had bought in Hyannis thirty years ago. There was at least this house, the one thing Joe had left her. Del chose to see it as a sign: *He had wanted her to come home.*

A faint sound, like a cat mewing, and Del stiffened. One ear was always cocked for her daughter, even when she slept. She turned from the guest room—she preferred it to her father's bedroom, still haunted by his smell, his lingering presence, perhaps even his ghost—and crossed the hall to her own childhood bed.

Sara's face floated like a small flower against the pillow, one fist tightly curled around the neck of a stuffed toy. Not that it *had* a neck, exactly; it was a whale Ralph Waldo had bought her at the Whaling Museum's gift shop. Ralph would spoil her unmercifully this summer, and Adelia was inclined to let him. Sara had gone too long without a grandfather.

Del smoothed the child's cheek, and her eyelashes fluttered. No sign of fear or discomfort; the mewing must have been part of a dream. On occasion she wondered what a two-year-old dreamed of; one more thing she would never know, and Sara could never tell her.

The doorbell rang.

Del turned swiftly and ran down the stairs, hoping it was Merry. But her brows knit in confusion when she opened the door, and she stepped back involuntarily.

"Hello," she said, surprised. "I didn't expect you at this time of night."

Rafe da Silva was no stranger to the dawn hour, and normally he took his time as the first light of five-thirty stole up from the shoreline to the east, enjoying the way it picked out the drops of dew glinting among the green cranberry vines. He'd drink his coffee, watch the sheep, and think about very little.

Today, however, he was hurrying through his duties with Peter's flock of merinos, intent upon the prospect of swordfishing with Adelia Duarte. Felix Harper had seen his way clear to renting her the *Praia* under a simple contract with Joe Duarte's estate—much as he had determined she could stay in her father's house free of rent or further obligation, as long as she paid the utilities. *Big of him*, Del had said, with a disgusted snort; it was galling to have to ask a perfect stranger if she could sleep in her own bed, or take out the boat she'd handled since she was a teenager. But that's how things were, and Felix, Rafe reflected, wasn't all bad; he might think about writing a will with him himself one of these days. Or would, if he knew where he and Tess stood. The girl still wasn't talking to him, and if the marriage was off, he didn't much care what they did with his things once his day was over.

That thought, he reflected, was an exaggeration, like most of his angry words about Tess. Even if he were dead, he'd want somehow to protect her and Will for as long as possible. At the thought of Tess he felt a familiar ache. He did not know how to reach her, other than to quit fishing, and everything in him rebelled at the idea. But he doubted whether a swordfish was worth trading for happiness, even as he loaded his gear into the back of the Range Rover.

He'd make an appointment with Felix Monday.

Rafe whistled for Ney, the big half-breed working dog both he and Peter adored, and the shaggy mutt's ears swiveled in his direction. He made the sign for bringing in the sheep, and Ney went into action, turning and wheeling among some sixty ewes with breathtakingly silent ferocity. Of all Mason Farms' inmates, Ney enjoyed his work the most.

And what about me? Rafe wondered. *Do I enjoy mine?* A question his father would never have had to ask; fishing, for all its backbreaking labor, its poor pay, its cold and wet and exhaustion, was a way of life, not work.

And that's the difference, he thought. *I work here, and it's fine. I can't think of a much better way to make money, or a fairer guy to work for than Pete. But out on the water, I'm living the life I was born into, the only one that feels as natural as breathing.* How to make Tess understand?

"Did you see this, Ralph? They're saying the Nantucket police are dragging their feet on the worst case of arson in the island's history. As if we've been sitting out on the beach all week working on our tans! This is all I need."

Merry Folger snapped the *Inquirer and Mirror* in irritation and bent over the article for a second time. It was Thursday morning, and the island's oldest weekly had just arrived at Tattle Court.

"Be glad they haven't got that fellow Field for an exclusive interview," Ralph Waldo said mildly.

"Oh, they have—that story is the sidebar to this one. He fed them a whole line about police persecution of political activists. Do me a favor, would you?"

"Hide the paper?"

"At least until I'm gone. Dad sees this, and I'll get another lecture over breakfast about the importance of public relations, particularly during tourist season, and I don't think I can listen to that today."

"Feeling beat?" He set a bowl of blueberries on the scarred oak table and pulled out a chair.

"It's been a long week, whatever the paper says."

With the discovery of Mitch Davis's murdered body, John Folger had turned the arson investigation over to the state police at the order of the Barnstable DA. To make Merry feel better, he appointed her liaison with the state police, and she had to scramble between South Beach and town and the state post out on Liberty Street. No link was found between Joshua Field and the fire. But the arson expert, Jim Hayes, thought he had figured out the bomb.

The device was enclosed in a bait box, which Tim Potts had found on Thursday in blasted pieces; and the detonator, Hayes informed her, was triggered by a curious apparatus he'd never encountered before. After twenty-four hours of study and attempts at reconstruction, he hit upon its mechanism by pure chance as he dangled it from the side of a substitute dinghy at the water's edge.

The trigger was encased in waterproof plastic and suspended straight down in the water from the mooring line, probably at high tide. The mooring line had detonator cord twined along its length that ended abruptly in the hinge of the bait box. As the water receded throughout the day, the boat lowered toward the bottom, until the trigger touched sand at mean low tide and blew the detonator. The cord in turn ignited what Hayes believed was several pounds of plastic explosive—it was the only form of nitroglycerin stable enough to use in a rocking boat—and fed on gasoline sprayed onto the dock by the exploding outboard motor.

"Very clever," Hayes said. "The boats in these first few slips are in five, six feet of water at the low, and a good bit of their lines are dragging on the bottom. With a dinghy as small as that one, it's way below the level of the dock even at high tide. Not the sort of boat anybody's going to study for very long, if they even notice. And no need for a timer, no need for remote control; just a guy with a tide table and an alibi somewhere else."

The timing of the tides suggested the bomb had been set up in midafternoon, a few hours on either side of the 2:54 P.M. high.

Merry could envision it all: an average guy—Field or an accomplice—strolls down the dock, bait box in hand, in the middle of a busy Sunday when most of the boat owners are out on the water. He putters around the dinghy, stows the bait box, checks the mooring line—and takes the opportunity to attach a wire with a trigger mechanism and a deadly leash of detonator cord. Then he goes home to Monomoy, and when the plastic bag and its trigger hit sand that evening, he's enthralled with two hundred others by the flickering images on the Dreamland's wide screen.

"It hasn't been a picnic for your dad, either," Ralph said, breaking into her thoughts. "Remember that the next time he's dressing you down. Now, what are you doin' on your day off?"

"Swimming at Surfside," she said, stretching luxuriously, "with a magazine and an umbrella and nothing else. I don't want to speak to anybody, I don't want to run into friends, I don't want to have to read anything longer than two-syllable words. How 'bout you?"

"Young Sara is coming to call," Ralph said, "on account of Del's fishing. Matter of fact, they're probably at the door."

But it was Rafe da Silva standing on the front step, Sara in his arms, and Merry knew as soon as she saw him that something was terribly wrong.

"What is it?" she said, her voice as flat as the look in his eyes.

"It's Del," he said. And that was all.

* * *

Rafe had pulled shut the door of the house on Milk Street, though he'd found it just barely ajar upon his arrival at seven-thirty that morning. Merry made a mental note about his fingerprints on the knob, knowing he'd have smeared any left by someone else. She wrapped a bandanna around it now—she carried one in the makeshift evidence kit that sat in the back of her Explorer—and walked into the Duarte living room.

Her sharply indrawn breath, the half-swallowed cry of anguish, was the only sound she heard, as though all else—a bicycle clattering on the brick sidewalk, the voice of a child raised in protest across a neighboring backyard—had been muted to silence by the fear of death.

Adelia Duarte lay sprawled in the middle of her father's living room, one arm bent under her and her eyes staring at the ceiling. A rich swath of dark hair spilled across the carpet, the last flag she'd left flying in the moment of surrender. The ends were smeared red with dried blood. She was wearing sweatpants and a sweatshirt of dark green that Merry recognized; after-dinner, before-bed clothes she pulled on to watch TV. She'd never gone to bed last night, and she'd ignored Sara this morning, so intent was she upon studying the spider making its way with excruciating slowness across the white plaster far above her head.

But the most incongruous aspect, the fact that had forced Merry's breath from her body with a half-choked mutter, was the harpoon canted rakishly in the middle of Adelia's chest. The lacquer-tipped fingers of her right hand were still clenched around the shaft, as though in her death throes she had attempted to wrest it from between her ribs; but her time was too short and the dart had been thrust well home. There was a look of wonder on Del's face. In her final moment she'd understood that the line was truly on, the surface growing closer, and the hand of the fisherman inexorably reeling in, reeling in.

Merry felt Rafe's fingers grip her arm, and she shook him off without even thinking, stooping to kneel at Del's side. She reached toward her helplessly, knowing in the back of her mind that she shouldn't touch anything, mustn't pull the harpoon from her body, couldn't close Del's eyes. She could only sway over the body, her tears furious and hot, saying her name over and over, *Del del del del del*, while the fear and disbelief churned her stomach and the recognition of an old pain swelled in her head. She had been here before, keening over her mother, over the telegram about Billy, over Sylvie. Keening over blood. She wanted Ralph Waldo and her father. She crumpled in a heap and allowed herself to sob.

"Mere," Rafe said, low and urgent. "Mere, I'll call the station, okay?"

When she didn't answer, he sidestepped toward the kitchen phone, cursing himself for his stupidity. He'd thought of the Folgers first when he'd opened the unlocked door and seen Sara sitting cross-legged in fouled diapers, one thumb in her mouth and the other twirling a piece of hair, by the side of her mother's body; but he should have called the station. John Folger would kill him when he saw the state Merry was in.

CHAPTER THIRTEEN

"**D**ARNED IF I KNOW," Dr. John Fairborn said to Chief Folger. "She was a strong, healthy woman. Rigor usually begins fairly quickly in that case, and lasts longer. I'd say it's fairly well established."

"Thanks, John," Chief Folger said in exasperation. "That tells me nothing."

"I can't give you an exact time of death. Only the detective novelists do that," the doctor said. He stood up from his kneeling position by Adelia Duarte's corpse and tiptoed backward, mindful of the evidence. "The normal range for onset of rigor is two to six hours after death. It's pretty well established two to six hours later, and can last for twenty-four to forty-eight hours after *that*. So *you* tell me when she died."

The chief knit his brows with the effort of mental calculation, working backwards from seven in the morning. "Sara was hungry this morning, but she wasn't starving. Her diaper needed changing, but I wouldn't say she'd spent more than a few hours in it dirty. So we'll rule out the idea that Del was killed before dinner yesterday and skip the twenty-four to forty-eight hours bit."

"Even assuming she was killed no earlier than dinnertime last night, the state of her rigor still fits a range of anywhere from seven P.M. to three A.M.," the doctor said. "Not to mention the cadaveric spasm."

"The what?"

"Cadaveric spasm. See the way the hand is clenched around the harpoon shaft? It went through her ribs and into her heart, Chief, and she died almost instantly, clutching at the weapon. Her muscles contracted and froze. That looks like rigor, even if it happened only two minutes ago. She might have been killed by the guy who discovered the body. Though I doubt it. She's cooled too much for that to be likely."

"Okay, okay," John Folger said, with sudden distaste. Fairborn's casual familiarity with a corpse never failed to disturb him. He glanced at Del's expressionless face, the hand still clenched on the harpoon, and turned away. She was too close to be discussed so irreverently. Why did he care *when* this had been done to her, anyway?

"You've got to realize, Chief," Fairborn said, "I just don't assess rigor that often. I attend *births*, not deaths. Other than that Mason guy last year, we haven't had a murder in a decade. Not that I'm complaining. Give me an induced labor anytime."

Nantucket had no coroner. Unattended deaths—bodies discovered by a neighbor, for example—were routinely examined by Fairborn and a few other island doctors on call to the police, and then shipped to Barnstable for autopsy. In serious cases—where murder was suspected— the corpse flew to the state crime lab in Boston. Adelia Duarte would be following Mitch Davis's corpse there.

"She's got several slashes on the right forearm," Fairborn continued, "and a puncture wound in the left shoulder. The slashes are probably defensive—she was holding the arm up before her face—and the punc- ture is where he missed the first time."

"You figure it was a guy?"

"Not necessarily. I was just being sexist," the doctor said. "The wound is *very* clean. Even without looking at the dart, I'd say it's got to be pretty sharp." He hesitated, assessing Del's chest. "It went right through the ribs here, and angled upward toward the heart. Not a blow that had to pen- etrate the sternum. A woman could have done it. *This* woman sure could have. She was adept at using this thing, wasn't she?"

"So I understand."

"It doesn't seem like a woman's weapon, all the same. More like something the victim picked up to defend herself with, and then had it turned against her. That's my bet."

"So there was a fight. She wasn't just surprised."

"By a six-foot-long harpoon aimed at her chest? I don't think so."

"She was supposed to go harpooning with Rafe this morning. That's why he found her."

"Then she probably had the weapon waiting by the door, and tried a little preventive action when whoever it was threatened her. Big mis- take."

"Preventive action" sounded every inch like Del Duarte. John felt a wave of sadness wash over him. A less confident woman might have called the police when trouble started. A less confident woman might be alive.

"What about her hands?" he said, hunkering down to examine the scarlet-nailed fingers clenched around the harpoon.

"You want me to open them?" Fairborn looked for Clarence Strangerfield, the crime scene chief, and found him on the other side of the living room, labeling a plastic jar containing a brownish liquid that was probably Del's blood. "Clarence!"

"Ayeh?"

"You're done photographing and sketching?"

"You wouldn't have gotten neah her, doctah, if I waren't," he said comfortably. "She's all yars."

Fairborn bent down and reached for Del's fingers with a grunt. "I'll have to break them," he said.

Chief Folger nodded once, and then studied the far wall intently. Anything but look at Del, or toward the door where Merry still sat with Rafe on the front steps, her weeping made more terrible by its silence. There was the cracking sound of small bones. He winced.

"Clarence," Dr. John called over his shoulder, "we need a plastic bag. And your labels."

When the fire department's black body bag had zipped closed over Del and the emergency crew had pulled away, John Folger stood a moment in the doorway and stared down at his daughter's blond head. It was bent to her drawn-up knees, the curtain of hair hiding her face. He saw that her shoulders were still; no sobbing or grief to read from above. Her hands were linked over her ankles, the slender, tanned fingers pressed white from the effort of holding on.

"Meredith," he said, cupping his palm over her hair, "we need to go home now." She didn't move. He looked at Rafe da Silva. The younger man said nothing, his eyes worried. With a grunt of pain for his bad back, John Folger lowered himself to the steps between his daughter and the foreman and threw an arm over her shoulders. "Sweetheart." He shook her slightly.

Her head came up from her knees, eyes unfocused and reddened from weeping. "It's my fault," she said.

"*Your* fault? There's *no way* this is your fault." John Folger shifted around to hold her close, his hand stroking her hair. "Meredith. You couldn't have known this was going to happen to Del."

"Oh no?" She reared away from him. "Because I'm too stupid, right? You'd have to be an idiot not to have seen this coming. She thought Joe was murdered. She told us that. God knows who else she told when we didn't believe her. *Somebody* must have known she wasn't happy with the accident story. She'd even gotten a threatening letter—and *I*, I told her to bolt her door at night. She must have thought I was nuts. Her instincts were right. I mean, what would it take for me to believe her? *Getting killed?*"

"She bolted her door?"

Merry nodded.

"And it was unlocked when you arrived?" This to Rafe da Silva.

"It was ajar."

"She must have let the guy in, then," John Folger said.

Merry thrust away her father's restraining arm and stood up, pacing back and forth on the brick path in front of him, wiping the tears from her eyes with furious fingers. "I'll tell you one thing, Dad, I'm going to find whoever did this to Del and I'm going to make sure he fries. He's not going to get away with this."

"With what, Meredith? With making you feel responsible?"

"With Del. Lying in there like that—like a—like an *animal*—"

"Meredith."

She looked at him then, the tears she'd just dried welling up once more.

"Calm down."

She hesitated, glanced at Rafe, and then studied her Top-Siders, angry and embarrassed at once. "You know what I mean," she said.

"Yes, I think I do. But I also know that you're in no shape to investigate anything."

Her chin shot up, questioning.

"I can't give you this case, Meredith," he said, as gently as he knew how. "Even if the DA in Barnstable lets us handle it. You're too upset about Del—which is natural. But in this frame of mind you'd go after Jackie Alcantrara without a thought for the evidence."

"Dad!" She was aghast.

His stomach knotted, but he pushed on. "I'm giving you two weeks' vacation, Merry. You can help Del far more by settling her affairs and taking care of the baby. That's what she'd have wanted, I think."

"Since I failed her so badly?" his daughter said bitterly, and laughed, a harsh, choking sound that died almost before it began. Her face went white and then red. She opened her mouth to say something—an appeal, John Folger sensed—and then read the futility of such words in his face. She turned away, one fist slicing through the air in a gesture of rage and hopelessness, and walked off toward the Civil War monument on Main.

Rafe got to his feet with a grunt. The two men stood looking after her—the tall, thin frame, moving swiftly and surely across the uneven brick sidewalk, graceful even in the midst of abstraction.

"Poor little Girl Scout," Rafe said.

Peter Mason looked for her where Ralph Waldo had told him she would be: in the shallows off Jetties Beach, swimming laps vigorously up and down the shore. He had walked through the few sunbathers of early June to stand at the base of the lifeguard's chair, eyes narrowed against the glare off the water, searching for the form knifing through the waves. The sound here was calmer than anywhere else on the island, buffered by the curve of land, the series of bars reaching toward the Cape, and the outflung arm of the stone jetty that kept the harbor channel from completely silting closed. Windsurfers wheeled and rocketed in its protected waters, and toddlers played. It was the perfect place to lose oneself in hard exercise.

.It wasn't difficult to find her; she was the sole swimmer in the water. She'd gone out past the bar, where dark water folded seamlessly into golden, wanting a place her feet couldn't touch. Calling to her would be useless, and disturbing to the sunbathers. Peter pulled his T-shirt over his head and kicked off his shoes, stepping onto the smooth pebbles that marked the beginning of the surf.

Even the sound was chilly in the first week of June—less than sixty degrees, he guessed. The shock of cold crept up his legs to the edge of his corduroy shorts; a surging wave slapped at his groin. He gave up and dove into the sound, moving powerfully in a crawl, out past the line of breaking surf and the bar. Where the sandy bottom abruptly slid away, Peter stopped, treading water and shaking his hair out of his eyes, his breath coming in quick gasps.

He surged upward to look for Merry. She was moving toward him, having turned in her lap while he edged out from shore, and her golden arms were slicing purposefully through the water. Heading for the jetty as she was now, she moved with the current, and in a very few seconds she would be upon him.

Peter waited, wondering why he'd come and what he would say. He hadn't thought clearly when Rafe had told him about Del. He'd gotten in the car out of blind instinct, certain he could help if only he could find her. *Hubris*, he thought. Why should she talk to him at such a time as this?

She was wearing goggles, and saw his body motionless in front of her. She swerved to avoid him. He reached out a hand as she passed and she came to a spluttering stop, outrage on her face until she understood who he was. She lifted the goggles to the top of her head.

"Peter." She was breathless from exertion, her eyes wide and green under the black brows. There was a dent in her eye sockets where the goggles had pressed, bruising the flesh. Wet, her hair had darkened to the color of blond wood, swept back from her forehead and revealing the hard, unvarnished structure of her face. Cheekbone and brow hollow and lips blue from cold, the cords in her neck straining with the effort to keep her head above water.

What do I say?

He reached for her instead, pulling her toward him, her body like carved stone in the wet Lycra; and incredibly her legs slid around his waist. She clung to him, all of her chilled by seawater and death, her cheek against his shoulder, and as Peter breathed deeply to ease the knot at his center, he felt her begin to shake. Salt tears and salt sea, the mingling of life with life. Merry, alive within the circle of his body. He felt pierced by joy, a sensation made strange by long absence; he closed his eyes against it, aware that it sprang from a terrible pain—the dead sorrow of his past, the unspeakable sorrow of her present. *In the midst of death we are in life*, he thought, inverting the Biblical phrase with purpose. It seemed the only honest thing to do.

* * *

Peter carried her halfway to shore, until the furrowed mouth of the bar bit at their feet and she dropped away from him. She was done crying, but kept her face averted for all that, the sun and wind sweeping wisps of wet hair like a veil across her eyes. He should have felt awkward, should have retreated from the feeling that had gripped him in the water; but he knew that *that* had been real, and this was not.

"I've only got one towel," she said abruptly.

"I'll use my T-shirt."

"Then what will you wear?"

"A wet T-shirt?"

Her lips started to tremble with what might have been laughter, but a horrified expression superseded the smile and she turned away, pulling her towel from a bag lying on the sand.

"Del wouldn't want you to stop smiling, Merry," Peter said gently, "even though she died and you didn't. You know that."

"She didn't *die*, Peter," Merry shot out. "She was *murdered*. Stuck through with a harpoon like a butterfly on a pin." She turned back to him, her rage on her face. "And here I am swimming with you, *laughing* at you—"

"—as though it had never happened. Yes. That doesn't make you a criminal."

"No," she said. "No, my stupidity did that."

"Merry—"

"I should have saved her, Peter. I should have known."

She fell silent, toweling off purposefully, pulling a shirt over her head, slipping on her shorts. She looped the handles of the beach bag over her right shoulder, ran her fingers through her hair, and set off for the parking lot without looking at him. He followed, sobered, his wet shorts clinging to his legs uncomfortably. He'd go shirtless.

He caught her up at her gray Explorer, and held on to the car window frame as she opened the door. She looked at him finally from her place behind the wheel, her face a picture of misery. He slid the back of his hand up her cheekbone, and she flinched, leaning away from him.

"Your father won't give you the case."

"Why should he give the case to somebody who's already bungled it? I had my chance. In my own kitchen, when Del told me Joe's death wasn't right. I blew her off."

"I thought you looked into it."

She laughed in contempt. "I verified my own conclusions. That she was in denial out of grief. Then I went to work on something more important, because my daddy told me to." She lifted the keys to the ignition, then dropped them back on the seat. "She'd be alive if I'd taken her seriously, Peter. I can't get around that."

"Why? Because you'd have stayed with her night and day? There's nothing easier than killing a person, Merry, no matter how many people are alert to the possibility. Look at the Kennedys. All the bodyguards in the world couldn't have saved Del if someone wanted her dead."

"Don't tell me what I want to hear, Peter," she said. "I can listen to that all day. From you, I expect the truth."

She pulled the door away from him, head down, and he let her go.

CHAPTER FOURTEEN

"**T**ESS," RAFE SAID.

She was sitting slumped over the kitchen table, chin resting on one hand, and she stiffened perceptibly at his voice. He waited for her to look around. She didn't. But she didn't tell him to leave, either. Rafe approached her slowly and stopped a few feet behind her chair.

"Del Duarte was killed last night," he said, and waited. "Or maybe early this morning. They don't know."

Tess did not respond.

Rafe reached a hand toward her shoulder and then lost courage, his arm dropping to his side. The rigidity of her neck, her immobility, caused the hair to rise on the back of his head.

A pile of fresh beets lay leafy and red on the table, their spiky roots tarnished with soil. The eleven-thirty lunch crowd was only an hour away, and Rafe knew the salad Tess intended to fix—the beets boiled and napped in a raspberry vinaigrette, on mesclun, with a bit of goat cheese—but she hadn't made much progress.

"I found her. We were supposed to go fishing today."

Tess's chin dropped and she studied her hands, palms upward, as though her fortune could be read there. She might never have heard him. Then she pushed back her chair and started to walk out of the room. Something in Rafe snapped.

"Don't you even give a goddam?"

A hesitation, and then she looked at him. "How was it done?" she said, voice low and without inflection.

He was appalled by the avidity glittering in her eyes. "She was stabbed through the heart with her harpoon."

A light came over Tess's face, like the lifting of a cloud; it might almost have been joy. Rafe felt slightly sick. The corners of her mouth twitched, and he thought she was about to say something; but to his horror, she threw back her head and began to laugh.

"Tess," he said, shocked.

The laughter grew more hysterical, uncontrolled, and she beat her knees with her fists, overcome by hilarity. "*Vengeance is mine; I will repay, saith the Lord,*" she gasped out, tears streaming down her face. "Oh yes, I will. Do I give a goddam, Rafe? You bet I do. I could scream her death from the housetops. There *is* a God. I've never been so happy about anything in my life."

"You don't mean that."

"Oh, yes, I do." Tess drew a deep, shuddering breath and closed her eyes.

Rafe backed toward the door, flooded with the fear of what her words might mean. That Tess was angry about his fishing, he had understood; that his attention to Del Duarte had nearly driven her mad, he had not begun to suspect.

"I've wanted her dead in every waking hour, in every obsessive thought of the past week, in every burning vow of hatred I've nursed during the sleepless nights," Tess said. "*And now she's dead. I'm free.*"

Will was standing at the door, his face white, his stark eyes fixed on his mother. "Jesus," the boy breathed.

Rafe steered him toward the hall and pulled the door shut behind him. "She been this bad before?"

Will shook his head. "Not exactly. But the past two days it's been really weird. She's been whispering to herself, staring off into nothing, looks like hell. I don't think she's been sleeping. Then she drinks coffee all day to stay awake, and her nerves are completely shot. She fired *Sammy* yesterday for saying an order was late, then called him this morning and begged him to come back. We might as well close the restaurant down."

"I didn't know," Rafe said.

"Of course you didn't," Will snapped. "How could you know anything? You're just *gone*. Like we don't even matter. Like Mom's just somebody you can take for granted. *You're* the reason she's such a mess. I could—" He stopped, frustrated and spluttering, his fists clenched.

"You could punch me a stiff one," Rafe said dryly. "I don't blame you." From behind the closed kitchen door they heard the tearing sound of Tess's weeping, harsh and guttural, as frightening as her laughter had been. Rafe imagined her arms outflung on the table, the beets scattered, her shoulders heaving. "Listen, Will," he said, throwing an arm around the boy and walking toward the front door where his truck was parked, "I'll call Dr. John. Have him stop by and talk to Tess. Maybe she needs something to quiet her down, let her sleep. In the meanwhile, stick the 'Closed' sign on the door. We'll figure this thing out."

Will nodded, his dark blue eyes too large. The kid never got out from under trouble, it seemed. Rafe pulled Will's head to his chest in a quick embrace, ruffled his hair, and opened the door.

The relief he felt at leaving scared him.

Merry sat on the left side of her bed, near the night table and the open window, her knees drawn up and her hands lying uselessly in her lap. A breeze sent the smell of wild roses wafting through the room, the pervasive scent of Nantucket in summer; the June sun was pitilessly bright. From the kitchen below came the hot, bursting odor of blueberry muffins and the sound of Ralph Waldo dragging a chair across the floor. He was singing to Sara, and her childish, tuneless voice attempted to keep pace.

> *"O do you know the muffin man,*
> *the muffin man, the muffin man,*
> *O do you know the muffin man,*
> *Who lives in Drury Lane?"*

A squeal of laughter and the sound of clapping hands. The day proceeded, full of heart's ease and the delight of summer; Merry felt it, heard it, breathed it in. Del was dead. The sharp pain of having survived, of *being* when Del had stopped, overcame her, and she shut her eyes. Peter Mason's hawklike face hovered on the closed lids, his expression as careful and contained as when she'd left him in the Jetties Beach parking lot. He would wait, and watch, and be ready whenever she felt weak.

Merry groaned and rolled into a ball, her back to the window, as though that would keep her safe from him. Peter was *life*, sharp, inexorable, overpowering; and to want life was to betray Del.

The smooth wet skin, the hard slope of his shoulder where her cheek had lain; the sensation of peace in his arms like nothing she had ever known. For a few seconds, while the water buoyed them and they drew breath in unison, she felt a relief and a completeness as solid as remembered childhood. She was inches from abandonment, from crawling into his bed and never coming back; she clung to his strength, and for the first time that day, her tears eased her pain.

But relief had turned to self-loathing and guilt, the desire to flee. She had failed Del; Del was dead; and her first impulse was to use Peter and hide. She was despicable.

She had driven aimlessly around the island after leaving him, heading first out to Madaket and then back along the Milestone Road to Siasconset, the monotony of the familiar moors maddening in their confinement. She had struggled just to *think*—of who might have wanted Del dead, and made the terrible decision to end her life. That the murder was spontaneous rather than planned she thought self-evident. The murderer could not have anticipated the harpoon would be waiting, sharpened for the morning hunt, by the front door. Whoever killed Del was moved by sudden passion—the violence of rage, or the panic of fear. The door ajar, the lights burning, the baby unharmed—all spoke to an unforeseen calamity. The visit wasn't intended to end in death.

Jackie Alcantrara was given to sudden rage, Merry knew. Her father's cautionary words came back to her now as she lay on her bed; but she shrugged them off. Jackie was the most obvious suspect. He disliked Del, and she had all but accused him (to the Folgers, and how many other people?) of having arranged Joe Duarte's death. Merry herself tippped Del's hand when she confronted Jackie on the *Lisboa Girl;* she told him outright that Del was requesting a murder investigation. Suppose Jackie had stopped by the house on Milk Street last night, hoping to talk things over—suppose he'd tried to strike a deal with Del, the *Praia* for her silence, perhaps—thinking that he could buy her off. It would be like Jackie's limited intelligence. If *he* could be satisfied with a boat, no questions asked, why couldn't she?

But Del flew into a rage, brandished the harpoon, and when Jackie tried to disarm her, was killed in the skirmish. With Del lying in a pool of blood on the floor, Jackie panicked and ran out the door. The neighbors might even remember him.

"Meredith!"

"Up here, Ralph."

"You're wanted on the telephone."

She thought of asking him to take a message, but it might be Matt Bailey, the most obvious of her fellow detectives to be assigned Del's case; and much as she despised Bailey and chafed at the notion of his handling a murder investigation, it would not do to ignore him. She rolled off the bed and headed for the phone in her father's room.

"Merry."

"Peter," she said. She looked about her wildly, the receiver to her ear, as though in search of protective cover. "Did you find a dry shirt?"

He laughed, and the carefree sound felt like a blow to the solar plexus. "I do own more than one."

A pause.

"You still there?" he said.

"I don't feel much like talking."

"I called to see if you felt like coming over for dinner tonight. You needn't speak, just eat."

"I can't."

"You can't eat?"

"Well—actually, I'm starving," she said, surprised.

"Life reasserting itself, Merry. It's not something to fight."

"But you are, Peter," she said, and bit the words back too late.

"I thought I might be," he said, his voice grown very quiet. "That's not what I intended when I came looking for you this morning."

"I know. You wanted to help. But you can't help me right now, Peter, you can only make things worse."

"Because I make you happy."

"Because you make me guilty."

"Same thing. Merry—"

"Don't argue this one, okay? It's how I feel."

The terrible stillness of a phone line burdened with too much to say. He cleared his throat.

"Look," he said. "You need to do something *positive*. Sitting around helpless for two weeks will only make you crazy."

"And you think dinner at your house is something positive?"

"No," he said patiently, "but I think finding Del's murderer might be."

She hesitated, confused. "What are you saying, Peter? That I ignore my dad, run roughshod over the department, and light out on a personal vendetta?"

"Sounds good to me."

CHAPTER FIFTEEN

☙

MERRY SLIPPED OUT THE
back door in the 6:00 A.M. silence of Friday morning, her Top-Siders in
one hand and her car keys in the other. She felt like a teenager or an
errant spouse; but Sara Duarte was still asleep upstairs, and she didn't
want noise to set off a baby alarm that would rouse the household. She
needed to get to the station before her father was even showered.

She had tossed and turned all night, debating Peter's words. "Your
knowledge of Del could be vital to finding her killer, and you'll feel in
the long run like you've helped," he said. "Once you've got the information, you can hand it to the guy running the investigation, and nobody'll be the wiser."

The idea was compelling. But she would need to be back on duty to
make it work. The station meant access to files—Clarence's forensics—
and a plausible reason for tooling around the island asking questions. She
would tell John Folger the arson case was a necessary distraction from
Del's death, and that she'd defer the vacation he'd offered until she was
better equipped to enjoy it.

But first she wanted to see those files.

Yesterday's paperwork, untyped and unorganized, sat on Matt
Bailey's desk in the darkened office he shared with another detective.
Merry outranked him, and had a private room—one more reason he
resented her. His first and foremost grievance was her refusal to have
dinner with him; the second, that she was the chief's daughter; and the
third, that she was a woman masquerading as a professional.

Merry set her enormous plastic purse on the floor next to Bailey's
desk, fished around in its depths for her half-glasses, and switched on

the Tensor lamp. A spotlight fell on Del's wide-eyed face. They'd gotten the pictures developed quickly.

The force had neither an official crime photographer nor a darkroom. Every officer was expected to master a 35mm camera, use it when necessary, and have the film developed commercially. Clarence must have gone to a one-hour place; Merry wondered for an instant what the lab technician had thought when he'd hung these up to dry. She shifted through the images quickly, not wanting to see them just yet, and found the crime scene chief's summary.

It was written in Clarence's dry manner. Del's injuries were noted sparingly, pending the state crime lab's autopsy findings. Merry recognized the significance of the defensive cuts on the right forearm; Del had not been taken completely by surprise. She paged quickly to the end of the report, where Clarence described the blood retrieved from Del's floor—and noted two different samples, A positive and O.

Merry flipped back to the top and began reading in a more organized fashion. Clarence's sketch of Del's living room, with the position of the body carefully triangulated and a notation of the blood pattern on the floor, she gave only cursory attention. She knew the living room well, and the image of Del's form was seared in her memory. It was the rest of the house that interested her.

Clare had dusted the doorknob for fingerprints and come up with nothing. When he sprayed the weathered wooden shaft of the harpoon with ninhydrin, however, he hit pay dirt. The killer thought to wipe the doorknob but didn't know unpainted wood retained prints—not surprising, really. Most people thought a surface had to shine in order to show the ghost of a finger. The problem with the harpoon, however, was the sheer volume of prints it revealed.

Merry sat back, chagrined. The first element to be lost from a print was water; some fingerprint processes depended upon reaction with it, and could only pick up fairly recent deposits. Ninhydrin, however, reacted to the amino acids fingers left behind when they touched a porous surface. The spray was capable of picking up traces of touch that were days old. Her own prints were probably on the harpoon somewhere; she'd undoubtedly gripped the shaft during the swordfishing expedition, as had Peter. And Rafe. And Del herself. There was no telling how many

people had handled it recently, and very little hope of proving con-
clusively that a particular print was deposited in the act of murder. She
read on.

Joe Duarte's study had been rifled, the contents of a filing cabinet
strewn across the floor. The cabinet's metal surfaces were carefully wiped
clean of prints.

This brought Merry up short. In her mind's eye, she'd thought of the
killer—all right, she'd thought of Jackie—harpooning Del in the midst of a
fight, and running out the door. She hadn't allowed for a jaunt farther into
the house, dying woman ignored and caution thrown to the wind, in order
to steal some files. *Files?* What crime of passion turned on *files?*

Clarence had endeavored to find out. In Del's room, which the murderer had apparently not entered, the crime scene chief discovered several items of interest neatly stacked on her bureau. First among them
were two threatening letters, composed of newsprint, and reproduced in
Clare's notes.

I WARNED YOU ADELIA DUARTE GET OUT OF TOWN. I'M LOSING
PATIENCE, the first simply said.

LEAVE UNDER YOUR OWN POWER WHILE YOU STILL CAN, the second
began. THE LIFE YOU SAVE MAY BE YOUR OWN.

Both were signed *The Avenging Angel.*

"A cliché wrapped within a mystery inside a cliché," Merry muttered.
The poisoned penman might have cribbed his—or her—notes from a
Threatening Letters for Beginners manual. These two must have arrived
in the days following the Town Pier fire; Merry hadn't spoken to Del
since she'd shown her the first letter that night.

Clare had sprayed the paper with ninhydrin—again, few people
thought of fingerprints when they forged a check or sent an anonymous
note—and come up with some beauties. He intended to search for a
match among the station's existing prints, but these should also be mailed
to the state crime lab for comparison with its database. That could take
some time, of course; and it would be useless if their killer wasn't already
in the computer. More than likely he wasn't.

The final item on Del's dresser was an inventory of the file cabinet.
Trust a former office administrator, Merry thought. She must have gone
through Joe's papers at some point after the funeral. Everything he'd
stored was carefully noted, as were the items Del discarded and the

files she added for herself. Clarence had cross-referenced the inventory and the cabinet's remaining folders, and discovered that only one was missing. Del had labeled it "Personal Documents." Whether Joe's or her own, Clarence couldn't say. The inventory told them nothing more.

In the galley kitchen, everything had appeared ordinary to the crime scene chief, except for a bottle of Glenfiddich scotch standing open on the counter. Near it stood two clean glasses. Clare had poured the scotch into a sterile container for analysis, dusted the bottle and glasses, and transported them to the station in plastic. The bottle revealed beautiful thumb and forefinger prints that bore no relation to Del's or those he'd found on the threatening letters.

Probably Joe's, Merry thought sourly.

The glasses had no prints at all.

Now, that's bizarre, she thought. *Del offers the murderer a drink, which he pours; and after a bit of scotch, the killer stabs his hostess, rifles her filing cabinet, and carefully washes the glasses, drying them with a towel to remove all prints. But he— or she—thoughtfully leaves the bottle for Clare to dust. Huh?*

The remainder of the report concerned the particulate matter vacuumed from the scene and the body. Clarence was struck by the lack of surface dirt on the premises—Del had apparently cleaned thoroughly only a little while before. Nonetheless, the crime scene chief found a few large links of copper chain embedded in the rug near the body, probably torn from a piece of the perpetrator's jewelry (*parpahtratah,* Clare would have said); some fine blond hairs; and sandy grit—probably from a shoe. Del was wearing green cotton fleece. Her hands, unclenched by Dr. Fairborn, had torn at clothing made of beige raw silk and linen.

Merry sat back in disbelief. Jackie Alcantrara's hair was mousy brown, and she doubted he had ever worn silk of any color in his life. Linen might be a possibility—but on a Wednesday night, when he'd probably been mending net or working winches on the *Lisboa Girl* all day? Indigo from a pair of jeans was more like it, or the cotton fibers of a Hanes T-shirt.

She pulled her half-glasses from her nose and flipped them shut. First thing to do was discover Jackie's whereabouts Wednesday night. She glanced at her watch. Seven o'clock. Time to beat it before Matt Bailey accused her of turf-jumping. She snapped off the Tensor light and threw her bag over her shoulder.

*　*　*

Jackie Alcantrara lived in a twenty-year-old frame house off the Surf-side Road, not far from the high school. Merry seized the excuse of a drive out of town and stopped for Scotch oatcake and coffee at the Downeyflake—exiled to the Milestone Road rotary after a gas main explosion destroyed its beloved Water Street digs. She pulled up in Jackie's drive at eight o'clock.

His truck was gone—like any fisherman, he'd have been up at dawn and on the road not long after. She eyed the house and noted what appeared to be a fresh paint job. The lawn, too, was neat and newly landscaped. Either the Alcantraras had a generous landlord or they'd bought the place and put some money into it. But where had *that* come from?

Merry rang the bell.

"Mrs. Alcantrara?"

She was a short bleached blonde with sharp brown eyes, a tendency toward plumpness, and a fixed simper. In her cotton knit stirrup pants and matching large tunic she looked, Merry judged, a good five years older than Jackie's twenty-eight. She stared at Merry blankly.

"Yes?" Hot pink fingernails with small gold charms at their tips grazed through the blond fringe.

"Detective Meredith Folger. Nantucket police."

Wariness replaced the blankness for an instant, and then the simper returned. She had probably been called "Daddy's Dimples" as a child. "What can I do for you, Detective?"

"I'd like to talk to you about Adelia Duarte."

She stood back and held the door wide, the smile more fixed. "Please come in."

The living room shared space with the dining area, and both were done in baby blue and pink. Hearts and flowers in the same shades were stenciled on the walls at ceiling line, and sprays of lace and dried blooms were tucked into pictures, nailed above doorways, and springing from every corner. The sofa was of ruffled gingham, and magazines were stacked in a rack coyly made in the shape of a pig. American Country with a vengeance, and all of it ordered from the Spiegel catalogue, Merry guessed. The massive spring issue was spread on the sofa, near a depression that corresponded to Constance Alcantrara's weight. Katie Couric chirped from the corner where the television set had been draped with a baby's quilt. An open box of chocolates and a mug of coffee proclaimed it breakfast hour in the Alcantrara household.

Constance bent to clear the sofa with a hostess's flutter. "There!" she said brightly. "Now we're ready for guests. Would you like some coffee, Detective? Or herbal tea?"

Merry declined and sat down in a padded rocker. She winced.

"Oh, let me take that for you."

Merry reached back and felt for the hard knob that had driven into her back. The head of a rag doll, tough plastic surmounting calico and nylon lace. She handed it to Constance and pulled out her notebook.

"I feel just terrible about Adelia," Constance began, without waiting for a question. "But then, everyone does. The poor dear had such a *difficult* life—though I always think we make our luck, don't you? Perhaps her life was difficult because she made it that way. Not that we're all responsible for *everything* that befalls us—but still—"

"When did you hear about her death?" Merry said.

"Well," Constance said, leaning forward conspiratorially, "I ran into Margot Grant yesterday afternoon—you know, she works as dispatcher at the firehouse, and she'd just run across the parking lot to the Finast to buy some tomatoes—and she told me there'd been a rescue squad sent to the Duartes' that morning. She filled me in on all the details." Her round lips were pursed and her eyes avid. "I understand she was *impaled* by a harpoon. Would you like a chocolate?"

"No, thank you," Merry said, feeling slightly queasy. Never in a million years would she have imagined bullet-headed Jackie, with his simmering rage and blunt words, tied to this refugee from a bad soap opera. "And did you tell your husband, Mrs. Alcantrara? Or did he hear the news elsewhere?"

"Call me Connie." She reached for a piece of Russell Stover's and sat back into the cushions, primed for a long gossip. "Jackie's been out fishing for the past few days, but I managed to raise him on the radio and give him the news. He said he'd start back today when his lockers are full."

Not immediately upon hearing of the death, but only once he'd made a full trip. How like Jackie. "You have a radio here in the house?"

"In the kitchen. That way he can let me know when he's due, and I can have something nice and hot waiting when he pulls up in the truck."

"Whereabouts was he when you raised him?"

"The Bank."

A full day's trip out of port. "And he left to fish when?"

"Wednesday morning."

Twenty-four hours before Del's body was discovered. He'd have made the Georges Bank by the time she was killed, if indeed he didn't fish somewhere nearer shore that first day, and return to the harbor under cover of darkness for the express purpose of harpooning her. Then he could have reached the Bank during the night and had his alibi fixed. Merry would get Terry Samson at the Coast Guard office to check a log of radio calls. The fishermen always gave their coordinates when they buzzed the Brant Point station.

But that sort of calculation and scrupulous timing didn't fit with the found weapon, or what seemed to be the spontaneous nature of the crime. *Damn.*

"He managed to find a crew, it seems," Merry said.

"Not really a *crew.*" Connie pulled a face. "Just that Swede. He has nothing better to do, I understand. I declare, after what he did to Joe Duarte, I'd rather Jackie fished alone."

"What the *Swede* did?"

"Letting the doors in careless like that. It's criminal."

"Happily, it worked out to Jackie's benefit," Merry said carefully.

"Well, it's an ill wind as doesn't blow *somebody* good. Jackie deserves everything he gets, believe me, Detective. And once that lawyer said he could fish—as if he should have to ask anyone's permission—there was no talking sense to him. Wait another week, I said, and hunt up some real crew, but Jackie was heading out, and I wasn't going to argue with him."

"The news about Del must have been a shock."

Connie shrugged. "I don't think so. He always said she'd come to a bad end."

Her indifference made Merry burn for an instant, and she had to look away from Connie Alcantrara's smug face. *"She would of been a good woman,"* The Misfit said, *"if it had been somebody there to shoot her every minute of her life."* Flannery O'Connor, apt as always. Connie needed a shotgun against her butt. Merry collected her thoughts and tried to regain the thread of her inquiry.

"Why did your husband have such a poor opinion of Ms. Duarte, Mrs. Alcantrara?"

"Connie," she said automatically. Merry's interest in Jackie's whereabouts and attitudes seemed hardly to disturb her. Merry wondered for an instant if she'd expected the police visit or simply enjoyed the attention. "Well, you can hardly blame him after the way Del behaved."

"Her concern about her father's death?"

"What concern?"

So Jackie hadn't told his wife about Merry's visit to the *Lisboa Girl*. Interesting. "She couldn't quite believe her father died by accident."

Connie laughed and took another chocolate. "Those Duartes. Always acting like they ruled the world, and both of 'em dead. No, Detective," she said, dusting chocolate crumbs from her fingertips, "I meant the shameless way she ran after Jackie a few years ago. Practically threw herself at him, trying to get him into bed. As if she'd be the sort of woman he'd find *attractive*. So swarthy and voluptuous, and never bothering to keep herself well groomed. It was absolutely disgusting. But she never had any morals, did she? I mean, *that baby* came along somehow, didn't it?"

The idea of Del throwing herself at Jackie was too ludicrous to be believed. But why had Jackie seen fit to tell his wife such a tale? "Did you know Jackie at the time?"

"Oh, I met Jackie three years ago this past April, at the Rose and Crown," she said, with a coy smile. "*All* the girls were mad for him. He couldn't *shake* them off. But I knew just how to handle *him*. I acted like I'd seen his sort a thousand times before, and I was looking for something *better*. He bit right away. We were married two years ago."

"And was Jackie working for Joe Duarte at the time?"

"No," Connie said, and clammed up, a slight sharpness in her eyes. Of course not. He was skippering the boat he would sink a year later.

"This is a lovely house," Merry said.

"Isn't it?" She leaped at the conversational change. "We were so lucky to get it. The owner came down a bit in the price. Not that there was anything wrong with it, you understand," she said hastily, "just that—well, he liked us, and knew we were just starting out."

A sympathetic gesture. Something no Nantucket property-holder would be fool enough to make, with real estate prices as they were. "How long have you been here?"

"Just a year."

So right after Jackie sank his boat and lost his job, he'd bought a house.

"Do you work, Mrs. Alcantrara?"

"Connie," she said. "No. I used to do nails at the On-Glaze"—this was a salon on West Creek Road—"but Jackie wouldn't have his wife go to business. A man should be able to support his family, Jackie says."

Then he's one of the few fishermen who can afford to be a chauvinist, Merry thought. Like almost everyone else, draggers depended on two incomes to make it. As first mate, Jackie might have cleared forty thousand dollars the previous year—if it was a good year. So how was he keeping his wife in Spiegel catalogues and dye jobs?

"Thank you, Mrs. Alcantrara," she said, flipping her notebook closed. "You've been very helpful. Just one more question, if I may."

"Of course."

"What do you do in the evenings when Jackie's at sea? They must be very lonely."

"Oh, heavens," she giggled. "I can never find enough time for all I do. This week, for example, I was tied up every night."

"Really?"

"Uh-huh. Monday was my reading group—we're doing Danielle Steel, she's *so thrilling*, I think, and the sex is so tasteful—you can just imagine it without feeling dirty, which I always think is important in a writer."

"And Tuesday?"

"I went and saw that *Forrest Gump* at the Dreamland with Margot. Now what did I do Wednesday? Oh, yes. Wednesday is 90210. I never miss 90210."

"Did Margot watch it with you?"

"Dick'll only let her do girls' night once a week."

So the evening of Del's death Connie Alcantrara was alone. Merry could have asked her for the 90210 plot, but it was probably a rerun at this time of year, and Connie would have mastered it whether she'd been in the house Wednesday or not. When did 90210 air? Nine o'clock? Ten? Plenty of time to kill someone and get back to the tube. But she couldn't quite see Connie wielding a harpoon. *Too icky.*

"And last night I worked the bingo table at the high school. A benefit for the Worship Center." The Nantucket Worship Center was an interdenominational group that held services out of the school.

"May I ask *you* a question, Detective?"

"Feel free," Merry said.

"Now that Adelia's dead, what will become of that lovely house on Milk Street?"

"I suppose it will be sold."

"And her estate goes to—?"

"Her daughter, I would think. I don't know if she left a will, but even if she didn't, Sara's her next of kin."

"Well, that might be enough to bring the father forward," Connie said, interest lighting her eyes. "That house is worth a bundle. Which means the baby is, too."

"I hadn't thought of it that way," Merry said stiffly.

"Then I suppose you'll be arresting that Dave Grizutto," the other woman said comfortably.

"Excuse me?"

"The baby's father. *Dave Grizutto*. He bartends at the Brotherhood of Thieves. Don't tell me you didn't know? Jackie says it was all over the island once she left."

"I never heard Dave discussed," Merry said firmly, her thoughts racing. Not for the first time, she wished she'd been more involved in Del's life the past few years. She knew Dave slightly—and remembered vaguely that he and Adelia had dated—but thought they'd broken up long before Sara was conceived. Del had never even suggested that poor Dave was the father.

"Why would I arrest Dave?"

"Because he wanted the money, of course. Or he wanted Del. And she'd spurned him. So he killed her. It's obvious, isn't it?"

"Nothing about murder is obvious, Mrs. Alcantrara."

"Connie," she said.

Merry stood up.

"You're sure you won't have anything?"

"I'm fine. Thanks."

"Detective," Connie Alcantrara said as she opened the door, "do let us know if anything is decided about that baby. Dave is *not* the person to handle so much money. But we'd be happy to give the poor little mite a home. She'd be far better off in a *stable* family, don't you think? And we're practically family anyway. Joe *did* leave Jackie his boats, after all. Which tells you something, doesn't it? He didn't trust that girl. I can't get over him leaving her the house."

CHAPTER SIXTEEN

❦

"**D**ETECTIVE FOLGER,"
Bill Carmichael said, slapping an empty manila file against his thigh, "I
thought you'd gone on vacation." *Fine time for it, too,* his tone suggested.
The state policeman in charge of the arson investigation looked harassed.
His eyes were deeply embedded in their sockets and threaded with red-
dened capillaries.

"I decided work was more important right now than time off," Merry
said.

"I see. Or rather, I don't, but never mind." He brushed past her to
his office and slumped behind his desk. Involuntarily, his eyes fluttered
closed, and he grimaced, rubbing a hand against his forehead. Carmichael's sandy hair was receding, and the dome of his skull had burned
and peeled. Merry took the chair opposite his desk and waited for his
eyes to open.

The phone rang. He ignored it.

"You alone here?" Merry said, glancing around.

"Well, there *are* only three of us, and a secretary," he said irritably.
"Sam's on patrol, Chuck has the day off, and Dottie stepped out for a
cigarette. I assume you dropped in to hear what we've got, right?"

"If there's anything new," she said.

He laughed shortly. The phone continued to ring.

"Things pretty hectic?"

"In a word. The phone never stops," Carmichael said. He reached
across the desk and took it off the hook. "I'm not supposed to do that,
but what the hell. It's either silence or insanity. I've got boat owners
calling when they can't get anywhere with your emergency center; I've
got reporters calling; I've got my bosses calling, and the fire chief, and
your dad, and Lisa Davis. *She's* calling me at home—not that I blame her.

And I can't tell her a thing, except that the bullet that put Mitch away was a thirty-eight to the back of the skull. Small hole where it entered, helluva mess inside. The guy is toast and he's got no nose, Merry, but can I tell her why? Nope."

"The weapon didn't turn up in the water or on the beach."

Carmichael shook his head. "And it won't. It's probably in somebody's boat locker. And the boat's probably out on Long Island Sound by now."

"What do you mean?"

"I mean it was a random killing, that's what I mean. It can't be anything else. Think about it. Mitch is out there on the beach in the middle of a bunch of panicky boaters who're trying to cross the fire barricade to save their stinkin' boats. He tries to stop some guy, words flare up, the guy's half nuts because he's losing a fortune in fiberglass, and so he hauls off and shoots the jerk who's trying to save his life. Then he gets in his boat and beats it."

"And yet the body was burned, not left on the beach."

Carmichael shrugged. "What wasn't burned that night? Mitch couldn't exactly get out of the way." He shoved a toothpick between his teeth and commenced rolling it from one side of his mouth to the other, his eyes hard and bright. "There's no way we're going to track this one down."

"We could broadcast an appeal for witnesses," Merry said. "If he was killed the way you think, somebody might have seen it."

"I've done that," Carmichael said patiently. "Posted bulletins on the radio and the news. Now I've got the joy of sifting through all the garbage that'll come in for the one nugget of real information."

"I'll help."

He looked at her from under his eyebrows, glowering. Nothing was going to cheer Bill Carmichael today.

"Have you talked to Mitch's wife?"

"I told you, she keeps calling me."

"I mean about who might've wanted him dead."

"Oh, for crying out loud," he said, slapping the desktop in frustration and thrusting his chair back against the wall. "Nobody wanted Mitch dead. *That's the problem.* According to Lisa, he was the local pick for Miss Congeniality. Everybody loved him. The town will never recover from his loss. And you know, she's probably not just painting a rosy picture. Sometimes nice people die for no reason at all, Detective. And we can't assign the blame."

"I know," Merry said. "So you've decided Scottie Flanagan's theory is not worth looking into."

"What, that he was killed in revenge for his toilets?"

"Hot-water showers. And ice machine."

"Maybe you guys have time to follow up leads like that," Carmichael said, "but the *state* police do not, my dear."

"Okay, okay," she said. "It was just a thought. Anything further on Joshua Field?"

"Abbie Hoffman in Birkenstocks?" Carmichael said. "Nope. There's nothing to tie him to the bomb—to its construction, that is. Just to ownership of the boat it was in. Even there, it's his uncle's boat. He'll probably be sued for civil damages, and he'll get a lawyer who'll show that anybody could've rigged that device without the Baldwins' knowledge. It'll go nowhere."

"Were his fingers tested for plastic explosive trace residue?"

"My, my, my, didn't *we* study hard at the academy," Carmichael said sarcastically. "Your arson guru had it done. I think he hoped he'd find a dead Iranian at the bottom of the harbor, with a note proclaiming 'Death to the Great Satan' tacked to his head. He was sure the explosive was Semtex imported from Slovakia. When in fact he's now determined it was American-made plastique you can steal from any construction site. And the timer was from Radio Shack, not Switzerland."

"Joshua Field works construction."

"And we do so much blasting on Nantucket. That sand sure gets tough for the backhoes to handle. Come on, Mere."

"So what about Field's hands?"

"Clean, of course. That's not surprising. Three days elapsed between the bomb and the test."

Merry waited a second while Bill Carmichael toyed with his toothpick, his eyes drifting elsewhere. She recognized the expression. He was half attending to her and half focused on the thoughts that couldn't stop whirling in his brain. She was the same way herself—asking questions about Field, and wondering whether Dave Grizutto had been in touch with Del since her return to the island.

"Bill," she said, rising from her chair, "somebody built a bomb and destroyed the pier. *Somebody did that.* Until we can figure out why, we can't begin to focus on who."

"Maybe there was no *why*, Detective. Maybe there was just a torching for kicks. The classic profile of an arsonist is a guy who gets a sexual high from watching things explode and burn. You've got to admit the pier put on a helluva show."

The station door opened and shut. "Bill!" a woman's voice called. "I brought you coffee!"

Carmichael groaned. "Just what I need," he said. "More Colombian speed bean. You taking off?"

Merry nodded. "I'll be in touch."

"Heard your friend bought it the other night."

The casual way of describing Del's death struck Merry like a slap on the cheek. Tears smarted under her lids, and she blinked quickly.

"Actually, somebody bought it for her."

"Sorry to hear it."

"Thanks, Bill," she said, and left, avoiding his eyes.

Once back in her gray Explorer, she sat for a moment with her hands in her lap, staring blankly at the steering wheel. Nothing could be simpler than finding out whether Del had seen Dave Grizutto before her death. She had left her Filofax on the Folgers' dining-room table Sunday night. In the aftermath of the fire, Merry had never found time to return it to her. And she knew Del well enough to expect every one of her appointments to be carefully noted somewhere in the calendar. A chill rose up Merry's back. *My God*, she thought. *She might even have put down a date with death, days in advance.*

Rafe da Silva stood up to ease his aching back and rested his chin on the handle of his spade. "So you think I ought to talk to Merry?"

He sounded doubtful and anxious, even to himself. Peter squinted up at him from his place in the dirt, halfway down the row of tomato plants he was staking. "Well, talking to Tess hasn't gotten you anywhere."

"Except deeper in the hole."

He had stopped by the house on Quince Street that morning and found Will sitting morosely in the empty kitchen and a *Closed* sign on the restaurant door. The second weekend of the summer season, and the Greengage was turning away business. Tess was upstairs in bed, half conscious under the effect of Dr. John's Valium. When Rafe bent over her pillow, he was shocked at the ravages the past twenty-four hours had written on her face. Tears slipped unheeded from the corners of her eyes, and she stared fixedly at the ceiling, her fingers limp, her chest barely rising and falling with the effort of breath. Every inch of her cried out *depression*. He held her fingers and received no pressure in response; nor did she bother to turn her gaze in his direction. He brought Will back to the farm for a few hours and put him in Peter's study with a book, under the careful eye of Rebecca.

"I wonder if this hasn't been coming for a long time," Peter said.

"Tess's blowup?"

"The whole thing. She had nerves of steel those first few months after Dan drowned. You remember. Sold the scalloper, refinanced the debt, put in a commercial kitchen. All between March and June, with Will walking around like a zombie. Then Will gets sent to the mainland for psychiatric work, and she runs the restaurant alone."

Peter ripped at a piece of sheeting with his teeth and tore it into a thin strip. The rag went under a tomato plant's armpit and looped in a figure eight around the six-foot stake.

"Just as she's through her first successful season, and Will's back on the island starting school again, he gets pitched from his bike and ends up in Mass Gen. So Tess has to be stoic for the next six months until he's out of the woods. And make ends meet somehow in the off-season, when the restaurant's closed. *Anybody'd* have a nervous breakdown once they got a breather."

"Maybe," Rafe said. "It's just not like Tess."

"Of course it isn't," Peter said. "If it were, you wouldn't think she was crazy. And you certainly wouldn't think she was a murderer."

There it was, the word he'd been skirting. *Murder*. The fear that had gripped him since he'd heard Tess's weird laughter yesterday morning, seen her rejoicing at Del's death. *Murder*. He couldn't seem to get away from it.

"Go talk to Merry," Peter said, standing up and dusting off his bare knees. Small grains of grit had embedded there and left a pattern like ostrich skin. "She'll probably tell you Tess didn't do it. You need to hear that, Rafe."

"I'm not sure it'll help," he said, swallowing. He lifted his chin from the spade and turned back to the beans he was cultivating. "She scared me bad, Pete. I'd never seen Tess so—*evil*. I can't get it out of my head. Maybe I've never known her at all."

"You know her," Peter said. "You just don't know all of her. There's ugliness in every one of us. Deep feeling—like envy, the fear of loss—brings it out." He stopped, feeling slightly foolish. Rafe had seen more of the ugliness of life than Peter could possibly imagine—in Vietnam as a boy of eighteen, and in New Bedford only a few years ago. "Very few of us admit that we're happy when someone we hate is lying dead. It's a nasty little secret, isn't it?"

"Very nasty."

"But Tess's honesty about it—however repugnant—suggests to me that she had nothing to do with killing Del. And with Del gone, the source of her jealousy and insecurity is gone as well. You'll find the Tess you knew again, Rafe."

"But can I trust that it's the real Tess?" the foreman said, stabbing at the dirt with his spade.

Peter said nothing. He understood that trust could be broken as easily as a dropped glass, past all mending.

"Guess I'd better call the Girl Scout," Rafe said, "and get it over with."

Ralph Waldo Folger peered down at Sara Duarte as she lay sleeping in her collapsible crib. To his relief, her breathing was steady and shallow. The previous night she had cried out in her sleep, a terrible sound that brought all three Folgers running from their beds, afraid of what they might see. Sara did not even awaken with her shriek; whatever fear grazed her unconscious with dark wings flapped on into oblivion.

Ralph wondered about the memory of a two-year-old. Had Sara seen or heard something the night of Del's death? Probably not. She would certainly have cried out and run to her mother's side. And in that case, she would be dead.

They had brought the child's things to Tattle Court before the Duarte house was sealed, and Sara seemed to have adapted to her new surroundings happily enough. Del had died without appointing a guardian for her daughter; even now, Felix Harper was discussing the formal adoption process with Del's New Bedford cousins.

A sound in the doorway behind him; Ralph Waldo turned and saw Merry. "She's sleeping," he said in a gruff whisper, and backed out of the room in stockinged feet.

"No more nightmares?"

"Not yet."

Merry looked past him toward the crib, her black brows drawn down. "What'll happen to her, Ralph?"

"Felix is handling it."

"I'm not sure he should be."

"Now, Meredith—"

"*We're* the people who loved Del," she said. "We should be taking care of her child. It's what she'd have wanted."

"Her family loved her, too. Don't discount that. Those cousins took her in three years ago, and stood by her, when you had less to say to Del, as I recall."

"I guess," she said, unconvinced. "But Sara's so small, Ralph. She can't say what she wants, so we decide her life for her. She may hate us someday."

"You've just pronounced the ancient law of parenting," he said dryly. "Take it as cautionary advice."

"I think I'll go see Felix Harper," Merry said, her chin up.

"How's the arson investigation?"

"Fine. Bill's got everything in hand. Not much news on the prosecution front." She glanced at him, the green eyes softening. "You don't have to remind me, Ralph Waldo. I'm not on Del's case. I'll behave."

"Never occurred to me you wouldn't," he said, fibbing. "Why see Felix?"

Her eyes slid away. "I'd like to keep track of Sara's affairs," she said, "and talk to him about the estate. The house will have to be sold. Dad told me to spend the next few weeks settling Del's business. I can do that and keep up with Bill Carmichael at the same time." She turned toward the stairs.

Ralph followed her, not certain whether he believed her. She spent rather too much time explaining how little she had to do with Del's murder investigation.

CHAPTER SEVENTEEN

F ELIX HARPER'S OFFICE
was in a Federal-style shingled house on South Beach, with roses growing
up both sides of the door and a miniature brass lightship basket for a
knocker. Other than the discreet wooden sign at the foot of the slate
walk that read FELIX HARPER, ATTORNEY, it might have been any other
island home—of a wealthy off-islander resident for a month, Merry
thought. The place had the carefully tended perennial borders lining its
picket fence, the fresh paint trim, and the clipped expanse of lawn that
characterized the retreats maintained *in absentia* for the fashionable sea-
sonals of New York and Connecticut. Felix was doing well.

Merry lifted the handle of the lightship-basket knocker and let it fall
with a thud.

Del's Filofax showed several appointments with the lawyer, one reason Merry wanted to talk to him. Other entries in the appointment book
were equally interesting. Del had lunched with Tom Baldwin a few days
after his nephew had thrown fish guts over Merry's head—looking for
her old job, perhaps? She had also seen Dave Grizutto—or so Merry
assumed. The notation said only "Dave, 7:30"; but it sent a chill through
her nonetheless. Del talked to him the very night of her murder.

It was Mrs. Harper who opened the door, a small, sparrowlike woman
with white hair the texture of cotton candy and bright blue eyes. Faded
pink lipstick was smeared in the crevices of her lips, and her skin had
softened into well-worn suede the color of parchment. She wore a Fair
Isle sweater and vivid pink linen shorts, and she held a trowel in her
hand.

"The peonies," she announced. "Just readying them for the show. And
how can I help you, dear?"

"Detective Meredith Folger," Merry said. "Nantucket police. I was hoping to see Mr. Harper."

"Fil!" she called over her shoulder. "Are you engaged? There's a lady to see you."

A low murmur from within, and the sky-blue door opened wider. "Through to the left, dear, and Fil will show you out. Mind you make him ask if you'd like some lemonade. It's sitting on the counter."

Merry worked her way past the dining room's Chippendale side chairs with their needlepointed seats to the study off the hallway beyond. A dim circle of light cast on a desk piled with papers illuminated a pair of hands, the left one holding a pen, and the right braced against a yellow legal pad. At her appearance, Felix Harper ducked into view and stood up, pulling his reading glasses from the bridge of his nose. Tall, gaunt, and abstracted, with dark hair just beginning to feather into gray, he was a good thirty years younger than the woman who'd answered the door.

"Yes?" he said. "How can I help you?"

"I'm Meredith Folger, Mr. Harper. With the Nantucket police."

"Ah, yes. Is this a follow-up, then, to that fellow who came by yesterday?"

"Detective Bailey?"

"That was the name."

"Only sort of," Merry said. "I'll be honest. I'm not assigned to Adelia Duarte's case. I was just an old friend of hers, and I wanted to talk to you."

A faint wrinkle on the pale skin, and he raised a hand to his brow. "Please sit down," he said. "I'm not sure I can help you, but perhaps—" He paused. "Mother did make some lemonade. Would you like some?"

"She'll be so pleased you remembered," Merry said, smiling. "I'll have a glass."

He tucked his height under the doorframe and disappeared down the hall. Merry looked around the study. Black-and-white photographs of a much younger Felix, racing a Swan in turbulent seas, were tacked to the walls. Floor-to-ceiling shelves held a motley collection of books, some leather-bound, some paperbacks, all of them carefully dusted. *Mother*, Merry thought. Mother probably had arranged for the framing of the two diplomas—one from Harvard College, one from Harvard Law—positioned over Felix's desk in full view of any client's chair.

An ice-cold glass of lemonade descended from the heavens.

"Thank you," she said, and smiled up at Harper. He looked uncomfortable, and hastened to put the desk between them.

"In what way might I be helpful?"

Merry took a long draft of her drink, sighed, and set it down carefully beside her chair. "My family is taking care of Sara Duarte at the moment."

Recognition and comprehension dawned on his spare face.

"I understand you've been discussing Sara's future with Del's relatives," Merry continued, "and I wondered whether you've reached any conclusions. Also whether the house will be sold, and how the funds from the sale will be disposed of, and so forth."

The lawyer cleared his throat and looked down at his hands. The right thumb and forefinger began to worry a signet ring on the third finger of the left, turning and turning it around the knuckle.

"Miss Duarte died intestate, as no doubt you know," he said. "In Massachusetts, that's not really a problem—her property will go to her daughter, once the estate is probated and the death duties are paid. I cannot envision the child having much to live on without the house being sold, and its proceeds retained in trust by her guardians."

"That's the question," Merry said. "Who are likely to be Sara's guardians?"

"There arises an interesting question," Felix Harper said, settling into his chair, "and one that I've been debating with Adelia's cousins, Yolanda and Manny Duarte. They're roughly the same age as the deceased, they're quite fond of young Sara, and they have two children of their own. They would be logical adoptive parents."

"But? Don't they want the responsibility?"

"They may not be allowed the chance. There is the issue of Joe Duarte's will to be considered."

"Joe's will?"

"Indeed. It may have some force and effect in the matter—although not in the way he envisioned." The lawyer leaned forward and cupped his hands. "Mr. Duarte's will provided for his granddaughter's care in the event that his daughter predeceased him."

"Wait a minute," Merry said. "Joe Duarte dealt with the issue of Sara in his *will*? He'd never even seen her."

"So I understand. Nevertheless, his will states that if Adelia Duarte predeceases him, his granddaughter's financial affairs are to be placed under the guardianship of Jackie Alcantrara, one of the legatees of his estate. Apparently Mr. Alcantrara was someone Mr. Duarte trusted."

"No way," Merry said, flabbergasted. "That's insane. Did Del know about this?"

"She was informed at the reading of the will. At the time, the provision seemed meaningless."

"Because she was alive. She hadn't predeceased him."

"Exactly. However, her death makes the will's provision an interesting one. Had Miss Duarte found time to draft a will of her own, assigning the child a guardian, it would, of course, have superseded this. Unfortunately she did not, and Sara Duarte is"— he hesitated before the colloquialism—"up for grabs."

"Along with her inheritance," Merry mused.

"The provision is not, strictly speaking, enforceable. Miss Duarte did not predecease her father. But there remains the possibility that Mr. Alcantrara will attempt to have it enforced, as the sole legal provision for Sara Duarte's future. I have informed Yolanda and Manny Duarte of that fact. If they proceed with their plans for the child, they may face a court battle."

"What a mess," Merry said. Connie Alcantrara's avid face and purposeful questions rose in her mind. She understood better now the woman's willingness to talk; her morning chatter was anything but idle. Had Jackie, who witnessed Joe's will, told her about the guardianship provision? Was this added incentive to murder—or a suggestion that the Alcantraras were innocent? For if monetary gain had been their primary object, wouldn't Adelia have predeceased Joe—and not the other way around?

"That would be too obvious. They'd be afraid someone would put two and two together. Better to get the boats and hope for the kid."

"I'm sorry?" Felix Harper said.

She looked up and realized she'd spoken aloud.

"Nothing," she said. "Just thinking too much. Mr. Harper—Del stopped by to see you twice in the week she was on the island. Did she come to talk about the will?"

"Yes," he said hesitantly. "About the house, and renting the smaller of the two boats. And some other—matters."

"Could you give me some idea what those matters were? It could be helpful in determining her state of mind before she died—what concerned her, and so forth. That might shed some light on her activities, and possibly on the identity of her murderer."

"I understand," he said.

"Was she thinking of writing a will herself?"

"I don't know."

Merry waited.

"She was certainly concerned about her daughter, however," he finally said, relenting. "She wanted to discuss the nature of trust funds—how they were administered, how funds were safeguarded, the appointment of trustees, and so forth. Almost prophetic, when one considers it."

"Right," Merry said thoughtfully. "But she never got to set anything up."

"No," he assented. "Which means that the twenty-five thousand dollars is just sitting there, waiting to be halved by death duties. It's a crying shame. A trust would have protected it."

"Twenty-five thousand *what*?"

"Twenty-five thousand dollars," Felix Harper said. "The amount she wanted to place in trust."

"Did Joe leave that much to Sara?"

"No, Detective," the lawyer said. "I don't know where Miss Duarte came by the money. She wouldn't say."

"Del had twenty-five thousand dollars?"

"She still does, I suppose. In an account in the Pacific National Bank."

"So the way I see it," Matt Bailey said, kicking his chair back and putting his feet up on Merry's desk, "this Alcantrara guy and his wife had everything to gain and nothing to lose. It's an open-and-shut case."

"Based on what evidence?"

He shrugged. "According to your dad, Del thought her father was bumped off, right? And then *she's* bumped off. Who benefits? *Jackie Alcantrara*. Both times."

"Right," Merry said. "But besides that, what *evidence* have you got, Bailey?"

"That's confidential until the arrest is made," he said, pulling his heels to the floor.

Merry rolled her eyes. "Get out of my office, will you?"

He stood up, his expression injured. "I didn't think you'd let a little thing like envy ruin your professional judgment," he said.

"Believe me, I haven't."

When he had slouched off to his own cubicle, Merry put her head in her hands. The chump would arrest Jackie Alcantrara on the basis of a hunch—except that her father wouldn't let him. He couldn't. She wondered what John Folger would think when he read Bailey's report, the better part of which would concern information Bailey had gleaned from Felix Harper. She was fairly certain that Harper had told the detective nothing about Del's twenty-five thousand dollars, but he had latched onto two facts: Jackie'd gotten the boats, and Jackie might eventually get everything else if he went to court for custody over Sara. Her father, however, would be looking for more than just motive—he'd expect to find opportunity and means in Matt Bailey's report. And Merry very much doubted he'd find them.

She picked up the phone and dialed Clarence Strangerfield. The crime scene chief was off-duty today, but she might be lucky enough to catch him at home.

"Come on, Clare," she said. "Quit holding out on me."

"I would nevah hold out on you, Marradith. I'm merely practicin' the rules of police procejah. Yar not on this case."

All she could see of Clarence Strangerfield was his hindquarters—considerable when viewed from the best of angles, but truly formidable in his current position in the rose bed. He had an insecticide pump firmly in hand and was sending clouds of something noxious billowing about the leafy canes.

"Neither is Matt Bailey," Merry said. "He signed off about twenty-four hours after he signed on."

"Now, Marradith. Bailey may lack yar pahtickulah interest in finding Miss Duarte's murderah—"

"The jerk's going to arrest Jackie Alcantrara."

Clarence sat up so quickly he stabbed his forehead on a thorn and swore under his breath.

"I know he can't have talked to the guy—Jackie's been at sea for the past several days, and isn't due in until tonight. Never mind that he was supposed to be on the Georges Bank when Del was killed. I figure Bailey thinks he was lying, and that the coordinates he gave to his wife were pulled out of the air. I haven't had time to check whether he radioed them to the Coast Guard as well. I can understand skepticism about the alibi—I was thinking up ways Jackie could've gotten in and out of port long enough to kill Del myself. What I want to know is whether Bailey's even bothered with the evidence."

"O' carse not," Clarence said. "Have you been doin' a bit of investigatin' on the side, Marradith?"

"I've just talked to a few people," she said evasively. "Dad told me to settle Del's affairs. I've been settling."

"And you wouldn't have peeked at my reparht, now would you?"

"Maybe peeked."

Clarence set down his spray gun deliberately and pulled off his gloves. "You'll get yarself fired one o' these days, Detective. And you'll *still* be pokin' yar nose in othah people's business."

"Clare, she was an old friend."

"I know."

"And I let her down."

"Ow, come off it."

"I did. She tried to tell me there was something wrong with her father's death, and I dismissed it. If I'd taken her seriously, she might not be in a refrigerated locker in Boston."

"Don't think about that paht, Marradith." He turned one knee to the earth and raised the other for support, grunting as he thrust himself to his feet. "Yar not responsible."

"Then if I'm not, no one is."

He looked at her, eyes narrowed, and nodded. "Whaddya want to know?"

"If, as seems obvious, Del was killed because she'd discovered something incriminating about Joe's death, then Bailey's right to look for suspects among Joe's crew—Jackie chief among them, since he benefited under the will. I would be doing the same. But I'd hate to see Bailey blow the case by arresting Jackie too early. If he can't make the charges stick, Jackie'll be free a few hours later and covering his tracks with a vengeance."

"Ayeh," Clarence said grimly.

"Jackie took only one crew member with him on this fishing trip. The Swede—the guy who operated the winch that accidentally killed Joe. But their stories differ. Jackie says the Swede brought the doors in too fast because he was careless. The Swede says he had no choice; the winch was jammed. Interesting that they're out on the Atlantic together when Del dies, isn't it? That way, the Swede can say Jackie was on the Georges Bank the whole time, and vice versa."

"You think they were conspirin'?"

"I'd like to know where the other two crew members were while Jackie and the Swede set up their alibis. Scuttlebutt has it they've taken jobs on the mainland—but that doesn't mean they weren't on Nantucket Wednesday night. Bailey isn't even bothering to think beyond his feet— which he'd prefer to leave propped up on the desk in front of him."

"Now, Marradith."

"Has Bailey checked Jackie's closets for linen or silk clothes?"

"Nothin's come to me for analysis, far's I know."

"Nothing from his wife's closets, either? *Her* alibi is nonexistent."

Clarence shook his head.

"What about fingerprints?"

"He may plan to get 'em aftah he arrests the fellah."

"Oh, that's brilliant."

"If you've seen the repaht, you'll know about the two different blood types," Clarence said carefully. "Guess they'll be drawin' blood, too."

"Clare, you've got to talk to the chief before Bailey does anything."

"He's *yar* fathah, Marradith."

CHAPTER EIGHTEEN

J OHN FOLGER WAS PULL-
ing at his salt-and-pepper mustache as he read over Matt Bailey's report. The detective prided himself on his intuitive leaps, as he called them. John's preferred words were less flattering. While Bailey saw himself as an intellectual path-blazer who cut investigation time in half, his chief considered him lazy. His failure to do the scut work of investigation too often resulted in a false arrest or an unresolved case.

John had given Bailey Del Duarte's murder in the hope that it might galvanize him. But as he read the cursory paragraphs, the chief admitted that handing Bailey responsibility was rather like giving pen and paper to a dog—you hope he'll learn to write, but more often than not, he'll chew the pen and urinate happily on the paper. Once Del Duarte's death was behind them, John decided, Bailey was going to be counseled. He'd been counseled before, of course, by the training officer; he'd done his forty hours of mandatory, in-line training the state expected every year; and nothing had changed. It was time he was counseled into another career.

The chief slapped the file closed in irritation and reached for his intercom buzzer, intending to call Bailey into the office; but he stopped in midreach. His daughter was leaning against the doorframe silently, watching him, and he didn't like the look in her green eyes. She was both wary and intent, which meant she had resolved to say something she was sure would make him angry.

"What is it, Detective Folger?"

"Do you have a minute, Chief?"

He nodded toward the captain's chair opposite his desk. She closed the door behind her and sat down, tucking her hands between her knees and drawing breath.

"I decided to forgo vacation," she said.

"So I see."

"Time off would just leave me thinking, without any distraction, and that wouldn't be good for me right now."

"Probably not," he said gently. "How's Sara doing?"

"She was asleep when I stopped by the house. No nightmares."

"Good." He waited.

"I talked to Bill Carmichael," she began again. "Nothing much has developed in the arson investigation. They've tracked the plastic explosive by its residue, and can say that it's American-made, probably construction-grade. They should have the manufacturer and batch pinned down soon."

"Uh-huh."

"Nothing can be traced to Field."

"Have you talked to Tom Baldwin?"

"Not yet. I'm planning to."

"Good. I'd like your sense of how he reacts to questioning. Maybe he knows more than he'd like us to believe."

"Maybe. Carmichael thinks Mitch Davis was shot by an enraged boat owner. Completely random."

"Could be." Not our jurisdiction, his tone implied.

"Dad—"

"Yeah?"

"Bailey told me he's planning to arrest Jackie Alcantrara."

"Really," he said, raising one eyebrow. "Feeling good about it, was he? Spreading the joyful news?"

"He called it an open-and-shut case," Merry said, meeting her father's bright blue eyes.

"And it's not."

"You know it's not."

John Folger sighed and tipped his chair back against the wall, legs dangling like a child's. "No, it's not, Mere. I'll be honest. I don't know what to do." His chin lifted and he studied her a moment. "I thought you'd be pleased to hear Jackie was being fitted for handcuffs."

"Not if it means the case is blown," she said.

"Ah."

"He's got an alibi, Dad. He hasn't been in port for three days. And he has a crewmember who'll say the same thing. That doesn't mean he's innocent—just that Bailey hasn't done his homework. No attempt to match fibers found at the scene to fibers in Jackie's closet. Or his wife's, although his wife has no alibi at all and is panting to adopt Sara and her future income."

Her father's face looked suddenly guarded. "You've talked to Jackie's wife?"

Too late, Merry caught herself.

"Isn't that Bailey's job?"

"Felix Harper told me the Alcantraras might contest Sara's adoption," she said, stretching the truth. "I thought I'd better check Connie out. You *did* tell me to take care of Del's affairs."

John Folger didn't answer.

She rushed on. "Bailey hasn't bothered to find out what the other two members of Joe Duarte's crew were doing on the night in question. They might have been at a pizza party with seventy witnesses. Or they might have been shoving a harpoon into Del's stomach."

"You sure you're working on arson, Meredith?"

Her eyes dropped to her lap. "I know it sounds like I'm ratting to Daddy about a fellow detective. I know how it looks. But Dad, he's screwing this up! And I can't stand it."

"I know," her father said. "And I know you came in here expecting me to be angry because you're walking around the margins of Del's case. Normally, I would be."

Merry didn't say anything. She didn't have to. Her face had flushed a guilty pink.

"But I'm so damned relieved somebody's thinking about the tough questions, I don't have time to be mad."

"So does Bailey arrest Jackie?"

"I don't think so." The chief tapped his fingers on the desk in a rough approximation of chopsticks, his face abstracted. "What if we do this? I tell Bailey he hasn't got enough to support an arrest. I send him out to Alcantrara's to collect samples. I have him hit the Cape to interview the remaining crew members."

"You have him get everybody's fingerprints," Merry said.

"I have him get fingerprints."

"And search the trash," Merry said.

"The trash?"

"Del received threatening letters. Three of them, in fact, before she died. They were made up of clipped newsprint, magazines—the usual thing from a first-time poison penman. Maybe the shreds are out back of Alcantrara's."

"You think Jackie would bother with that?"

"No, but it sounds just like his wife."

"Sounds like that visit yielded a lot of information."

Merry had the grace to look abashed.

"Will that satisfy you?" her father said.

"It's a start." She hesitated, then plunged on. "You could always have me take over the case."

There was a silence. John Folger looked at his hands. "I can't do that, Meredith."

"Dad—I'm not going to fall apart just because it's Del."

"I know you believe that," he said.

"It's not just belief. I'm fine."

"You don't look fine."

She rolled her eyes. "So maybe I haven't been sleeping well. Neither have you, if it comes to that."

He grunted assent. "Bailey needs to win or lose this one, Meredith. It's his last chance."

"Does he know that?"

"He should. But he probably doesn't. Judging by this report"—he flipped one edge of the manila folder contemptuously—"he thinks he's done a dandy job just by stating the obvious. He'll blunder himself right off the force."

Merry stood up, walked toward the door with her hands in her pockets, and turned. Her face was expressionless. "So finding Del's murderer is less important than finding a reason to fire Bailey?"

"You know that's not true."

"That's what I hear you saying."

"Meredith—" he said, and drew a breath. She was right, he'd had too little sleep, and his temper—volatile at the best of times—was hairtrigger right now. "I'm not going to tell you to keep away from this case, okay? If it makes you feel better to skulk around on the side, making sure you turn over every stone Bailey misses, go ahead. But trust me to do the same. I'm not going to let him arrest Jackie because he inherits under Joe's will. Give me some credit, Detective. We'll find Del's murderer."

Merry looked at him, her green eyes hard. "I won't meddle directly. But if I find evidence or information, I'm not going to look the other way."

"Just get it to me, okay?"

"Okay."

"When's Jackie due?" he said, thinking about the fingerprints.

"His wife figured this evening. He and the Swede left port the day before Del died, and with only two men working the tiller and the nets, they'll take a while to get a full hold."

"The Swede? Isn't that the guy who was careless with a winch?"

"So Jackie says. The Swede tells a different story. The winch was jammed, he says, and couldn't be slowed."

"Maybe they'll fight it out on the high seas."

The ghost of a smile crept across her face, and was replaced suddenly with a look of horror. "Of course!" she said. "Dad! I've been an idiot! I thought Jackie took the guy with him to provide an alibi while he killed Del. You know, 'Say I've never left the Georges Bank, and I'll forget you screwed up with the winch.' But the Swede's hardly the sort to back up a story he doesn't think is true. He'd be an odd choice for the job, even if he *is* the only crewman Jackie could find." She began to pace frantically in front of John Folger's desk, one hand scrabbling among her bangs and the other clamped in dismay over her mouth. "What if he took him out there for another accident, and then beat it across the Canadian line?"

"Meredith," her father said.

"He could. Or he could sink the *Lisboa Girl* in international waters, get picked up by a conveniently close foreign trawler, and be in Norway by the end of the week."

"You're overreacting."

"Why?" She pivoted to face him.

"Why sink a boat he barely owns? Why risk another accidental death? He'd be a fool."

"Or desperate. Think about it." She threw herself into the captain's chair and leaned forward in her agitation. "Jackie knows the Swede has spiked his story. So he has to get rid of the Swede. Then he panics, because the death list is growing too long, and he lights out."

"He kills the Swede on the same fishing run he uses as an alibi to kill Del? Why kill Del if he's not going to be around to enjoy Sara's wealth?"

Her enthusiasm faltered for a moment. "That's true," she said, sitting back in the chair. She sat still for the space of several heartbeats, mulling it over, and then looked up at John. "Okay, so I got a little carried away. I just had a sudden vision of the Swede on night watch, all alone in the middle of the Atlantic, and Jackie getting an itch to readjust his side of the story."

"Like I said, you could use a little sleep."

She stood up. "Too much to do."

"There's more than one day to do it in."

"I love it when you give advice you never follow." She turned at the door. "Dad—"

"Yeah?"

"Send Howie to find the guys who crewed for Joe Duarte. He's a better interviewer after one summer than Bailey is after ten years."

John Folger smiled as Merry left the office. A year ago she'd thought Howie Seitz was a millstone around her neck. Now she realized she'd trained him.

Rafe da Silva already had a table against the Brotherhood's long narrow wall, his dark hair and beard retreating into the dimness of the place, his brown eyes glittering in the light of a candle flame. His blunt fingers were clasped around a bottle of Michelob. Merry looked at him without the pain that would have accompanied their meeting a year ago; instead of wanting Rafe, the sight of him made her think only of Peter.

"Hey, Girl Scout," Rafe said, standing up to greet her. "You were great to come by."

"Anything's better than sitting at home."

"I hear ya. How's Sara?"

"Actually, better than I'd have expected."

"Good. I was afraid we'd have a lifelong psycho on our hands when I saw her sitting there next to Del. Not that she was acting crazy, but seeing that kind of thing can't be good for a kid."

"No," Merry said. "Nothing that's happened to Sara lately has been good." She pulled her purse off her shoulder and set it on the floor at her feet. "Buy me a beer?"

"What'll it be?"

"Sam Adams."

"Been hanging around Pete too much," he said, grinning.

"Oh, and Tess hasn't converted you?"

Rafe's smile faded. He motioned for a waitress and ordered the beer.

"So judging by your face, it's Tess you want to talk about," Merry said. "Are things still bad?"

"Gone from bad to worse."

"I'd have thought Del's death—I mean, you're not going to fish anymore, right? That hasn't helped?"

"Well—that's why I wanted to see you tonight, Mere," Rafe said.

The waitress dropped a bottle and a chilled mug before Merry's nose. She thanked her and poured some golden brown liquid against the frosted glass. "You know what I love? When the mug's this chilled, the beer forms little ice crystals against the sides. Like slush. It's got to be the best taste of summer."

"I thought gin and tonic was."

"That too." She set the bottle down. "Tell me about Tess."

"She went a little crazy the other day. Thing is, I don't know whether it happened *after* Del died, when I saw her—or before."

Merry's green eyes slid up from the rim of her mug and studied Rafe. "Crazy how?" she said.

He shrugged. "She's sedated, right now. Dr. John's orders. I can't get any response from her when I visit. Neither can Will. You can imagine what that does for the kid."

"How's she running the restaurant?"

"It's closed."

"Whew." Merry ran a fingertip down the side of the mug, tracing a pattern in the condensation. "And before she was sedated?"

"After I left Del's the other day I went by the Greengage to tell her the news. She went into some kind of fit, Mere, laughing and crying, like she'd won the lottery or something. She said she knew now that there was a God."

He paused, the air between them filled with the clatter of cutlery and chairs scraping against brick flooring. The Brotherhood was flooding with dinnertime tourists.

"So Del's death made her happy," Merry said slowly. She took a sip of beer. "I don't like that, but I can't say it's crazy. I've hated people out of jealousy before. It can make your reactions a little—extreme."

"Right," Rafe said. "I figured that's all it was. I mean, it's not like she must've killed Del—right?"

"Frankly, if she had, she'd have giggled her way to sleep the night before and been completely composed in the morning when you arrived," Merry said. "Not that I'm a psychiatrist. Maybe Tess killed Del in a fit of fury and forgot all about it until you showed up, the bearer of good news. Who knows?"

"That's the problem," Rafe said, rubbing at his eyes with both hands. "I just don't know. I figured maybe you could find out."

"Whether Tess killed Del?"

He nodded, unable to put it into words.

"That's a hell of a job to hand me, Rafe da Silva. Find out whether one friend killed another."

"But it *is* your job, Merry," he said suddenly. "When you're a cop on an island this small, it's always going to be people you know doing things you don't want to know about."

"And you'd rather I looked into it than Matt Bailey."

"*That* stupid son of a bitch? He couldn't find his own mother in the supermarket," Rafe said.

"I know. He'd send a complete stranger home with the groceries before he realized his mistake."

"I can't believe your dad put him in charge of Del's case."

"Well, there's a story about that. You don't have time for it, believe me."

Rafe bottomed out his beer and set it down on the table with a sigh. "Want another one?"

"I'm not done with this. I always get three-fourths of the way through and stall."

"I don't know why this had to happen," he said wistfully, looking over her shoulder at something only he could see.

"Del's death?"

"That too."

*   *   *

When Rafe had left, Merry walked the five feet to the bar and slung a leg over a stool.

"What'll it be?" the barmaid said.

"Can I have a glass of water?"

With the patience of a saint clearly written on her face, the woman complied. She slammed the dripping glass on the bar, where it settled into a pool of wet.

"Thanks," Merry said. "Is Dave Grizutto on tonight?"

"He comes in at seven."

Merry looked at her watch. "Ten minutes. Do you know if he's here?"

The barmaid sighed and slammed her way out the half-door toward the kitchen. Merry watched her lean through the service entrance, her throat working. The kitchen door swung closed and the barmaid returned.

"He's coming," she said. "Want some chips?"

"Sure."

She recognized him immediately, walking with easy grace through the low-ceilinged room, head slightly bent to accommodate the space. Dave was tall, tanned, blond, and good-looking, with a casual dimple in his resting expression that widened to dazzling charm when he smiled. It was a manner that served him well tending bar. He could defuse a drunken argument, calm a harried waitress, mollify the recipient of a late order. College-age girls hung on his stools and left sizable tips in their disappointed wake. He belonged on a beefcake calendar, bare-chested and lazy-eyed for the camera, but Merry sensed he would be profoundly uncomfortable there. Dave's looks were an accident his personality had not quite caught up with.

"Merry Folger," he said, extending a hand. At close range, she saw the strain around his eyes, the hollows beneath them. Two lines ran from the corners of his mouth to his nose. He'd been keeping late nights, or broken ones.

"Hi, Dave. I hoped I'd find you here."

"Am I ever anywhere else?" A trace of bitterness in the words. He had to be about her own age, Merry thought, and he'd been tending bar at the Brotherhood for over four years.

"Do you have a few moments to talk before you go on? Somewhere less—public?"

"Sure. Let's head for the back. If I take a table, the manager'll kill me. Not that there's one to take."

Merry looked around and realized it was true. The usual line for seats extended out the door and up Broad Street. How could a hole-in-the-wall place with a slave trader staring evilly from its sign pack them in like this year after year?

She followed Dave through the service door to a small room off the kitchen. "The chef's office," Dave said. "He orders everything from here. The rest of us use it for phone calls." He sat down in a straight-backed wooden chair and motioned Merry toward its mate. The room barely contained them both, but it had a door that closed, and when Dave shut it, the silence rang welcomingly in her ears.

"You're here to talk about Del," he said quietly.

"Yes."

"As a cop or a friend?"

"I have to be both."

"I can understand that." He looked at her once, looked away. "It might almost be a relief, I suppose. To have something official to do. A distraction from dwelling on the pain."

"I'm sorry, Dave."

"Coming from you, that word almost has meaning." His voice broke, and he rubbed at the bridge of his nose with a thumb and forefinger.

"Dave," Merry said, aware that time was short, "did you get to see Del while she was back on the island?"

A deep, shaky breath, and nothing.

"I only ask because she said something about dropping by here the night she died," Merry said. A white lie, but so what. "I wondered if she'd seemed nervy. Or frightened. Anything out of the ordinary that might give us a clue to what happened."

His hand came away from his face, and he looked at her with an expression closer to agony than any she'd yet witnessed. "How's Sara, Merry?" he said. "What's going to happen to her?"

"She's staying with us. Del's lawyer is working out the adoption."

"So *you're* taking her?" The shock was close to outrage.

Merry shook her head. "I'd love to, but Del's cousins are first in line.
And there's some chance that a clause in Joe Duarte's will may foul things
up. He named Jackie Alcantrara Sara's guardian in the event of Del's
death. It's not clear whether that's enforceable, but there's a chance Jackie
will try for it."

"What could he possibly want with Sara?"

"Her money. That's pretty crass, but it's what I'm guessing."

"As if Del had money to leave."

So the twenty-five thousand dollars hadn't come from Dave. "There's
the Milk Street house," Merry said. "It's worth quite a lot."

"Jackie Alcantrara, of all people," Dave burst out. "I won't allow it."
He stood up and reached for the door, as though he intended to hunt
Jackie down that very minute.

"Dave—"

"She's mine, Merry," he said, turning and stabbing at his chest with
a stiff finger. "Sara is *mine*. And the last person who should have her is
Jackie Alcantrara. The bastard. If he goes to court, he'll find me there."

There was a moment's silence, during which Merry studied the tor-
tured face and compared it reflexively to the baby's waiting at home.
There was not the slightest resemblance between them. Where Sara's
features were slight and delicate, Dave's were large and blunt, much as
Del's had been. Where Sara's eyes were green, Dave's were bright blue.
She was petite, he was enormous. And her auburn hair bore no comparison to his blond.

Blond hair was found on the floor, however, near Del's wounded
body.

"Did Del tell you this?" Merry said when he'd turned from the door
and sat down.

He shook his head. "She denied everything."

"Then why are you so certain?"

"Who else could it have been?" he burst out. "I was always with her,
Merry. I loved her. I wanted her, for God's sake. I wanted to marry her.
Even after she told me she was pregnant, and that she was leaving. I
tried everything I knew of to make her stay. I even followed her to New
Bedford, did you know that? For three months. I worked at a bar down
near the seaport, just so I could see her, try to talk some sense into her."

"But you finally came home."

"What else could I do? There's only so long a guy can feel like an idiot."

"And she never admitted you were the father?"

"No. Even I began to wonder, after a while. I mean, why wouldn't she tell me the truth?"

"Maybe because the truth would hurt."

"There was no one else," he said in a small voice.

"Dave," Merry began, and stopped, searching for the words. "Del and I grew apart over the past few years. She never told me who the father was. But I did think she'd ended her relationship with you several months before Sara was conceived."

His eyes slid to hers, slid away. He shrugged, nodded assent. "She decided to stop seeing me. That's true."

"Do you know why?"

He laughed shortly. "Because I loved her. Del was always threatened by real feeling. I asked her to marry me, Merry, and she told me not to call her again. *You* explain that."

Perhaps she couldn't marry someone she didn't love, Merry thought. *Perhaps she'd met someone she did.* "When would this have been?"

"Three years ago."

"And Sara is two."

"Right. Which means we broke up in June and Del got pregnant somewhere around September. It wasn't by me, is that what you're saying?"

"I don't have to."

He stood up, turning in the small space like a caged animal. "It may still have been me," he said. "I wasn't done with Del. I've never been done with Del. I stopped by, on and off, saw her now and then. I couldn't keep from loving her, Merry. Do you know what it's like to ache for someone like that? To ache *physically,* until you think you'll scream or smash a glass in a customer's face from the pain of not having her? I couldn't live with that. She had no right to expect me to."

A cold finger moved up Merry's back as comprehension dawned. "Did you rape her, Dave?"

"It wasn't rape," he said swiftly, turning on Merry. He was very tall against the office's single swinging bulb, and she shrank away from him involuntarily. "It wasn't rape. I'd never do that to Del."

There was a note of defensiveness in his voice Merry could not entirely trust. She wondered, for a moment, if he was prone to violence; if the calm exterior and the easy charm hid a volatile temper. Perhaps this was what Del had seen, and why she wanted to break away. There was no way of knowing, now. But Matt Bailey could look in Dave's closet for fibers that matched those on Del's floor. He could take a sample of his blood, a piece of his hair, an imprint of his thumb and forefinger.

"Sara doesn't look much like you," she said.

"She doesn't look much like Del, either."

"So you've seen her."

Too late, he caught himself. His eyes flicked to Merry's, then flicked down to the ground. "I've seen her," he whispered. "I had to see her."

"Did Del bring her to the bar?"

He shook his head. "I wasn't working the day that—that day. I stopped by Del's house."

"What time, Dave?"

He did not meet her gaze. "Around seven," he said.

"And how was she?"

"Same old Del. She turned into this person I could never reach once she knew she was pregnant, Merry," he said, sitting down opposite her once more. "She'd stand in front of me with her arms crossed and her face distant, and she'd make small talk. Like we'd never been more than passing strangers. She built up an amazing wall. And all I wanted her to tell me was why she thought it was so necessary. But I could never get her to talk about anything real—to be herself with me. She was polite and untouchable and a complete stranger. Sometimes I wanted to shake her until her teeth rattled in her head—" He stopped, and looked down at his hands. "That is not an admission of guilt."

Merry swallowed uneasily. "Did you argue, Dave?"

He shook his head. "We never got that far. I was trying to give her space, keep my distance, reestablish contact. I played with Sara. I figured with Del back on the island, maybe with time, whatever had gone wrong three years ago could be put right. Maybe she'd see me with Sara and recognize that the kid needed a father. I was trying so hard, Merry, and it was like talking to myself."

"There was nothing wrong when you left?"

"Not a thing."

"What time was this?"

"About eight. An hour was long enough. Besides, Del had been housecleaning all day and she looked pretty beat. She wanted a bath and an early bed."

"Did she say anything that suggested she was worried, Dave?"

"To me? She said nothing even remotely personal to me. You forget, I'm the stranger." He smiled crookedly. "All I heard about was swordfishing. And how good your grandfather was with kids. And how tired she was, and shouldn't I be going? She gave me the politeness and the door."

"And a drink," Merry said. "Let's not forget the scotch."

"Scotch? What scotch?"

"The Glenfiddich. It was sitting on the kitchen counter when we found her."

"Well, it wasn't when I left." He snorted. "Del didn't drink scotch. She rarely drank hard liquor, and when she did, it was Stoli and cranberry juice with a dash of club and a lime."

"You're sure about that?"

"I'm a bartender, Merry," he said patiently. "I've got half the resident population's drinking habits memorized, not to mention the preferences of some steady tourists. Del didn't drink scotch. She couldn't take it."

"I suppose the bottle was Joe's," Merry said thoughtfully, "or left over from the post-funeral reception. Though that still doesn't explain why it was out."

"Joe drank Jack Daniel's, and he was too cheap to keep much of anything else in the house," Dave said. "Believe me, I know. When I went to dinner there, I always brought the wine. It was the only safe thing to do."

Merry looked over at him, at the cleft chin and the warm blue eyes. He was deceptive, Dave Grizutto—nothing about his appearance, his temper, or his life was quite what it seemed. He revealed only a bit of the truth, to himself as well as to her.

"I've kept you too long," she said. "Your manager will be screaming."

He shrugged. "I don't really care anymore," he said. "I kept this job in the hope that Del would come back to Nantucket one day. She did. Only things didn't turn out the way I'd planned. Maybe it's time I moved on."

"Just don't do it for a few weeks, okay?" Merry said, attempting to keep her voice light.

"Because you suspect me of murder?"

"I don't suspect you of anything. I'm not on Del's case."

"I doubt that," Dave said, and opened the office door.

Sleep eluded Merry, as it had for several nights past. Her brain was filled with a constant command, urgent and unanswerable. *I have to find Sara's father. I have to find Sara's father.* The best way to avoid all the court battles, the tug-of-war over a child, was to know the truth.

Jackie would want to see the will enforced, and the Duartes would do everything they could to stop him. Dave Grizutto would insist on his paternity in an attempt to prove that Del had really loved him. Merry very much doubted that Sara was Dave's child. It was not like Del to deliberately lie; but to avoid causing him pain, she could easily justify keeping the truth from Dave. Instead, her silence had allowed him to ignore reality, up to the very night of her death.

—Unless Del finally told him about Sara's father, hoping that hard facts might slap him into sense. She might even have shown him the birth certificate. Had jealousy and rage taken over? Had Dave snatched up the harpoon and plunged it into Del's chest, fleeing with the file marked "Personal Documents"?

As the town clock tolled midnight, the refrain hardened into conviction. *I have to find Sara's father.*

CHAPTER NINETEEN

T OM BALDWIN STARTED
life as an unskilled construction worker, with a day that went from six-
thirty to four, and though the afternoon hours at his office now stretched
until dinnertime, he still left the house while most of the world was
asleep. This Tuesday morning in June was no different. The streets of
the town were empty of life as his heavy tires wallowed along the cobble
paving stones, halting patiently at every stop sign before moving through
the empty intersections.

He imagined the traffic that would choke the one-way streets for the
rest of the summer as vehicles snaked from Steamboat Wharf along South
Water, up Main, and out Orange Street to all the island points beyond.
Block by block, every car would stop—for the pedestrians, who believed
Nantucket was an island for walking, and the bikers, who thought cars
should be banned. Life in high season would be far more efficient if the
selectmen would allow traffic lights, but commercial lights of all kinds
were expressly forbidden by the historic preservation ordinances. Tom
grimaced. If he had his way, Nantucket's future would pay less homage
to its past.

The island was governed in traditional New England fashion, by a
board of selectmen who presided over a few elected officials and the
annual town meeting. Tom had crossed swords with the selectmen in the
past—over zoning ordinances, sewage and water rights, tax provisions.
He proposed enlightened schemes for the management of the island's
property that would have brought in significant tax dollars, and he was
thwarted as often as he was pleased. He was an outsider—by birth and
occupation—and that marginal status cost him. But soon he would enter
the holy of holies.

One of the most significant posts in island government was that of

finance director. The finance director was appointed by the selectmen
and served, in essence, as the chief financial officer for Nantucket, town
and county. The finance director supervised everything to do with
money—long-range planning, budgeting, all the contracts and procure-
ment for government projects—and so finance director was the job Tom
Baldwin wanted. The incumbent had died suddenly, to his intense satisfaction, and the head of the board of selectmen was a personal friend.
Over drinks at the Surfside Beach Club two days ago, Jerry Swain had
all but told Tom that the post was his for the taking.

The developer crossed Broad Street, heading for his office on Easton,
and took a moment to glance toward the yacht club on his right. The
boats hardly bobbed in the slack tide; a gull posed on a piling, arcing
its wings and opening its beak in a soundless cry. A redheaded waitress
moved among the breakfast tables on the terrace of the White Elephant,
the hotel perched on Brant Point, and he felt a sudden pang. The beauty
of young, redheaded women, moving with sinuous grace among the tables; like his mother, before too much hard work and childbirth turned
her creamy Irish skin to leather. His eyes flicked back to the road and
he cleared his throat, shaking off the past.

There was a car parked next to his reserved space—a gray Ford
Explorer. Not a staffer's car; he knew them precisely. A client? Too early
in the morning. A tourist, perhaps. He'd have to have it towed.

"Good morning, Tom."

"Meredith Folger! You're up and at 'em."

"I've a lot to do." She stood with a hand extended, professional and
neat as ever in her straight khaki skirt and silk camp blouse. She managed
to endow the simplest clothes with a bone-deep elegance, he thought,
like Greta Garbo. It was no accident he'd thought of the reclusive actress
in looking at Merry; something about the cheekbones and the hollows
of the eyes was the same, the uncompromising line of dark brow under
the cap of light hair. She was perhaps an inch shorter than five feet
eleven, about the size of his Jenny. But he had never seen her quite so
poetically. Perhaps it was the unexpectedness of her presence, or the
breath of memory that had stirred his thoughts earlier, gazing at a red-
haired waitress.

"What brings you to my neck of the woods?"

"I'd like to talk about the Town Pier, if you don't mind, Tom."

"Of course," he said. "It *would* be about Josh, wouldn't it?"

He showed her into his office and shut the door. "My girl isn't here yet, but I can make some coffee," he said.

"Don't bother. I've had some." She settled into one of his leather club chairs and pulled a notepad out of her large purse. Half-glasses perched on the end of her nose.

"What can I say, Merry?" he began. "Josh left an old dory at the Town Pier, but he didn't wire it up. You're barking up the wrong tree if you think he's an arsonist."

"I don't," she said. "At least, he doesn't strike me that way. Maybe he's got a psychological fascination for the blue glow of flame, but if so, I can't detect it. He doesn't seem desperate for attention, or in search of a tool over others, or in need of venting deep-seated hostility through destructive behavior. But then, I'm neither a psychiatrist nor a parent."

"Neither am I."

"No. You're just a relative who's given him board and a job for the summer. How come?"

"Alice—my sister—was recently divorced by her husband of nearly thirty years. Josh hasn't taken well to the change in his home life."

"I thought he was pretty much at school."

"He is. Funny, but a lot of marriages fall apart when the last child leaves for college. That's what happened to Alice. Jack looked around, saw the kids were gone and his only responsibility to them was financial, and he decided to seize on a second youth. Ward off death for a while. He changed jobs, changed towns, changed partners. It's not uncommon."

"No. And Josh?"

"His grades started slipping. He switched majors, from business to political science. Started protesting anything and everything. Alice thought he needed some focus—a different place, new interests, hard work for decent pay. I figured it was the least I could do."

"And how's it been?"

"Fine."

"Just fine?"

"I'm a little old to become a parent overnight. I'm not very good at it, Merry. I don't know how to talk to kids—at least, not like a dad. You know. Fatherly. Inspiring. Warm. Reassuring. So I settle for being a ger-

iatric older brother, and I'm not too good at that either. I imagine Josh
sees through both."

"Has he made any local friends?"

"I don't really know. Jenny might."

"I just wondered. If he'd fallen in with someone who knew he had
the boat, and saw it as an opportunity, it might give us a lead."

"You really think this was done by a kid?"

She shrugged. "I'm not in charge of this investigation, Tom. The state
police have it. I'm just helping out."

"Which means you're not at liberty to tell me anything."

She smiled by way of an answer. "Do you ever use plastic explosive
on your construction sites?"

He looked his surprise. "On Nantucket?"

"I understood you had building sites elsewhere."

"On the Cape, yes. There's one or two developments off Route 28."

"And outside Boston."

"Braintree."

"And—in the Berkshires?"

He shifted behind his desk and raised one foot to the opposite knee,
cradling the ankle. "I've a site in the planning stages just outside of
Lenox."

"There's a lot of rock in the Berkshires."

"There is."

"If it's not inconvenient, Tom, we'd like to have the name of the site
manager there."

"What's going on, Merry?"

"I just do what I'm told, Tom."

"That's a damn lousy attitude to take with a friend."

"Sometimes friendship is lousy."

He looked at her a moment, assessing. He'd always dismissed her
status as a cop, considering it a sinecure provided by her father, equiv-
alent to a college kid's lifeguarding at Daddy's country club. He realized
now that Meredith Folger was in her early thirties; she'd outgrown the
college-kid phase when he wasn't looking, and assumed the family mantle
of authority. If she was asking for the manager's name, he knew her father
wanted it, too; and if he stonewalled, he'd only bring the chief of police
to his door. He reached over to his Rolodex and flipped through it

impatiently, though he could have recited the man's name and phone number from memory.

"Here it is," he said, copying it onto a slip of paper and straining across the desk. As he did so, a pile of paperwork slid to the floor at Merry's feet. She bent to collect it. "I'll get that," he said quickly. "Don't bother."

She looked up at him from her kneeling position and smiled, handing him a sheaf of blueprints. "Looks like a hefty piece of work," she said.

"All speculative at the moment." He thrust the pile back on his desk. "It's been delightful, Detective, but my day starts early for a reason. Forgive me, but I'll have to cut this short."

"No problem, Tom," she said, smoothing her hands down the length of her skirt. "Just one more question. Did Del want her old job back?"

He stopped short and stared at her. "Del?" he said.

"Del. Duarte. She had lunch with you a few days before her death. I just wondered why."

"We were old friends," he said.

"I know. That's something we have in common. You're handling her murder very well, by the way. I thought you might bring it up, but when you didn't, I realized you were respecting my feelings. I appreciate it, Tom."

Was she mocking him? The green eyes were as cool and careful as ever; he couldn't tell. He felt the skin on his forehead moisten slightly, and a wave of anger washed over him.

"I handle *everything* well, Detective Folger," he spat out. "I lose a hundred-thousand-dollar boat to fire, and I shrug it off and talk about insurance. My nephew's facing a criminal indictment, and I tell my sister with a straight face that he's adjusting to life quite well. A young woman I regarded almost as a daughter dies a brutal death, and I'm back at work the next day. Handling things is how I get through *life*, Detective. How do you do it? By turning the knife in the wounds of everybody you meet?"

"It was just a thank-you, Tom," she said quietly, and picked up her purse. "I take it Del didn't come looking for a job?"

He shook his head, his breathing rapid, and reached for a handkerchief to mop his face. "She didn't need anything from me, Meredith," he said. "She'd decided to make her own way."

After she left, he picked up the phone and dialed Jerry Swain at home. Swain was independently wealthy and spent the summer sailing; he never left the breakfast table before nine o'clock. It was time to tell him that Tom Baldwin was his man. He'd waited a day, to make it convincing; but he wasn't kidding anybody. The finance director post was everything he'd ever wanted. Strange, to be worth ten million dollars, and still feel that way.

Merry's brow was knitted and her gaze distracted. She drove the familiar roads without seeing them, thinking about Tom Baldwin. Her job had been to study his reaction to questioning, and he'd given her plenty of material. The notion of Josh and arson did not ruffle his calm; the request for the name of his Lenox site manager irritated him; but the mention of Del positively blew a fuse. What had happened at that lunch to make Tom Baldwin so defensive? Had Del in fact *asked* for a job, and had he refused her—and felt guilty in retrospect? It didn't seem likely.

And what in the hell is Windy Harbor? Merry thought. The name had leaped out at her from Tom Baldwin's blueprints, scattered at her feet. A development of some kind, but she wasn't able to study it long enough. The name didn't ring a bell. The day before, she'd obtained a listing of Baldwin Builders' fifteen current projects from Tom's helpful secretary— the source of her knowledge of Lenox, the one place the developer might conceivably use explosives. She'd swear Windy Harbor was not among them. *Speculative*, he'd called it; and he'd been anxious to tuck it out of sight. Not before she noticed an unfamiliar name—Oceanside Resorts— and a Delaware incorporation, written in small block letters on the lower left-hand corner of the top sheet. Had Tom come by a competitor's plans? Or was he forming a partnership with another developer? Big business was very hush-hush.

And with everything else on her plate, Merry thought irritably as she parked the Explorer on Chestnut, why did she care?

CHAPTER TWENTY

MATT BAILEY WAS LEAN-
ing against the blue mailbox that served the Nantucket force as evidence
locker when Merry walked in. He had a mug of coffee in his hand and
a bleary expression around the eyes, both habitual at eight in the morning; he rarely looked fully awake before noon, nor did he make much
effort to work until after lunch. He claimed that he accomplished more
in a few hours of focused attention than the rest of them did with half-
hearted efforts throughout the day, and no one was interested or out-
raged enough to challenge him. It was simply one more way Bailey
attempted to turn failure to success.

"Mere! Hey, everybody!" he yelled in the general direction of the
dispatch room. "I want it known that I was actually in the office today before Detective Meredith Folger, that celebrated morning person
and worker bee extraordinaire. Sleeping on the job, Mere? Not
enough to do?"

"I had a breakfast meeting," Merry muttered, wishing for the strength
to ignore him. She tried instead to sweep by, head high. He grabbed
her arm.

"Got the case just about wrapped up," he said, in a confidential tone.

"Oh yeah?" Poor Clarence must have been working overtime. Jackie
Alcantrara had limped into port Saturday morning with a thunderous
look on his face, the Swede in smiling good health, half a hold's worth
of bottom fish, and a busted oil pressure gauge. His engine had died, off
and on, for the better part of twenty-four hours, and he was ready to
walk away from the *Lisboa Girl* without a backward glance. Bailey had
chosen that moment to request his fingerprints, and Jackie had actually
swung at him. Without the Swede to restrain him, he might have started

a fistfight in the middle of the boat basin. Bailey was presently nursing a grudge.

He had followed Jackie home in order to hear both crewmen protest their innocence and affirm each other's whereabouts on the night in question. Then he surveyed Jackie's closets and found candidates for beige linen and silk fibers among his wife's clothes. The trash was next, where he'd come up with plenty of magazines to store in his police-issue Crown Victoria, without explaining to Connie Alcantrara why her outdated *Redbooks* and *Cosmopolitans* interested him. Then he'd rousted Clarence from his Saturday peace and told him to get to work.

The crime scene chief had replied mildly that most things could wait until Monday, *except* his weekend, and had shut the door in Bailey's face. He'd been closeted in his tiny lab most of yesterday, however, and despite her antipathy for Bailey, Merry admitted she was interested to know what Clarence had found.

"You want to talk about it?" she said.

"Sure. Never too busy to offer a few pointers to a colleague."

"Drop by my office when you've got a chance."

"So the way I figure it, Jackie goes to sea in search of an alibi and has Connie do the number on Del," Bailey was saying. "She's wearing her beige silk blouse and her beige linen pants, and some of her blond hair gets left behind on the floor. We haven't found a piece of copper jewelry yet, but if it broke in the struggle, she may have gotten rid of it." He sat back in his chair and raised his heels to Merry's desk, the picture of complacency.

"Her hair is dyed."

"What?"

"I mispoke. Forgive me. Her hair is bleached, and *then* dyed."

"So?"

"Oh, for crying out loud, Bailey, don't you remember any of your training? Bleached hair has dark roots. The blond hairs at the scene didn't. Which means they were from a *naturally* blond person. Like the Swede. I suggest you take a sample from *his* head." Merry pulled her half-glasses from her nose and stared at him balefully. "Or wait until Howie gets back from the Cape and ask him if one of Jackie's old shipmates happens to be blond. Connie didn't do it. The mere notion of her shoving a harpoon in Del's chest is laughable. Del would have had her disarmed and decked in thirty seconds."

"I wouldn't be so certain, Detective," Bailey said stubbornly, staring over her head. Lines of pique settled around his nose and mouth, and with a resolute gesture, he stood and turned for the door. "You can't know what Del or Connie would have done, and it's unprofessional to suggest your *feelings* should carry any weight. I'd hoped the daughter of the police chief would look at the evidence instead of following her gut instinct. But women are usually emotional first, and rational when it's too late."

"Has Clarence had a chance to look at the prints, Bailey?"

He stiffened. "I've asked him to send them to the state crime lab for expert matching."

Meaning that Clarence was no expert in Bailey's mind. Jackie's prints must not have looked like those on the threatening letters or the scotch bottle. Interesting. Maybe he hadn't done it after all. At the very least, he'd bought himself some time. Even in the case of murder, Bailey wouldn't get the results back from Boston in under a week.

Sometimes an alibi is just an alibi, she thought. *But if not Jackie, then who? It has to be one of Howie's guys. He's been gone all weekend. Maybe he'll show up today.*

Bailey let himself out.

Funny thing about plastic explosives. They were useful in the detonation world because the plastic medium stabilized a highly volatile substance—nitroglycerin—into something that could be cut, torn, molded like putty, and dropped on its head without destroying its handler. No need to worry about transporting *this* stuff like a newborn baby. Those sweat-tingling moments immortalized in a thousand movies, when the nitroglycerin tube falls through the air under the close-up lens, only to be caught at the last second by an agonized hand—those moments had gone the way of John Wayne's rattlesnake smile.

Merry had pored over the technical manual Jim Hayes left for her education. The arson expert had taken a liking to her—perhaps because she was so openly humble on the topic of his expertise, so frank in admitting she knew nothing about explosives beyond Hollywood's special effects.

Though it burned with destructive force once triggered, plastic explosive left behind a residue that the clever could read as readily as a signature. The bait box recovered from the shallows of South Beach, for example, which had held this particular bit of explosive, told Jim Hayes not only the name of its manufacturer, but the number of its batch. Plastech Explosives Incorporated—the manufacturer in question—was only too happy to avoid liability for arson and sent its shipping records to Bill Carmichael at the Massachusetts State Police. Merry now had a complete list of those professionals—road engineers, construction companies, Navy SEAL units, and the like—who had received explosive from the batch. Baldwin Builders was not among them. Nor was the name Joshua Field. She had even searched the list for Boston University, thinking perhaps a chemistry lab had obtained the explosive and Field had pocketed it before leaving for the summer. But here, too, she struck a dead end.

It was just possible, she reasoned, that Baldwin's Lenox site manager ordered plastique under his own name. And so she was riffling through the list—which was organized not by alphabet but by shipping date— for a Barry Heinecker. Or Hemecker—it was tough to tell from Tom's handwriting. There were three hundred entities listed over ten pages. She went through them several times, ticking off the names with a pencil point. No Heinecker. No Hemecker. Nothing to connect Lenox to Nantucket. And that left her—or Bill Carmichael—with a case-by-case investigation of each recipient of naughty explosive, hoping against hope that somebody'd had some plastique stolen, or failed to receive the expected shipment, or could point to an employee with a lifelong grudge against Nantucket Island. Prospects, at the very least, looked tedious.

She picked up the phone and dialed Lenox. Nothing but an answering machine in a closed office. Merry tugged on her bangs and studied the list of names for a moment; it swam beneath her eyes. Interesting as Jim Hayes had managed to make bomb investigation, her heart wasn't in this one. After a moment, she thrust the list under a pile of reports and pulled the Boston phone book down from a shelf. Time to start looking for Sara's father.

* * *

"Did you ever get to the fruit salsa? With the cranberry dressing?"

There was no answer from the inert form in the queen-sized bed. Peter Mason shifted uncomfortably in his chair and glanced out the window, preferring the bustle of tourist life to Tess Starbuck's silence. Then he cursed himself for a coward and got up.

Her face, when he sat down on the edge of the mattress, was turned away from him. He knew she was awake by the line of eyelash visible against the pillow; the lids were at half-mast. But for all her connection to the conscious world, she might as well be in dreamland. He reached a finger to brush back her hair; its auburn brightness was dimmed and slack. She flinched and moved away from him.

"What do you want us to do, Tess?" he said softly.

No answer.

"Leave you alone, right?"

Her breathing quickened for an instant, then fell back into shallowness. Peter felt a wave of impatience grip him, and thrust it away with effort. He wanted to pull Tess out of bed, show her Will sitting despondent in the empty kitchen below, show her the blank tables in the restaurant, the produce rotting in the refrigerators. Instead he sighed, and looked away. And the doorbell rang.

Will's light feet, running to answer it with the haste of every sixteen-year-old. A murmur of voices, indistinguishable. And then Merry Folger, standing in the bedroom doorway in a slim khaki skirt that made her seem taller and thinner than she was, a blouse the color of melon, her hair like corn silk.

Merry nodded in his direction, her face carefully composed, and looked at the woman in the bed.

"Tess," she said. "I know you're not feeling well, but I need to talk to you. It's important."

Tess's eyes fluttered, but she made no sound. Merry pulled up a chair, set her purse on the floor, and leaned toward Tess's face. "I've got to talk about Del." She looked at Peter. "Has she been given medicine recently or something?" she whispered.

He shrugged his ignorance. "I've been here for fifteen minutes, and she hasn't spoken yet."

Merry nodded and looked back at Tess. "I hear you had an interesting reaction to Del's death," she said carefully. "Under the circumstances, I can pretty well understand it. I can even see how you'd be happy she was dead."

Merry might have been talking to a mannequin, for all the response she drew.

"I'm partly responsible for that, I suppose. That's one reason I'm here. I suggested Rafe help Del out, as a friend. But you saw it differently, didn't you? You think Del lured the man you love back into a world you don't trust, and he seemed to like it there. And he was in no hurry to reassure you about what that meant. Your distance and your silence didn't do a thing to keep him off the water, and in fact, they seemed to drive him further away and closer to Del. That must have been pretty threatening, Tess."

Merry paused—assessing how far she should go, Peter thought.

"I mean, Del was a good ten years younger, and Portuguese to boot. It must have played on your worst fears. And instead of abandoning the whole business in order to save his relationship, Rafe decided to be macho and force you to accept his point of view. So you decided to work on Del, isn't that right?"

Tess shifted under the covers and looked full at Merry. Her eyes were devoid of expression, but her gaze was steady.

"She got the first threatening letter two days after you first fought with Rafe. What did you do—walk out of the Brotherhood and fume all the way home? Think of all the things you'd say to Del Duarte if you just got the chance? Only a cat fight would be demeaning, wouldn't it, and hardly the sort of behavior for a middle-aged woman. Better to look cool and unconcerned. Beat Rafe at his own game. But Rafe didn't call to apologize that night, and when he stopped by Saturday you warned him off the premises with a kitchen knife."

Tess's head turned away.

"You probably tossed and turned until midnight, thinking about the ring you'd thrown at his back, feeling remorse, feeling scared, feeling anger. I bet you got up at two in the morning and started leafing through magazines. Crazy ideas always seem logical to the sleep-deprived, don't they?"

The still form on the pillow moved; it might have been a nod.

"'Get out of town and take your brat with you,'" Merry said. "I started thinking about the tone of those notes after Rafe told me how worried he was. I'd assumed they were sent by whoever killed Del. But they sounded like the words of an angry woman—a woman who resented Del's sexuality and youth and freedom, a woman who wanted her to disappear. Even the last one—'The life you save may be your own'—had the predictability of a cliché.

"They were like the threats a cheerleader would leave in a rival's locker. What were you going to do when the notes failed, Tess? Egg the front of her house?"

Wincing at Merry's harshness, Peter looked at the woman in the bed. He'd instinctively been gentle with Tess, fearing her fragile spirits, avoiding the outbreak of emotion he sensed was building.

"She had no right," Tess whispered. It was a dry and guttural sound. In the dimness of the shuttered room, Peter could not be sure that she was weeping, but he thought it likely from the break in her voice. He looked at Merry in alarm, but the detective was unmoved.

"No right to take Rafe away from you."

"No right."

"And that made you hate her."

"I wanted to hurt her."

"Call her a slut, talk about her past, make her feel shame and anger and a desire to leave."

Tess nodded.

"She didn't take Rafe away from you," Merry said. "Rafe loves you. He always will."

Something between a grunt and a snort emanated from the bed—a laugh, Peter realized. "Not after what I've done."

"Rafe won't love you?"

"Can't."

"He liked to fish with Del. But that's over now, isn't it? Because Del's dead."

Tess was weeping in earnest, now.

"Did you go to see her the night she died, Tess?"

"Never saw her. Never—"

"You never faced her in person, did you? Just through the patchwork notes, like a coward, unsigned and left at her door. Do you feel like a coward, Tess?"

A shuddering sob. Tess turned her face to the pillow.

"Did you kill Del?" Merry's voice was very quiet; the words might almost have been unsaid.

A pause, filled with shaky breath. "I wanted her dead," Tess said suddenly, clearly, raising her head from the pillow. "I wanted her dead. I'm glad she's dead. I'm not sorry."

"I don't think that's true," Merry said. "I think you're so sorry she's dead that you can't get out of bed in the morning. Or the afternoon. I think you need Dr. John to help you live with how sorry you are, until you've had enough Valium to believe you're not sorry at all. But wanting her dead isn't the same thing as killing her, Tess. Even though you think it is."

She reached for Tess's hand and pressed it, hard. "Stop feeling guilty about what you can't help. Guilt won't bring Del back. Guilt will only poison your life and accomplish your worst fear—it'll drive Rafe away permanently. Admit that you got what you wanted, talk over your feelings with Rafe, and go on. That's the only way to live with what's worst in yourself."

"Won't want to," Tess whispered, slumping back into inertia again.

"Rafe? Rafe won't want to talk? You're the most important thing in his life, Tess. He told me so himself."

Merry stood up and looked at Peter. He nodded once, and bent to kiss Tess on the cheek. She closed her eyes, the tears visible even to him, now, and turned away.

"One last question," Merry said. "Why the fancy signature, 'The Avenging Angel' in italic script?"

"I wanted her to know," Tess said. "The sort of person she was dealing with."

"I see," Merry said.

Vanity, all is vanity, Peter thought. They left Tess where she lay.

CHAPTER TWENTY-ONE

❦

"DO YOU THINK THAT
was the right thing to do?" Peter said, as he followed Merry down the
stairs.

"I don't know," she said frankly. "I haven't the faintest. I figured I'd
say what Tess wouldn't, and see how she reacted. Maybe she'll wake up
and fix dinner for Will tonight. Or maybe she'll cut her wrists in the
bathtub, and I'll be the one decked by remorse in the morning."

"But you don't think so."

She looked over her shoulder. "No. I'd never have done it if I thought
that's how she'd react. It might be worth sending Rafe over tomorrow
morning, though. Just to see how she's faring after twenty-four hours of
thoughtful consideration."

"I'd no idea Del was getting threatening letters. How did you hit on
Tess?"

"There were three altogether. None of them sounded like a man, and
since the chief suspects in Del's murder are male, that left me looking
elsewhere. One other woman was a possibility, but I couldn't quite see
the motive. Then, when Rafe talked to me, I just knew."

"I thought cops avoided gut instinct."

"Do me a favor, okay? Don't tell anybody down at the station that
I guessed about this. Particularly a guy named Bailey."

"Who's he?"

"The jerk trying to solve Del's murder."

"Ah." Peter followed her to the door of the gray Explorer and
watched as she got in, her narrow skirt making it a tricky business with
the Ford's high running board. This was the everyday beauty of life, he
thought; the appreciation for a strong thigh outlined in strained khaki.

"Had lunch?" he asked suddenly.

She shook her head, staring at the wheel.

"Thinking about it?"

"Peter—"

"I know. You don't want to see me right now. Too busy, too distracted by death. Too scared to eat with me."

"Scared?" Her chin went up.

"That's what I said."

"I'm not scared. I'm just not hungry."

"Right. Since when have you ever turned down a square meal? You've got fear written all over you."

She slammed the car door and rolled down the window. "It'll have to be quick," she said.

"Follow me."

He led her up the Cliff Road past his shuttered ancestral home—inhabited now only in July when his sister, Georgiana, arrived with the children—to the gentle overhang of trees and the hand-painted whale that marked the quahog-shell driveway of Something Natural. The shingled house with the wide porches and the constantly banging screened doors had been an island institution for nearly twenty years, serving fresh-baked bread and sandwiches to bathers returning on their bikes from Madaket or walking up the twisting roads from Jetties Beach.

Peter had miscalculated, thinking that one o'clock in the afternoon was past the daily rush; there was a crowd lounging in polo shirts and Docksides on the porch by the pickup door, waiting for completed orders. Sunburned girls, their hair matted with seawater, perched on the railings near too-tall boys, leather thongs braided around their wrists and baseball caps worn bill-to-the-back. He was recalled sharply to his own college summers, the immortality of every moment, the sense of expansive future, the pleasure of a good sandwich when hunger was sharpened by sea air. At least the last remained to him.

"It's not going to be quick," he said, when Merry appeared from the parking lot.

"Of course's it's not," she replied. "And don't tell me you didn't know that."

"Want to go somewhere else?"

"I want a cheese, avocado, and chutney sandwich on seven-grain," she said. "Make that half."

A whole sandwich on Something Natural's bread was impossible to finish. Peter ordered half a lobster salad for himself and two bottles of Nantucket Naturals lemonade, then walked back to the picnic table where Merry was sitting. She was surveying the sky doubtfully.

"Gonna rain," she said.

"Nah." He set down some napkins and put the lemonade on top as an anchor. "It can't. There are no tables inside."

"Peter—why this? Why now?"

"Because I have to eat every four hours. I get light-headed if I don't."

"That's not what I mean."

He looked at her, saw the panic in her eyes, and knew it for what it was. "Why *you?* is what you're asking."

She waited, her green gaze steady. The force of it was too much.

"I should have ordered chips or something to tide us over. They said it could be twenty minutes."

"Now who's scared?"

Peter stopped and took a deep breath. She was right.

"I've never been less scared in my life," he said. "*That's* why this, why now. Because I'm ready." He swung a leg over the bench and leaned toward her across the plank table, wanting to feel her cheekbones under his fingers. "You know the names of all my ghosts, Meredith. You know when they walk and how to call them from the grave. But they have no power over me anymore; I've given myself up entirely to the living. To you."

That silenced her; she looked away, unable to hold his gaze, and fumbled for the lemonade jar on the table beside her.

"It's taken me a while," he said. "I know that. My timing could have been better. But most things have their season of growth. All winter, while the rain and snow fell and the ice formed over the cranberry vines, and gray day followed gray day, I'd sit by the fire and consider taking a walk. And it would occur to me that I wanted to walk with *you.* I wanted you in an oversized sweater and a pair of boots tramping through the moors in the mist. I wanted you sitting by the fire afterward with your hair burning in the reflected light of the flames; I wanted you rolling my glass of sherry between your hands; I wanted your laughter and words to fill my silence."

Peter's voice grew quieter. "I wanted you warm beneath the down of my bed in the dark. I wanted to chafe your skin with my touch and rob your mouth of its breath. I just didn't know how to begin." He closed his hand over her wrist and felt her pulse, racing like a bird's.

"I'm not going to tell you I love you, Merry," he said quietly, "only because I can't bear to watch you run."

Merry took a deep, shuddering breath and stood up, loosening his hold. "I can't do this, Peter," she said. "I can't give it the attention it needs. Never mind that I can't even *begin* to understand what you see in me." She turned her back to him, her arms crossed protectively over her chest. "I don't have the mental energy to explore any of it. No—that's not it. The whole question *saps* me of mental energy. It consumes my thoughts. And I need all my ability to find Del's murderer. Nothing can be allowed to stand in the way of that."

"Fair enough," Peter said. "I'm not so selfish as to demand your attention when it's justifiably disposed elsewhere."

She looked at him quickly, suspicious of such ready retreat.

"As long as you're honest with me."

"Haven't I been?"

"I hope so."

"What do you mean?"

"I wouldn't want you to use Del's death as an excuse, Merry. Nothing would be easier. Telling yourself you're focusing on what's meaningful, when in fact you're avoiding it."

"Nothing is more meaningful than Del's death," Merry said tensely.

"Work can be an admirable way—a face-saving way—to ignore the truth."

"What makes you so goddam certain I give a shit about you anyway?" She was angry now, the black brows knitted contemptuously, her back up like a cat's.

"I'm an egotistical bastard."

"You are, you know. And you have no idea what I think or feel."

"Oh, yes, I do."

"You *can't*."

"Why not?"

"Because it's all I have left."

He saw it then, like a flash of light—how Merry fought him, fought herself, to keep hold of her stability; how the arms buckled under her breasts were a metaphor for her entire emotional state. She'd girded herself with an iron resolve *not to feel;* because if she once allowed feeling in, it might consume her. He was overcome with the desire to cradle her out of her darkness. He so wanted to love her.

"Merry," he said.

She saw in his face all that she had told him, and sat down on the bench. She put her head in her hands. "I can't, Peter," she said. "I can't face it."

"I won't hurt you."

"You can't *help* but hurt me. That's all people do to one another."

"Not all," he said. "There's the joy."

"I can't see that," Merry said, looking up at him. "It's crowded out by the pain."

He reached a hand to the nape of her neck, feeling the warmth of it, the coolness of her blond hair grazing his skin. Her mouth was like a partly opened shell, awash with seawater and mystery, giving up nothing; it drove him deeper and deeper, drowning.

Merry broke away. The first drops of rain fell on his cheek, and he let them, stunned.

"Aren't our sandwiches ready yet?" she said.

It was midafternoon by the time Howie Seitz arrived back on the island. He'd spent the past three days traveling from Gloucester to Mattapoisett to Provincetown, and had managed to catch the one-fifteen ferry out of Hyannis by the skin of his teeth, weaving his way among the line of packed cars waiting patiently to board in the rain that had already doused the Cape for much of the morning. He found a seat on the lower deck by the port rail, the side for disembarking, and settled his large frame with a copy of the *Globe.* Once they were an hour out on the sound he'd think about lunch; but the crowd at the upper-deck snack bar was always heaviest at departure. Something about taking to sea—even for two hours and fifteen minutes—drove people to eat; the lesson of Robinson Crusoe, perhaps. If by some inexplicable mischance they were all wrecked and cast away, at least the bulk of them would be well fortified with chili.

Howie mulled over the past few days with a flutter of uneasiness. He was uncomfortable with Bailey running this investigation—the detective would never know if he had missed something vital. The guy cut corners, neglected evidence, ran with his first idea and fit the pieces to the size of his personal puzzle. That made Howie feel too responsible, like a tightrope walker without a net. It was Merry Folger he hated to fail. She would listen to his recital, read his notes, and find the gap he should have noticed. He wished the chief had put her on the murder.

Howie found Merry sitting in her office, staring at a crack in the opposite wall, since she had no window to serve as a suitable focus for daydreaming. He rapped a knuckle on the open door and hovered.

"Seitz! Just the man I wanted to see. How was Gloucester?"

"A dead end. The guy had already left. But I found him in Mattapoisett," he said. "The fishing business is pretty unstable, I guess."

"Pull up a chair. You talked to Bailey yet?"

He turned red. "Your office is first along the hallway."

She refrained from comment. "Why don't you run through it from the beginning."

"Okay." He pulled his notebook from his back pocket, even though he knew the contents by heart, and sat down, shoving a hand through his dark curls. "Let's see. Charley MacIlvenny is the guy in Mattapoisett. Formerly Gloucester, for all of a week. Formerly Nantucket, where he joined Joe Duarte's crew last October. Formerly Hyannis, where he captained a boat that unfortunately sank in that same month of October."

"It *sank?*"

Howie nodded, uncertain of the significance. "Hit an unmarked wreck while racing for port in a storm, and sank pretty quickly, apparently."

"Did MacIlvenny own the boat?"

Howie looked back at his notes. "I don't think so. He talked about the owners, how after the boat sank he couldn't get hired as captain anywhere, so he went to work for Joe."

"Go on."

"I asked about the night of Joe Duarte's death, and his story pretty much tallied with Jackie's. Said he was standing across from the Swede waiting for the net to come up, and that it was winched in too fast and Joe got clobbered on the left side of his head."

"He said nothing about *why* the net was winched in too fast?"

"Just that it was a pretty confusing night. The storm was hitting hard, and Jackie and Joe were yelling at each other, and first the order was to drop nets, and then it was to pull them up, and they weren't sure who to obey."

"Jackie and Joe were yelling about the net?"

Howie nodded. "Jackie wanted it dropped, and Joe wanted it raised. From the way Charley tells it, Joe was so mad he wouldn't have seen Moby Dick coming over the side that night. He was right in Jackie's face, telling him he'd better figure out who was captain, who gave orders on his boat, and so forth, and Jackie was giving it right back. Charley figures the Swede was just distracted."

"So that's why Joe Duarte was messing around the net," Merry said thoughtfully. "Del couldn't figure out why he hadn't left something that routine to his crew. Jackie never mentioned a fight. I wonder what else he's keeping to himself?" Her eyes flicked back to Howie's. "What'd Charley have to say about the night Del died?"

Howie looked uncomfortable. "He was busy," he said.

"Getting to Nantucket and back? Or what?"

"Busy. You know."

"No, Seitz, I don't."

"He was with a—girl. Woman. Whatever."

"Ah. All night?"

Howie nodded and looked away.

"You talked to her?"

"I had to track her down first, and that wasn't easy, believe me. Charley remembered she was called Kiki, and he had a rough idea where she lived, but couldn't tell me the address or her full name. Talk about drunk. Those two must've been—" He paused, and reddened again. Merry wondered how much older than himself he thought she was.

"But you found Kiki?"

"Yeah. I had Charley drive me to what he thought was her apartment complex, and then I waited around until the manager came back, and found out her name is Christine Benson. Kiki's her stage name."

"I see. An *artiste*."

"She's a sort of—dancer."

Exotic, by the look on Seitz's face. "Gotcha. And according to Miss Benson, Charley was not on Nantucket at the time of Del's death."

"So she says."

"Okay." Merry blew out a breath that lifted her blond bangs and sat back in her chair. "Let's hear about number two."

"Rick Berkowski. New Bedford born and bred, currently crewing on the *Jenny Lyn* out of Provincetown. Joined Joe Duarte's crew in January after his boat sank—"

"No way," Merry said, though she'd been half waiting for the words. "Where'd this one go down?"

"Hit an unmarked wreck near the Nantucket Shoals. Pretty far from port."

"About forty miles."

"There was a New Bedford trawler near enough to pull off the crew."

"Lucky for Rick. Men die in a matter of seconds in January water."

"They couldn't save the boat, though. Sank in ninety fathoms."

"How convenient for the owners—since I very much doubt Rick was skippering his own boat. When it came time to file for insurance, the wreck was probably hard to locate. Sending divers ninety fathoms down in the middle of the winter is no picnic, either. Wonder how long it took the insurance company to pay out?"

"You think the sinking was deliberate?"

"I think it's just too much of a coincidence that three of Joe Duarte's crew were former captains who'd sunk boats in the past year. It's not that common. Scuttling vessels for their insurance *is*, however."

"Wow," Howie said. "You think Joe put that together?"

"If he didn't, it's because he chose not to," she said. "A man who's been on the water as long as Joe was knows to mistrust coincidence." She leaned across the desk. "I've got a job for you, Seitz. Find out who owned those two boats—you should be able to get the information from Terry Samson at the Coast Guard. And note down who insured them. Something stinks about the whole story."

Howie stood up, his face alight. Merry was pleased. He'd done good.

"Where was Rick the night of Joe's death?" she said.

"Down below. It was his turn to sleep."

"And last Wednesday?"

"He doesn't remember."

"What?"

"That's what he says. Can't remember what he did last Wednesday. Thinks he might have been watching TV."

"Alone?"

"He's not married."

Merry sat very still. "What color's his hair, Seitz?"

"Dirty blond," he said.

"Thanks. Be sure and tell Bailey that, would you?"

"Of course, Detective. Anything else?"

"Don't tell him about the insurance stuff yet, okay?"

Merry found Ralph Waldo in the backyard, culling lettuces from his vegetable garden. It occurred to her that he'd been practically housebound since Sara Duarte had come to stay. Not that he couldn't have taken Sara with him on most errands—he could, and did. But he had abandoned many of his normal pursuits, his quiet routines, his visits to old cronies or to check library books out of the Atheneum.

"Hi, Grumpus," she said to the white head bent over the soil. "I decided to come home early."

"Glad to hear it," he said, rising with a grunt. "I could use the help."

"Sara giving you trouble?"

"Apparently the honeymoon is over," Ralph Waldo said. "She's been fussy all day. Started crying after breakfast, and its been like King Lear ever since—howl, howl, howl, howl, howl. The worst of it is, I can't help her, my dear." He tossed some Bibb lettuce in a basket and turned toward the back door. "All she says, over and over, is *I want my mommie. Mommie.* And to that, Meredith Abiah, there is no answer in the world I can give."

"No," Merry said. "I'm so sorry, Ralph. We've left you here to hold everything together, Dad and I, while we ran around looking official. It isn't fair. Should we get a baby-sitter tomorrow?"

"Oh, it's all right," he said. "I'm fond of the little thing. One more stranger right now is the last thing she needs. It'll pass, with time. If she could get more sleep she'd be less unhappy. But she had nightmares again last night."

"I slept through them," Merry said, feeling guilty. "Did you get up?"

"Twice. Both times she'd fallen back to sleep."

"I wonder what she sees."

"I don't think she has the vocabulary to tell us yet. I only hope it passes before too much longer."

"Ralph," Merry said, following him to the kitchen, "I called the state Registry of Vital Records this morning."

He set the lettuce down on the counter near the sink and turned on the water. "About Sara?"

"Yes."

Ralph Waldo turned the leaves under the water. Tiny black grit flowed out, a dead bug or two. He shook the heads lightly and searched in a cupboard for the salad spinner. "You sure that's a good idea?"

"I didn't get far enough to do any damage," she said. "I was told that when the parents of a child aren't married, access to the birth certificate is restricted."

"They wouldn't send you a copy."

"No. I'd have to get a court order to see Sara's records. From a Boston court."

"Even though you're a police officer, and this is a murder investigation?"

"Even though."

He dropped the lettuce in the salad spinner. It was an old-fashioned one, with a pull cord that turned the inner basket instead of a handle. "Sara loves to pull this, you know," he said. "She laughs and laughs."

"We can't keep her, Ralph."

"There was never any question of that."

"But she's going to be tugged in several different directions, whether she's aware of it or not. Jackie Alcantrara's going to try for her, according to Felix Harper, and with the provision in Joe's will, he's got a fighting chance. The Duartes won't let her go that easily. And then there's Dave Grizutto."

"Who's he?"

"Bartender at the Brotherhood. He thinks he's Sara's father."

"Is he?"

"I doubt it."

"And you think finding the real father would help," Ralph Waldo said slowly.

"It might save a two-year-old a lot of mess. You know what'll happen. She's living here on borrowed time. She'll be declared a ward of the state, and put in foster care while the hearings and the trial dates are set, and Dave Grizutto's DNA is tested for paternity purposes. Then she'll be taken from her foster parents and awarded to *somebody*—the Alcantraras, quite possibly. Connie Alcantrara doesn't have a motherly bone in her body, but she sure knows how to spend money. It'll be a nightmare."

"Even if you find Sara's father, she could still face a trial," Ralph Waldo said. "He might not want her. Or his custody could be contested. He hasn't exactly been active in Sara's life."

"True. I still think it's worth a chance."

"Do you?" Ralph Waldo's voice tightened with anger. When he turned to face her, she saw how offended he was. "Is it Sara you're thinking of, Meredith Abiah, or are you just itching to know?"

"Hardly *that*." She studied him an instant. "I'm surprised you're so opposed."

"Those records are restricted for a reason," Ralph Waldo said. "Del didn't tell anybody when she was alive, and I'm not sure she'd want it known once she was dead."

"She certainly wouldn't want Sara made a bone of contention," Merry said.

"Then she should have named a guardian."

"But she didn't." He was being very stubborn; but Merry knew what was right. "I'm going to request the court order, Ralph."

"Fine," he said, his bearded chin jutting out. "Just don't blame me once Pandora's box is open."

But it was Jenny Baldwin who really took the lid off, the following morning—though it was not the box Ralph had in mind.

CHAPTER TWENTY-TWO

❦

I T W A S M E R R Y W H O R A N
into Jenny Baldwin at the Downeyflake.

Ever since the bakery-cum-breakfast-place had moved from its digs
two blocks from the police station, her morning walk to work had lacked
color and interest. Coffee and fresh baked goods seemed particularly
necessary this Wednesday morning—Del's autopsy report had come in
late the previous afternoon. Overcome by longing for a raspberry bramble, Merry rose an hour early and drove out to the rotary.

She took a long draft of coffee, gazing through the window at the
fire station across the street. It was a gray morning, with yesterday's threat
of rain realized. Along the South Shore beaches, fog had rolled in off
the Atlantic; by nightfall it would blanket the town, racing like a hasty
ghost under the occasional streetlight. The perfect night to stop by Del's,
for a warm dinner and some good conversation; the sort of visit Merry
had intended to make, and put off because of the Town Pier fire.

The state crime lab's report said that Del had suffered a punctured
lung, a broken rib, and a ruptured chamber of the heart. Her death had
taken perhaps a moment from harpoon thrust to completion. Analysis of
her stomach contents showed primarily half-digested pizza and some
alcohol—but it was determined to be red wine, not scotch, despite
the two carefully washed highball glasses on her kitchen counter. Del
had probably put her wineglass away herself. She rarely left dishes
out to dry.

Pizza and red wine, Merry thought. *The mundanity of final moments never
recognized as final.* Del had cleaned all day, felt exhausted, ordered pizza
for Sara and herself, and washed it down with table wine she probably
kept corked on top of the refrigerator. Had she known it was her last

meal, what would she have eaten? A beloved dish from childhood? Something fattening? Nothing at all?

Merry sighed and bit into the bramble. It was an airy, smooth pastry in the shape of a hockey puck, filled with raspberries and what she thought was walnuts. She needed a second one to be sure.

"Detective Folger! Now if that isn't a coincidence!"

She looked up and saw Jenny Baldwin's bleached blue eyes staring at her intently. The developer's wife was wearing neat and emotionless separates of the kind seen everywhere among a certain class of people in New England—flowered skirt in pink and blue, deep pink polo shirt with the collar buttoned clear to the neck; tennis shoes, which she would call "tennies," or "Keds"; and a deep blue hairband drawn severely back from her forehead. A lightship basket dangled from one arm, its chocolate patina and modest ivory decoration suggesting respectable age and provenance.

"I was planning to stop by the station and talk to you right after I got these doughnuts home for the boys," Jenny said. "Do you have a moment?"

"Sure. Sit down."

Jenny transferred the purse from her right arm to her left, tucked one hand behind her skirt, and slid into the banquette opposite Merry.

"Want some coffee?"

"Had some. What's that you're eating?"

"A bramble." Merry didn't offer her any. She could get her own. "What can I do for you, Jenny?"

"Well, it's probably nothing, and I really should talk to someone less senior than yourself, I'm sure—"

Flattering me already, Merry thought. *Must be really thankless.*

"—but you're the only person I know down there, and I'd so much rather talk to a woman."

"I understand."

"I just feel so *violated.*"

Dear God, don't tell me she was raped. Merry sat up and put the bramble back on its plate. "Did something happen, Jenny?"

"My upper left-hand drawer," she said.

"Your drawer."

"It's been pilfered."

"Really?"

"Well, it must have been. I mean, I always keep a little store of money tucked into my glove box, just for emergencies, and when I happened to put some cleaned gloves back yesterday afternoon, I noticed the money was gone."

"How much are we talking about, here?"

"A fifty-dollar bill."

"And you last saw it when?"

"Oh, I don't know. Maybe a week ago. I haven't actually used the money for ages. I just keep it there."

"You don't think Tom could have taken it? Intending to replace it, I mean," Merry added quickly, not wanting to offend. "Maybe he was short of cash, and didn't have time to stop at an ATM."

"Well, I thought so too. And so I asked him, last night. He actually laughed at me. 'You think I'm that desperate for money?' he said, and that was the end of it."

"And—your nephew?"

"Joshua didn't know it was there. How could he?"

Merry relaxed against the seat. Every petty thief knew to check the upper left-hand drawer of a woman's bureau for valuables. Over the past ten years on the island, more upper left-hand drawers had been robbed of cash and jewelry than she could count. Tourists wrapped their treasures in bathroom towels and hid them behind the headboards in their hotel rooms. The crooks knew that, too. But if the loss of fifty dollars felt like violation, Jenny had led a charmed life.

"Did you notice whether anything else was missing?"

"Well, that's it. This morning I decided to do a thorough search of the drawer. After all, I keep some jewelry in there. And the bracelet is gone."

"What sort of bracelet?"

"My copper one. It's not very valuable, which makes it so strange. They left my pearls, and an emerald pendant, and some *rather* good pieces of onyx. And they took the worthless copper."

Merry's attention was suddenly riveted. "Could you describe it for me?"

"It was very simple, really. Just copper links with a bar in the middle that had my name on it. Tom gave it to me for back trouble. They say that copper worn around the wrist can cure you of pain."

"Did it?"

"Not at all. It just turned my wrist black. So I stopped wearing it. I'd almost forgotten about it until this morning."

"You know, Jenny, I'm glad you stopped to talk," Merry said, gathering up her purse. "But I think we'll have to go to the station anyway. We found part of a copper bracelet the other day, and I'd like to see whether you think it's yours."

Merry sent Jenny Baldwin home with her doughnuts and instructions to appear at the police station as soon as she could. Then she drove into town herself and relayed the news to Matt Bailey.

"We'd better print her," he said grimly.

"Oh, come on, Matt," Merry said. "You really think Jenny Baldwin would innocently report the theft of a bracelet she knew she'd worn to kill Del Duarte? *That* makes a lot of sense. About as much as her motive for Del's murder. She has none."

"It makes more sense than a burglar stealing it, and then leaving it by Del's body."

To that, Merry had no answer.

Jenny duly arrived, and was shown the tiny plastic evidence bag Clarence produced, with its pitifully few links of chain.

"Well, I don't know," she said doubtfully. "You didn't find the bar with my name?"

Be glad we didn't, Merry thought, *or Bailey would have drawn your blood days ago.*

"Thaht's all we have, I'm afraid," Clarence said. "Makes it hahd to say, doesn't it?"

"It certainly does. Where did you find it?"

Clarence looked at Merry, and Merry at Matt Bailey. The latter's expression was portentous. "On the living-room floor of Adelia Duarte's house," he said. "Do you have any idea how part of your bracelet was present at the scene of a murder, Mrs. Baldwin?"

"A murder? My bracelet? But I didn't *say* it was my bracelet," she squeaked, bewildered. "I can't know that from these few links. I just came down to talk about a burglary."

"I'm afraid I'm going to have to fingerprint you, Mrs. Baldwin," Bailey said.

Merry groaned.

"And I'd like permission to take a few samples of your clothing from your closet."

"You can't do this," the woman gasped. Her fingers clenched and unclenched convulsively on the handle of her lightship basket.

"Jenny," Merry said, "is there any chance you wore the bracelet to Joe Duarte's funeral reception? Perhaps you lost it then."

"Maybe I did," Jenny said, grasping at straws. "I'm sure I did."

"Could you come with me, Mrs. Baldwin?"

"You can't take my prints unless you arrest me," she said. "I want to speak to a lawyer. Merry—"

"You're right," Merry said. "He can't. But there's no reason to be afraid of prints, Jenny. You've got nothing to hide, right? So the prints don't mean anything. It might be better to do as he says."

The woman's eyes were wide and frightened, and ten years seemed to have dropped into the lines of her face. Little as she liked Jenny Baldwin, Merry felt moved by pity. If the woman objected and got a lawyer, Bailey would simply write up a request for a search warrant an hour later, and be at her house by the following day. It would be a simple matter then to find prints everywhere.

Jenny took a deep breath. "Of course I've nothing to hide," she said, avoiding Merry's eyes. "I'll do as you say. But believe me, Tom will have quite a conversation with your father. This is the first time we've asked you people for anything. *A simple burglary.* I understand now what Josh meant about police persecution."

"It doesn't help to threaten the police, Mrs. Baldwin," Matt Bailey said stonily. "Come with me, please."

Clarence watched her go thoughtfully. "She cahn't have lost the bracelet at Joe Duarte's reception, Marradith, though it was nice o' you to suggest it. Thaht house was clean's a whistle. Del had vacuumed. If she hadn't, we'd have found more fibahs and whatnot from that crowd a' people than we'da known what to make of. Those links were dropped ahftah Del cleaned."

"That doesn't make them Jenny Baldwin's," Merry said stubbornly.

Clarence grunted. "Guess I'll be wanted directly." He braced himself against the arms of his chair and thrust himself upright. "Not that young Bailey is so enahmahed of my opinion. He'll be wantin' to send those prints to Bahston next."

But the state crime lab's expertise was unnecessary, as it turned out. Jenny Baldwin's thumb and forefinger clearly matched the prints on the bottle of Glenfiddich. It was merely a matter of time, Bailey said confidently, before they found the right fibers.

Merry wasn't so sure. She looked at the sensible cotton clothes Jenny was wearing, and had always worn. Beige linen and silk? It didn't seem likely.

Bailey went ahead and arrested Jenny, despite Merry's protests. He didn't have enough of a case, she said; there was too much unexplained. But Bailey felt that Jenny Baldwin was spooked and scared and acting guilty. She had tried to avoid having her prints taken, threatened the police with retribution, and virtually taunted him to arrest her. And if he sent her home now, with *her* money she'd be out of the country in a matter of hours.

Tom Baldwin arrived, breathing fire and demanding to see John Folger; Felix Harper arrived, blinking as though from too much exposure to sunlight, and sat by Jenny while her statement was taken. Bailey took away her lightship basket and locked her in one of the two cells reserved for women, where she huddled like a skittish dog on one corner of the steel bench, staring at the commode and the opposite wall.

"This is ridiculous," Merry said angrily to her father. She was in his office with the door closed, knowing full well she was violating collegial protocol. Bailey was running the investigation; Bailey thought he'd found a murderer. If he was wrong, let him hang himself. Only she couldn't quite leave Jenny Baldwin in the role of gibbet.

"Ask him *why* Jenny Baldwin killed Del. He doesn't know. Neither does Jenny. Because she didn't, Dad."

John Folger looked at her from under his heavy eyebrows—Folger eyebrows, *her* eyebrows—and sighed. He wanted the whole thing to go away. "How'd her prints get in the house?"

"Her story is that she brought the bottle to the funeral reception as a gift," Merry said. "Everybody brought something. She didn't know the

Duartes never drank scotch—that sort of thing happens all the time. Look at all the well-meaning bottles of Campari we've got sitting in the pantry at home. The *real* question is why the Glenfiddich was placed out on the counter, with the murderer's prints nowhere in evidence, when the autopsy says Del didn't drink it that night. Bailey doesn't want to think about that. It's too complicated. He'd rather believe Jenny drank enough for two, washed and wiped the glasses, and helpfully left the bottle there with her prints all over it."

"Where was she the night Del died?"

"Lying down in a darkened room with a compress to her head, according to her statement," Merry said. "No witnesses. She was supposed to go to a private party at the yacht club with Tom, and begged off at the last minute because of a migraine, which she says she often gets. Her nephew was out with friends. So she has no alibi. In your experience, isn't that often the case with the innocent? I'd be more suspicious if she produced three complete strangers all willing to swear she'd sat next to them at the Boston Symphony."

"Why are you so sure she didn't do it, Meredith?"

"Because I can think of no reason for her to kill Del." Merry sat back in her chair, arms folded, a challenge in every line of her body. Her father plowed ahead anyway.

"And it wouldn't be because this lets out Jackie—who, I must say, *has* an alibi and left no prints or fibers at the scene?" he said.

"You know what I think of alibis."

"I also know what you think of Jackie."

"I think we're looking at something a little more complex than Jenny Baldwin virtually handing us evidence that incriminates her."

"Meaning?"

"The murderer deliberately left a bottle on the counter that was filled with something Del never drank. Why do that? Unless the murderer knew it had Jenny's prints on it. He left it for the same reason he dropped a part of her bracelet on the rug by Del's body—not enough to look too obvious, not the part of the chain that had her name, for instance, but just enough to look plausible."

"You think she's being framed," her father said slowly.

"Don't you?"

"I don't know, Meredith. Like you, I stumble over motive. Why would Jenny kill Del? I've no idea. But why would someone want us to *think* she did? That's even harder."

Merry ran her fingers through her blond waves in exasperation. "I don't know, Dad. But I'm sure Bailey won't give either question the consideration it deserves."

Her father rubbed at his eyes wearily. "She's being arraigned tomorrow?"

Merry nodded. "The sheriff is escorting her by plane to Barnstable. Then, unless I'm very much mistaken, Tom will post whatever bail is necessary. And we'll have two very angry people back on the island, with power and influence to turn the entire Nantucket establishment against the police. You know what this could do to our funding?"

"Don't even talk about it. It's worse than you know."

Merry leaned toward him. "What do you mean?"

"Tom Baldwin's already been here. He informed me he's just been appointed town finance director. And I'm under no illusions as to what his wife's arrest means for the police budget. Particularly coming as it does after that fiasco with his nephew and the fish guts. The arson accusations. We're beginning to look like we have a vendetta against the Baldwins."

John Folger stood up and rubbed balled fists against his aching lower back. "It is not too much to say that my job may even be on the line. What a mess, Meredith. What a mess."

Merry's breathing was suspended, and her skin felt cold. For her father to be imperiled by Bailey's stupidity was insupportable.

"You could release Jenny, Dad," she said. "Apologize to Tom. Tell Bailey to build more of a case before he reads people their rights."

"I could," he said slowly, looking off into space, his attention focused somewhere between L3 and L4 of his vertebrae. "In fact, I think I have no choice. As for you, young lady . . ."

"Yes?"

"That business of the scotch bottle. Find out *why*."

CHAPTER TWENTY-THREE

A MASS OF VEGETABLES, again spilled out on the table; and as the previous week, Tess was sitting in a chair with her back to the door. Rafe stood there, paralyzed by the sight of her, uncertain how to begin. It was too much like the last time he had seen her—only today the vegetables were zucchini, not beets. He must have made a small movement, or expelled a heavy breath, because she turned; and that quickly relief washed over him like a sudden summer storm.

"Hey, girl," he said, and Tess smiled, extending one hand. His ring was shining from her third finger. "You feelin' better?"

She nodded. "Much."

"You look good."

She stood up when he didn't approach the table, and clasped her fingers together awkwardly, as if aware of the light of the diamond and uncertain of its effect. "It's good to see you."

"And you. Life hasn't been the same."

"No." Tess looked behind her at the squash, and then faced him. "We should talk about all of this."

"Only if you want to."

"I don't. But I need to say some things, and you need to hear them."

Rafe nodded, too thrilled by the peace in her eyes and the color in her skin to care much what penance she felt compelled to perform. But at the thought of penance he remembered his own conviction, seized that morning in the shower and acted upon not long after breakfast.

"I came here to talk myself," he said. "I've some explaining to do." He took the three steps across the kitchen to her side and put his arms loosely around her. She sighed like a tired child and sank into his chest;

a circle of quiet and peace, of rightness such as he only knew with Tess. Rafe closed his eyes against the pain of it.

"I should have tried harder to understand what I'd done to you," he said carefully. "The fishing business, I mean. I was trying to settle a score with my father, seems to me, only I was using you to settle it."

"No, Rafe, it was me—"

He laid a finger across her lips, silencing her.

"I didn't have enough courage to face the Old Bastard himself and tell him how much he'd destroyed me when he threw me off his boat. He tried to cut my legs out from under me, Tess, as you know better'n anyone. I forgot that for a while, out on the water; felt like I'd come into my own, on my terms, and the hell with everything else."

"I understand. I—"

"The hell with everything else, including you. So what if you didn't want to see me ruin my place with Pete, or throw myself into a thankless job with lousy pay and worse prospects? So what if I stirred up a lot of bad memories—of Dan and his death and the way he lived his life?"

Tess opened her mouth, and Rafe let his arms drop to his sides, turning away from her. "I was back on the water, doing what I was supposed to do years ago, before the mess in New Bed and everything after. That feeling of getting my own back—despite my father and his pride—was pretty powerful. I think I lost you somewhere in the bloodlust, Tess."

It was a long speech for Rafe da Silva. He felt drained and sat down, staring at a mango-colored squash blossom half unfolded on the wooden table. He traced a finger along its green veins and waited for her voice.

"I lost faith too quickly," Tess said, sitting down opposite him. Their knees in faded denim were almost, but not quite, touching. "You're not Dan. You don't have his crazy optimism, his dogged persistence in the midst of financial ruin and defeat. It was the optimism that killed him, I think. He couldn't understand when he was beaten, and turn to something new." She met Rafe's eyes an instant, her own filled with pain, and then looked down at her hands. They were reddened and chapped from the hard work she had done all her life, struggling to make ends meet.

"He kept taking the scalloper out, year after year, and painting houses in the summer, and the bills kept mounting. He always believed something would break—an act of God that had nothing to do with reality. And in the end, it was a storm and a freak accident and Dan lying broken on the beach."

"I'm sorry, girl," Rafe said.

"But you're not like that." Tess took his hand and gripped it tightly. "You see the storms coming. You know that life isn't fair. You know what people can do, and how to protect yourself. I should have trusted that."

"There's something else." Rafe covered her fingers with his, smoothing the rough skin. "You should have trusted me to love you. What did Dan do, to make you so certain I'd be gone with the first pretty face?"

A look of wariness came over her at that. She looked away. "That wasn't Dan," she said. "That was the green-eyed monster. Every woman's vulnerability. There's so little place for women over forty in this world. Especially among men. Men want taut thighs and flat stomachs and smooth skin. They want breasts that are high and full. They want *youth*, Rafe, and youth is something that has escaped me."

"You're the youngest person I know," he said, his mouth dry.

"Look at me," Tess said, holding his gaze, challenging him. "I have brown age spots on my hands. My hair is turning gray. I have lines that run from the corners of my mouth to my nose; they used to disappear after a good sleep, but I don't get much of that anymore. I have a stomach paunchy from childbirth and saddlebags on the backs of my thighs. I *saw* Del Duarte. I remember what that was like—to feel beautiful, strong, worth looking at. Don't tell me otherwise," she said, as he started to protest. "I don't want to hear well-meaning flattery. I know what I am. I'm not thirty-one. Or was it thirty-two? I'm not Portuguese. I can't give you little black-haired children, or a darling two-year-old, or a day in the sun in the back of a boat. I can't harpoon swordfish. I can't read navigational charts. That woman was everything I wasn't. And it scared me to death. I couldn't see straight because of it."

"I should have understood that, too," Rafe said.

"Why? I never talked about it. I couldn't. How can you point out to the man you love every way in which you're lacking, and someone else has you beat? I was completely dumb. And the thoughts and the fears just grew and grew in my mind. Until I did what I thought was certain to make you hate me."

"The letters."

Tess nodded. "Silly things that they were. Merry Folger was right. I took the coward's way out."

Rafe cleared his throat and shifted; he had no answer for this.

Tess smiled and patted his hand with her free one. "Never mind," she said. "I've had plenty of time to think about them. I can't change what I did, how I felt. I can't live in regret because Del ended up dead. I didn't kill her, although there was a time when I felt like it. I can accept that I felt that way, understand it for what it was, and go on. Merry showed me that, too."

"I guess the Girl Scout was something of a help," Rafe said.

"She was invaluable. She told me you still loved me, when I thought that was impossible. And from that moment on, I began to hope. Hope is what deserts us in our worst hours, Rafe," she said. "Hope is all that stands between us and the abyss. I learned that, last week."

He leaned forward and kissed her brow. "As long as you don't forget it," he said. "I never wanted Del Duarte in the way you think. And I don't want a generic thirty-year-old, or twenty-year-old, or anything in between. I want Tess Starbuck, always have. That's something you've got to *know* as well as believe."

"I'll try," Tess said.

"Want to have dinner tonight?"

She shook her head. "I'd love to, Rafe, but it'll have to wait. I'm completely booked. The high season is kicking in, and I'm back in business."

He surveyed the table. "Need help?"

"Have you ever stuffed a squash blossom?"

He wrinkled his nose. "What for?"

"Deep frying."

"For crying out loud."

Tess threw back her head and laughed, a sound he hadn't heard in weeks. "Tell you what," she said. "Go home. You'll be saving me a trip out to Peter's. I've got that salsa he's been waiting for. Finally."

Howie Seitz was at something of a loss. Merry Folger had told him to find the owners of the crew members' sunken boats and to learn the result of their insurance claims. Matt Bailey had told him to return to

Provincetown, in search of Rick Berkowski's blond hair and fiber samples. But when he'd stopped by Matt's office to say he'd be setting off for the mainland the following day, the detective had snarled at him and nearly given him the back of his hand.

It seemed Matt was stewing about some setback with the chief. He'd had the entire case sewn up, he told Howie, until Merry Folger had stuck her goddam nose in his business and worked her way around her father. She should be fired, and would be if Daddy weren't protecting her. And if a real chief were ever appointed to take Folger's place, and his daughter was out on her ear, she'd probably scream sex discrimination. Or *gender* discrimination, to be more politically correct. These women were all the same. Why did she think she was on the force in the first place? Much less a detective with a rank senior to his own? *Because* of sex discrimination—against white men. She'd gotten the preferences and the breaks because she was Daddy's little girl and the force wanted to show it could hire and retain women. Well, what went up must come down. She'd get what was coming to her one of these days, and so would he.

Howie broke into this rambling diatribe as politely as possible, and asked the obvious question. Were the crew members of the *Lisboa Girl* no longer under suspicion?

"They never would have been," Bailey said contemptuously, "if Merry Folger hadn't wanted Jackie Alcantrara's balls in a sling."

Howie refrained from pointing out that Matt himself had been eager to arrest Jackie only Saturday morning.

He adjusted his sail to the shift in wind direction. "What would you like me to do?"

Matt rubbed his chin and looked thoughtful. "Find some dirt on Merry Folger," he said. "That bitch deserves to be brought down."

Howie escaped as quickly as he could.

He was surveying the Coast Guard's computer files now, thanks to Terry Samson, who had adopted a knowing air at the mention of Merry's name and winked repeatedly at Howie, as though they shared confidential information that could not be discussed outside a soundproof room. He logged into the LEISII computer, plugged in the names of the *Lisboa Girl's* shipmates, and found their accident reports. MacIlvenny's dragger was owned by a company called SeaCon, Berkowski's by Oceanfree Shipping, Inc. Both companies were listed as having offices in New Bedford. The insurer for each was the same: a company called Water Rights, based in Boston. Howie checked the information about Jackie Alcantrara he'd copied from Merry's file earlier that morning. Jackie's boat was also owned by SeaCon and insured by Water Rights.

"This is too weird," Howie breathed, and tore off the printout from the LEISII. "Thanks, Terry. You've been very helpful."

He rode his patrolman's bike back to the station and tried calling New Bedford information for the phone numbers of SeaCon and Ocean-free. He was informed by a disinterested operator that neither company was listed under those names in that area. Perhaps they had moved. Howie tried calling Boston. Then he tried Hyannis. And Provincetown. And Gloucester. Nothing. He was stumped.

"Call the insurance company," Merry said, barely looking up as he hovered in her doorway. "If they settled the claim, they'll know where they sent the check."

Howie went back to the phone and called the Boston directory. This time he was successful.

"So in all three cases, SeaCon and Oceanfree were reimbursed for the replacement value of the boats," Merry said, her black brows drawn down over her green eyes.

"To the tune of four hundred thousand dollars apiece," Howie said. "A total of one point two million."

"After which, they appear to have gone out of business."

"Yep."

"This stinks."

"I thought so too."

"Did the insurance company offer any contacts at either company?"

Howie peered at his notes. "A guy named Jerry Dundee from SeaCon. Nobody at Oceanfree. I've got a number in New Bedford for Dundee, but when I dialed it, it was disconnected."

"Wasn't it just," Merry said, bemused. She tapped a pencil against the desk for an instant, in a gesture so like her father's Howie almost gawked; then the green eyes slid back to him. "It's time to talk to Jackie Alcantrara," she said matter-of-factly. "But I'm going to have to ask you to stay here. He might not be as forthcoming with two people taking notes. Not that he's forthcoming anyway. But I've got a hunch he'll talk to me."

"What do you want me to do while you're gone?"

"Doesn't Bailey have anything for you?"

Howie swallowed. "Not really."

"Well here," Merry said, sliding out from behind her desk. "You can learn how to fill in these forms sooner rather than later."

"What are they?"

"A request for a court order. In the case of a murder investigation, when the police are the requesters, the probate court should waive a hearing and issue a summary judgment. That'll save us a trip to Boston. But I need these filed as soon as possible."

"You want to see the baby's birth certificate?" he said, wide-eyed. "Why? You think the baby's *father* killed Del?"

Merry stopped stock-still, her face frozen, thinking of Dave Grizutto, who she'd been certain was *not* Sara's father. She'd imagined Dave tearing out of the house clutching a birth certificate that told him the truth. She'd never considered that someone else might kill to *suppress* the same information. Had Del been blackmailing the father of her child? So strenuously that he had appeared Wednesday night in an attempt to talk reason, and when tempers flared, had stabbed her with a convenient harpoon? Impossible. Blackmail was completely unlike Del. But there was that twenty-five thousand dollars no one could explain, sitting in an account at the Pacific National Bank.

Merry collected herself. Howie was staring at her. "I don't know, Seitz," she said. "I never quite thought of it that way."

CHAPTER TWENTY-FOUR

M

ERRY FOUND JACKIE
Alcantrara the first place she looked—at his new berth in the boat basin,
mending net under the eyes of gawking tourists. No wonder, Merry
thought; the *Lisboa Girl* looked like a vagrant wandering among the sleek
and pricey bodies lined up along the Old South Wharf, the sort of rusty
fellow picking among dustbins that tourists self-consciously avoid, sensing the arrival of an unpleasant odor on the next shift of wind. Whether
Jackie was aware of his effect was uncertain; he appeared oblivious to
everything but his nets.

"How long do you think you'll hold out?" Merry said.

Jackie looked up, located the source of the voice, and studied her
dispassionately.

"How long will you?"

"That's different."

"No, it's not. The costs are just as high for both of us. You could do
better on the mainland, maybe even get your own place. You're what—
in your thirties? And still living at Dad's."

He stated it as a simple fact, and she had to admit he was right. She
had spent close to six years on the Nantucket force, which made her a
veteran. The island was considered a first tour for young officers. Real
estate prices and the cost of imported goods made it impossible to buy
a house or raise a family on a policeman's salary. Merry was different
because of her father and grandfather, the house on Tattle Court. But
how long, as Jackie said, could she stick it out? She wasn't getting any
younger. She'd turn thirty-three in a few months, and had no home, no
boyfriend, no marriage, no kids.

Peter Mason's face flashed into her mind, and she thrust it aside
brutally. He wasn't a solution. He was everything she would never be—

wealthy, self-possessed, independent of all worry. He had the complete freedom of knowing that he could do whatever he chose, without the constraints of financial hardship, while she considered cost before she considered anything else. Perhaps that explained their present conflict. He had decided to acquire her, much as he might a new car. His voice rang in her memory. *I wanted you in an oversized sweater and boots, I wanted you sitting by my fire, I wanted you in my bed.* He'd made it sound far more beguiling, of course, but the basic thrust was the same. Want, want, want. She would be another one of his possessions, living in *his* house, as dependent as ever. Another brick in the wall of her resistance to Peter slid into place.

"Can I come aboard?" she said.

"I was just about to leave."

"Can we talk for a bit?"

Jackie shrugged. "I'd like a beer. Feel like the Rose and Crown?"

Merry waited while he locked the pilothouse and swung himself over the side, as incongruous as his boat among the crowd on Old South. She wasn't particularly fond of the Rose and Crown, a cavernous beer hall on South Water named for a famous shoal off Nantucket. But she followed Jackie down Straight Wharf, happy to stay one step off his pace, and up Water Street to Broad. Maybe a little alcohol would loosen his grip on the truth.

Jackie chose a high table near the door with four barstools grouped around it and took up a position staring out the window. He ordered a Bud and knocked back half of it when the waitress set it down, immediately ordering another. Then his gaze drifted back to the window. He was, Merry realized, checking out girls.

"When did you decide you wanted Del?" she asked.

He started as if hit with a cattle prod, but his gaze never wavered. He took a swig of beer. "That's bullshit," he said.

"I think it was Connie—your wife—who gave me the first clue. She talked about how Del had thrown herself at you and made you feel like a hunted man. It was the sort of story I could see you telling, to explain something of Del's that Connie might have found—a picture forgotten in a drawer, maybe, a token kept for memory's sake."

Jackie belched.

"Or the sort of story you'd use to heal your wounded pride," Merry said. "Even a suspicious wife would prefer it to the truth—that Del didn't think you were worth a second glance. Have you always impressed women with your sexual prowess, Jackie? Or just Connie? Is that why you married her?"

He slammed down the beer and stood up. "I don't have to listen to this shit."

"I'm requesting Sara's birth certificate from Boston," Merry said, clear above the bar's din. "Joe Duarte thought you were the baby's father. That's why he gave you his boat and named you Sara's guardian. Isn't that right? He hoped one day Del would come back and you'd all be a family." She laughed deliberately, to provoke him. "Where did he ever get such an idea?"

"You think it's so impossible?"

"Yes. I do."

"Because Del was too high-class, is that it? Too good for me? That's a laugh."

The waitress returned with Jackie's second beer, and he hesitated, eying it. "She wasn't so high-class she couldn't get knocked up with a bastard. The slut. Walking around like a princess, with those tits and that ass waving in the breeze, wearing those shorts and her hair hanging loose, acting like she's too good to touch, and all the while—" He looked away, at the door.

"Sit down," Merry said. "You can abuse Del all you like. You can abuse me, if it makes you feel good. But we're going to talk about this one way or another. It can be here, over a beer, or it can be two blocks away at the station, on tape. You decide."

He took a long draft of the beer, still standing, still eying her, un-committed. She thought for a moment he'd fall back on his customary swagger and head for the street, but her tone had implied too much. Merry was just another woman to him, and he had contempt for them enough, but she was also the police chief's daughter, with a murder on her hands. Jackie sat down.

"You couldn't forgive her for ignoring you, could you?"

"She was just a bitch."

"All that frustration. All the wanting, and the refusal. The anger at not having. The knowledge that she gave someone else what she would not give you. And then she left, probably for good, and you knew you'd never have her. So you picked up Connie—poor Connie, who's so easily impressed. Did you tell Joe you'd fathered the baby when you needed a job on his boat?"

"He'd have thrown me overboard if I'd tried that," Jackie said, snorting. "I worked up to the idea. He knew I'd always been hot for Del. He could tell. I used to hang around their house, do chores for the old man, hoping I'd run into her. He knew. Everybody knew. And *she*—"

"—acted like you didn't exist. It must have been galling."

"I wanted to shake her," Jackie said, his fingers white around the sweating glass. "I wanted to bust her till she couldn't move. I wanted—" He stopped, breathing heavily, his eyes slightly glazed.

"Let's not go into exactly *how* you wanted to hurt Del," Merry said matter-of-factly. "Did you?"

He shook his head. "I never got to touch her. Then, or when she got back."

"But you let Joe think you had."

Jackie shrugged. "Once I had the job, I got close to the old man. He was lonely enough. Once in a while I'd let things drop—like I'd talked to Del, or knew more about her than he realized. Just a few words, here and there. Finally he asked me about it. Forced me to tell him what he wanted to hear. I let him think what he chose. Told him Del figured I didn't make enough money, and that's why she refused to marry me; she wanted more than a fisherman for a husband. So she left me, and I married Connie. That made him mad. Like she'd turned her back on her father's way of life. And he got to thinking. Maybe if I was better off financially, maybe—"

"Del would come back. Connie would conveniently disappear. Joe would no longer be lonely."

"He thought the kid should have a proper father," Jackie said defensively. "And he was right. I *should* have custody of the kid. The way Del was living, can you blame her dad for wanting to find it a good home?"

Merry looked at his bestial face, thought of Sara, and stifled the urge to scream. "So he died thinking all this was true?"

"Guess so."

"And that's why you have a boat."

"He left it to me, fair and square. Anybody'll tell you the same."

More swaggering self-justification. She could see how his life had gone—Jackie a poor fisherman's son in the middle of an increasingly wealthy resort; his father's death, his father's debt; the boat he'd counted on inheriting sold to pay off its mortgage; the dogged reliance on the only trade he had ever known; the chance at easy money skippering for SeaCon. The rationalizations, the years of self-deceit, the fantasies used to shore up a flagging ego. Jackie was all-powerful, Jackie was always right, Jackie made the rules. Jackie was a winner, not like the rest of the poor schmucks making an honest living.

"You're used to taking things that aren't yours, aren't you, Jackie?"

"What's that supposed to mean?"

"I'm just thinking of SeaCon. Your former employer. How much did they pay you to scuttle the boat?"

He stared for a moment, flabbergasted. "You're full of shit."

"Am I?"

"You know it."

"They collected four hundred thousand dollars. What was your percentage? Forty thousand? Or less? Enough to put a down payment on Connie's house, but not enough to buy your own boat. Of course, you'd made other plans. You were getting a boat from your future father-in-law. Once he was dead, of course."

"I didn't kill him," Jackie said automatically. "What happened was an accident—"

"—and anybody'll tell me the same," Merry finished for him. "Right. How much did they pay you, Jackie?"

He said nothing.

"Come on," she said patiently. "I know about Rick Berkowski. And about Charley MacIlvenney. We've talked to them." (*Not about this exact topic,* she thought, *but it's true enough.*) "Everybody got a nest egg once they scuttled the boats. The mortgages must have been low for SeaCon to make a profit. What were you guys skippering—boats repossessed by the bank and sold at auction for a fraction of their value?"

Jackie didn't answer. Merry wasn't certain he was even listening. She plowed on.

"Say SeaCon and Oceanfree picked them up at bargain-basement prices, paid for them with mortgages, and insured them at replacement value. Then they paid their captains to scuttle the boats in a convincing fashion—preferably in deep water during the winter when the weather made it hard to locate the wrecks—collected insurance for the boat's full value, paid off the low mortgages, and pocketed the difference. And promptly went out of business."

Merry paused for breath, waiting. Jackie looked slightly whipped— by her words or too much beer, she wasn't certain.

"How much is left after the Spiegel catalogue takes its share, Jackie?"

"Not enough," he whispered. "Not a goddam enough. Charley and Rick tell you all this?"

"They didn't have to," she said. "It's pretty obvious. Someone was going to figure it out sooner or later. You're just killing time, Jackie, until you're indicted for fraud along with SeaCon and Oceanfree. You know that, don't you?"

He laughed harshly. "Those guys'll never take the fall," he said. "It'll be jerks like Charley and Rick and me. They'll be long gone by the time you catch up with them."

"Unless you help me," she said. "You could make a better deal for yourself with the DA if you tried, Jackie. It wouldn't take much."

He looked at her, considering. "What'd you give Rick and Charley?"

"I haven't yet. I wanted to talk to you first. I figured you'd know more. And have more to lose."

"What do you want to know?"

"Where's Jerry Dundee, Jackie? Where do I find the big fish?"

He snorted. "You really think he's the big fish? You think Dundee's your man?" He threw back his head and laughed. Something in his face made her realize she'd lost him, and she sat back, disappointed, casting about for another hook.

Jackie leaned close to her, his breath oppressively beery. "You've got a lot more work to do, Merry Folger." He reached out and actually pinched her cheek, in a gruesome attempt at condescension. She reared backward. "Good luck," he said. "If all you've got is Jerry Dundee, I'll sleep easy. You're not gonna be indicting *me* anytime soon. Call me when you've got a case."

"I know about the fight, Jackie," she said.

"What fight?"

"The one you had with Joe Duarte, the night he died. The shouting match that drew him out of the pilothouse in the middle of a storm, to handle a job he should have left to you. Only you weren't following orders, were you? Was it deliberate? Did you hope he'd be distracted, not notice when the winch brought the doors in too fast?"

Jackie shoved his stool away from the table and slapped down a ten-dollar bill.

"The Swede says the winch was jammed." Merry grabbed his sleeve. "That he *couldn't* control it. Did you have a hand in that, Jackie?"

"You're out of your fucking mind," he said.

And with that, to her mingled relief and dismay, he really did walk out of the bar.

Merry fled the Rose and Crown, turned left on Broad, and walked the few blocks to the Brotherhood. It was too early for Dave Grizutto to work his shift, but she was in luck; he'd arrived early and was having dinner at the bar.

"Looks good," she said.

"The Bostonian. Burger topped with blue cheese. Amazing what a little mold can do for a meal, isn't it?" He set the burger down and wiped his mouth with a paper napkin. "You're becoming a regular."

"Thought I'd test your fabled knowledge of the island's drinking habits. Does Jenny Baldwin like scotch?"

"Only if it's Glenfiddich," he said immediately. "Why? Need a hostess gift?"

"Not exactly. You know her well?"

A wariness came into Dave's eyes, and he studied Merry's face a moment before answering. "Why do I think this isn't an innocent question?"

"Because I'm a cop," Merry said, exasperated. "I can't ask somebody the *time* without causing panic. Come on, Dave."

"Sorry," he said, his smile widening. "You're right. Anybody else asked me that, I wouldn't think twice. I know Tom better than Jenny. He's in and out of here all the time, talking business, meeting clients, that kind of stuff. Jenny just comes looking for him once in a while. Sometimes she seems to expect him, takes a table in the corner and drinks her scotch, and he never shows."

"That happen often?"

"Three times that I can remember."

"Funny," Merry said thoughtfully. "She's not the sort of woman I'd think would be comfortable here."

"Because the bar is near the tables?" he said, amused.

"Because it's kind of a hip place. You know. The tourist crowd, young people, everybody here around midnight trying out the various liqueurs you guys keep."

"And she's too garden-club," he said.

"Something like that."

"The blouse buttoned to the neck, the sensible shoes."

"Exactly."

"I think Mrs. Baldwin has everybody fooled."

Merry sat up and looked at him; but his eyes were turned carefully away. He took a bite of his burger and a swig of Coke. "You want anything?" he said.

She shook her head. "You go ahead and eat before it gets cold. Tell me what you meant when you're ready, instead of changing the subject."

He laughed at that, head thrown back, showing strong white teeth. "I should have known," he said. "Never make a comment you can't explain to Merry Folger."

"Well, I *am* a cop."

"And I guess you're more interested in Jenny Baldwin than you admitted."

"Yep."

He set down his glass, sighed, and pushed his half-eaten burger to the side. "Let's just say that I think Jenny is feeling a bit lonely. All does not seem to be well in the Baldwin household."

"Did she come on to you, Dave?"

"As much as that sort of woman ever does," he said. "Her signals were subtler than a twenty-two-year-old's, but she was signaling all the same." He looked at her with something like embarrassment. "You'll think I've got a big head."

"Not at all," Merry said, mulling it over. "I figure you can tell the difference between friendliness and suggestion."

"She drank a bit too much scotch once," he said. "Back in May. She was here late into the evening, and it was pretty obvious that she was waiting for Tom and he wasn't going to show. She finally abandoned the table when the waitress pressured her to order, and moved over here. Quite a sight. All that Talbot's clothing bellied up to the bar."

"And that's when she—signaled?"

"She asked when I got off and what I intended to do that evening," he said carefully. "I consider that a signal."

"And you told her—"

"That I would be here another three hours, had to close up, and was exhausted. I was going home to bed. I thought that was a clear enough refusal."

"Jenny didn't?"

"She said that sounded like a lovely idea."

Despite herself, Merry grinned. She could imagine Jenny's bleached blue eyes bloodshot with drink, her loosened inhibitions, the voicing of a thought she'd never have allowed to the forefront of her brain in normal circumstances. She *would* use the word "lovely," as though a tumble with Dave were comparable to a fine piece of china, or a good view of the sound. She had no vocabulary for the coarser things in life.

"So, Dave?"

"So what?" He ran his fingers through his blond hair, and then grimaced, studying the strands caught on his fingers. "I'll be bald in a few years, Merry," he said. "This hairline just keeps receding."

"Did you take her home?"

He snorted. "I excused myself, called Tom Baldwin at the Yacht Club, and had him pick her up. Apparently he'd forgotten they had a date."

"How did Tom treat her?"

"Pretty grimly. I don't think relations are all that amicable."

"That's sad."

"It always is, Merry. You want to believe marriages have staying power. Then you look at the ones that have lasted twenty years, and it eats away at your hope."

"Maybe if they'd had children—"

"Who knows? There'd just be a few more lives damaged by the mess."

Merry thought about the Baldwins as she drove toward Tattle Court. Were Tom and Jenny close to divorce? That might give Tom a motive to frame Jenny for murder. But why go to such lengths to effect a break— and why choose Del as the victim?

Or was Dave Grizutto only giving her half the story? He admitted he'd visited Del the night she died, and he knew about Jenny Baldwin's taste for Glenfiddich. Perhaps his relationship with the developer's wife had gone farther than Dave said—so far, in fact, that he was ready to be done with it. When he'd killed Del in a fit of passion, and taken Sara's birth certificate, he'd set Jenny up for the murder.

It was still too speculative. Merry had no evidence that Dave killed Del; he had only said he'd been in her house. She looked at the passenger seat of her gray Explorer, where a napkin and a glass sat carefully wrapped in plastic. She'd said good-bye to Dave and watched him walk back toward the kitchen. Then, taking advantage of the Brotherhood's habitual semidarkness, she'd casually dropped his empty Coke glass into her voluminous purse, in case the prints it held matched any Clarence had found on the harpoon. It was a matter of seconds to wipe a Kleenex across the bar, scooping up a few blond hairs for comparison with the ones found near Del's body.

Dave was right. That hairline *was* receding. Merry wondered what else troubled him about his advancing age.

CHAPTER TWENTY-FIVE

O N THURSDAY MORNING, Chief John Folger released Jenny Baldwin, purse in hand and muttering darkly about the future of the police budget.

Matt Bailey sulked and appeared unlikely to move forward on a case he thought was blown.

Merry, feeling guilty about Bill Carmichael and the overloaded state police, glanced at the list of Plastech Explosives customers, considered starting at the top with a call to a contractor in Madison, Wisconsin, and decided she couldn't face it.

Feeling grumpy and dissatisfied, she looked over the Request for Court Order forms Howie Seitz had completed, dated them and signed her name, and filled out a fax cover sheet with the number of the Boston probate court. Mailing the forms was out of the question—they had to be filed as soon as possible—but she'd have given anything for the excuse to walk to the post office. It was a glorious June day, and her windowless cubicle was more than usually oppressive. What she needed was a drive out into the moors. Rebecca's face at the screen door of the Mason Farms saltbox rose in her mind, but if she drove anywhere, it would be to Tom Baldwin's offices to inquire about his schedule the previous Wednesday night. And, in a roundabout fashion, the state of his marriage. She thought again of the weather, and decided to walk.

Tom was unavailable, his assistant told Merry when she entered the air-conditioned dimness of the South Beach Street office. Merry gave the woman the once-over, curious to learn something of Del's replacement. She was a neat, cool, elegant blonde, dressed in androgynous separates; the sort of woman who went with the neutral-toned furniture and the generic prints on the walls. Everything about Baldwin Builders was rose and beige, including Tom's assistant, as though she had been acquired with the lamps. An off-island import, Merry decided; very unlike Del. But then, Tom's lifestyle these days was more upscale than it had been when Del worked for him—and he would use the word "upscale," a term that applied to improved real estate. In Del's day he'd rented a place on Washington Street, not far from the Town Pier, and it hadn't looked like the interior of a Hyatt.

"Do you know where he can be reached?"

"He's at a selectmen's meeting," the assistant said. There was an overtone of the British Isles in her accent, not pronounced enough to be native, but quietly suggestive of breeding and culture. Probably as bottled as her hair color.

Merry's brow wrinkled. "I thought they met on Wednesday nights."

"They do. This is a special meeting. To consider the future of the Town Pier. Something has to be done as soon as possible, and as Tom's finance director—"

"I see."

"He should be back in an hour or so, if you'd like to call round again."

There it was, "call round," a carefully cultivated Anglicism. Wouldn't Del laugh, Merry thought.

She thanked the woman and left, making her way toward 16 Broad Street and the Town Building, past Steamboat Wharf, where a car ferry had just arrived. A flood of early weekenders rolled off its gangplanks, cars packed to the gills, pedestrians pushing baby strollers and bikes, a huddled mass waiting impatiently at the taxi stand for one of the few vans circulating the island. The taxi problem was notorious; every summer it grew worse. Merry had seen new arrivals actually come to blows over a place in a cab, and more than one driver had been accosted when he refused a fare.

When she arrived at the Town Building's conference room, it was to find the door barred and the sign CLOSED MEETING propped up on an easel.

"Excuse me," she said, walking back to the lobby receptionist, "is it the selectmen's meeting that's closed?"

It was.

"I had understood it concerned the fate of the Town Pier."

It did.

"But isn't that rather important? I mean, shouldn't they call a special town meeting or something?"

The receptionist looked at Merry coldly over her glasses and inquired whether she represented a news organization. Her temper flaring, Merry pulled out her badge and flashed it at the woman.

"The selectmen are merely considering preliminary proposals for the pier's replacement, Detective . . . *Folger*," the receptionist said icily, lifting her glasses to peer more closely at the badge. "Proposals do not concern the public. Once the pier becomes a budgetary matter, it will of course be under consideration as business for next spring's town meeting."

"I thought the point was to get the reconstruction under way quickly."

"That is correct."

"So conceivably it could be done *before* the next town meeting?"

"I could not undertake to say. That is a matter for the selectmen to consider."

Decidedly hush-hush. Too much that concerned the Town Pier was hush-hush. Merry thanked the receptionist, walked back down the hall, and pushed open the door marked LADIES, all with exaggerated emphasis for the woman's benefit. By the time she emerged, the receptionist was occupied by the telephone. Merry crept up to the conference-room door and crouched with one ear to the crack between the double doors.

She was in luck. Tom Baldwin was speaking.

"The plan submitted by Oceanside Resorts is admirable in several respects," he said. Strange how a familiar voice altered when detached from a face; instead of Tom's avuncular heartiness, this voice sounded suave, persuasive, commanding. "It provides for multiuse facilities that will bring significant tax dollars to Nantucket and improve the shoreline along South Beach. A condominium complex with private moorage, a boat-servicing complex including a dockside restaurant, a shopping arcade providing goods to residents, a small, sixty-five-room hotel, and retail space for galleries, clothing stores, upscale food emporiums, lightship basket shops—"

Oceanside Resorts. Oceanside Resorts. She'd heard that somewhere. She groped for it in her mind, half listening to the conversation behind the door.

"You still haven't explained how you're going to turn a piece of town property into private holdings." This from Patrick Mayhew, a longtime

Nantucket resident near the end of his tenure as a selectman. There was an audible sigh from his fellows.

"It'll be *leased*, Pat," came one impatient voice. Jason Summerfield, a recent transplant from Manhattan. "We'll sign a long-term lease with Oceanside, oversee the construction and cleanup, and sit back while they take care of our problems."

Oceanside. Merry sat back on her heels as though she'd been sucker-punched. Small print at the lower left-hand corner of a blueprint sliding from a pile in Tom Baldwin's office. Blueprints that looked pretty final only days after the fire. Blueprints that must have been drafted months earlier.

"Have you run this by the zoning office, Baldwin?"

"Not yet. This is merely a preliminary sounding of the board—"

"Well, I for one don't like it," Mayhew said testily. "We don't need more building along the harbor. Those fishermen's shacks selling T-shirts and whatnot on Old South are eyesore enough. They serve a purpose, of course; they keep the day-trippers occupied and out of the upper end of town. But do we need more of that, I ask you?"

"This is entirely different, Patrick," Tom Baldwin said. "The plan under consideration is geared toward an affluent clientele."

Upscale again, Merry thought.

"We're talking condos with harbor views, starting at four hundred thousand dollars. This is no gimcrack operation. Eventually, perhaps, it could be extended to Old South and provide a welcome face-lift to the area."

"And what about all the seasonal boats coming in and out of the moorings? Fifteen hundred boats a summer."

"The moorings will be unchanged," Baldwin said. "Oceanside will simply run them."

"And take the jobs from a few more Nantucketers."

"Why are you so opposed to a plan that admirably solves our problems?"

"Why are you so ready to embrace this Oceanside? What do we know about them, anyway? You've only been finance director for a day and a half, and already you're jumping up with a contract to fill. Sure you're not acting as their agent?"

"Good God, Patrick, what are you suggesting?"

"Patrick," Jason Summerfield broke in, "Tom is merely doing his job, and superlatively at that. He's presented an option for solving a major headache. You mentioned fifteen hundred boats mooring off South Beach. That's an accurate number. Only they're unable to moor off South Beach right now, and if we don't move our tuckuses, they're not going to come in all summer. The place is a wreck. We need action, we need improvement, we need a deal that'll bring in *more* tourist dollars than the old pier ever did. And we need it yesterday, not next spring."

"Detective Folger," said an icy voice behind Merry.

She tried to leap to her feet, shamefaced, and discovered her legs had gone numb from the knee down. To sprawl in supplication about the ankles of the lobby receptionist was the cherry on the sundae of her day.

Merry took refuge in Congdon's Pharmacy, blessedly air-conditioned and provided with a spare, neat 1950s lunch counter where real islanders ordered grilled cheese sandwiches and old-fashioned sodas. She had both, stirring her black-and-white desultorily with a straw, licking the foam from the bottom, and trying to fit Tom Baldwin into arson. She'd taken a moment to call Howie Seitz at the pharmacy's pay phone, and he'd found Oceanside Resorts halfway down the list of Plastech Explosives' customers. Coincidence was not an option here.

For her money, Patrick Mayhew had Tom Baldwin pegged. He was an agent for Oceanside, and he must have believed a bomb was the best door-opener to the South Beach property. There was the obvious tie, of course; it was Tom's dinghy that had blown. The fact that he'd been miles away in Boston was irrelevant. He could have hired someone to destroy the pier, and allowed his own expensive yacht to go up in flames in order to look more convincingly innocent. His boat had undoubtedly been insured—and maybe he was tired of it, anyway. But how to establish his connection to the bomber? And what did the pier have to do with Jenny Baldwin's prints showing up in Del's house?

That was the immediate problem. If Merry revealed how much she knew about Oceanside, Tom would run before any connection with Del was made.

She sighed, pushed away the remains of her sandwich, and thrust her fingers through her blond waves. Her head hurt. A sure sign she was unconsciously working out the tangle. Deciding the best antidote for weariness was to ignore it, she paid her bill and headed back to Tom Baldwin's offices.

The master builder was at leisure, Merry was told, and would be with her in just a few minutes. After perhaps half an hour with a magazine in her lap, she was ushered into his private sanctum.

"Detective," he said, not bothering to rise from behind his desk, "I understand the Nantucket police are now eavesdropping on the town government. Are things going completely to hell over there on Water Street, or is your father just past his prime?"

Hence the half-hour wait. She was intended to feel humbled. "I know you must be upset about your wife's arrest," she said, taking a chair he didn't bother to offer.

"Upset? I'm *irate*. The poor woman has done nothing to deserve such persecution. She came to you thinking she was coming to a friend. And she got a night in a jail cell. It's something she won't soon forget, I assure you."

"Tom, her fingerprints were found in Del Duarte's house."

"On a bottle she brought to Del," he said dismissively.

"There is also the bracelet."

"Which no one can say is hers. It's not a bracelet, it's a few links of chain."

"What I'm trying to say, Tom, is that the bottle and the chain were deliberately left there to incriminate your wife. Del didn't drink scotch. There were no other prints on the glasses. So whoever murdered Del wiped the highball glasses clean and left Jenny's prints to be found on the bottle, along with the remains of her chain."

"Why would anyone do that?"

"I don't know. Any more than I know how the murderer knew Jenny would be home alone in bed that night."

"I suppose everybody at the Yacht Club knew it," Tom said, thinking. "I explained why I was attending Paul Harris's party alone."

"Paul Harris?"

"Old friend from Boston. Just got married for the second time. Cutest little thing you ever—" He stopped, realizing who he was talking to, and recovered. "There were about twenty or so people."

"When you arrived, or throughout the course of the evening?"

"When I arrived. The invitation was for seven-thirty. I showed up a good fifteen minutes later."

"And were some of the guests friends of yours and Jenny's?"

"Just about all of them."

"Any of them have a reason to kill Del and frame your wife for it?"

"What the hell kind of question is that?"

"The sort I'm forced to wrestle with every day."

"No."

"Any of them leave early?"

"What's early?"

"Before midnight, I suppose."

"Hell, yes. I was home myself by ten-thirty. I get up every morning at five."

"And Jenny was in bed?"

"Of course," he said dismissively.

"Was Jason in?"

"Not yet. His crowd don't call it quits until the wee hours."

"Did you have any reason to step out, Tom, during the party?"

"Did I take a whiz, are you asking? I should think so. And no one came along to hold my hand."

"The bathroom wasn't exactly what I had in mind."

"Are you accusing me of murdering Del Duarte and framing my wife?" At this, he finally rose from behind the desk and leaned menacingly toward Merry. Tom was not a tall man—not much taller than herself— but he was bulky, his shoulders broadened by years of hard lifting and pounding. He was aware of his strength, she knew, and was consciously using it. Merry decided to ignore it.

"I'm not accusing you of anything," she said mildly. "Should I be?"

"You people don't know when to stop," he said, his voice choked. "But the rest of us may do it for you. There's more than one way to control a rogue elephant. You can trip it, you can trap it, or you can shoot it in the head."

"If by 'the head' you're referring to my father, Tom, I'd be careful what you say. He has more friends than you do."

"That's a laugh," he said, coming around the desk toward her. "We'll see how many he has when I'm through with him. And now I'd like you to get out, Meredith. And don't come back, will you?"

CHAPTER TWENTY-SIX

❦

Iᶠ Tʜᴜʀsᴅᴀʏ ᴡᴀs ʙᴀᴅ, Friday morning looked positively awful. Bailey had stirred himself enough to collect fabric samples from the Baldwins' closets, and Clarence was hard at work attempting to match fibers. Merry had given Bailey her notes about Tom Baldwin, though she had little hope he'd grasp their significance. The knowledge of Bailey's ineptitude sat in her gut like a half-digested sausage—sickening, persistent, and ruining her day.

So when the phone rang in her office and Peter's warm, dark voice came over the line, Merry was frustrated enough to resent him wildly—merely for having a life independent of murder and fraud.

"I'm pretty busy, Peter," she said, doing her best to sound both efficient and irritated.

"I'm sure you are. I won't ask you to dinner."

"Good. Can I do something for you?" There was the hint of a clock ticking behind every word.

"I ran into Lisa Davis yesterday afternoon while I was out riding. She used to baby-sit for Georgiana at the Cliff Road house."

Training on his bike, of course. Running into the help, chatting over a rose-covered fence, enjoying the summer day without a care in the world beyond the betterment of his quadriceps.

"Who's Lisa Davis?"

"You don't know? I thought you'd have talked to her by now. Mitch Davis's wife. Remember Mitch? Got a bullet through the head during that arson case you're investigating?" Peter never sounded irritated himself. His voice simply got quieter when he was angry.

"I'm not heading that investigation. The state police are."

"What exactly is making you so busy, then?"

"Cleaning up after everybody else," she snapped. "All the work and none of the recognition, if you must know. What about Lisa Davis?"

"She's not doing too well, Merry. I thought you might drop by and talk to her."

"Because it takes a woman to understand another woman's grief?"

"No," Peter said. His voice was almost inaudible. In another mood, Merry would have heard that as a warning. Today, fed up with the smug Baileys and the bike-riding Masons of the world, she didn't care.

"Because nobody seems to give her any information," Peter continued. "Whoever is handling it over at the state police has told her it was a random killing in the middle of a crisis, and that they doubt they'll ever have a lead."

"Sometimes that's the truth, Peter," Merry said. "I'm certainly not going to second-guess the state police."

"What has gotten into you today, Meredith Folger? I'm trying to have a simple conversation here. About something I think matters. I'm asking for your help, and you're biting my head off."

"I said I'm busy, Peter. I realize that's something you can't understand. Thanks for calling." And she hung up.

Merry studied the name Oceanside Resorts on the list of Plastech Explosives customers. She should give the information to Bill Carmichael over at the state police, though she would be unable to answer his obvious questions—why Oceanside, when she had no clear link to a bomb other than Tom Baldwin's pushing their bid for the pier reconstruction, and Tom Baldwin's boat blowing sky-high. It was too soon for the Massachusetts police to muscle their way into Oceanside's doors; more of a case should be built. And despite herself, Merry admitted, she didn't want the state disturbing Tom Baldwin's complacency. She was certain he was into something fraudulent up to his neck, and his wife's fingerprints had been found in Del's house. If the state police rolled up his network prematurely, she might never find out why. She could explain all that to Bill Carmichael, of course, or at least let him know Lisa Davis's concerns. But he'd already said Mitch's wife was pestering him unmercifully; and knowing Bill, his phone was probably off the hook.

Mitch Davis. He'd been shot in the back of the head. Bill thought he'd walked away from an irate boater just as the guy pulled the gun out and fired at him; but in the smoky dark, would an irate boater manage to hit the exact center of the base of the skull? The entrance wound *had* been rather precise, hadn't it? And what about the burn marks?

Merry walked down the hall to Clarence's office and knocked. He looked up from a report he was writing and smiled at her. "I'd love to be able to tell you that Dave Grizutti fellah's prints are on the hahpoon," he said, "but they're not. Hairs are a pretty good match, howevah. He was definitely thayre."

"Never mind that," she said. "Do you have your notes on Mitch Davis?"

"Mitch Davis? O' carse." Clarence was scrupulously neat. Everything was labeled, everything sorted, everything filed. He pulled open a desk drawer and reached into a mass of folders. "Here 'tis."

Her brows knitted, Merry studied the crime scene chief's notes. Though the murder had been turned over to the state police, Clarence had obtained a copy of the crime lab's autopsy report and appended it to his file. Mitch Davis *had* been shot in the center of the base of the skull by a .38 caliber pistol, at close range. He had the burn marks to prove it.

An execution, Merry thought. Bill Carmichael must have recognized it. So why wasn't he doing anything about it? She flipped the file shut. Peter was right. She should talk to Lisa Davis.

The Davises owned a neat new Cape Cod off Bartlett Road—the paved part, before it turned into a sometime track through the Miacomet Golf Course. This was the southwestern end of the island, abutting Bartlett Farm's acres of produce, the Ram Pasture conservation area, and eventually, down Hummock Pond Road, Cisco Beach. It was a part of the island Merry rarely frequented.

A child's three-wheeler lay overturned in the gravel drive, and the pots of geraniums on the front stoop looked parched and neglected, their dead flower heads left to wither and straggle above the riotous petunias. Merry walked up the slate path, wondering if anyone was home. She should have called first. But as she mounted the steps, there came from somewhere inside a high-pitched wail, followed by the distinct sound of a slap. Good thing Peter's sister had found another baby-sitter.

Lisa Davis was a younger woman than Merry had expected, perhaps all of twenty-eight. Mitch had been a good two decades older. His wife carried a little girl who looked to be about two, and a boy of perhaps three clung to one leg. It was the latter who had been crying; the track of tears stilled trailed from his wounded eyes.

"I'm Meredith Folger, Mrs. Davis," Merry said. "With the Nantucket police. Would you have a few minutes to talk?"

"*Would* I?" she said, her eyes widening. "I've been trying to talk to somebody for days. Ever since Mitch—" Her eyes welled with tears. "Ever since Mitch—" She stood back and held open the door. "Please come in."

Merry followed her to a spare living room, furnished with the sort of furniture newlyweds consider necessary—a careful dining-room table and chairs, from their appearance hardly ever used—mixed with the odds and ends of a bachelor's existence.

"You're Peter Mason's friend," Lisa Davis said, leading Merry through the dining area to the small kitchen. She slid the two-year-old into a high chair and pulled out a stool for the older boy. Two grilled cheese sandwiches cut in fours sat on plates beside small glasses of milk. "We were just having lunch. I hope you don't mind."

"Go ahead."

"It was such a relief to run into Peter yesterday. He's so comforting, isn't he? I always feel things are okay when I talk to him. Even when they're really bad. I suppose it's because he's the closest thing to family I have on the island."

Merry looked sympathetic.

"He thought you might know something," Lisa said, recovering her train of thought. "I can't get any information out of that Carmichael guy."

"What is it you wanted to know, Mrs. Davis?"

She slumped down in a chair opposite her son and leaned her head against one hand. "Why no one wants to believe Mitch was killed for a reason," she said. "The same reason the wharf was burned. I mean, come *on*." Lisa looked at Merry in exasperation. "You think the whole thing was random? All that destruction? If they want to find out who torched my husband's pier, they'd better find out why somebody thought they had to shoot him. Chalking it up to some faceless boater doesn't work. At least, it doesn't work for me."

"You think Mitch's murder and the arson were linked," Merry said.

"Of course they were linked."

Merry pulled out the remaining chair, slid her purse to the floor, and sat down. "Tell me about Mitch's work."

"That's what's so sad," Lisa Davis said. "It was going so well. He was so proud of it, you know? All the changes he'd made."

"How long had he been marine superintendent?"

"Almost five years. Ever since he left the Coast Guard, right after we got married."

"You met here?"

"Oh, no," she said, surprised. "I'm from Providence. That's where Mitch was stationed. We met when I worked at the Coast Guard head-quarters as a secretary, right out of college."

"And when he got out of the service, he took the marine superin-tendent's job here."

Lisa nodded. "He liked the idea of living on an island, and staying close to boats, that whole harbor sort of life. I understood it. I thought Nantucket was beautiful. Of course, I had no idea what it was going to be like in the winter months." She smiled ruefully. "But winters were good in another way—Mitch had so much free time. Other than issuing scal-loping permits and making sure the catch quotas were kept, there wasn't a lot to do. He was able to be much more of a parent to Tod and Whitney than most men ever are." At this, her eyes filled with tears again.

"Daddy," said the boy faintly, and dropped his sandwich. He pushed his plate away and put his head down on the table, arms hanging slack at his sides.

"You can be excused, Tod," Lisa said firmly, and turned toward her daughter, attempting to force a corner of bread into an unwilling mouth. "They eat next to nothing these days," she said to Merry. "And they're so quiet. It breaks my heart. Not that I'm Little Mary Sunshine myself. It's been hard on all of us."

"Could you go back to the mainland for a while? See some family?"

"I will," she said, "just as soon as I figure out what's going on with the police. They haven't released Mitch's body yet. I can't even plan a funeral." She set down the rejected sandwich and wiped her daughter's mouth. "Would you like some iced tea?"

Merry shook her head. "How did Mitch feel about the job once he got into it?"

"I think he saw it as a challenge," Lisa said. "He had to work against a lot of attitudes. People in town tended to disregard the pier area—other than collecting the trash and whatnot. The selectmen, for instance, never wanted to part with a dime."

"Scottie Flanagan told me."

"Mitch got the harbor designated a Federal No-Discharge Zone. He was very proud of that."

"A Federal what?"

"No-Discharge Zone. For sewage," she said. "Boaters couldn't enter the harbor if they didn't have contained sewage systems. There was a sewage-processing facility at the pier, and they'd bring their sewage there instead of dumping it in the water. I think it was pretty much destroyed in the fire. But before Mitch, the harbor was one big toilet."

"I had no idea," Merry said, feeling vaguely queasy.

"He was very proud of that. It was only the second in the commonwealth, and the fourth in the nation. That and the hot-water showers were what he really pushed for."

"The showers," Merry said. "Scottie Flanagan said he'd ruffled some selectmen's feathers over that."

"Oh, Scottie," Lisa said, shrugging. "They just didn't want to pay for the new bathrooms, so Mitch went to Visitor Services. Got tourist money to pay for a tourist facility. I think the selectmen were pleased. There really weren't any hard feelings."

"Then why do you think someone might have wanted Mitch out of the way?"

Lisa hesitated before answering, assessing Merry's face. Whatever she saw must have reassured her. "He was being pressured about something he wouldn't discuss with me," she said, her voice dropping. She glanced at her daughter, then reached over to pull her out of her high chair. "Go play with Tod, sweetie."

She waited until the child ran out of the kitchen, then turned back to Merry. "He told me he couldn't afford to have me know. That it would be dangerous. But whatever it was clearly upset him. He'd meet with that Jerry Dundee, and afterward he'd be in what I called his simmering rages. So angry he couldn't speak."

"Jerry Dundee," Merry said dully. "Jerry *Dundee?*" The SeaCon employee Seitz had tried and failed to locate.

"You know him?"

"I wish I did. His name keeps turning up in the oddest places."

"He wasn't an islander," Lisa said. "But he used to show up at the marine super's office and bother Mitch."

"Your husband told you this?"

Lisa shook her head. "Dundee called here once and left a message. Mitch got really mad—that's how I found out all about it. I heard him call the guy back and tell him he was never to bother his wife again, or come near his home, and that if he did, he'd have Mitch to reckon with."

She paused, choosing her words. "Mitch was very strange after that phone call. He went into the children's rooms and held them in the dark, as though they were very precious. I couldn't get it out of my mind. He was threatened by that guy. And he wouldn't tell me why, or how; he wouldn't let me help."

Lisa looked down at her nails, bitten to the quick, and picked at a cuticle. "And then he was killed—"

"How soon after his last conversation with Dundee did that happen?" Merry said.

Lisa looked thoughtful. "The call to the house was a while ago— April, maybe. But Dundee probably bothered Mitch down at the pier after that. I didn't always know when he'd had a run-in. I used to be able to tell—he'd come home so mad. But I think Mitch started covering up. So as not to worry me."

"Dundee had been harassing him for a long time, then."

"At least a year."

Merry sat back and mulled this over. Jerry Dundee, insurance defrauder and sinker of boats, had been pressuring the marine superintendent for the past twelve months. Pressure that culminated in Mitch's death and the destruction of his pride and joy. A warning to others, similarly ill disposed to accommodate Mr. Dundee? Or a means to an end?

"Mrs. Davis," Merry said, "you mentioned that Dundee left a message in April, and that Mitch called him back. Is there any chance that you still have that number?"

She shook her head. "He didn't leave it. Just his name and that Mitch should get in touch. Mitch must have known the number."

"Did your husband carry a calendar of any kind? An address book?"

Lisa hesitated. "Yes," she said. "Normally he'd have had it on him when he was—" She paused, looked down, recovered. "But the fire came after dinner, when he'd already been home and changed out of his uniform. I'll check his bureau. I've left everything just as it was, all his clothes. I can't face going through them."

She disappeared into the bedroom, down a hallway off the kitchen, and reappeared almost immediately. "It might be in here," she said, dropping a small black leather calendar before Merry. It was the sort that could be purchased at any card shop, about the size of a billfold. "He had his wallet with him, so if he kept the number there, we're out of luck."

"They haven't returned his things to you?" Merry said.

"His wallet was stolen. I thought you knew."

Merry leafed through the calendar's pages, starting with January. Mitch Davis's handwriting was surprisingly clear for a man's—as crisp and precise as he'd always kept his uniform. There were cryptic references to shellfish permits, boats' names, and what Merry took to be National Marine Fisheries Service regulations, the minutiae of the scalloping season. He'd even noted the weather for various days. But there was no sign of a darker presence, no unexplained threat. Jerry Dundee's name appeared nowhere. Merry turned through the months, stopping longest at April, and came to a halt at Memorial Day weekend. She didn't want to know the dates Mitch Davis had looked forward to, the hopes he'd had for June.

"Mrs. Davis," she said, "there's nothing here. But it only covers the past six months. He wouldn't have kept last year's calendar?"

"I can look."

She found it in his sock drawer. And on a day in July, nearly a year earlier, Merry discovered what she was looking for. In his precise hand Mitch had written the single word "Dundee." The number had a Providence area code.

Merry studied the notation an instant, debating her next question. But there was no avoiding it; she would have to be brutal. She looked up and met Lisa Davis's eyes.

"Why did your husband leave the Coast Guard?" she said.

There was an instant's tense silence, short enough for someone less observant to ignore, long enough for Merry to notice. The other woman's eyes slid away for the first time, unable to hold her gaze.

"He'd been in twenty years," Lisa said. "That was enough."

On her way back to the station, Merry called Howie on her cellular phone and gave him the Providence number. Then she called Terry Samson at the Coast Guard station. Maybe Mitch Davis *had* simply retired; but if not, Terry would find out. She was willing to bet that Jerry Dundee had something on the marine superintendent—an episode in Providence Davis dreaded reliving—and used it for blackmail. Unsuccessfully, it would seem. Mitch had faced him down, and Mitch had died. The flaming pier rose vividly in Merry's mind, the memory of choking smoke and horns blowing chaotically. The prize must be worth a hell of a lot to spawn such madness.

CHAPTER TWENTY-SEVEN

"MITCH DAVIS LEFT PROV-
idence under something of a cloud," Terry Samson said quietly—or as
quietly as a man with his cracking voice could manage. He stood up and
crossed to the door of his office, looked both ways down the hall, and
closed it. "This is highly confidential, you understand."

"I do," Merry said. "I appreciate your telling me anything. I know it
isn't easy to talk about a colleague's record, even a dead one."

"I spent four years in Providence," he said, "and another three at
Woods Hole. I don't need to twist any arms back there or ask for any
favors. I remember what happened to Mitch."

"Did you see him much once you were both working here?"

Terry shook his head. "Not in the way you mean. Not socially. But
the Coast Guard deals with the marine superintendent all the time—he's
the harbormaster. He has jurisdiction within the harbor, we have it beyond the jetties. And sometimes things overlap. If Mitch ever thought
force would be necessary in apprehending a nasty boater, he didn't hes-
itate to call. He was smart, was Mitch. We respected each other's turf."

"So what happened?"

Terry hesitated. "I don't really know. I only know what the Coast
Guard *said* happened. But I have to believe there was another story."

"Of course there was. There always is. But the Coast Guard's version
is what matters—if that's why Mitch left."

"Oh, it's why he left, all right. Though he'd had a clockwork career
up to that point. He was a lifer—graduated from the Coast Guard Academy, served with the service in Vietnam, did tours in Hawaii, Miami,
Woods Hole, Providence. That's where he ran into the wrong end of a
propeller, metaphorically speaking."

"Personal differences with a boss?"

"I wish." Terry looked over his shoulder, though they were completely alone. "He was in charge of a mission to apprehend some heroin dealers—Dominican Republic guys, they run the stuff up from the islands and hand it off to relatives in the states—who were going to meet at a certain coordinate off Providence Harbor. He made the arrest, seized both boats, locked up the money and the drugs, and headed for port. Only when he got there, the money was gone."

"How much money?"

"Close to a million."

"Whoops."

"Mitch couldn't explain it. He'd had the only key to the evidence locker on the boat. The entire vessel was searched. So was every man jack of the crew. Nothing. The service undertook an intensive investigation of Mitch's private life—found out he was recently married to a much younger woman, had significant credit-card debt, a mortgage on a new house, the whole nine yards. They concluded privately that he'd probably tossed the money overboard to a confederate and that it was in a numbered Caymans account by that time. But they couldn't prove anything. They could only court-martial him for dereliction of duty. He resigned first."

"His home didn't look like the house of a man with a numbered bank account," Merry said thoughtfully. "What do you think of the story, Terry?"

"I think somebody else had a copy of the key, and wasn't telling," he said. "I'd be interested to know which of the crew resigned once the mess blew over and Mitch faded away."

"I would, too," Merry said, "but I haven't got time for that. I imagine this was a big deal in Providence, five, six years ago."

"It was all over the news for a few days."

"So anybody looking for dirt on Mitch Davis would find a significant paper trail."

"Unfortunately."

"How'd he manage to get the job here?"

"He'd resigned, he wasn't court-martialed. Enough people were suspicious of the official story and close enough to Mitch to give him a good recommendation. If he didn't want to talk about the past, I guess he didn't have to."

"But if he'd deliberately kept the knowledge of it from the selectmen, he might be a little worried he'd lose his job if the word broke."

"He might." He leaned toward her. "Was he being blackmailed?"

"I don't know."

"This isn't related to the other questions you were asking, is it? About insurance fraud?"

"I'm beginning to wonder," Merry said.

In the intensity of following Jerry Dundee's tracks, Merry had momentarily forgotten Del; but as she walked into the police station, her friend's face rose before her with a painful urgency. Clarence was standing before the blue mailbox that served as evidence locker, dropping a package into its depths, and through the clear plastic he held in his hands, Merry could plainly see beige clothing. Linen and silk beige clothing, she had little doubt.

"Jenny Baldwin's?" she asked.

Clarence looked at her and winked. "A-no," he said. "Guess again."

"I don't have time."

"Pawh spahrt."

"Come on, Clarence."

"Her husband's."

"Tom's? Tom's fibers were near Del's body?"

"Ayeh."

"You realize what this means."

"Don't have time, Marradith," he said, giving her some of her own medicine.

"He *framed* her. Jenny, I mean. He killed Del and left his wife's bracelet sitting by the body. He left her fingerprints in the kitchen."

"I reckon that's what young Bailey thinks, too. He just left to arrest the poor bahstahd. Fax arrived, by the way."

"From Boston?"

"Ayeh. Yah got that ordah you were lookin' fahr. I left it on yahr desk."

Merry dashed down the hall and up the stairs to her office. There it was, and in record time, too.

"There is no Jerry Dundee at the number you gave me," Howie said, leaning around her doorjamb.

"Aw, shit," Merry said, looking up from the fax. "You're kidding."

"Nope. I called up and asked for him, and they said, 'Mr. Dundee is no longer employed by Oceanside Resorts.' Period. I asked for a forwarding number, I asked how long he'd been gone, I asked—"

"Wait a minute. Did you say *Oceanside Resorts?*"

Howie nodded. "The name you had me look for on the Plastech list. Was this guy sinking boats with explosive?"

"Seitz, you're marvelous," Merry said. "Call Oceanside back. Tell them you're an interested investor, tell them anything that comes to mind. Ask them to fax their quarterly report. Then dig up everything you possibly can about who runs the operation. Go to the Providence police, if you have to. And plug Dundee's name into the NCIC terminal, okay?"

The National Crime Information Center computer sat downstairs near the dispatcher's office. It could tell Merry most of what she needed to know about a suspect in a matter of minutes.

"Where are you off to?"

"To send another fax," she said, waving the court order. Though it hardly mattered. The only possible connection was staring her in the face.

At Merry's request, Tom Baldwin's questioning was delayed until the following morning—Saturday. She and Howie spent the remainder of Friday researching the corporate history of Baldwin Builders, and what they discovered was highly intriguing. The fax worked overtime, between incorporation offices in Delaware, business offices in Providence, and the Water Rights Insurance Company in Boston. Merry and Howie ordered pizza at five o'clock and spent the next three hours deciphering the paper trail they had received over the telephone wire. The final piece of information they got was from the Registry of Vital Records and Statistics in Boston. Although she had known what it would say, Merry stared at it, unseeing, for a while.

Matt Bailey had long since departed, after depositing Tom Baldwin in one of the men's bright blue and yellow cells. His demands to see her father were met with silence.

And so, at eight o'clock Saturday morning, Baldwin was sitting handcuffed in the station's upstairs conference area. Felix Harper was beside him, fastidious as a cat. Merry would have been distinctly uncomfortable in their presence, but for the anger she felt over Del, the Town Pier, and Mitch Davis; it seethed within her like a hot nausea, barely contained by her desire for the interview to go exactly as she planned. For that to happen, she needed icy calm.

She had been unable to brief Matt Bailey prior to the session; he hadn't answered his phone the previous night, and arrived late to the interrogation, eyes bleary and a coffee cup gripped in one hand. He placed himself directly opposite Tom, with a tape recorder between.

"Where were you the night of Adelia Duarte's death?" Bailey began.

"I've told you. At Paul Harris's party at the Yacht Club. Surely you can verify that. Perhaps then you'll explain why the Nantucket police have decided to arrest the Baldwin family for every crime committed this summer."

"I've spoken to Mr. Harris, and I've spoken to a number of his other guests. Apparently there was a period of time during which you stepped out of the club to examine a boat, Mr. Baldwin?"

"I looked at a yacht that was for sale, yes," he said impatiently. "If you recall, I recently lost a vessel in that fiasco at the Town Pier."

Merry, sitting next to Bailey, touched him lightly on the arm. He looked at her and gave way.

"Was that boat insured, Mr. Baldwin?" she asked.

"Of course."

"And the insurer's name?"

"Water Rights. A Boston firm."

"I'm familiar with Water Rights. Interestingly enough, they also insured several commercial fishing boats that sank off the Massachusetts coast during the course of last year. Boats skippered by the crewmen of Del Duarte's father, Joe. As you know, Joe, like Del, is recently deceased."

"What of it?"

"Does this pertain to the matter for which Mr. Baldwin was arrested?" Felix Harper said.

"If you'll allow me to proceed, Mr. Harper, I believe you'll see that it does."

"Be assured that if it does *not*, I will advise my client not to answer your questions."

"Fine." Merry turned her chair slightly in Tom's direction. "Are you familiar with the corporations SeaCon and Oceanfree, Mr. Baldwin?"

"Can't say that I am." His eyes flicked away from hers, and he rolled his shoulders, as though to ease the ache of his arms, cuffed behind him.

Merry deliberately gave him an instant to chew on her question. "You haven't heard of them," she said, lifting a publicity folder from a file, "even though, according to this quarterly earnings statement to which I'm referring dated May thirteenth, they were recently liquidated by their parent company—Oceanside Resorts? A company that lists Tom Baldwin as a member of its board of trustees?"

Baldwin studied her face an instant, and his own grew cold. If he could have, Merry thought, Tom would have punched her.

"The trusteeship is a recent appointment," he said. "I can't be expected to know everything Oceanside has done."

"That's a very curious statement, Mr. Baldwin." Merry ignored Matt Bailey's restive movement beside her. "A Jenny Dundee is listed as the chief executive officer of Oceanside. Am I right in believing that Dundee is your wife's maiden name?"

A hesitation. "It is."

"How does this information bear upon the matter for which Mr. Baldwin was arrested?" Felix Harper broke in. "I must ask you to confine your questioning to the matter at hand."

"I'm with Felix," Matt Bailey said.

"And so the business of your wife's company is something you've ignored," Merry continued, her eyes never leaving the developer's face, "since its incorporation, which I see here was back in"—she paused, making a show of studying the earnings statement—"1987."

"Where did you get that thing?" he said suddenly, leaning painfully across the table, as though to snatch the quarterly report with his teeth.

"This information *is* a matter of public record, Mr. Baldwin. And faxes make communication so much more immediate, don't you think? I don't know how business—or the police—survived without them."

"Merry," Matt Bailey said, almost seething, "could we hold the stuff about Baldwin's business and get on to the murder, please?"

"Certainly, Matt," she said graciously. "I was merely establishing background. And a motive for incriminating Jenny Baldwin."

"I did not incriminate my wife," Tom said.

Matt looked at her, then at Baldwin, and opened his mouth. Merry preempted him.

"Would you excuse us a moment, Tom?" she said, smiling sweetly. "Look after him, would you, Seitz?"

Matt followed her into her office. She closed the door.

"Here's the scoop," Merry said. "Baldwin's been hiding assets in a series of spurious corporations, most of them subsidiaries of a company incorporated under his wife's maiden name. SeaCon and Oceanfree owned commercial trawlers that were deliberately sunk for their insurance value—three that I know of, but probably dozens insured by different companies around New England. The money was absorbed by Oceanside Resorts, Jenny's company, of which Tom's a trustee. Just yesterday at a selectmen's meeting, he was pumping a bid by Oceanside to rebuild the Town Pier. It sounded like they bought it hook, line, and sinker. Tom denied any personal connection to the company in pushing for the contract, which we know is a lie."

"I still don't see what this has to do with Del Duarte," Matt said stubbornly. "You're derailing my line of questioning."

"Matt, try very hard to concentrate on what I'm about to say. From what I hear, the Baldwin marriage has been none too steady these past few months. A divorce proceeding would put Jenny on the defensive and make her cling to any money she could. It would also throw unwelcome light on Baldwin's corporate investments. But if Jenny goes to jail for murdering Del, Tom will get control of her assets."

"So he murdered Del and framed his wife?"

"Yes."

"He just screwed up on the fibers?"

"I guess so. A lot of people don't realize they leave a fabric trail everywhere they go."

Matt mulled this over.

"Why Del?"

Merry flipped open her file and handed him the Registry of Vital Records fax. "He's Sara Duarte's father."

Matt Bailey whistled under his breath. "And did Del want him to divorce Jenny?"

"I don't know," Merry said. "I've no idea how she really felt about

Tom Baldwin. I never even knew they were lovers. She worked with him for five years, but when she left to have Sara, she stayed away for quite a while. If it was marriage she wanted, she went about it in a rather circuitous fashion."

Merry paused, remembering Del's tight-lipped reaction when Tom tried to feed Sara at her father's funeral. "From everything I know about her, Del wanted to be left alone to raise her daughter as she chose. Tom may not have trusted that. He may have been afraid she'd tell Jenny, and Jenny would file for divorce, and he'd lose his house of cards. So he tried to get rid of one problem—Jenny—by framing her for the murder of his other problem—Del."

"I think we should ask him," Bailey said.

"I've got one more area of questioning, Bailey."

He looked at her, and to her surprise, she saw a grudging respect in his eyes. "Go ahead," he said. "Just explain it to me later, will you?"

When they returned to the table, Tom Baldwin was staring intently at its surface, the furious working of his brain written in every line of his brow.

"Did you kill Mitch Davis, Tom, or was that your brother-in-law Jerry's work?" Merry said as she slid into her seat.

"What in the hell—"

"Detective Folger, I really must protest," said Felix Harper. "Mr. Baldwin has not been charged with the murder of Mitch Davis."

"Mitch Davis's death is related to the murder for which he has been charged."

"I would like my protest noted in the record."

"The Town Pier, Tom," Merry said. "The bomb. Oceanside received a shipment of the plastic explosive used to blow up a boat you owned. The marine superintendent was shot point-blank in the back of the head. Execution-style. Almost like a Mafia hit, I thought when I read the coroner's report." She waited for Tom Baldwin to react. He didn't.

"Poor Mitch. He was slated to lose, whatever he did. You had Jerry Dundee work on him for a year, telling him that if he didn't back the Oceanside Resorts plan for developing the pier—a plan that would bring you ridiculous amounts of profit, and that you'd finance from insurance fraud—you'd revive the scandal that ended his Coast Guard career. He had two young children. He couldn't afford to lose his job."

"This rambling is really inexcusable," Felix Harper said.

"I imagine he thought about it a long time," Merry continued. "Weighed the pros and cons. He'd worked so hard to give the pier a facelift; he'd outmaneuvered the selectmen, taken criticism from ignorant taxpayers, been the target of a lot of envy. He'd successfully rebuilt his life after a crippling mistake. And Jerry Dundee was asking him to destroy the fruits of his labor." She leaned into Baldwin's face, forcing him to meet her eyes, to hang on every word.

"But eventually you wore him down, didn't you? Mitch Davis set the bomb that torched the pier. He'd been with the Coast Guard in Vietnam. He understood explosives. And after Jerry got him the plastic and saw that the job was done, he made sure Mitch would never talk about it. In all the smoke and confusion and chaos, nobody would hear a gunshot. And nobody would see who pulled the trigger."

"You've gone completely mad," Baldwin said. "You've made a single family the center of a fantastic conspiracy."

"That's not what Jerry Dundee says."

There was a moment's painful silence. Tom Baldwin drew a shaky breath. "Jerry? You've—talked to Jerry?"

"I haven't. The NYPD has. We put out a national warrant for Dundee's arrest on the NCIC computer yesterday afternoon, and they picked him up last night. Told him you were in custody. He didn't hold out very long. Did you know he's an alleged hit man for the Castiglione crime family, Tom? Execution-style shootings are his specialty. New York was pretty glad to talk to him. They've been looking for a reason to put him away. I think he just gave them one."

Something in Tom Baldwin's face shattered and fell apart. "Jerry talked? That son of a—"

Felix Harper placed a restraining hand on his client's arm. "I wouldn't say anything right now, if I were you, Tom," he said. "None of this touches on the matter for which you were arrested." He looked at Matt Bailey, and Bailey looked at Merry.

She nodded, an enormous weight lifting from her chest. Tom knew it was all over. Whether he confessed or not, the paper trail was there. Jerry Dundee's testimony would drown him deeper. However good a lawyer Felix might prove to be, his client was trapped.

Bailey cleared his throat and looked down at his notes, trying to regain his focus. He'd last asked about a boat that Baldwin said he'd considered buying—while in all probability he was on Milk Street, killing Del and framing Jenny.

"The evening of Del Duarte's death, approximately how long would you estimate you looked at the Yacht Club boat that was for sale?"

"I walked around it a few times. I glanced into the main cabin long enough to see it had an icebox instead of a refrigerator, and that was enough. I don't need an outmoded secondhand piece of junk."

"Guests at the party put your absence at roughly half an hour."

Tom shrugged. "Who's a judge of time at a party? They don't know how long I was gone. *I* couldn't tell you how long I was gone."

"Long enough to get to Milk Street, murder Del, wipe your finger-prints from the harpoon, and leave clean glasses by a bottle of your wife's favorite scotch," Merry said, her anger rising.

"You needn't respond to that, Tom," Felix said soothingly. He looked increasingly less comfortable in his role, however.

"I had no reason on earth to murder Del Duarte."

"How would you characterize your relationship with Miss Duarte?" Bailey asked.

"Characterize? I don't know. She was an employee for years. A good kid. I was very fond of her. Felt bad as hell about the trouble she was in when she left. But she wouldn't take any help from me."

"Just twenty-five thousand dollars when she got back?" Merry broke in.

"What?" Tom Baldwin looked perplexed.

"Twenty-five thousand dollars, Tom. In her bank account. It corre-sponds to some certificates of deposit that were cashed in last week at the Pacific National Bank. Certificates in the name of Tom and Jenny Baldwin."

"I don't know what you're talking about."

"And you're saying Del was just an employee?"

For the first time that morning, Tom looked genuinely bewildered.

Merry pulled out the facsimile of Sara's birth certificate. "Mr. Harper," she said to the lawyer, "I'd like you to note that this is a copy of Sara Duarte's birth certificate. Please note the name of the father."

Felix settled his glasses on his nose and studied the fax. All expression dropped from his pale face, and his eyes slowly rose to meet Merry's. He understood.

"What is that?" Tom said.

"A copy of the form you stole from Del's filing cabinet. The one that shows you fathered her child."

"I fathered her child? I did? That's not possible," Tom Baldwin said. A look of panic came over his face. "I can't have children."

There was a moment's silence around the table.

"Are you certain?" Merry said.

"I don't have any, do I?"

"That could be your wife's difficulty, not yours."

"My doctor wouldn't agree."

"What exactly is the nature of your—problem, Mr. Baldwin?"

He looked intensely uncomfortable. "I had mumps as an adult."

"That wouldn't preclude fathering a child. It simply makes it highly unlikely."

He considered this, picked up the certificate, stared at his name typed on its face. "Little Sara," he whispered. "Mine. She never told me. Oh, my God." Tears pooled in his eyes. Unable to blot them with his hands cuffed, Tom was forced to let them trickle down his cheeks. It was a curiously humbling sight, coming as it did after so much bluster and anger. Merry glanced at Matt Bailey, and at Seitz, who shrugged his shoulders in mute shock. They had watched Tom Baldwin bluff his way through an hour's worth of questions, with varying degrees of transparency, but his emotion now seemed absolutely genuine.

"Are you saying, Mr. Baldwin, that you had no idea Sara Duarte was your daughter?" Merry said.

Tom nodded. Felix Harper reached over with a pristine white handkerchief and dabbed at his client's eyes.

"You didn't take the birth certificate from Del's filing cabinet the night of her death?"

"I told you," he said, his voice high-pitched and dry, "I didn't kill her. I'll confess to everything else—Felix, don't try to stop me, it doesn't matter anymore. I'll confess to the insurance fraud, the mess at the Town Pier, the plans for Oceanside. It's all true. I spent years laying the groundwork for it. But I never killed Del—I loved her. And I had no idea that beautiful little girl was mine. If I had, I'd have thrown everything to the winds for her."

Despite the awkwardness of his cuffed wrists, Tom dropped his head to the conference table's cool surface, his face turned away from them, eyes staring at the wall. "Sara," he said. "Little Sara."

CHAPTER TWENTY-EIGHT

ERRY LEFT THE STA-
tion feeling more confused than when she had arrived. If Tom Baldwin
was guilty of Del's death, his denial made no sense in the face of all that
he had admitted. He was willing to claim responsibility for the Town
Pier arson, not to mention insurance fraud and Mitch Davis. So why balk
at confessing to Del's murder—unless he was truly innocent of it? And
if Tom didn't kill Del, who framed Jenny Baldwin?

She stood blinking in the sunlight of Chestnut Street, where a summer intern was busy washing a patrol car. She watched as the Crown
Victoria turned from a dirty gray to its original medium-blue, thinking,
thinking, and getting nowhere. It was then that Merry saw Joshua Field.

He was leaning in the doorway of Jungle Jim's, the T-shirt shop
across Water Street, looking like any other kid on a summer's Saturday
morning, a cup of something steaming in his hand. His hair was tousled
as though he'd just rolled out of bed. His entire air was casual, but behind
his narrow tortoiseshell glasses, Merry could feel him scrutinizing her.
He'd been watching the station.

She walked the few steps to the corner of Water and Chestnut,
looked for traffic, and crossed to where he stood. "Hi, Josh," she said.

He ducked his head in greeting, and seemed at a loss for words.

"Waiting for your uncle?"

He shrugged and looked down the street, as though searching for a
friend, or afraid of being seen by one.

"He's not going home, I'm afraid," Merry said. "He'll be escorted to
Barnstable by plane later today, under the sheriff's protection. He'll be
held there and arraigned on Monday."

"He didn't kill her," Josh said. His eyes met Merry's, then slid away.

Merry looked at him thoughtfully. "How do you know?"

"He wouldn't, that's all." Josh took a swig from his cup, crumpled it, and cast about for a trash can.

"Over there," she said, motioning. He tossed it like a basketball, knees bent and hands arcing high, and missed. Merry caught the rebound and went for the completion.

"Josh, tell me about the night Del Duarte died," she said, leaning against the wall next to him.

"I've been wanting to," he said slowly, studying his sandals. His feet were tanned dark brown, making the nails seem blush pink. "I just didn't know if I should, or who was in worse trouble. I still don't. Do you think Uncle Tom'll be convicted?"

"Could be. He's admitted to a lot of other things. Things that might make a jury believe he was capable of killing Del."

"That's not right," Josh said. "She wasn't home."

"Del wasn't home? The night she died?"

"Not Del. Aunt *Jen*. She wasn't home when she said she was."

"You mean, she has no alibi. No one could say she'd been home. That's slightly different."

He shook his head. "Nope. I mean *she wasn't there*. I went back, you see. Around nine o'clock. I left the house at seven, met some buddies, had burgers at the Atlantic Café, and ran out of money. They wanted to see the movie at the Dreamland and hit a couple of bars afterward. Nobody had anything to lend me. So I went home."

"And your aunt wasn't in bed with a headache," Merry said, understanding now.

"The bed was unmade, like she'd been lying on it. I know, because I went up to her room. She kept fifty bucks in her upper left-hand bureau drawer, and I figured I'd put it back Monday when I could get to the bank. I don't have an ATM card," he added, by way of explanation.

"She wasn't somewhere else in the house? Or out back on the terrace looking at the stars?"

"Her car was gone, Detective. I didn't think anything about it at the time. Just took the money and went back to the Dreamland—the show was starting in twenty minutes, and I had to get a ticket. She was in bed when I got home, though. And later, when she was arrested and said she'd been there all the time, I got to thinking about it. But I didn't tell anybody. I didn't want to contradict her, you know? It was too serious."

"Yes, it was, Josh," Merry said. "Serious enough to put your uncle in jail."

The Baldwin house seemed deserted when Merry drove up the drive with Matt Bailey and Howie Seitz. Mindful of the Dundee expertise with guns, they all had the instinct to move cautiously. Jenny met them at the door before they had time to ring.

"Where's Tom?" she said, looking past them. "Surely you've released him by this time?"

"Unfortunately not, Mrs. Baldwin," Matt Bailey said. "He's being flown to Barnstable on multiple charges of arson, fraud, and conspiracy to commit murder. Quite a list. But that's not why we're here." He cleared his throat and stood a little straighter. "Jenny Dundee Baldwin, I arrest you for the murder of Adelia Duarte. It is our duty to inform you of your rights. Patrolman Seitz?"

"You have the right to remain silent," Howie said. "You have the right to obtain counsel and—"

"Good heavens," Jenny said, with an amused smile. "We're not going through that rigmarole, are we? I heard it on Wednesday. You didn't have a case then. You don't have one now. Run along and find somewhere else to play. I have to pack for the Cape."

Despite herself, Merry was impressed. Dave Grizutto was right; Jenny Baldwin had everybody fooled. The private-school air and the conservative clothes, the unmade-up face and the plain brown hair. Unimpeachable marks of a respectable pedigree, cloaking the sister of a Mafia hit man. Money must be terribly important to her. And money had been her downfall.

"One question, Jenny," Merry said. "Why did you bother to tell me about the fifty dollars? It was a small detail, but one you shouldn't have missed."

"I beg your pardon?"

"The fifty dollars. You said it was pilfered from your drawer. That was the word you used—*pilfered*. A word for a theft in the family, not a burglary. Did you know Josh had taken it? I suppose you did. You just didn't know when."

"I don't know what you mean. The money was taken when the bracelet disappeared."

"Actually, Josh just told us he took it while you were at Del's. He came back around nine that night, before the Dreamland's second show, to get some cash he knew was in your drawer. Only you weren't there to ask permission. You were committing murder."

"That's absurd."

"I know. The whole thing is absurd. You must have discovered the money gone a few days later, and wondered when it disappeared. Did Tom take it? Or Josh? Or had you spent it and simply forgotten? But if you were going to report the theft of the bracelet as you planned—to begin the process of incriminating your husband—you couldn't ignore the fifty dollars."

Merry put her foot on Jenny's doorstep, leaning toward her, and disconcerted, the woman edged backward.

"Tom or Josh might mention taking it, and seeing the bracelet when they did. You had to admit you'd discovered the money's loss up front. Or so you thought. But it was a detail that didn't fit with the story we were expected to believe—that Tom murdered Del and framed you. We were supposed to think he'd taken the bracelet for that purpose, and left it near her body.

"But fifty dollars? To what end? It was a detail that kept surfacing in the back of my brain."

"I don't know what you're talking about," Jenny said.

"I'm talking about your plan." Remembering the harpoon in Del's chest, Merry's green eyes were hard and cold. "The plan you executed by coming down with a convenient migraine the night you knew Tom had a party and Josh was out all evening. The night you appeared on Del's doorstep, wearing Tom's beige linen pants and silk knit sweater— he's only an inch or so taller than you, isn't he? Heels would take care of that. And everything these days is oversized. You probably looked quite fashionable, quite unlike yourself. And Del let you in."

"I was in bed."

"Not at nine o'clock. Josh will swear to it. Your car was gone from the garage."

Jenny Baldwin's hand slid from the doorknob, and she looked about her, as if seeking help. There was none apparent. She stood back from the door. "I suppose you'd better come in."

Howie pulled out his notebook and pen.

* * *

"All right," Jenny Baldwin said, sitting on a sofa in her cool, airy living room with the view of the harbor beyond the windows. "I hadn't calculated on Josh." She sounded very weary. "I thought I'd worked everything out, but there was always the nagging fear. What had I forgotten? What had I missed? What couldn't I control? What would trip me up at the last moment? The past twenty-four hours have been the worst."

"With Tom exactly where you'd wanted him."

Her head came up at that, and she locked her eyes on Merry's. "Yes. I was so close."

"You hate him that much?"

Emotion rippled over Jenny's face like seawater over a rock. "He brought it on himself," she said. "All that I feel. The way he's treated me."

"What was it?" Merry said. "The affair with Del, or the fear of losing the money?"

Jenny took her time answering. "Both, I suppose. He'd done the unforgivable—the *unforgivable*—thing. He'd given her the child he could never give me. Or never *would* give me. He didn't know what he'd done— I realize that. But *I* knew, from the moment I saw that child at Joe Duarte's funeral. She looked like Tom's baby pictures, every inch of her. She had the same bowlegged gait, and his mother's extraordinary red hair. *And he didn't see it.* I thought the entire room must know, must be looking and comparing and taking notes. I wanted that woman off the island, and her brat with her."

"And so you gave her twenty-five thousand dollars to leave."

Jenny looked up. "You knew about that? I suppose you know about everything." Her eyes dropped back down to her tanned fingers, obsessively smoothing a pleat in her cotton skirt. "She wouldn't keep it. She told me she'd decided to stay. I'm afraid that made me—very angry. And so I had to come up with a plan."

"How did you know she kept a harpoon in her house?"

"I didn't. I intended to spike her drink. But we never got around to having one, you see. She refused to drink scotch. I lost my temper—it's always been a trifle uncontrollable—and she picked up the harpoon. I think she thought I'd be afraid of her. I wasn't."

"There were two types of blood on the floor," Merry said.

Jenny raised the long sleeve of her blouse and revealed a neat bandage on one arm. "I had a bit of trouble taking the harpoon away from her. I grabbed the shaft and wrestled her for it. I'm much stronger than I look, you know."

"You look strong enough."

She studied the bandage intently. "My, that dart was sharp," she said. "I had no trouble at all shoving it between her ribs."

"And then you left the scotch bottle with your fingerprints on it, and the pieces of copper chain."

"Well, that *was* the plan."

"Why, Jenny?" Merry said. "Why did you have to kill Del? Did the affair matter so much?"

"I didn't expect it to," she said, sounding surprised. "Tom told me about it after the girl left—but of course, he never thought the baby was his. He thought she'd two-timed him, and it hurt his pride. That's why he made a clean breast of it to me. He felt like an ass, and it made him honest." She laughed, a brittle sound. "He decided to wash his hands of her and make a new start. But I never could."

"Forgive him?"

"Oh, I suppose I forgave him—in the incessant way of married women. I forgave him. I just couldn't forget it. Couldn't trust him again. Every time he was out late, or missed an appointment, I'd wonder who it was this time. Until eventually I ceased to care. Or thought I did."

"And then you saw the baby."

"Yes. Tom would have thrown me out like a torn shirt if he realized Del had been faithful and the child was his. There'd be nothing to keep him, then. And suddenly I realized I didn't really *want* Tom anymore. What I *really* hungered for was revenge—to be rid of him with my life intact, not savaged and lessened by the divorce. I wanted the money, the house, and the knowledge that his life was destroyed. As mine has been."

"You killed Del out of selfishness."

Jenny Baldwin shrugged slightly. "She didn't matter very much in the world's scale."

"She mattered to me," Merry said softly.

"I'd like to say I'm sorry," Jenny said, folding and refolding her pleat with deft fingers, "but I haven't felt that way in weeks. I've felt—powerful.

I've felt like I had a purpose. I could show the world that I was a hapless victim, and all the time it was Tom who would pay. I knew the shell game he'd been playing with his money, the boats that sank, the plans for the pier. He'd used my brother. No one would believe he'd stop at a simple killing. And framing me was entirely plausible."

"Just one thing," Merry said. "Why did you take Sara's birth certificate?"

"I wanted him to die not knowing," Jenny said. "I never wanted him to have the *satisfaction* of knowing." She lifted one wrist to rebutton the cuff of her blouse, hiding the bandage, and then stood up. "He knows now, I suppose," she said, looking at Merry.

Merry nodded.

Jenny Baldwin reached for her lightship purse and placed it firmly over one arm. "That's that, then. I've failed all around. Well, gentlemen," she said, turning to Matt Bailey and Howie Seitz, "I think that's enough for now. If we hurry, the sheriff can take us both on the same plane."

❦

CHAPTER TWENTY-NINE

SUNDAY WAS REBECCA'S
Quaker day of rest, and she was nowhere in sight when Merry pulled
up before Peter Mason's door. Rafe, she knew, was at the Greengage;
she'd seen the red Rover parked on Quince street, with its distinctive
CRNBERY vanity plate. Peter was completely alone. She reminded herself
to leave as quickly as possible.

He was in the kitchen at the back of the house, whistling cheerfully
over the sound of running water, and her knock went unheeded. So she
walked around to the deck and tapped on the screen, watching as his
head jerked up in involuntary surprise, his eyes narrowing against the
glare beyond the door.

"It's me," she said. "I came to tell you it's all over."

He shut off the water and stared at her, hands dripping. "Come in
and talk to me," he said.

She pushed open the screen and walked into the kitchen slowly. Set
her bag down on the table. Pulled out a chair and slumped into it.

"What happened?"

"Do I have to go over it?"

"Eventually. I won't be kept in suspense forever."

Whether he was discussing Del's murder or something else she didn't
like to think. She brushed her blond hair back from her eyes and looked
at him.

"I want to thank you for sending me to see Lisa Davis. Talking to
her unlocked the whole case."

"She called me after you'd stopped by. Apparently you made her feel
a lot better."

"Only temporarily, I'm afraid. Mitch torched the Town Pier, Peter.
And then was silenced by Tom Baldwin."

"By *Tom?*"

"Well, his brother-in-law, actually. It's too complicated."

"You need a gin and tonic."

"What time is it?"

"Late enough," he said firmly. "Medicinal purposes." He fetched a lime and a knife, filling the room with the stark freshness of citrus. "Let's talk about murder some other time, okay? You need a break. I propose dinner *à deux*. Meaning, we both pitch in and scrounge something to eat."

"Is it dinnertime?"

"It could be," he said equably. "It's a summer evening with nothing ahead of us. Everything is open to negotiation."

"I'm so tired, Peter," Merry said, putting her head in her hands. "I hadn't taken time to realize how spent I feel. And all I can think of is Del. I thought at first she'd died because she'd stumbled on something important about Joe. But he probably *did* just fall overboard; sometimes the obvious is what happened. Instead she was killed because Jenny Baldwin was growing old and childless and unhappy in her marriage, and Del had youth and the love of her husband, and a child he never thought he'd create. She died because she had reasons to live."

"This is going to take some telling," Peter said. "Here's your drink."

He listened without a word while Merry rambled through the history of SeaCon and Oceanside, Sara's birth certificate and Jenny Baldwin's brother. When she had done, she looked up and saw the shadows lengthening across the polished wood of his kitchen floor, and Peter's face very still.

"A long tale. And none of it important, really."

"I wouldn't say that. You've solved several crimes at once."

"I have no sense of victory from it." Merry felt suddenly weak, and laid her head on the table. "I just feel completely alone. When I was very little—probably about six—my father was called to a house on Milk Street where a woman had just died of cancer. She was lying in her bed, with a sheet over her face, and her little girl was crying in the room across the hall. They were all alone. Dad brought Del back to our house and put her to bed with me, and went off to find Joe drinking himself sick in the pilothouse of his boat.

"He could have locked Joe in a cell, but he didn't. Instead he slapped him into shape, got him back to our kitchen, and poured coffee down his throat until three o'clock in the morning. And when my mother committed suicide, Joe Duarte was right there in our kitchen, with Del, to pour coffee for my father."

Peter reached for her hand, held it.

"Who'll pour coffee for me, Peter?" Merry said. "In the middle of the night, when disaster strikes again?"

"Is that why you're here?"

"I don't know."

"I wouldn't have you go to anyone else."

The intensity behind the words brought her eyes up to his. She saw the unguarded feeling written on his face, and the decision he made not to take it back. He held her gaze an instant, and her stomach turned over. *Oh God*, she thought. *Oh God, no.*

Peter rose from his chair and knelt in front of her, her legs against his chest, his hands taking hers. He was alert and passive at once, the way an animal holds itself before springing, all the possibility of power and release poised in a muscular stillness. He said nothing, but the space between them filled with a static current, singing, alive, dangerously binding. Merry leaned away, fighting something akin to terror at his touch.

And then she took refuge in indifference. She could break this mood—reach for her purse, comment on the time, say something flip about murder making strange bedfellows. She opened her mouth to do it.

He saw the sardonic expression gathering, and laid his forefinger gently, inevitably, against her lips.

"You could break this mood in a minute," he said. "I know. And leave me jagged as a broken glass. You could do that. Merry, Merry—don't. It isn't necessary."

The touch of his finger on her mouth was like a cool seal to a pact struck long ago. She closed her eyes and reached for his palm with both hands, burying her face in it. She'd backed away from Peter once before, in the rose garden of a murderer, when he'd handed her a flower complete with thorns—a gesture implicit with the intensity and pain of offering himself. She had been afraid of him then, an instinctive fear born of ignorance. She knew him far better now, and knew why she was afraid. She wanted him more than anything or anyone she had ever known in her life. Peter Mason had the power to strip her of everything she was; the power to take her over, body and soul.

He lifted her face, a hand framing either cheekbone, his long fingers tangled in her hair. The gray eyes were burning now. "There's my girl," he said.

He took her in the shadowed half-light of his room under the eaves, the early June moonlight throwing his profile against the sloping wings of the ceiling, the sharp planes of his face picked out in black and white. He took her slowly, spinning out the midnight, making something holy from the ritual of shed clothing. He ran a finger like a burning match down the curve of silk covering her breast, then tore at the buttons of her blouse with his teeth until they fell in a rainy patter on the floor. He curled a hip under his palm, found the crease behind her knee with its faint dampness of sweat, dipped his mouth in the hollows of her collarbone.

Merry saw him outlined against the rafters, dark as a thunderhead hovering over her body, the power of his frame leashed by a terrible gentleness; it occurred to her that he was afraid that he might break her in half. She fought him over this—wanting to tear him loose, to force him into the tide that was sweeping the length of her body. She was a small boat, a wooden dinghy, the kind that fishermen used to launch in the surf years ago, meeting the sea just before its crest, knowing survival meant going through the wave, not foundering in it. She tried to tell him of the sea, of the wave curling in whiteness over her head, but her mouth was locked in his and he had taken her breath. She clung to him, to the pull and thrust of the current, feeling herself spiraling in a whirl-pool, drowning him with her. His fingers found her hair again, arching her neck back and her mouth up to his; she opened her eyes and saw his staring into her own, gray as the Atlantic under rain.

Much later, as Merry sat in her Explorer with the engine idling, forcing herself to go home, she watched the dog, Ney, round up the sheep in the early-morning sunlight.

"Stay," Peter said, leaning in through her window. "Stay here forever."

"I know why Alison left you." Her mouth felt dry.

"What does that mean?"

"You have power, Peter. I'm not talking about sex—or not *just* sex. I'm talking about the soul. About self-possession. Anyone who loved you would be completely controlled by you. That sort of feeling is what some women look for all their lives—a consuming passion to lose themselves in. I just find it frightening."

"Is that how this feels?"

"It does this morning."

"Consuming?"

"You bring me to my knees."

He turned to the climbing rose that trailed over the post-and-rail fence, tore off three perfect blooms, and brought them to her wordlessly. They spilled through the Explorer's open window in all the headiness of June scent. She looked at them and felt her throat constrict. Another offering of himself in the rose, an act painful in its honesty. He would never tell her he loved her, and weight her with a sense of obligation; he would make her choose him for herself. But the knowledge of love was there all the same.

Peter stood away from the car. A thorn had torn his finger, and a bright bead of blood was gathering there. He seemed not to feel it. The sight of his hands brought back the sense of them on her skin, and she took a deep breath. She could not look at his face.

Merry turned the car toward home and fled down the drive, her lap filled with flowers.